He stopped her barely halfway up. "Too...slow," he said. "You go get Janine. Bring her and your mother and... boyfriend here. I'll...guard the front."

"With what?" Nina said. She'd noted his shoulder holster was empty and Nina hadn't felt any other sort of gun. Nor had her mother returned with either gun she apparently had in the house.

Mackenzie reached down painfully and tugged up his right pant leg. From a concealed sheath, he pulled out a dagger with what was maybe a five-inch blade.

"Oh, that'll scare them," Nina said.

ALSO BY TERRI DARLING

Downhill Rush

What a Man Wants

Second Chances

COLLECTIONS

Love Sneaks In

Love Sneaks In Again

Love Snuck

Love Steps Up

Love Steps Up Again

Love Steps Up Deluxe

TERRI DARLING

LAST ONE TO HIDE

fiero PUBLISHING

Published in electronic form 2012 by Fiero Publishing
Published in trade paper 2013 by Fiero Publsihing
www.fieropublishing.com
Book and cover design copyright © 2013 by Fiero Publishing
Cover design by Terry Hayman/Fiero Publishing
Cover art copyright © curaphotography/123RF Stock Photo and ca2hill/depositphotos

ISBN-13: 978-1927920053

ISBN-10: 1927920051

First Print Edition: December 2013

For my honey, who makes
every day something special.

LAST
ONE
TO
HIDE

1

Bethesda, Maryland
late morning
Sunday

THE PHONE.

When it jingled out through the heat of the backyard gardens, Richard Mackenzie's head snapped up. If that was his brother's mysterious "Deep Throat" contact, he was twelve minutes past his scheduled call time. Richard had already let his brother's family stand down from reception mode and resume their normal lives on this hot Sunday afternoon.

"I got *you!* I got *you*, Daddy!"

"Oh yeah? Well take *that*, you little squirt gun monster!'"

Richard's brother, Tom Mackenzie, a handsome, twenty-eight-year-old government lawyer, chased his whirling-dervish of a daughter, Janine, in and out of the rhododendron bushes that lined the back of their property...just inside the detection wire Richard had strung up around the whole perimeter.

Richard was helping Tommy's wife, Marie-Ange, weed the gardens closer to the house itself.

The phone rang again.

Tom still obviously hadn't heard it. But Tom's wife had. She knelt, frozen in place among the impatiens in the dirt of the long flowerbed directly behind the stone patio. Her back and curly blonde hair were to Richard, her heart-shaped face hidden from him, but he saw her tremble. And why not? Even though she knew nothing, Tom had made her his backup for these calls in case something happened to him.

Stupid. You give someone a job, you owe them the intel to do it properly.

On the third ring, Richard made a snap decision and leaned towards her from where he'd been bagging the weeds she pulled.

"You answer it," he whispered.

Visibly pale, Marie-Ange mopped her sweaty forehead with the back of a gardening glove, then tugged off the gloves, stood, and hurried inside the kitchen door of her and Tom's modern colonial.

Richard followed.

As she stopped at the butcher-block counters and reached for the wall phone, he held up a hand. "Wait."

Stepping beside her, he flicked on the modified Public-Safety Answering Point he'd insisted Tom let him set up this morning. The PSAP was a three-foot box of gray metal and plastic a friend of Richard's from U.S. Navy intelligence had "borrowed" from a mobile 9-1-1 unit. It stuck out like an eyesore in the homey kitchen. But the auto number and auto location controller (ANI/ALI) could still trace incoming calls in ten seconds if the call came from the greater DC area. And while its cell phone tracking was slower and dependent on which carrier brought the signal, it could still pinpoint the nearest cell tower coverage area within fifteen seconds, or the location within five meters if the user's phone sent a GPS signal.

The data flowed to the connected laptop computer. It also recorded calls and used a voice-stress analyzer to function as a crude lie detector.

Placing his hand on the PSAP's tapped-in second receiver, he caught his sister-in-law's gaze and said, "Go."

Marie-Ange picked up the phone receiver with Richard picking up his simultaneously. He stood almost shoulder-to-shoulder with her, noting distantly the slight gap in the front of her blouse, the smoothness of her cheek and neck, the smell of her floral perfume—violets, roses, something light. Once upon a time that would have stirred something in him. But that was before Afghanistan and the deadening of all such responses. Now the best he could do was say a silent congratulations to his younger brother. And swear to keep him alive to enjoy the life he'd built.

"Hello?" Marie-Ange said.

An intriguing contralto voice answered, "Hi, M.A."

There was a long beat of confusion on Marie-Ange's face and Richard frowned. According to Tom, his Deep Throat used some kind of voice distortion to protect his or her identity, hardly the show of trust Richard liked in someone Tommy was preparing to risk his life and his family's life for. So this wasn't Deep Throat?

Marie-Ange's eyes suddenly blinked wide. "Nina? Is that you?"

"Hey, Sis."

"Oh my God." Marie-Ange's face, pasty white split seconds ago, now flooded with color. "Neens! I didn't think you'd come! When you didn't call me back. Nothing. And it's been..."

"Almost seven years, like you said."

"Just after Janine was born!" She was staring at Richard now with her eyes wide—forget-me-not blue, by God. Glistening with tears. His own face hardened and he thought that even if he'd still had the emotional freedom to lust, it wouldn't have been for this kind of woman. Marie-Ange was too sweet. She was like spun sugar that would crackle and melt when the going got tough. And in Richard's world, it always did.

He refocused on the phone call and the voice of this woman he'd never met, supposedly Marie-Ange's estranged sister.

The voice carried elevated stress levels. Richard didn't need the machine to tell him that. He could hear it as "Nina" began to talk, telling how she'd watched Marie-Ange's DVD. *Her what?* How they'd have to talk about that.

Something in the controlling tone of voice made Richard flash to a photo Tom had shown him once—Nina at some college function with her friends. She'd been taller than the other girls, thick brown hair and glasses, with a real presence that made her sexy. But it had all been ruined by her haughty expression. Richard had guessed, and Tom had confirmed, that she was an over-educated snob who wouldn't have been happy to know where Richard and Tom really hailed from.

Not that any of this would be hard to imitate on the phone by an impostor planning to draw Marie-Ange out of her protected zone. Was whoever Tom feared that devious? If it was the Russian mob, like Tom had hinted, they could be.

The ALI had pinpointed the caller in the 7400 block of Wisconsin Avenue, Bethesda, barely two miles away, a cellular call with GPS signal. Richard touched Marie-Ange's shoulder and pulled the receiver away from his ear, covering the mouthpiece and indicating she should do the same.

She did, staring at him in exasperation.

"Ask her where she's calling from."

Marie-Ange took her hand off the mouthpiece. "Where are you calling from, Nina?"

The voice gave a little snort. "Bethesda Station. I flew into the Reagan an hour ago and took the Red Line up here. *Such* a treat. I was going to just drop in on you, but figured I better give you some warning first in case your super-soldier shot me on sight. Is he there?"

"Yes, he's— Bethesda Station? You're right here?"

A cross-reference on the computer confirmed it. Which meant nothing if the whole point was to draw Marie-Ange out there, take her as a hostage. Almost like she'd read his mind, the voice on the phone asked for a pickup.

"Of course. Of course!" Marie-Ange gushed. "My God, I can't believe it! I'll be right out in just as quick as—"

Richard shook his head—*No*—and Marie-Ange frowned.

"Just a minute, Nina." She covered her receiver, with Richard copying the move. "Why not? It's ten minutes away by car. I'm wearing my beacon. This is my sister."

"Tell her to grab a taxi."

"But—"

"The phone line needs to be clear for Deep Throat's call. Clearing it in ten seconds." He held the phone to his ear with his shoulder, held up his ten fingers, and began silently counting them down.

Marie-Ange hurriedly spoke into the phone again. They had car trouble, she blurted, but lots of taxis came to the front of the Hyatt Hotel just across the street from the Station exit, Nina should take one, Marie-Ange would cover it when they got here, she was so thankful Nina had decided to come, and they'd catch up on everything just as soon as she arrived.

Then she slammed down the phone with a gasp of breath just as Richard's last finger fell and he too hung up.

Almost the same second, the phone rang again.

~~~~

Okay, Nina Tauredaux thought as she flipped her cell phone closed and pushed back her thick black hair. It was official. Marie-Ange was worse than ever and Nina was crazy for agreeing to come to her rescue.

The ribbed white roof of the Bethesda subway station converted the sounds of rushing people into garbled laughter, agreeing with her. But Marie-Ange's DVD-recorded plea hadn't really left her a choice, had it? It hadn't been the first time Nina's little bouncy, pretty, cheerleader, man-stealing sister had reached out with an apology and plea for Nina come back, but it was the first time Nina had tried to make it life and death.

And Marie-Ange had a child now, a six-year-old girl whom Nina had never even met. How could Nina not respond to help protect a little niece who, in another lifetime, could have been Nina's own?

Was it very sick that Nina was coming back as much to see that "might have been" as to help out her sister?

And if Tom Mackenzie just happened to do a double-take over how much Nina had improved herself these last seven years—she turned to catch a group of boys ogling her as they boarded the train, and she gave them a wicked smile and wave—well maybe that wouldn't be so bad either. He'd divorce Marie-Ange, sue for custody of little Janine, marry Nina, and move out west with her so they couldn't hear Marie-Ange howling in despair 24/7.

Or maybe they'd give Janine to Marie-Ange as a consolation prize. And Nina could give Tom electroshock treatments to wipe his memory. Then Tom and Nina could start over again, all fresh as dew and perfect as a rainbow.

Cue the Disney soundtrack.

Nina stopped in annoyance as her eyes started to leak. Damn pointy shoes! She knew she shouldn't have bought new shoes for this!

She sniffed, pushed back her unruly hair again, and grabbed the extended handle of her suitcase.

Okay, fine. So Nina was a bitch who was only coming back for all the wrong reasons. But Marie-Ange *did* ask her. So whatever happened, it was as much her fault as Nina's.

Dabbing lightly at her eyes to make sure her mascara hadn't run, he headed for the escalators to find a taxi.

~~~~

Richard saw Marie-Ange reach for the phone automatically, probably assuming it was an automatic call-back because the line hadn't disconnected properly.

Richard scooped his receiver up at the same time.

"Hello?" said Marie-Ange.

"Who is this?" came an electronically distorted voice. Deep Throat! Richard's earlier distraction was gone instantly. He saw the PSAP trying to get a fix on location. A DC lock! No. A router. At least one. The call had originated somewhere else. Whoever Deep Throat was, he or she obviously knew how to hack the carriers, or had the help of someone who did.

Marie-Ange, meanwhile, had almost dropped the phone in fright but Richard's free hand had steadied her wrist, feeling the sensation of her smooth skin, the delicate bones. Uncomfortably fragile. He noted that the shrieks and laughter had vanished outside. Tom and were probably on their way in.

"M-Marie-Ange here," she said.

Silence. Then, "I saw a flock of birds today."

Tight panic in Marie-Ange's eyes at the code words. Richard squeezed her wrist lightly. He knew Tom had given her the code answer. Richard just hoped she hadn't blanked in fear.

"Better...better birds than bombs," Marie-Ange said.

"Yes," the voice said. "Listen carefully. No more data drops. Someone hacked my security this morning. They know what I've been sending and they know your husband took the stuff. They'll be coming for him any time now, probably for you and your little girl too. You have to leave your house immediately."

With a click the line went dead.

2

UP AT GROUND LEVEL, Bethesda Station, Nina impatiently tugged her suitcase away from the top of the escalator and struggled for breath. God. Six years on the West Coast had made her forget how thick the air was here in mid-summer. She shaded her eyes from the sun. You could broil an intern on this sidewalk. Wash her down with a soggy cigar.

A quick look around showed her the Hyatt hotel Marie-Ange had mentioned with, sure enough, a line of two taxis parked near the front.

"Give you a hand?"

She turned to see one of the drooling boys she'd waved at in the subway. Oh, please. She'd only waved because they'd been getting on a train. Did they really think she'd made herself this magnificent for the likes of them?

"Please leave," she said.

"You sure?" He tossed his cute curls and stuck his thumbs into the top of his Levis.

"You're too young and height challenged, okay?"

"Re-e-eally?"

"Really."

"Hey..."

"Listen," she said and dropped her voice into a serious *sotto voce*. "I've got genital herpes with really big warts, and gummy red ulcerations. They're sticky, gooey, gross and bleeding."

The boy grimaced and backed away quickly.

"Yeah. Thought you'd like that."

Nina spun back to the street with an evil grin, gripped the handle of her suitcase and set off for the street, the suitcase rocking and bouncing across the paving stone behind her. If there was one thing you gained from not being a roll-over Barbie doll, it was the freedom to—

"Hey!"

She turned to see the punk kid jogging after her and lost it. "This is not persistence! It's stalking! Now get out of here, before I kick you in the nuts!"

Then she bared her teeth at him until he stopped, muttered something under his breath, and hurried off.

She growled and smoothed back her hair again. Whatever he'd muttered was probably true and she frankly didn't give a damn. She wasn't her sister. She was better.

The traffic broke. Nina hurried across the street to grab a cab.

~~~~

"Was that the call?" Tom's voice. He was suddenly in the kitchen doorway, all curly brown hair and grinning like a kid, the irresponsible kid brother.

Janine stuck her head out through his legs, grinning just like her dad. The lost-tooth gaps on either side of her mouth showed. "Hello-o!"

Richard took Marie-Ange's phone from her trembling hand and hung up both phones at the same time. He stared long and hard at his brother. "That was Deep Throat. He said they're onto you and could be here at any moment. We go to Scenario One immediately."

"You traced the call?" Tom said. "Sure it's not just some weird test? Because—"

"It's not a test."

"But—"

"No!" Richard snapped. And as Janine pulled her head back to hide behind her daddy's legs, Richard fought away all the flashes of how *he* would approach this house if he were assigned to apprehend its residents by any means necessary. Sniper rifle to blow out their legs? Tasers? No. No survivors. In his mind he hustled through these rooms, rifle raised, taking down each target with a shot, two at most. Screams. Bodies fall. In a familiar twist, he saw Tommy falling from his father's fist. Richard had been too slow to stop that one.

"We go to Scenario One," Richard said. "Evacuation. Now."

Tom closed his mouth, held Richard's eyes, and finally nodded. Good. There was the grit that had to be there if he was as good at his job as this enormous house attested to.

And even as he thought it, he fought down the little voice that was still turning over Deep Throat's strange pronouncement—*They know he took the stuff.* Tommy, government lawyer with the Criminal Division of the Justice Department and...on the take?

It hurt to even think it because it exposed just how much Richard had lost touch with Tommy's life. With the lives of everyone outside the intense zones of combat Richard had been operating in for what seemed like forever now. If Richard had been a normal man and a real brother, he wouldn't be questioning Tommy's guilt or innocence now. Because he'd never have let Tommy become wrapped up in something like this in the first place.

And damn it, when this was all over...

"Okay," Tom said now. He swiveled and became the lovable rogue again as he reached down to take the pigtails on either side of Janine's head. "JJ, you gotta go upstairs with Mommy. Get all your stuff. We're going on a little trip."

Tom caught Marie-Ange's eyes and Marie-Ange sniffed once, nodded, and stepped forward to get Janine. Tom headed for his main floor study.

When they'd gone, Richard jogged downstairs to the basement where he'd been staying. Sixty seconds later he was back upstairs in everything but his Canadian Special Forces beret. Combat boots, knife in a boot-sheath under his jeans, a SIG P225 concealed in a shoulder holster, black market M16 carbine (not as good as the C8, but damn close) concealed in a hand-carry duffel bag, and a pack full of ammo and other supplies strapped to his back, more in his vest pockets. If they met a hit squad on the way out, it was the squad that would get hit.

"Tom?" he called from the front hall.

"Here!" called his brother. Tom thumped out of his home office with his prepared backpack. Richard had made all three family members prepare such a pack two days ago—change of clothes, essential records, money, something comforting. Presumably Tom had also included whatever it was Deep Throat had given him on his "data drops." A bunch of thumb drives? Microfiches?

"I should carry that," Richard said, pointing to Tom's pack.

Tom was still staring wide-eyed at Richard's gear, probably wondering whether he'd smuggled it off base or (the reality) bought it after he'd arrived here. Then he registered Richard's suggestion and shook his head with a grin. Breezy kid-brother mode again.

"You just keep me safe, bro'. I keep my family safe. Even little Snuffles." Tom held up the short-haired, stuffed armadillo that was Janine's teddy bear. Dark green and brown with black marble eyes. She refused to sleep without it.

Richard nodded and the two of them hurried through the laundry room and into the double garage. Marie-Ange and Janine weren't there yet.

They jogged back into the house just as Marie-Ange came flying into the hall from the back door in near hysterics. She saw Richard's get-up and it just about sent her over the edge.

"No!" she cried, grabbing onto Tom. "No! We can't go yet!"

"What is it?" Richard snapped.

"Janine w-won't come. She ran out back to hide somewhere and I c-can't find her."

Blown sugar collapsing. Great timing.

Marie-Ange turned towards the kitchen and back yard door again and screamed, "*Janine!*"

No response.

Mentally clicking through the time that had passed since Deep Throat's call, Richard made a decision.

"Tom," he said evenly, "you take Marie-Ange to the van and go to Rendevous One. I'll find Janine and meet you there."

"No!" Marie-Ange screeched, ripping away from her husband raising up her hands either to fight him off or plead. "She won't come to you! She's probably scared! She needs her mother! Let me! You both go! Let me!"

Tom's own face showed indecision. Richard stepped forward and grabbed both of Marie-Ange's slim wrists, willing his calm through to her.

"You're right!" he said. And again, "You're right, Marie-Ange. She's more likely to come to you. But if anyone shows up, I can fight them off and protect her. You can't."

"I'll hide! They won't find us!"

"These people wouldn't stop until they did," Richard said. "You know I'm right."

"I...I can't leave her."

"It's okay," Richard said, giving her wrists a squeeze and making her meet his eyes. "I will find her. And I'll protect her. There is no way on heaven or earth I will let anything happen to your little girl. Do you understand?"

Or to you or Tom.

Her eyes flicked from his rifle, to the strap of his shoulder holster, and back to Richard's eyes. "I... Yes."

"Then go. Now."

Richard saw Tom nod from behind Marie-Ange. His brother looked suddenly a hundred years old. But then Tom gritted his teeth and nodded.

"Give me Snuffles," Richard said. "As bait."

Tom blinked, hesitated, then handed it over. "Don't lose it. Or her."

Richard took the stuffed armadillo, gave a last nod, and jogged for the kitchen door to the backyard. He paused there and ensured Tom and Marie-Ange had actually gone for the van. Then he loped outside.

~~~~

The taxi Nina rode in smelled like cloves and cinnamon. The seats were immaculate, the windows clean, the driving safe and swift. And Nina's taxi driver was middle-eastern—Barzin Ruh al-something-unpronounceable. He had a wide, square face with a short curly beard and limpid brown eyes that danced with kind of barely-suppressed laughter.

Omar Shariff by way of Osama bin Laden?

She bit her lips to stop the grin. Oh, behave. He was probably married.

And what, after all, must it be like for Barzin, working around the capital district of the country that had stormed into two of his possible homelands and threatened three or four of the others?

As if reading her curious stares from the back, the driver flashed a toothy smile and nodded. "I come from Iran, yes. Are you a Jew?"

Nina grinned and shook her head. "I just have this Gallic nose." She ran a finger down it. "My father's side of the family."

"Because, you know this story of the Iraqi taxi driver who found and returned the briefcase full of diamonds in the back of his cab? Left there by a Jew diamond dealer, yes? This was my cousin."

Nina snorted. "No kidding. You hear about Mother Theresa helping the Muslim cleric lost in New Delhi?"

"No."

"Yes. That was my aunt."

"Mother Theresa?"

"They just said it was Mother Theresa. My aunt didn't mind."

"Ah."

As he said it, two limousines with windows tinted black squealed out of the cross street ahead and into the taxicab's lane. Nina's driver slammed on his brakes, throwing Nina into the seat back in front of her, then swerved to the side of the road, cursing and looking in the rearview mirror at the cars braking hard behind him.

Nina pulled herself back upright as her driver spun around in his seat.

"You are okay? You are fine? You are not hurt?"

"Yeah. I'm fine," she said. But in the pit of her stomach she wasn't. Something line she'd read once about black harbingers of death kept jumping into her consciousness. She tried to keep her voice calm as she said, "Can we get going again, please?"

3

GUT TIGHT, Richard did a loping, silent sweep of the backyard, checking each bush along the privacy fences on either side, looking in the brightly-painted playhouse Tom had built, doing a quick scout of the back greenbelt.

The red-haired six-year-old hadn't gone back into the house or Marie-Ange would have found her.

Richard also thought it unlikely she'd have snuck around the side of the house. Janine didn't like dark or narrow places. Yesterday, playing hide-and-seek with the family to impress on everyone the limits set by the detection wire, Richard had encouraged Janine to squeeze into the space between the playhouse and the fence. He'd become more forceful as Marie-Ange's countdown neared zero. Janine became hysterical, screaming at the top of her voice until Marie-Ange came running.

Richard Mackenzie—world's best uncle.

He *was* a trained observer, though. And just as he heard the sound of the garage door opening and the van with Tom and Marie-Ange leaving out front, Richard caught a movement from a bushy cedar in the back border of the property.

He ran up to it and stopped at the bottom. Looking up, he could see a dangling running shoe. As he watched, the shoe moved and the needles shook. Probably Janine trying to look down to see if she'd been caught.

"Janine?" he called up. "You remember we all talked about maybe having to leave the house quickly someday. It's nothing to—"

He stopped at the sound of screeching brakes and skidding tires. Not just one set, but two. Three.

Oh, shit.

"Janine, you wait just where you are," he said. "Stay there and *don't make a sound.*"

He hid her stuffed toy at the back of the tree, pulled his M16 out of its duffel and looped its strap over his neck and shoulder. Then he loped to the side of the house and shuffled along it, his back flat to its brick wall.

Too late.

The Mackenzie family van had screeched to a halt not ten yards out of the driveway, blocked by two dark Cadillacs with tinted windows that had skidded sideways into the cul-de-sac.

Five men wearing ski masks and carrying submachine guns had already surrounded the van, smashed the driver's side glass, jammed the barrel of a submachine gun into it, and started shouting manically. In Arabic. Their wrists and hands were dark.

Shit. A *Hadji* hit squad? Here?

Fighting a trained urge to take them all out as quickly as possible, Richard locked his finger away from the trigger and raced through scenarios, trying to find one that let Tommy and family get out alive.

Neighbors were running for their houses. Some peered out their windows, maybe calling 9-1-1. Not that they'd ever arrive in time.

The masked man with his gun in the window yelled at Tom again, hit him with the gun muzzle.

No good options. Richard sited down the barrel of his assault rifle and squeezed off two quick shots. The thug spun backwards out of the window. Down. Alive, maybe, but no more threat.

Unfortunately, the other men this side of the van reacted fast, ducking for cover. One had already had managed to open the passenger door.

With a scream that plunged through Richard like ice, Richard knew Marie-Ange was taken. He felt the roughness of the brick against his right shoulder, smelled the sharpness of his own sweat, as the gunman who'd grabbed her out around the front. He had his arm around Marie-Ange's neck with his gun pointed at her right temple. His eyes darted back and forth, looking for where Richard's shot had come from.

A second man followed him, jamming his own gun muzzle up into Marie-Ange's rib cage.

Stalemate. Too close. No good shot from this distance. Richard pressed himself flat back against the wall, breathing hard. Had to assess. Wait for an opening.

"Come out!" the men were saying with heavy accents.

Richard come out? Unacceptable. Operationally unsound.

"Come out of the van, Thomas Mackenzie! Now!"

With a growing sense of hopelessness, Richard saw his options narrow as the front driver's side door of the van open slowly and his younger brother stepped out. With dignity, damn it.

As Tom cleared the door, one of the two remaining men who'd been hiding behind the van now surged out and grabbed him. They twisted Tom around and bound his wrists together with handcuffs. The other hiding man, shorter, dove into the van. Richard could see him tearing Tom's backpack apart inside. Obviously nothing in there after all. Marie-Ange's purse. The glove compartment. The man gave a howl of rage. The seat cushions. The carpets.

With each failure, the skinny man holding Tom hit him with his gunstock.

Just tell them what they want to know, Richard thought furiously. Tell them where you hid the evidence. Online? In a vault? On your person? It wouldn't make them leave, but maybe it would split them up to look for it. Increase my options.

Another brown-skinned man climbed from one of the Caddies. Much heavier than the others but still wearing a ski mask. He squinted around the cul-de-sac, eyes passing right over where Richard hid, then stomped over to Tom and began questioning him with a quiet calm Richard could barely hear.

"Where is it?"

"I don't know what—Ungh!—you're you're talking about."

"What you stole. And everything this 'Deep Throat' told you. Where is it?"

"I don't...have...anything."

As Richard gritted his teeth in awful foreknowledge, the fat man turned towards the men holding Marie-Ange and nodded. The man with the submachine gun at her temple re-aimed the gun at her right foot and pulled the trigger.

The thud of bullets and Marie-Ange's screams pummeled the base of Richard's skull, urging him forward. Attack! He raised his rifle and sited first on the heads of the men holding Marie-Ange, then the man holding Tom. Still too close. This wasn't a sniper rifle. Any drift, any wind...

The masked men were staring around, expecting the torture to draw Richard out, disclose his position.

He kept the rifle up, breathing raggedly, as Marie-Ange slumped, sobbing hysterically, and Tom lunged at her captor, only to be jerked back and hit again in his gut and on his face. When the fat man was done, and Marie-Ange had been pulled up straight again.

"Tell them, Tom!" she sobbed. "Jesus oh *tell them!*"

The fat man leaned his masked face in close to Tom's bleeding one and spoke too quietly for Richard to hear. But the man gestured obviously towards Marie-Ange.

When Tom raised his head, Richard could see he was broken. Tears streamed down his baby brother's face. Richard's own gut tightened dangerously. His finger twitched on the trigger.

Now. Tell him, brother. Or fight. Give me an opening.

But Tom was shaking his head, twisting it to look at Marie-Ange. Richard's heart fell out of him when Tom suddenly cried out, "I can't! I'm sorry, Marie-Ange!"

Shit. Time's up.

Richard swung his aim to the two men holding Marie-Ange and popped one of them. But before he could get the other, the man had shoved his gun muzzle further up under Marie-Ange's rib cage, pulled his trigger, and fired a sustained burst that made Marie-Ange's body dance like a marionette.

Richard shot the man. He fell. Marie-Ange fell. Dance over.

Too late. Too *late.* Doesn't matter. Move. Take them out. Finish it.

Richard swiveled and fired a burst that ripped apart the fat man's neck as he tried to run. Whether from a sense of self-preservation or grief, Tom dropped to his knees. It gave Richard a clear shot at the skinny guy who'd been gun-butting him earlier.

Richard shot. The man staggered backwards, firing a wild spray of bullets into Tom's back as he went down. Tom pitched forward.

No!

Richard ran for him, blasting out the windows of Tom's van and hitting the fifth thug there as he went, and yelling, "Get up, Tommy! Get up!"

But now the two Cadillac sedans had squealed forward, aimed straight for Tom.

Richard reached Tom first and hauled him sideways towards the van as the first Caddie hit the men Richard had downed and went airborne past them. The second Caddie skidded to a halt and its rear doors swung open.

Reaching the front of the van, Richard heaved Tom's too-still body around the fender, then spun and squeezed off three quick bursts that spider-webbed the Caddie door windows as yet more bad guys rolled out.

And rolled. Opposite directions. He couldn't get a lock as he traced after them with suppressive fire.

Damn. They were trained.

He dove back behind the fender with Tom. Alive? Dead?

"Richard..."

Alive. Tom's mouth was bubbling, coughing blood. And he smelled like death. Goddamn it. Richard knew the smell.

"Just lie back, bro." Richard switched in a fresh clip from his combat jacket pocket. "Got some business first. Then we talk."

"N-no." Tom coughed more blood. Few wounds on his front, but Richard didn't even want to think what his brother's back looked like. "Janine."

"She's safe."

Tom gripped Richard's pant leg as the fender above them rattled with gunfire. Richard rose to kneeling, swiveled, and shot the wounded man who'd finally stumbled out of the far side of the van.

"Listen!" said Tom, shaking Richard's leg. Richard turned to him. Tom's eyes blazed as he whispered, "They knew Marie-Ange was a backup. They'll assume you were too. And Janine. Save her!"

"Damn it, Tommy. Then tell me what they're after. What did you take?"

He wiped his mouth. "You know when Dad died..."

"Fuck that! Just tell me what you took? Secrets? Money? What?"

Tom spasmed and spat more blood. Bright red. "Home," he gagged out. "You have to...reach it first. It's there."

"You left it *behind*?" Richard spun and shot the running gunman he'd seen in his peripheral vision, trying to flank them.

"Richie..."

Spatters of bullets on the ground nearby. Richard raised up and sputted a response, then whipped back to his brother. "You stay with me now!"

"Love you, bro'. Sorry for...never telling..."

The sound of death was like the smell. Even in the midst of explosions and ear-cracking insanity, you couldn't miss it. The stillness. Then you saw the absence in the eyes.

Damn it, Tommy. Damn it.

Then, even through the icy chill sinking slowly into his gut, Richard heard the distinctive ring of a cell phone, then the rough voice of a Hadji answering it in what sounded like Farsi, then English. He closed it. Yelled out a command to the others and pointed at the house.

Richard looked back that way and saw Janine at the corner he'd run from. She stood in plain sight with her stuffed armadillo clutched in both hands, her eyes wide, her face white.

Richard jumped up, spattered a wide swath of pavement with suppressive fire, and sprinted to save the niece he barely knew.

4

Georgetown
Washington, DC
8 days later

SOMEWHERE HERE.

Nina blinked around at the murmuring people in black who filled her parents' living room and thought, *I have to find it.*

It was late afternoon, eight days after she'd arrived in a taxi to see her sister's house blown apart in a series of air-thudding explosions. Since Nina had staggered out of the taxi to identify, finally, that one of the two dead bodies in front of the wreckage was indeed Marie-Ange. The other was Tom. Spots where other dead bodies might have had been marked out with police lines. The bodies were gone. Only the bloodstains remained.

Nina herself felt like that. Just bloodstains. Her real self gone.

Or was she just circling, trying to figure things out? The news said the attack was terrorists, but no one could say why they'd targeted Tom Mackenzie and family. Or where they'd come from, where they'd gone, or anything except that two people were dead and the region was in shock.

No one knew anything. And then the funeral was done, Tom and Marie-Ange laid to rest, and...

Where is it?

Nina shook hands with the last of a long string of black suits and dresses who'd come to pay their respects. Judge Fitz-something-or-other and his wife. Nina nodded as they retreated. All the power players in this room, the sense of law and policy being shaped *sotto voce* even here—it was so familiar. Like slipping on an old pair of favorite gloves. Only...not?

My fairy hut.

What?

My fairy hut, Neens. C'mon out back. Daddy helped me. The front of a teeny house, built against the bottom of the dogwood tree. It's so cute. Like you can just imagine there's a fairy living inside? Come see.

M.A., that is so strange.

Aw, come on.

"Are you all right, Princess?" said a rich male voice. A whiff of spicy Polo cologne.

"Hi, Pops," Nina said and looked up into the crinkled eyes of her godfather, Senator Gordon Farthering, speaking of power players. He'd been five delegates short of being the GOP's candidate for President in the last election. And if he'd won, if he'd been guiding the country eight days ago, there wouldn't have *been* terrorists in Bethesda, would there?

"What are you thinking?" he pushed gently.

She looked away from him. "My daddy didn't stick around long after the funeral."

"At least he came."

"If I can stand my mother, you'd think he could."

Pops didn't take the bait on that.

"Did you know Marie-Ange used to call me Neens?"

Pops shook his head. "No. I didn't."

"And I wanted to punch her out so badly. Never got the chance."

He gave her a moment of silence, probably thinking she held back tears. Which showed how little he knew the Nina she'd become. This Nina didn't cry. This Nina just felt a great sucking guilty space in her gut.

He finally gave her shoulders a quick squeeze. "You come see me if you want to talk, okay?"

"Sure."

He drifted back to his handlers and an older woman with an over-bite who seemed to be calmly arguing the lot of them down. A Democrat congresswoman, surrounded by Republicans. Reese? Rose? Something. Shriveled hard by power. Fighting. Always fighting. Rumored to be the President's point dog in the House. Was that what Nina's mother had wanted for Nina?

And Nina remembered again the concussive heat of the blast that had ripped apart M.A.'s house just as Nina had arrived. *Boom! Boom! Ba-room!* Three linked explosions. That's what the DC cops had confirmed before the FBI took over and issued a lock-down on all statements. And then...

She took a jerky breath. Oh God. The thing she was missing? That no one talked about? It was Janine. Her niece. No body found. Possibly abducted by Tom's brother. *Fairy huts. A little person hiding.*

It was like the thud from the explosions hit Nina all over again.

"He's a man. What does he know, right?"

Nina pulled herself together to turn and see who'd just addressed her. It was a pale-skinned female about her own age but with a smaller nose and even better clothes. Her black dress was shorter than Nina's. Her choppy hair was bobbed just under her ears. And even with stiletto heels, she only came up to Nina's chin. Assertively so. She held a thick-looking drink in her left hand.

"Farthering, I mean." The woman stuck out her right. "Denise d'Alvay, aide to Congresswoman Reis. The women's contingent."

"Ah."

Reis. Right. The Democrat. She and Pops argued now in the middle of a small knot of people near the grand piano. Nina's elegant, red-haired mother was there too, clinging to Pop's arm. Oh, yes. Because Nina's absent father hadn't stuck around after the funerals, after all. So Nina's mom, Grace Tauredaux, could ignore her current boyfriend and do what she did naturally—cling to power like a mosquito to a bug strip.

And Pop's wife?

Yes, there she was by the wet bar at the far end of the room, Elaine Lawrence of the Lawrence Electric Lawrences, a plump woman with black, curly hair. She and Pops had a twenty-four year marriage that included a geekish seventeen-year-old son, Shane. He was over by the sandwich table where he'd been eating nonstop. Probably so he wouldn't have to watch his father's public semi-affair.

Good grief, Mother.

"Hello?"

D'Alvay still stood with her right hand outstretched. Nina took and shook it quickly. "Sorry. Distracted."

"My Gawd, of course." D'Alvay gave a sympathetic snigger. "Aren't we all. Farthering's fighting Congresswoman Reis and the President tooth and nail over shifting more troops to Afghanistan, and then we get *this*? Terrorists attacking us at home again. Do we use it? Will Farthering use it? Will it look bad if we do?"

Nina squinted down at her. "Will it *look* bad? I just lost a sister and brother-in-law. And my niece is missing."

The aide's body froze for a moment, her face rigid. Then she swiveled smoothly to take in the entire room. "Of course. Of course. And it's a tragic loss. I met your brother-in-law once or twice, you know. Your mother introduced us. At some party, I think. He was hoping he'd leave the DOJ and become a lobbyist."

"A lobbyist..."

"You didn't know? Didn't you and your sister talk?"

"Um...not much."

"She didn't call you and invite you to come back to see her? *Some*thing must have been going on."

Nina stared. The woman's smile looked shark-like now. Congresswoman Reis behind her was looking their way now like she too wanted to rip some flesh off. They knew something. Had sources. But what exactly did they think Nina could tell them?

"I don't know what you're talking about," Nina said.

"Oh, come on!" D'Alvay took a long pull on her drink. "You didn't know they were having marital problems? You didn't hear about the drug dealing? The coke parties?"

Nina's face flushed red. She could feel Reis's eyes were on her and shook her head. "You're done. Walk away now while you can."

"Excuse m—"

"Bitch."

Nina leaned into it and this time there was no mistaking d'Alvay's answering expression—cold hatred. The aide stared at her with her upper lip curled back, then smiled like cracking ice, turned up her little chip of a nose, and strode away across the Persian carpet. Her bubble butt twitched angrily as she pushed past a waiter with a tray of canapés and headed for the wet bar where Nina saw her mom's boyfriend, Chester Bund, had joined Elaine Farthering. Both drank steadily.

Nina took some punch from a passing tray, downed it in a secret toast to them, then to Congresswoman Reis, then to herself for at least standing up to d'Alvay. She'd forgotten what it was like back here in DC. The government was obviously already testing the waters with the stories about Tom and drugs and marital problems. Anything to shift attention, make things explicable. Nina couldn't understand how her sister had survived all these years in this environment.

How could anyone survive?

~~~~

On the street out front, fifteen yards down, a man in a borrowed raincoat appears to be putting out the trash and casually checking out all the politicos going into the house. In fact he's confirming that the FBI's watch on the front of the Tauredaux house has been replaced by something else—two men who look military. Better trained than the feds. Hiding in the park across the street.

Someone obviously still expects him to bring Janine back here.

Damn.

He's given them no cause to be sure, though, so hopefully they're relying on passive reconnaissance and electronics. And unless they're very good, there's still at least one way in.

So thinking, he shrugs his borrowed raincoat higher up around his ears and ambles back into the shadows, then flits down to the end of the row of stately townhomes to where he left Janine.

She crouches in the dark shadows by an electrical box in total silence. When he appears, she looks up at him with wide, trusting eyes. Waiting.

"We're going in," he whispers.

~~~~

A wreck of a man suddenly stepped in front of Nina. "Ms. Tauredaux?"

He was chunky and pudding-faced, with pock-marked skin and glasses. Mid-forties. A conservative blue suit that was far too cheap for this crowd of black suits and dresses. Had to be government or...

"My name is Special Agent Leonard Junk, Ma'am. I'm sorry about your loss."

Junk? That fit. Wait—F.B.I. Oh, God. Nina's heart quickened. "Are you a friend of my mother or here for something else?"

"I'm afraid 'something else', Ma'am."

He discretely flipped open a badge for her of the sort she'd seen more often in the last two weeks than in all her former years.

"My niece?" She held her breath.

"Is still missing, Ms. Tauredaux. But we've gotten more background about your other brother-in-law, the one you said Tom Mackenzie brought in as protection—Richard Mackenzie." He spoke quietly and kept his face down. "He hasn't turned up yet, ma'am. And we don't believe he will unless it's by choice."

"By choice? But I thought the FBI were working on the theory they were taken by...whoever killed my sister."

Junk shook his head. "No, Ma'am. That's what I wanted to pass on. I was brought in as a military specialist because a witness turned up..."

His voice trailed off as his gaze shot to something past Nina's shoulder.

Nina turned. But the only new face she saw was an almost-comically square man chatting with the group in the square arch of the front entryway. He had broad shoulders, a thick neck, obviously all muscle. *Me Hulk! Me smash!* And, like Junk, this newcomer was also not dressed in black. He wore military, four-button dress blues. His was dark-featured, swarthy in way that made him look almost Middle-Eastern, yet his eyes were strikingly blue, the crew-cut a shade too light, as if bleached by the sun.

Junk cleared his throat but kept his face down, pretended to adjust his glasses, and spoke quickly. "As I said, a new witness. She claims she saw a man matching Richard Mackenzie's description carrying a little girl out of your sister's backyard."

"But then why hasn't he...?"

"We think he may be holding her for trade."

"What? Trade?"

"Yes."

"You think he's working with the terrorists?"

Junk shook his head. "Witnesses think he shot a large number of the terrorists, so no. But one witness thought he heard the brothers discussing something valuable that Tom Mackenzie had taken from the terrorists. Hid somewhere. We're thinking Richard Mackenzie might be looking for it now."

He raised his face and stared directly into her eyes. Held it. And Nina felt a shard of gritty ice go through her.

"You think I know something too. Everyone thinks I know something."

"Ma'am?"

"You think I have something that Tom took?"

He said nothing but held her gaze.

"Goddamn you," Nina said quietly, fighting not to explode all over him. "You probably think I've been in contact with Richard Mackenzie too, don't you. That we've been carrying out negotiations in-between me finding my sister dead and helping arrange her funeral. You honestly believe Janine's own uncle is cold-blooded enough to watch his brother die then barter his little girl for something. What? Drugs? Drug money?"

"We don't know, Ma'am. But we do know that Richard Mackenzie is

Canadian Special Forces, JTF2s they're called up there. He's trained to maximize opportunities, he's on the run, and his priority is survival or possibly payback, by whatever means necessary." His eyes twitched to look past her head again and his manner shifted. "Just remember that, whatever he says, he's very dangerous."

Junk magically flicked out a business card from somewhere and held it out to her. As Nina took it, he faded sideways through the crowd near the drawing room door and was gone.

Nina turned back to the big blocky man who'd scared Junk, trying to figure out where he fit in. He was obviously military, so...

At that moment Denise d'Alvay slunk up to the blocky soldier's right arm and wrapped herself around it like a taut lamprey. Ah. Her boyfriend. Or what passed for it in DC.

Survival. Payback. Very dangerous.

Like trying to negotiate these stupid political waters where no one said what they really meant. And oh, shut *up*, Nina! She was sick of herself, sick of mourning, of worrying about Janine, of second-guessing everyone and everything. In a fit of claustrophobia, she strode through out of the room through the side door and made her way to the French doors of the back patio.

It was getting dark outside. Breezy. And...was there something moving along the fence in the neighbor's back garden?

She stepped outside to look.

~~~~

Chance and timing. She's seen him.

He clasps his hands together, holds them out palms up, and his little ward steps into them automatically. He hoists her up into the branches of the tree that arcs over the privacy fence between the yards. She grabs on and pulls herself the rest of the way up.

He doesn't know if she truly understands what they're about to do, but he knows and his heart is pounding hard, muscles tensing.

5

Nina blinked her eyes at the night, willing them to adjust to the semi-darkness.

When they finally did, she saw no movement and it was almost a disappointment. Because now all she had here were memories. Her and Marie-Ange playing for hours amongst the grass, dirt, roses, wild lilies, azaleas climbing the privacy fences all around, chicory and dogwood. God, it was still the same.

Except that Marie-Ange would never see it again.

Kicking a shoe at the flagstone, she tripped forward along the gravel path that led into the rose garden along the back. Stupid games they'd played. Stupid life. An unreal little haven that was nothing, *nothing* like the cutthroat political world beyond its fences. That's why, if Marie-Ange were still alive, Nina would tell her to grab Tom and her child and just run away. Anywhere but here. Anywhere but where Nina was.

She mentally counted out the first two of the five, evenly-spaced wooden arbors that she and Marie-Ange had run through as children. Then the third arbor, farthest from the house. She wanted to reach out and *grab* it. *Shake* it. Have the roses prick her flesh. Make her—

Leaves rustled along the back fence.

Nina clutched at her wool-covered chest and stepped back, pulse rushing. There was something up in the squat dogwood, something—

A pink form, no longer than Nina's leg, dropped through the black lower branches of the dogwood with crackling and a tiny thud. A girl! Red pigtails. Filthy. She clutched an equally filthy stuffed animal.

"What—?"

Before Nina could finish it, the long, blue and black form of a man followed the girl down.

As awkwardly as the girl tumbled, the man hit the ground silently, like a jungle cat in combat boots. He wore loose blue jeans, a black tee-shirt that exposed taut and bulging arms, a large backpack cinched tight. A large branch suddenly fell after him, heading for the girl, but the man's hand shot out and caught it like an eye-blink. He tossed the branch away then reached down for the girl and pulled her to her feet. The girl immediately clung to his leg with one arm. She clutched her stuffie with the other.

And Nina's heart stopped.

All the world seemed to stop. No sound. The dying afternoon light a solid thing. The breeze frozen on the rose petals.

Even without having seen the pictures all over her parents' house, even without the warning Junk had so propitiously given her, Nina thought her heart would have recognized the little girl and man for whom they were.

Janine, her niece.

Richard, her brother-in-law. Janine's rescuer...or kidnaper?

The man was staring at Nina so hard now that she felt pinned in place. It wasn't sexual though. No, Richard Mackenzie's eyes probed like they wanted to dissect her, examine her very core to see if...what? She'd scream? Betray them?

And how would he respond if she did? The set of his shoulders was still, but his knees, where Janine clung, were flexed, not locked. Nina remembered how fast he'd grabbed the falling branch. She knew he could cover the few feet between them just as fast to silence her.

Her heart thudded in her ears. And despite her annoyance at doing so, she imagined this man's powerful hands over her mouth. His long body pressed to hers. His leg pressing the bottom of her dress up between her legs.

He was taller than Tom. Taller than Nina, refreshingly. But his body looked hard and cold; his chiseled face blank and set; eyes cold. And he smelled of blood and sweat, not cologne.

Dangerous!

"You're Richard Mackenzie," she finally managed.

His eyes narrowed. He nodded.

"And Janine?"

The young girl—six!—looked at her with wide eyes and clung tighter to Richard's blue-jeaned leg. Freckle-faced, but with the unmistakable look of her mother around the eyes and mouth. And mute. Nina realized she'd made no sound even when dropping from the tree. Not a whimper. It brought back a wave of the soul sick feeling. That this girl, Nina's only niece, didn't even recognize her...

Mackenzie seemed to be waiting for something from her, as if she held the key to his fully entering this garden. What did he want?

"The FBI are looking for you," she said.

"No they're not," he said quietly and she had to hide how his certainty both thrilled and scared her.

"They believe you kidnaped Janine. That you're trying to trade her for—"

"That's absurd."

"*Don't* cut me off," Nina snapped.

His mouth corners shot down and Nina felt a flush of adrenaline as she recalled Junk's warnings about him. *Witnesses say he killed a large number of the terrorists.* Just him. A killer. And he'd been living with Tom and Marie-Ange right up to the attacks. No wonder Marie-Ange had wanted Nina to come and be with her.

"I was just questioned by Special Agent Leonard Junk inside," Nina said. "Five minutes ago. He implied the fact you hadn't turned yourself in with Janine was proof you were desperate, paranoid, and highly dangerous. So why haven't you turned yourself and Janine in?"

Mackenzie waited a beat, emphasizing his mock deference to Nina before saying, "This guy Junk. Hefty. Soft around the edges, right? Glasses? I've seen him. Not sure which branch of intelligence he's with, but it's not field. And not FBI. He's alone."

"You didn't answer my question. What have you been doing for eight days?"

Mackenzie frowned again and for the first time his eyes left her face, glancing down at Janine, then towards the house and around the backyard garden. "Staying alive. Keeping Janine alive. Looking for answers. And this house has been watched."

"But not now?"

"Still. But the funeral was a distraction. I figured I might slip in."

"Oh, you did. Why, if it's such a big risk?"

He ignored her question, studying what he could see of the back of the house from where they stood in the garden. "Do you know how much time Janine spent in your mother's house?"

"Pardon me?"

"Would she have considered it a second home?"

"I...don't know. I've been away."

"Since Janine was born. I know. I was listening on the phone line when you spoke with your sister from Bethesda Station."

It stiffened Nina's spine and she glared hard at him until he finally looked at her. Then she almost regretted pulling his attention, it was so fierce. "Wh-what do you want here?" she demanded.

"What do I want? I thought that would be obvious."

"It's not. You're frightening. This whole situation is creepy. You make it sound like any minute men with guns are going to storm into this garden after you. And while I'm glad you've returned my niece to us, where she belongs, I don't understand why *you* are still here."

He tilted his head, reached down to where Janine still clung to his leg, and gave her the smallest smile. Nina was both shocked and annoyed at the quivers of doubt it shot through her.

"We, both Janine and myself, need a place to hide," he said.

6

THIS WAY."

Nina stopped to the right of the rear kitchen door and fumbled around for a key that... Yes! It was still there, hidden behind the drainpipe. She took it to the narrow servant's entrance that looked like it hadn't been opened since the last time the house was painted. With a bit of wiggling in the lock, the rusty key still worked, though. Nina shuddered the door inwards.

He half-shoved her ahead of him into the gloom of the narrow staircase heading up, then stepped after her, pulling Janine in behind him. Nina gasped with a sudden growing panic and fumbled about the wall for the light switch. Found it. Flicked it. It sputtered on but barely cut the gloom at all. It just made Mackenzie loom huge and thick behind her.

Oh God what had she just gotten herself into?

"Is...is it really both of you who need a place to hide?" she asked, licking her lips. "Or just you?"

"What are you suggesting?"

He didn't move but his presence just kept growing in the tight space. *He's trained to maximize opportunities.*

But surely not with a little girl present.

No? He's been dragging her around in hiding for eight days. Who knows what he's capable of.

Who knows what *I'm* capable of, Nina thought fiercely. I'm going to save Janine from him.

"You didn't answer my question earlier," she said, turning to face him, "about whether you thought they were after Janine as well."

"Tom thought they were."

"Why?"

"Can we go up now?"

Something in his voice. In his eyes. A defensive pain. Nina gasped. "You know. You know who killed them."

"If I knew that, they'd be dead right now."

"Then you know *why* they were killed."

The pain again, blazing through the gloom despite his squint. She could almost feel it rolling off his body.

"And why doesn't Janine speak?" she pressed.

Rather than answer, he took Janine's hand and pushed past Nina, heading up the stairs. The little girl re-clutched her stuffie and scrambled to keep up as best she could.

Nina scrambled up behind them as fast as her tight dress would allow. Her good sense was telling her to run back out the way she'd come, dash into the post-funeral gathering and call 9-1-1. But that risked Mackenzie taking off with Janine again. And...if Mackenzie was telling the truth...

She growled under her breath loud enough for Janine to turn around at the top of the stairs and look back in fear. Which made Nina force a smile. But damn it, she was mad. Furious actually. She hated being in a situation where a strong male had all the cards. Where he was telling her what to do and her only choice was to play along or lose everything.

It made her insane.

She reached the top to see Mackenzie had left Janine to do a sweep of the little apartment. Not that there was much to see. A worn carpet runner ran down the short hall. Bedroom and kitchen doors on the right wall. A cramped three-piece bathroom dead ahead. A door connecting these quarters to the main house's upper hall halfway down the left wall.

Mackenzie had circled around to that door.

The party! It was on the other side of that door, just down the stairs! Nina lurched forward with her hands up. "You can't go through there. People."

He stopped. "This house—built back in the mid-1800s?"

"Um...yes?"

"Eight houses in a row," he ploughed on. "Stone block fronts. Shared side walls. Two-by-six construction. Used to be all dirt roads and horse-drawn buggies in front. And these are the servants' quarters. No longer used." He reached up a finger and confirmed it by running a finger along the top of the door casing. Looked pointedly at the thirteen foot ceiling laced with spider webs and cracks.

"You're an expert in architecture now?"

His gaze snapped to her. "I know how to read and observe."

"Whoah. Okay! Okay, Mr. Smartypants with muscles!"

"Excuse me?"

"I don't see why I should!" Nina fumed. Inside, her little voice was screaming at her that no, she had to win his trust, not make him run, not anger him enough to hurt her. "You disappear with my niece for eight days so that everyone thinks you're both dead, then that you're a cold-blooded kidnapper—which maybe you are; the jury's still out on that one—then you drop out of a damn dogwood tree and say you need a place to stay, then you lecture me about the history of the house I grew up in?"

"You grew up in this part of the house?"

"My sister and I had a nanny when we were kids," she said. "She used to live here. We'd come and play."

Mackenzie snorted and left Janine and her stuffed animal standing by the door to brush past Nina and stride to the bathroom dead ahead. He slid up the double-hung window there, doubtless to check the line of black limousines and taxis which had taken over from the buggies and horses of yesteryear for the influential in downtown DC.

Take Janine. Run!

No. Way. I don't run.

Besides, he'd catch her. And, despite her better judgment, she didn't *want* to run. Richard Mackenzie mesmerized her. His powerful legs. The way his muscular shoulders rolled, making the backpack shift like a declaration of disgust for the well-heeled.

Of which Nina was one, wasn't she. Which was maybe part of why she sparked off him so badly. She disgusted him, and Nina picked up on that disgust. Hated it, the injustice of it. Even as she loathed what he did for a living. War. Killing people. Blowing things up. America needed its warrior-destroyers, but she didn't have to mingle with them. Besides, he wasn't even American.

"Anyone acting strange at the party?" he called back to her.

"It's a post-funeral party. What do you think?"

"Was anyone asking about me or Janine?"

"Besides Agent Junk?"

He waited.

"It's mostly a 'be seen' crowd," she said. *Way above your station. How could you and Tom have ever been brothers?* "Political obligations. My father was a big player on the scene here for years. My mother still wants to be."

Richard's gaze shot back to her with those piercing eyes and her own nostrils flared. She glared back at him. He broke contact to check out the bedroom again.

"No one comes up here," Nina said to his back. "If you're quiet, even my mother won't know you're here. It's a big house. Thick walls. Soundproof. The door on the other side of the hall from you enters the main area of the house upstairs but it's locked off from this side and I doubt my mother even knows where the key is anymore. I'll bring you both food. I'll keep you informed of what's going on."

He turned back to her.

Again those eyes! "How...long will you be staying?"

Mackenzie's twitched into an unreadable smile that sent a flood of warning through her. And when he slung his backpack to the floor and squatted beside it to check something, she saw that some of the straps over his shoulder weren't for the backpack after all; they held a loaded gun holster under his left arm.

Dangerous. However pissy she felt towards him, she couldn't afford to forget that a warrior-destroyer could destroy *her*.

"Janine's eaten but she's tired. She'll sleep. I might too." His gaze flicked around the bedroom. "When everyone's left the gathering downstairs, I want you to do one thing for me. Go out to the nearest mall and pick up a disposable cell phone. Prepaid. No contract to sign. Bring it back up here along with a phone book. Can you do that?"

"I— Yes."

"Good."

He stood and walked to Nina, took her by the shoulders.

Nina froze. It was the heavy physical thing again—the feel of him dominating her made her heart race and anger boil at the same time. His hot grip through the light wool of her mourning dress. The sharp smell of his sweat. If he were to draw her in close now, take her by force...

Nina!

She shook her shoulders but he didn't release her. Instead he gave them a gentle squeeze.

"Ms. Tauredaux. Nina. Listen. The attack on your sister wasn't random terrorism. Just before I ran to rescue Janine, I heard the leader of the attackers ask for a delay on bringing in the police. You understand what that means?"

Nina frowned hard, trying to connect that to her memories of the rushing sirens, the sympathetic officers. Besides the feeling of overwhelming grief that swelled up, there was something else. A disconnect. The leader of the attackers controlling the police?

"Exactly," Mackenzie said as if he read her mind. "They were working *with* the police. Possibly with a government agency. Tied to the reason they attacked. It's why I've been watching and waiting, trying to figure out who's in charge. It's why *you* can't trust anyone unless I've cleared them first. Do you understand?"

Nina swallowed and was mortified to feel herself shiver under his hands. Like she believed this? He was a Canadian (Tom's *brother*), had abducted Nina's niece (*saved* her), raved about a government (unless it *was* a conspiracy), and treated her like...like...

"Why did they attack?"

He flinched and hid his eyes. "I don't know it all. And I can't tell you what I *do* know without putting you in even more danger. Just that I think Tom was trying to do the right thing. He called me to help him. I failed."

Nina felt the truth of it and struggled to breathe. All the might-have-beens came flooding back. Her and Tom. Her and Marie-Ange. She gasped and her heart thudded hard in her ears. She had to reach a decision, any decision.

With a violent twist of her shoulders, she freed herself from Mackenzie's grip and stumbled backwards, half expecting him to come after her. When he didn't, she got her bearings and looked hard at him, then down at Janine, who'd snuck up behind him and wrapped her little free arm around his leg, her other arm still clutching her stuffed animal. Yet her face stayed as blank as stone.

Stockholm syndrome—in love with her abuser?

Nina had to get her away. Had to sort things out away from Richard Mackenzie's eyes and dominating presence.

She swallowed and nodded. "Will you let me take Janine to the other part of the house?"

"She stays with me for now."

"But—"

"She stays. The fewer people who know where she is, the better."

"I'll...get you the cell phone."

"After everyone else is gone," he said.

"After everyone else is gone."

"Without talking to anyone."

She leaned forward. "La-la-la-la-*la*."

"What?"

"I heard you the first time, Rambo."

Enough craziness, Nina! You made your point.

But Mackenzie barely reacted. He just lowered his voice and said very clearly, "I know you think that one of those power players down there can save Janine, maybe turn me in."

Nina clenched her teeth hard. *Pops!*

"I'm telling you the truth," he said. "About everything. You bring in the wrong person and not only will I be dead, but probably Janine. Maybe you too. This is not paranoia, just fact."

"Right."

Forcing her own face to go neutral, Nina turned back to the stairs and hurried down them and out.

~~~~

When Nina had left, Richard let out a long, hard breath.

Damnation. From the moment he'd dropped out of that tree and seen Nina Tauredaux up close, he knew he was in trouble. Seeing her a few times from a distance as she spoke with police or the FBI hadn't done her justice.

She was tall, yes, and had lost a lot of weight from the pictures Tom had shown him. Lost the glasses too. And had turned into something like a tall, cool drink in that dress that he wanted to run his hands up and down. Feathered haircut with reddish highlights, long straight nose, and full lips he'd found himself focused on far too much.

Mostly it was the maddening *presence* of the woman. The way her eyes had locked onto his and kept doing so, with barely a hint of fear.

Where had she gotten that strength? University? Was that what you got when you had all that education? A sense of entitlement? Added onto her rich upbringing, of course. So she thought she knew what was going down. Thought she knew what to do. What Richard had to do.

Goddamn! Cynicism and arrogance, Tom had said. Richard had worked with officers like that in the field. They usually ended up dead and their men with them.

So? Was he an idiot to stay?

His instinct said Nina might not trust him, but she clearly cared about her niece. She wouldn't risk Janine's safety by possibly alerting people out there who might do her harm. It's what Richard had gambled on in coming here.

But he wasn't going to risk Janine's life on a gamble, either.

He separated Janine from his leg. "Go explore around this place, okay? There might be some toys or picture books or something." Then he knelt by his backpack again and pulled out the receiver for the eavesdropping bug he'd hooked into Nina's dress when he'd clutched her shoulders.

He stood and popped the small receiver into his ear. The battery pod clipped over the waistband of his pants. Fiddling with the frequency, he got static, a crackle, then the scritching sounds of Nina's feet across the back patio steps. The whuffle and creak of the French doors opening...

A tiny hand tugged his pant leg. Janine had come back to him, now opening and closing her eyes like she could hardly see out of them. Her other hand still clutched Snuffles but was gripping and re-gripping it like she might drop it. Not surprising, since he'd gotten her up at four-thirty that morning to move out of their hiding spot before the house's residents were aware of their presence in the garage.

Richard grimaced. "Tired? Okay. Come on."

He hurried her back to the first bedroom Nina had shown them, listening to the ear bud throughout. Sounded like Nina had detoured into a washroom. Good.

"Just a minute," he ordered Janine. "Stand over there."

Janine did, like the good little soldier she'd been throughout. Other than the hair she was the image of her mother, Marie-Ange, but every once in a while Tom shone through too. And in those minutes, Richard had been hardly able to function. Jesus, he'd fucked up so badly.

Still listening to Nina's progress with one ear, Richard stripped the quilted cover off the bed, careful not to disturb the dust he saw layered into it. The blanket and sheet still on the bed smelled musty, but clean.

"Okay. C'mere. Shoes off."

Soundlessly Janine sat on the edge of the bed and he helped untie her little running shoes, filthy dirty and pretty pungent even though he'd managed to slip into a drugstore and buy her a few changes of socks and underwear.

She rolled back into a little fetus position around Snuffles, her stuffed armadillo, even before he'd gotten the last shoe off. Her eyes were still open, though, blinking sleepily at him.

Richard tugged off her last shoe and stared back at her, his chest tugging up inside his throat. "Sleep," he said. Through his ear buds, he could hear Nina finishing up in the bathroom.

Janine kept blinking so hard it looked painful.

"What?"

She blinked again.

"Not again. You really want me to?"

Blink.

"Fine. Okay? Just...stop the eye thing."

The blinking stopped.

Richard sat on the edge of her bed and rummaged through his mental attic for the Gaelic songs he'd sung as a boy with his mother, then as a fisherman, then as a sniper hiding in a cave in the Tora Bora mountains, and finally on the run with a little girl who'd crept out of her backyard tree to see her mother and father shot.

But the song that came to him now, as he looked up and around at the faded floral wallpaper, the quaint little dressing table in the corner, the dusty bone-handled brush still sitting on it, went even farther back for him. His mother sitting on his bed, stroking his hair as a fierce storm rattled the windows of their house, made the timbers creak, and made him wonder if his father was going to make it home.

"*Lullaby and goodnight...*," He crooned Brahms's *Cradle Song*. "*In the soft evening light...*"

He ached to stroke Janine's forehead as she closed his eyes but feared as always that his rough touch would somehow set her screaming. He wasn't her father. He was just her protector.

He finished the song and saw she was sound asleep.

"G'night, JJ," he whispered, just as a sudden tumult of murmuring voices in his ear told him Nina had rejoined the party.

Standing, he crept out of the room and shut the door behind him.

Then Nina spoke, her voice as clear as if she were standing right in front of him...

7

"I HAD TO VISIT THE LADIES' ROOM, Mother," Nina said stiffly. But her heart was pounding, her head spinning with the conspiracy stories Richard Mackenzie had woven for her in her old nanny's apartment. Even as he'd clearly protected his little niece, *Nina's* little niece, at what had to be great personal cost.

And Tom had trusted him.

And he'd killed a bunch of the terrorists. Clearly *tried* to save Tom and Marie-Ange.

"You wanted to escape Congresswoman Julia Reis," Grace Tauredaux said and gave her arm a squeeze. "I understand."

"No."

"She's a lesbian, you know. That aide of hers... She finds you very attractive, I'm sure."

"Is this somehow part of your latest plan to jump start my political career?"

Banter. Nina had to keep bantering until she figured out who here she could trust and who was sent to keep watch on this place from the inside. If what Mackenzie had said was true. If he wasn't, despite all his good intentions and actions, a raving paranoid.

Her mother waved away the waiter who offered fresh, Thai spring-roll hors d'oeuvres. "No. But as always, my dear, your chance to really make a difference is ready whenever you are."

"I make a difference where I am now."

"Do you really believe that?"

"I *make* a difference."

"If you say so, dear. Why don't you come and meet the President."

38

Nina blinked. "President. Of the United States?" And she was suddenly back to her immediate predicament. To Richard Mackenzie's conspiracy theory. How high up would something like that reach? To a fading President who wanted to give his war effort a boost by manufacturing another domestic terrorist incident? Was that why he was here now? To see what he'd wrought?

"Yes, baby," enthused her mother and primped her flame-colored hair. "He came to briefly pay his respects and got caught up debating policy with Gordon and Congresswoman Reis. Join them. This is your future."

But when Nina looked at the knot of people filling the center of the room, she couldn't see the President. She could see the three black-suited Secret Service men placed strategically around the room. She felt a quiet panic build inside her even as she tried to laugh it down.

Was this how the conspiracy theorists felt? Always afraid? Always imagining the worst?

"Nina, darling? Come on."

"I didn't vote for him, Mother. I can't stand the man."

"Of course not, but—"

"*No.* Why don't you just go...go comfort Elaine or something."

Grace sucked in her lips and marched off much as d'Alvay had done earlier, but this time Nina got no joy from it. Everything had changed in the last half hour. The world had gone from incomprehensible and tragic, to just plain threatening.

If Richard Mackenzie was right.

No, even if he wasn't, because then she was dealing with a dangerous paranoid who had Nina's niece in his control.

All these faces around her. If Mackenzie was sane and knew what he was talking about, they were all a threat. If Mackenzie was cracked, she could go to them now, get their help, get everyone's help, get the police, get the FBI and let them handle it. Things were so much easier if Mackenzie was cracked.

Easier...

Protect my child, MA's voice seemed to beg from the grave.

Meaning call the cops on Richard Mackenzie?

Protect her.

Meaning don't?

An entire group of suits shifted to the door and then the President was obviously gone. A gaggle of slimy d'Alvay types, men and women Nina vaguely remembered were lawyers with Tom's firm, began leaving too. Pops's son, Shane, was watching them with a baleful look like one or more of them had made fun of his long curly hair or too-long dress pants.

Then Pops raised his ear from Nina's mother's mouth and caught Nina's eye. Waved her over.

Nina took a deep breath and approached.

"Your mother said you didn't want to meet the old man," Pops said, meaning the President. His eyes crinkled as he said it, trying to be sweet. But she could see he was pumped from whatever the President had said to him.

"She's not a suck-up like you, Gordon," said Reis, standing beside him. She had twice the presence up close—frosted hair; subtle, perfect makeup; and dark eyes that now gave Nina a frank once-over, followed by a nod that somehow seemed to say a hundred things at once. *Good girl. You're keeping things together. You present well. You seem intelligent. I respect you...*

"But she's a good Republican voter, aren't you, Nina?"

Nina tore her eyes off Reis. "I would have been if you'd been running," she said to Pops.

Reis laughed, the others followed suit, and suddenly the incongruity of it all at a post-funeral reception, with her niece being held upstairs by a possible madman, was too much. Her emotion flooded up and he had to fight hard to keep it in.

But Pops saw it and glared the laughter down. "You know, Nina..." He paused for a moment, judging whether the time was right. Then he said, "We'll catch whoever did this. And we'll find out why."

Reis cleared her throat and looked away. Nina's mother nodded somberly.

Before Nina could respond, though, the whiskey-soaked corpulence of Chester Bund suddenly pressed up behind her. He took her by the shoulders and moved her aside. His bad comb-over straggled down his forehead.

"Oh, yeah, Gordo," he slurred. "An' then you'll make the slain into heroes, right? Whatever was really going on, they muss have been fighting the 'war on terror' right here on our native soil, right?"

Pops cleared his throat. "If the truth is..."

"Evil Iraquis! Iranis! Afghanis!"

"Why don't we talk about it later, Chester."

"The press'll dig it out!" Bund said.

"Someone will."

"And you'll make hay of it!"

"It's not—"

"Or your *advisors* will. Anything for power!"

"Chester, you're drunk."

"But *I'll* be sober later, an' *you'll* still be a right-wing, gun wiggling..."

Bund's tongue got tangled as Nina's mother finally lost her patience and physically shoved Bund away from the crowd, right over beside Shane, whispering something fiercely at him as they went until he began hanging his head like he wanted to vomit. Shane looked like he might vomit too.

On any other day, Nina might have felt for them.

"I'm sorry, Nina," Pops muttered. He took her arm and stepped away from the others. "This wasn't the place or time. I guess...the loss of Marie-Ange, as would the loss of you or your mother, knocks the wind out of me. It makes me fall back on this front we develop in the Senate."

He waved his hand over his face and Nina felt an overwhelming urge to confide in him as she had when she was a young girl. Let *him* decide if Richard Mackenzie was sharp or full of bullshit.

She cleared her throat, vaguely conscious of Congresswoman Reis watching her again. "Pops..."

"Yes?"

"Did you..." *Don't don't don't. Your decision. Yours.*

"What, Princess?"

"...talk to MA recently?" *Yes! Good call!*

Was it?

Pops seemed to take her cover at face value and nodded, looking down. "Two weeks before your sister and Tom were killed, Elaine and I had lunch with them. You know Elaine always loved Marie-Ange. She'd suggested I should get Tom on my team, help me run my next campaign. I pressed pretty hard."

"He said no?"

"He said he liked the law. He wasn't a politician."

Nina laughed at that, feeling it stab in her gut. Tom had been nothing if not a politician. Gift of the gab. Loaded with charm.

"Exactly," Pops said. "I'd planned to keep pushing."

"But never got the chance."

"No."

There was a long pause as Nina looked into his eyes. Pops said quietly, "There's something you want to tell me, isn't there?"

She almost swallowed her tongue. "What?"

"I've known you since you were pudgy little Buddha girl. You always have more going on behind those eyes than you let on. And right now you're bursting with something. You'll feel better if you just say it."

Your choice. Do you believe Mackenzie? Do you want to?

She opened her mouth to speak.

~~~~

"*I'm thinking, Pops,*" said Nina's husky voice in the ear bud in Richard's right ear as he pressed on it, the blood pounding there like it wanted out, "*that I and my mother are very fortunate to have you to share our grief with us. It's been difficult.*"

Richard leaned his head against the door that joined these quarters to the main house's upstairs hall and let his breathing slow. *Good girl*, he thought down through all the plaster and wood towards her. *Good girl.*

She was even smarter than he'd hoped. Which meant forever out of his league, of course, despite the strange little fantasies she'd sent blowing through his mind. Anyone who looked like that, with her background and education, *and* with the God-given good sense to keep it all together—well, a woman like that would never seriously say boo to a highly-trained swabby like him.

Not to mention the fact he was responsible for her sister getting shot. And Richard's own brother.

Oh, yeah. That little fact.

It didn't stop him wondering what Nina's hair felt like, the long curve of her back, her hot, long neck under that up-tilted chin...

Come *on*, Mackenzie! Focus.

Fact was that she was confirming with every conversation that he'd been right about her. So now, after eight days of ducking and hiding with a six-year-old in tow, risking too many times getting tagged to learn snippets of what was happening, he might actually have a chance to make serious headway. Find what exactly had happened and who was responsible.

He padded quietly back to his knapsack, still listening on his receiver to Nina's conversations. Squatting, he prepped for the night. He'd dumped his rifle because it was too hard to conceal, but he still had the SIG 225 pistol. Eight in the clip, one in the chamber. He got out extra ammo for it, small night-vision binoculars, wire-cutters, and something that had followed him all the way from his childhood romps with Tom up the shore through Inverness—smoke bombs.

Finally, a scrawled-on paper—a set of phone numbers he'd managed to pull off the internet at the local library the day before. Would have been nice to have the unmarked cell phone he'd asked Nina to get, but he'd decided that if he was actually here when she returned, she wasn't going to let him run out without telling her enough to put her into danger.

No, he'd just wait until he was sure she was on the way up to care for Janine, then he'd take off and find a pay phone on the street. Keep it short, untraceable. Whatever mistake the mysterious "Deep Throat" had made to get tagged, Richard hadn't spent the last seven years specializing in signals intelligence to slip up the same way.

He pulled out, unrolled, and slipped on, the cheap black windbreaker he'd picked up at a used-clothing store the day before, filling its pockets and his jean pockets with the smoke bombs and other equipment. Then he shoved the backpack out of sight under the bed where Janine slept.

Ninety-nine percent ready, he crept down the stairs to the back servants' entrance they'd come in by. There he paused, eyed his exit route via the black dogwood tree at the back, then went back up the stairs to the door that connected the nanny's quarters to the rest of the house.

With one ear he listened for any sounds of Janine stirring. With the other he followed Nina's movements in the main house and also listened through the door to see if anyone was upstairs.

He couldn't leave until he was sure Nina was coming back...alone.

And before that happened he also had one more thing to do.

~~~~

The grandfather clock in the front hall struck nine-thirty p.m. as Nina paced back and forth, watching the caterers carry their last box across the polished marble floor and out the wide front door.

She'd had a prickling feeling at the back of her neck all evening that wasn't just explained by the insanity of sheltering a fugitive and his captive niece, *Nina's* captive niece. No, there was more. Like she was missing something. Like Richard Mackenzie was spying on her or...

Grace, obscenely flushed and alive through the post-funeral party, stepped stiffly behind the last departing caterer, closed the double doors and leaned back against them like a propped-up corpse. Her drunk paramour, Chester Bund, had stormed out of the house ahead of Pop's departure so it was just Grace and Nina now.

Grace met her daughter's eyes, then looked away. "I'm...going to lie down for a bit."

"Kodak moment," Nina said.

"Don't be mean."

"I had a good teacher growing up."

"I was never *that* crass, my darling. That's all your own."

Then, sniffing, Grace Tauredaux shut the front door and walked with studied self-composure to the stairs. There she paused, huffed and squared her shoulders, and climbed. It was like she visibly carried the weight of her dead youngest daughter across her shoulders. Nina smirked and shook her head. It was one thing to love power; another to do it sloppily.

The second her mother had vanished up the last stair, Nina ran out through the drawing room again and back through the French doors to the outside servant's entrance. Upstairs on the servants' side, she hurried into the first room, her nanny's old room where she'd actually played a number of times as a child, and found Janine.

The girl was sleeping, shoes off but otherwise fully dressed, under the sheet and blanket.

Fully dressed. Why? Mackenzie's laziness? Wanting to be ready to run? A signal to Nina that this was the way he handled his niece?

Or—the mixed relief and panic of the idea made her heart flutter—had he simply decided Janine was too much trouble and left?

Nina jogged to the second bedroom. Richard wasn't there. She checked the bathroom, the first bedroom again. Then she saw it. Fastened, with a tack he must have found in the kitchen, to the wall in the hallway was a small, ripped piece of lined paper. *Back by morning* was printed in quick, neat letters.

Nina tugged it off, stared at it, then crumpled it up and tossed it to the floor.

And suddenly her decision downstairs to trust him, to believe him, crumbled to nothing. Because it had been based mostly, she realized, on his care of his niece. How could a crazy man bend himself so out of shape to watch over a little girl?

But then he'd just left her without knowing for sure Nina would come back. Without knowing anything. When? An hour ago? As soon as Nina had left him the first time?

And she'd believed him!

With tight lips, Nina ran to the sleeping girl and bent down to pull off the sheet and blanket. She reeled back a little from the little girl's B.O., but Janine slept on, oblivious.

Holding her breath and doing her best to be gentle, Nina leaned forward again and scooped Janine up. Then she turned with her, went through the door that joined to the upstairs hall of the main house, and went looking for her mother.

8

20:44. 1127 Connecticut Avenue NW.

One minute to rendezvous.

From the dark shadows of the bushes across the street, Richard raised his binoculars and surveyed the entrance of the Renaissance Mayflower. He'd done a full circuit of the place, checking all entrances and exits, looking for signs of the feds or any other group that might be watching for him.

There'd been no one. The spot-lit, flag-fluttering, stone facade with brown brick wings behind looked like an innocent, pompous older gentleman. Waiting for him.

But just as he'd done when he'd brought Janine to Nina Tauredaux, it was time to take another calculated risk. Confront someone who could be either a friend or an ally.

20:45. Time to move.

Flexing his toes in his new runners, he zipped the bottom of his black windbreaker to help hide the shoulder holster. Then he strode out from the bushes, across the near-empty street, and in through the venerable hotel's front doors.

The lobby was two stories high, overdone with potted greenery, stone and black metalwork, expansive area carpets over marble, a mullioned glass ceiling. And on this Tuesday night, it was virtually empty. A few late arrivals were checking in with the front desk staff. A couple giggled and stumbled in the long, high hallway to the right—presumably trying to find their rooms. Two white-haired gentlemen sat reading newspapers on either side of a garish electric floor sconce.

Then Richard saw his contact and felt his gut clench in anticipation. The unmistakable tank-like build, almost as broad across the shoulders as he was tall when he hunched. All muscle and deadly poise even here, his mixed Greek and Dutch ancestry giving him that dark skin and blue, blue eyes.

Major Misha Castinages.

The last time Richard had seen him had been on the C-17 flying back from Afghanistan to DC. The two of them had been the only human cargo on that flight and they'd shared the rumbling, dark hold with a decommissioned M1 tank. The Major had been smoking, against regs, and telling Richard about his family. Asking Richard about his.

And, despite the fact he only knew the man because Tommy had urged him to get onto the Major's Special Forces team for a mission or two, to check that team out, Richard had found himself unloading.

Maybe it was because they'd both come from similar working-class backgrounds and Castinages felt instantly like the father Richard should have had. Or maybe it was because Richard had seen only good things during the two missions he'd run with Castinages—professionalism, efficiency, commitment. On the second mission, a raid on Abdul Adeeb's drug-distribution compound deep in the Sulaiman Mountains near Kandahar, Castinages had saved his life once. Richard had then turned around and saved the Major's.

Whatever Tommy had been looking for, Richard had decided he trusted Castinages implicitly.

Of course, that was before Tommy and Marie-Ange were shot dead on Richard's watch. If Major Castinages had somehow been a part of that, all bets were off and Richard would count himself a fool. Again.

Now the Major stood in front of a rack of brochures to the left of the front desk and farther back, so still that you'd have to be looking for him to spot him.

He raised his head, caught Richard's eye, and gave an almost-imperceptible jerk with his chin. *Follow me.* He began walking back to his left, down a hall towards what looked like a bank of elevators.

Richard followed.

When Richard reached the elevators, Castinages was gone but an exit door was closing in the corner. Richard took it.

The floor ramped down along a poorly lit, narrow hallway. At the end of its carpet, by a fire door and stairwell going up, the Major waited, smoking his distinctively sweet Zimbabwean tobacco in the light of the red Exit sign over the door.

Richard stopped five feet short of the Major and snapped a quick salute. It was returned.

"Good to see you're still alive, Canuck," the Major rasped. Coughed.

"I'm glad too, Sir."

"But your brother's dead. And his wife."

"Yes, Sir."

"Guess you weren't fully on top of this one."

"I guess not."

"What can you tell me about it?"

Richard took a beat, then said, "My brother didn't tell me much. Only that it started with him investigating a politician about funding irregularities. He must have found some links to the military because he then contacted me."

Had Castinages raised his head at that? "When was this?"

"Two months ago. He wanted me to investigate Choke Force."

"Just like that."

"Yeah."

"That's why you became a pain in the ass about joining us on a couple missions."

"You could have said no."

"Your Captain recommended you. Our Colonel figured we should play nice with our coalition brothers." He glowered at Richard. "So what did you find?"

"A tight team. Highly effective."

"Bullshit 101."

"Higgs sleeps in the buff. Perky's phobic about scorpions and spiders."

"What did you brother expect you to find?"

"Some sort of Air America operation, I'm guessing. Intercepting drugs. Redirecting them somewhere for money. Not likely you'd be doing that with me aboard though, is it."

There was a long pause while Castinages took a drag on his cigarette then coughed like his guts were coming out. Richard tensed and unconsciously sank back into a defensive fighting stance.

The Major saw it and grinned nastily as he threw down his cigarette, wiped his mouth, and coughed again, still hunched over. "Sonofawhore. Stuff's going to kill me."

"Sir."

"Let me get this straight, Canuck." He stamped on the cigarette, bringing him a good two feet closer to Richard. "Your kid brother tells you to look into the best drug-busting team in Afghanistan, but tells you dick about what you're supposed to find? You find nothing and next thing you know he's calling you home because he's actually investigating some politician who wants to kill him. And does. That it?"

Richard stared at him, a chill forming in his gut. "My brother apparently took something from them and they wanted it back. Still want it back, I assume."

"What did he take?"

"You tell me."

"Right. Because I'm supposed to have smuggled it out of Afghanistan? Drugs? Military secrets?"

There was a long pause while Richard studied the Major and the Major waited calmly. And in that pause, Richard suddenly considered what it would mean if at least the Major himself was clean. It would mean...hope. That Richard had an ally. And not just any ally, but one experienced in tracking down the bad guys, one who had in's with the top brass, who could call on resources Richard couldn't even if he weren't on the run from everyone.

"Tommy didn't say what he'd taken," Richard said.

"Did he say *where* he'd taken it?"

"No place that made sense."

"Meaning what? What did he say?"

Home. The ice shifted uneasily in Richard's stomach. "It sounded like he'd left whatever it was in the house. Which means it's gone now."

Something flashed across the Major's face too fast for Richard to read. "What about the little girl? Does she know anything?"

"She's six years old. Traumatized. Can't speak."

"With you, then."

"She's...safe."

"And your brother's inside source? You know who was feeding him intel?"

Everything in the hallway was getting close now and Richard's heart sped up like it always did when he approached combat. "I never said anything about an inside source."

"Aw shit." The Major sighed. "Listen, Mackenzie. There are things going on here that you don't understand. That your brother knew fuck all about. If he had, things might not have gone down the way they did. But I guess the question is now, do *you* care? If you could be shown that everything that's happened had to happen, would you listen?"

The ice in Richard's stomach was flowing through his veins now, threatening to choke off his air supply. "My brother and his wife were shot dead in front of me. You're going to explain how that's a good thing?"

"Good? Fuck no. Necessary, yeah. Will you listen?"

Richard reached for his pistol. "Fuck n—"

The Major cut it off.

He was suddenly chest to chest with Richard, nose to nose, his right arm between Richard's left and his body, pinning Richard's holstered gun. The Major's other hand whipped Richard's right arm back and froze it.

The strength of the man was incredible. Cement. Immovable. Reeking of sweet cigarettes.

But even as the Major croaked, "Listen, Mackenzie...," Richard drove his head forward at his face, butting him on the bridge of his nose. He heard it crack. Felt a hot spray of blood.

Richard leapt backwards and snapped off a round kick at the man's thick torso, then spun a kick towards his head to finish him, but the Major had arched backwards and somehow had Richard's gun in his hand!

Using the momentum of the missed kick, Richard launched himself into a roll towards the fire door.

He felt, as much as heard, the *thud* of air that was a bullet from his own pistol just missing his head. Then Richard's feet were under him as he drove upwards towards the door...

Thud! Thud! Thud! Thud!

stiff-armed the bar release...

Thud! Thud! Thud!

and dove through.

Thud!

The ninth bullet caught Richard as he came up, half-turned, and caught him on the right side of his chest. Searing pain. A bubble in his throat. He staggered, half-expecting a finishing shot.

But of course the 225's magazine didn't hold the fifteen rounds of the 226, and Richard heard the Major swear, go for his own gun.

Richard found his balance and ducked right. Slammed the door behind him.

"Listen, Canuck!" came Castinages's muffled shout. "Don't you at least want to know what's going on? I saved your life at your brother's house, you know! You owe me!"

But a mental schematic of the back exit layout had already flashed through Richard's mind from his earlier scouting, and he was running. Even as the exit door smashed open, Richard had leapt to the walkway railing, then up to grab the lip of the stone wall of a walkway crossing over the exit door. Adrenaline pumping, he fumbled out a smoke bomb and threw it back down at Castinages. Heard it pop and the Major start coughing and swearing.

Richard ran.

He was steel. He was power. He was a god. The only people who dropped immediately from a bullet hit were those who believed you had to.

Still, as he ran the walkway crouched, he slapped his hand over the wound in his chest. Pain growing there. A wheezing sound from around his fingers. Bad. Open pneumothorax maybe—a sucking chest wound. He'd start losing breath. His lung could collapse. He'd suffocate. Had to treat it soon. Think!

He saw a door and ran for it, jerked it open, ducked inside. Upstairs utility room. Richard ran through, down the hall, and out a side door into a banquet room.

He grabbed napkins from a side table to wipe Castinages's blood from his eyes, then to staunch the bullet wound in his chest. He let go of the wound to reach over his shoulder and feel for an exit wound. Nothing. Damn. He clamped his hand over the wound again. The bullet was still in there.

But Richard still breathed. Heart still pumped. No vital organs hit except the one of hope. The one man in DC whom Richard had hoped would help him was one of the enemy.

Next door to another hall. Fire stairs. Exit.

He tore out into the night with his head reeling.

~~~~

It was dark and scary and Janine wanted to cry out, wanted to scream.

But she mustn't. Mustn't. *Couldn't.* Because she'd promised Mommy that she never would again. Never run away again. Not make a sound. Just stay close to Uncle Richard. Just be a good girl. Just...

The room door opened and someone dark and huge walked in, loomed towards her. Janine scrambled up out of her sheets, ready to leap. Ready to bite. To run.

The figure flicked on a little lamp and turned towards Janine. It was the auntie. The one who talked like Mommy a bit. Looked like her, but wasn't. She was tall and dark and...*not—Mommy!*

"It's okay, Janine," the woman said and sat on the strange bed beside her. "It's okay. I just moved you into the main part of the house and I've been making some phone calls. Have you slept in this room before? This was my room when I was your age."

Janine looked left and right and left and right again. Where was Uncle Richard? Where was he?

"You looking for this?" Her auntie pulled something soft out from under the covers beside her. Snuffles!

Janine hugged him tight, but he wasn't Uncle Richard. She needed Uncle Richard!

The big woman, her auntie, leaned over her and pushed Janine's hair to one side. "It's really okay, Janine. I wanted to see if I could call some people first, but no one's home. So I guess we'll just go now and wake up your grandma."

Just when she said it, though, there was a thumping and squeaking sound from somewhere, like someone big had just stumbled in through a door.

Bad guys!

"Wait here!" the auntie hissed at her. And she held her finger over her lips just like Uncle Richard did. *Be quiet. Don't make a sound.*

Then the auntie hurried to the door, slipped out, and came back a few seconds later. She whispered a swear word as she slipped inside the door and held it open just a crack.

Janine heard a sound like a big dumb man wheezing. "Sorry. I'll's'am sorry."

"You're still drunk." Her granny's voice!

"Cannn help it."

"Someone went through my room during the party. Was it you?"

"No. No."

"You wouldn't even remember."

"Make't up to you."

"In your condition?"

A snorting kind of growl.

"Oh, my god, Chester, you are an animal."

That confused Janine because Granny was laughing as she said it. And the auntie was swearing again in a whisper, over and over. Then a door closed somewhere, and something started creaking and banging.

The auntie prowled over to a bookshelf near Janine's bed, pulled out a big storybook and returned. Sat down on the bed again.

"I guess we'll have to wait a little before we go see Grandma," she said. "Let's read a story."

~~~~

"So?" said the voice on the phone.

"He got away," said Castinages. He tried to make his voice calm and straightforward, but his head was burning up with rage. That this Lieutenant from the Canadian forces, a fucking former swabbie, for Christ's sake, could have gotten the best of him... And it was because Castinages *liked* the sonofabitch, wasn't it. Because he'd wanted to give him a fucking chance to come onboard, use that sanctimonious chill of his to *end* this fucking war.

"That makes twice, doesn't it. You doing that on purpose, Misha?"

"Fuck you."

"You mean fuck up, don't you? Like the men you sent to retrieve our package. They weren't supposed to kill *any*one, much less blow things up."

"You wanted me to hire terrorists. That's what you got."

"I wanted our package too. I still want it. And I think your Richard Mackenzie has it—"

"No."

"—or knows where it is. Or his little niece does. Which means we need both of them, don't we. Alive."

Castinages's rage had burned itself through enough that he was thinking rationally again. "That may not be possible with this one. He's good. I might have to kill one of them to get what we need from the other."

There was a long silence on the other end of the phone line. Then, "If necessary. Do you know where they are?"

"Not yet, but I got some hints and I've got my team on it. By morning, I should—"

"Stop. Breathe, Misha. I have a gift for you. It turns out Mackenzie went for help to his sister-in-law, Nina. You may remember her from the reception after the double funeral you caused. Tall brunette."

Castinages racked his brains but couldn't come up with a face.

"She called my phone tonight and left a message. She has the girl with her at her mother's house. She's expecting Mackenzie back by morning and wants some protection from him before he returns. Do you think you might provide that?"

The mother's house? Shit, his team was supposed to have had that staked out. How the fuck had Mackenzie gotten in? Not that it mattered. All that mattered now was that he didn't get out again.

"I'm on it," he said and disconnected.

9

NINA LEANED BACK against the inside doorframe of the main bathroom and crossed her arms tightly over her chest as her mother bathed Janine.

After she'd heard Chester Bund's drunken thrashing die off and change to snores, Nina had changed into blue jeans and a plum-colored Ralph Lauren top and gone to summon her mother. She'd been prepared for the over-the-top theatrics of joy when Grace had seen Janine. Also for the recriminations towards Nina for not bringing the girl to her the second Mackenzie had arrived. What Nina hadn't planned on was her mother then insisting Janine be bathed before being taken anywhere.

Fine, I'll bathe her.

No, Grace had insisted in her scarlet robe and embarrassing filmy negligee. *She's used to me doing it when she visits.*

But...

There were no buts. The paranoid-psychotic Richard Mackenzie could be coming back at any minute, but Grace just had to make sure her granddaughter looked pretty for the police.

So now the old-fashioned claw-footed tub splashed warm water in around the naked little Janine, and Grace knelt on the thick pink bathroom rug beside the tub to squeeze warm water from a washcloth over Janine's head and body.

At least Janine had refused to give up her filthy stuffed armadillo, Nina noted. That had to be driving Grace crazy. The stuffie was half-soaked now, the wet part looking like a mud ball.

"I know what we'll do," Grace said brightly. She turned off the water, lay the washcloth over the edge of the bathtub, opened a cupboard under the sink, and dragged out a plastic boxful of water toys for Janine. There were rubber duckies, a hand-crank paddle-wheel boat, a floating book about Peter Rabbit, a wind-up submarine, some kind of sticky dot things, a squirt gun.

"Shall I choose your favorites?"

Janine, still half asleep, said nothing, so Grace plopped in the rubber duck, the floating book, and the submarine. Then she gently tugged at the armadillo.

"Let's give Snuffles a wash, shall we?"

Nina pressed her lips tighter together as Janine gradually relinquished it and Grace dunked it in the water, scrubbing it quickly with soap. Her mother even knew the names of Janine's stuffed animal. Nina could not remember her mother giving Nina a single teddy bear, much less bathtub toys. All Nina got were books. The only stuffies or squeak toys she'd played with as a child, she'd stolen from Marie-Ange.

Her mother finished the scrubbing, squeezed water through the stuffie until it ran clear and the toy looked vaguely two-tone—red and green—again. Grace wrung it out, and tried to hand it backwards to Nina.

But Janine wordlessly grabbed at the stuffie, clawing at Grace's raised arm, until Nina's mother relented and handed the washed stuffie back to her.

"Well you were a big help on that one," Grace mumbled back at Nina.

"You wanted me to help?" Nina said. "I thought *you* always washed Janine when she came to your place."

Grace turned at Nina's tone and stared in what looked like honest shock. "Why, my dear. You sound so petty. I just assumed, since you've never dealt with children..."

"Big assumption."

Nina strode forward, knelt beside her mother, and lifted the washcloth from the side of the tub.

"No!" Grace grabbed at it in a panic and tugged it back so frantically she fell over backwards. "No." She shook her head as she picked herself up painfully. "She's my granddaughter!"

"My niece."

"And you kept her from me!" Grace's lip quivered now as she knelt beside Nina. Janine clutched her stuffie and looked back and forth between them like she was ready to leap from the tub.

"I told you— Oh, you're going to cry now? That's your latest tool of manipulation? Terrify Janine so I'll just shut up and play along?"

Grace's eyes flashed and her lips stopped quivering. "I *never* asked you to just 'play along.'"

"Only my whole life."

Grace held Nina's gaze for a long moment, then slowly lifted the washcloth and handed it to her. "I'm so sorry you feel that way."

Nina fought the sudden prickling in the corner of her eyes and dunked the cloth in the water, rubbed it with soap, and began washing Janine.

"Me too," she muttered under her breath.

A few minutes later, upon Grace's insistence, the two of them managed to coax Janine to lie back in the water while they washed and conditioned her hair. When they finally pulled her from the tub, they gently dried and dressed her in a new set of purple overalls, stretchy yellow top, sweatshirt with the too-long sleeves rolled up, and running shoes. Then Nina watched with equal parts envy and admiration as her mother dried Janine's hair, brushed it out, and tied it up with a bow.

When her mother stepped back, Nina felt a flood of something hot and painful rush up through her. Because the moment before, Nina had been imagining herself as the sole object of her mother's attention. Now, suddenly, she saw Janine as she truly was—the spitting image of her mother. With Tom's mouth and chin maybe. The darker curl of his hair.

It was like Marie-Ange through a looking glass, all innocence and mute love, with her big sister and mother watching over her. Just too late.

Oh, MA, she thought, pressing seven years of regrets into the words.

But before she could touch Janine or tell her mother about this revelation, a loud pounding on the front door downstairs shot adrenaline through her. The police? The FBI? Pops? Who'd gotten her message?

Grace's mother turned to her, somehow snapping out of their shared closeness as she raised her carefully-plucked eyebrows. "This is someone you know?"

"I...I'm not sure."

Grace sighed, walked to the bathroom door, and pulled it open.

"Mother!" Nina finally moved, walking brusquely up beside her. "You can't answer the door like that. Let me. You look after Janine."

Grace walked back to her, took Janine's hand, and smiled. "We'll be in my room, darling. I keep a gun in the bedside table."

Doing a strained imitation of her mother's eye roll, Nina sprang out the door and hurried down the stairs. She paused in the front hall, uncertain. Then the heavy door pounded again and a recently-familiar voice called through it, "Nina!"

She sprang forward and unlatched it.

It was like letting in a dark hurricane. Richard Mackenzie plunged past her, wearing a ripped black windbreaker, his face pale and clammy looking. Eyes wild. Smelling like he'd rolled in a sewer. He grabbed her by her arms, but didn't fight when she jerked herself free of him.

"We have to get everyone out of here," he said.

"Why? More people chasing you?

"Forget *chasing*. They know we're here."

Nina stepped back from him, ready to run, but he suddenly leaned forward, hands on his knees, and took a wheezing breath. When he straightened, his face was just as pale and wet, but his jaw was tight and the eyes had gone calm. It was more terrifying than the excitement. And yet compelling. Where did that iron self-control come from?

"Nina," he said. "The two men watching this house were on full alert when I got back. Waiting for me. I took them out, but the others will be close behind. They'll capture anyone they find here. Kill them if they have to."

"Why would..."

"Who," interrupted a stentorian voice from the stairs, "are 'they'?"

Nina whirled to see her mother halfway down them, a more modest robe on now, in a deep purple.

"Major Misha Castinages," Mackenzie shot back at her. "Blocky military man. Buzz cut. Sun-bleached hair. Dark skin. Blue eyes. Hands like clubs. Ring any bells?"

Grace seemed unfazed by the rudeness. "He was here this afternoon. A friend of Congresswoman Reis's aide, I believe."

"Here?" Mackenzie seemed to wobble on his feet. He stuck a hand out to brace himself against the wall and Nina had to steel herself from rushing to his aid like some servant nurse. She didn't trust him, she reminded herself.

"It was a post-funeral reception," Grace clarified as she descended. "My younger daughter and her husband were killed. And if Major Castinages chooses to pay his respects, I'm not sure why—"

"Because the bastard controlled the group who shot Tom and Marie-Ange. And he took my gun and shot *me*! That's why!" Mackenzie slumped hard against the wall and opened his windbreaker, showing a bloody stain covering most of his upper right chest.

Nina swayed a bit herself, rethinking all her earlier conclusions. Her head said Mackenzie could still be lying, could be dangerously paranoid and had gotten himself into some crazy gunfight. But her innermost self believed him. And if what he said was true...

Grace, halfway down the stairs, raised her nose. "I don't believe you."

Mackenzie grimaced up at her. "Do you know who I am, Mrs. Tauredaux?"

"How could I not?" She reached the bottom of the stairs and swept across the floor towards him. "Your picture's been in the papers and on television at least twice a day since Thursday, giving this horror story new legs, another opportunity to drag the Tauredaux family name into the mud by association. Utterly charming."

Grace pushed Nina aside as she walked up to Mackenzie. There she stopped, drew back her hand, and slapped him so hard across his pale face that his head rocked to the other side against the wall.

Nina gasped and reached for her mother's arm but Grace shook her off. "That's for letting my daughter die, coward. And kidnapping my granddaughter."

"God, I see where Nina gets it from," Mackenzie said.

"What?" said Grace, her voice rising.

"Enough!" Nina said, blushing furiously. She grabbed her mother and pushed her back from Mackenzie. Then she stood, breathing hard, to stare down at the wounded man. "Is someone really coming?"

Mackenzie seemed to have difficulty raising his head. "I worried they might be so I went to check on the watchers and heard them talking. They somehow knew Janine was here, and that I was on my way back." He paused as he looked at Nina's face. "What?"

"I...made some phone calls."

"To who?"

"Police, FBI." *Pops.*

Nina's mother had recovered from her shove and was shaking with fury now. "I hardly think..."

"That's *obvious!*" Mackenzie snapped. "Mrs. Tauredaux, you're right. I should have saved your daughter...and my brother. Tommy called me in to protect them and...I didn't get them out fast enough. Now I'm telling you, as a professional soldier—Janine's life, mine, Nina's, *and yours*...are in danger! I *don't want to see more death! Do you get it?*"

Even weak as he was, it was like a lion's roar that even Grace Tauredaux felt. Nina saw her mother's fury drop as she took a shaky step backwards, looking like Nina felt.

"I— Yes," she said.

Grace promptly turned and strode back to the stairs. There she stopped with a hand on the guardrail, glanced over at the grandfather clock on the wall to her right—it was 11:53, almost midnight—then back at Nina.

"Darling, you need to pack for yourself and Janine. Chester and I will be ready to leave in five minutes."

"Chester?" Mackenzie said.

"Bund. Her boyfriend," Nina said.

"Damn it. Mrs. Tauredaux make sure you bring the gun from your bedside table."

Grace wrinkled back her nose again. "It was you who went through my room earlier."

"And get the shotgun from the downstairs office if you've got the firing pin."

"What...?" Nina said.

"Go!"

"I demand the right to know what's going on once we reach safety," Grace said.

Mackenzie nodded, "Fine," and mumbled something under his breath. Then, as Grace turned and regally ascended, Mackenzie turned to Nina and said through clenched teeth, "Help me."

Nina wavered. Even though she'd flip-flopped back to believing him, she didn't trust him. How the hell had he searched their house? That tingling feeling she'd felt earlier... *Had* he been spying on her during the party?

It all made her feel vulnerable and weak and idiotic. She didn't like that.

"Please, Nina," he said. "I'm not crazy...*unh*. Just injured."

"Are you," she said coldly. "Where? Here?" She poked at the wound, making him blanch. She had to bite her own tongue not to swoon at the smell and the pain on his face. "Oh, get over it," she said and wiped her bloody finger on a clean part of his shirt.

Then she grabbed his left arm and, taking as much weight as she could, started hobbling him up the stairs after her mother.

"Where...?" he grunted.

"The bathroom. Medical supplies."

He stopped her barely halfway up. "Too...slow," he said. "You go get Janine. Bring her and your mother and...boyfriend here. I'll...guard the front."

"With what?" Nina said. She'd noted his shoulder holster was empty and Nina hadn't felt any other sort of gun. Nor had her mother returned with either gun she apparently had in the house.

Mackenzie reached down painfully and tugged up his right pant leg.

From a concealed sheath, he pulled out a dagger with what was maybe a five-inch blade.

"Oh, that'll scare them," Nina said.

She caught his eyes and for just an instant saw him share her wry humor. It was like a whole other person existed inside that warrior shell. Nina almost gasped at the exquisite longing that rose up in her. For this man? Oh, she was twisted. Bring on the hardest, thickest skinned, impossibly alpha male she could—

He broke the moment with a croak. "So bring me the shotgun. And if you can get my backpack from under the bed where Janine slept…"

"How much time do you think we have?"

"Maybe just enough."

Gnawing on her upper lip, Nina finally nodded and ran for where she'd left Janine.

~~~~

Five minutes later, she'd packed a change of clothes for Janine and one for herself in a plastic Louis Vuitton bag, grabbed her purse, did a side trip to the nanny suite for Mackenzie's backpack—*heavy!*—and hurried back to the front stairs.

At the bottom, her impeccably dressed mother and bleary-eyed boyfriend knelt beside the prostrate, eyes-closed Mackenzie. The shotgun suddenly did not seem a priority.

Janine clutched Snuffles and danced from foot to foot right behind them. Mackenzie's blood-soaked top had been ripped off and Grace had taped a large square bandage over his chest wound. Nina saw his chest rise. He was breathing! Grace was just cutting the end of the medical tape that she'd wrapped around and around his thickly-muscled chest then over and under his shoulder to hold the bandage in place. A bottle of iodine and blood-soaked gauze pads lay on the carpet beside Mackenzie's windbreaker and bloody shirt. So did a honking big revolver she presumed was her mother's nighttime protection.

The sewer smell Mackenzie had reeked of earlier had become a chemical odor that still made Nina gag.

But now that she knew he was alive, she couldn't take her eyes off his naked torso. It was like his personality, she thought—taut, thick, hard, scarred…and calling out to her.

Sheesh. Was it possible to pick a more inappropriate time for a soldier fixation?

As if to reinforce it (or support it?), Janine apparently couldn't take waiting any long and ran to her uncle's face. She grabbed his cheek with her free hand.

His eyes blinked open, saw her, saw Nina on the stairs, and nodded painfully. "Have to...get going," he said.

"Right," muttered Bund, staggering up to his feet. Still drunk, probably. "Shizzle me."

"Get him dressed," Grace ordered Bund, and Bund sank back to his knees beside a pile of clothes Nina had missed before. Probably Nina's father's clothes her mother had somehow held onto—a dark polo shirt that Grace probably thought would hide any blood. Another windbreaker.

As Bund helped Richard dress, Nina's mother walked to the back hall with the bloody clothes and medical supplies. She was back by the time Bund was done and had pulled Mackenzie, grunting, up to his feet, one arm flung over the fat media baron's shoulders, Janine clinging to his leg.

"I don't know where the firing pin is for the shotgun," Grace said, so I suggest we leave now. The back door."

"Can't climb...the fence," Mackenzie said.

"Mother, they're not here yet. We hurry out the front—"

"No!" Mackenzie again.

"You'd rather just stay here?" Grace said.

"I stay," said Mackenzie. "Delay them."

"And I'll...uh...stay with him," Bund said.

Grace shot her boyfriend a withering look. "Just bring him," she said. She walked regally through the living room door to the drawing room and the French doors leading outside.

Biting off a caustic comment, Nina rushed to Mackenzie's free side, nudged Janine aside, and took his free arm. Together, she and Bund walked him out into the deep shadows of the back. Nina felt her own panic level rise until she saw her mother bee-lining straight to the back left corner.

The gate! Of course. When she and Marie-Ange had been little, their neighbors had had a girl and boy almost the same ages. The adults had gotten along too. So the neighbors had cut a piece out of the privacy fence and hung it back on with hinges. It was long overgrown, but presumably still functional.

After a moment of Grace's frustrated tugging, she called on her boyfriend again and he immediately shrugged Mackenzie's arm off his shoulders to go pull at the vines.

"Nice hand-off," grunted Nina as the sudden full weight of Mackenzie, as well as his backpack and her bag and purse, almost dragged her over.

A crash from the house made them all spin around. For the first time, Nina was glad Janine was hysterically mute because the little girl's eyes shot wide and Nina thought she would have screamed if she could have.

Bund worked faster. He'd grabbed Mackenzie's knife from its leg sheath and cut furiously at the vines around the door.

"Leave some," whispered Mackenzie at Nina's cheek. "Camouflage."

Nina repeated it so Bund could hear, then slid Mackenzie down to the ground and ran to the gate to assist.

"It's enough!" she hissed, pulling the gate towards them almost a foot before the ripping vines stopped her. "Let's go!"

So they did, her mother first, eyeing her strangely as she grabbed Janine's hand to pull her through. Then Bund with Mackenzie. Then Nina.

Nina pulled the gate closed after her just in time to see her mother and Janine throwing stones at the upper floors of their neighbor's house.

Nina looked back at the upper floors of their own house. A light went on there. Whoever was looking for them had entered the Tauredaux house. How long before they realized they weren't there and came out the back? Seconds?

Then her mother was hissing up to an open window. The window closed. No lights went on. But a moment later the back door by the neighbor's kitchen opened and an old man Nina vaguely remembered from her years here—Mr. Hayes?—beckoned them in as he looked fearfully back and forth.

More lights were on in the Tauredaux home. Nina's bedroom upstairs. Her mother's. The nanny's quarters where Janine's old clothes were.

Countdown.

10

CASTINAGES, his face a mess of bandages where an Army medic had taped over the mess Mackenzie had made of his nose, fingered the little-girl's panties he'd scooped up from the dirty clothes on the bathroom floor. He pressed the back of the same hand against the side of the old-fashioned steel bathtub. It was still wet and warm. That plus the bloody clothes in the back hall suggested a hurried departure.

Yeah, Mackenzie and the girl had been here recently. Minutes. Less. When Burton and Gomez, assigned to watch this house, woke up, Castinages was going to personally put bullets in their fucking heads.

He hit the commo button on his flak jacket. "Guardian here. Report."

The three stateside Green Berets he'd kept on a "need to know" standby for emergency ops like this came back one after another. All negative.

"Choke One, you've got night vision?"

"Affirmative."

"Back exterior."

"Roger that."

Castinages couldn't see them running out the back. These row houses, fancy as they were, simply backed onto other row houses, with no lane in between. The elite who lived here kept their vehicles in a valet-run parking garage a block-and-a-half over. Visitors parked on the street. (Or, in the case of the President, earlier that day, commandeered the street.)

Had they gone out the front then, just before Castinages had arrived? Mackenzie was smart. He'd have gathered from the operational readiness of Burton and Gomez that they'd twigged onto his hiding spot, and he would have run.

But how fast and how far?

Castinages coughed and thumped his chest. Given the blood trail leading out of the Mayflower, Mackenzie had to have lost a lot of blood. Castinages was damn impressed the man had not only made it back here, but also taken out two alerted Green Berets. Still, he had to be passing out soon.

Castinages coughed again and spat out blood into the panties in his hand. He hoped the blood was just from the nose Mackenzie had smashed. His commo squawked.

"Choke Three. Car out front starting up. Moving. Northbound."

Castinages hit his TALK button. "Guardian here. Intercept. Repeat. Intercept. Deadly force if necessary."

He stuffed the bloody panties into his left chest flak jacket pocket, hugged his C8 flattop up against it, and jogged for the door connecting the servants' quarters to the rest of the house.

Just like cleaning out the neighborhoods around Kandahar. The rats always tried to run.

~~~~

Alfie Hays, had always resented the parking arcade arrangement foisted on his ancestral home when the powers that be permitted the residential re-zoning of the laneway behind his row house. For this reason he frequently parked on the street and now enjoyed the opportunity to, as Grace Tauredaux's newspaper boyfriend put it, "tweak the government's Homeland Security, private-citizen-raiding, paranoid-right-wing-fascist nose."

For this reason Alfie gunned the engine on his ancient Citroen as he saw the commandos in black suits pile into their SUV and roar after him.

He was even singing to himself when they finally caught him in an early-morning traffic jam on the Pennsylvania Avenue roundabout.

"Gentlemen!" he cried when they dragged him out and threw him up against the side of his car. "Please remember that this is an advanced society." He waved his hand at the gawking people around them, all staring out through their windows at the unraveling scene. "People do have camcorder phones."

~~~~

Hiding in the back of Bund's Cadillac sedan, parked further south down the street from where Hays and then the bad guys had peeled out, Nina was intensely uncomfortable. Her mother and Bund sat up front, Bund driving. Nina had shoved Janine down to the floor in the back where she wriggled and breathed fast, sounding close to panic. Even worse, Nina herself lay stiffly on top of the hot, supine Richard Mackenzie, trying to keep her weight away from his wound.

Yes, she had planned on using her feminine wiles to break through his rock-solid exterior. Eventually. If she decided she could stomach his superior attitude.

Not like this, though.

Worse, was the fact that while the danger of their state seemed to have made her entire body hypersensitive to his—to every adjustment of his hips, his groin, his hands—he seemed virtually oblivious to her. And she couldn't just blame it on his wound. The pungent apple cider Mr. Hays had urged on him, or the momentary rest, second wind, whatever, had brought him back from the edge. His breaths were shallow but even. His eyes glittered keenly in the darkness.

But they weren't looking at her. They stared past her at the roof of the car, like he was both listening and thinking hard.

He painfully reached a reassuring hand down to Janine, then turned his face to the front seats. "Turn all the running lights off, start her up, and pull a slow U-turn. Head for 34th and Wisconsin. If we're lucky, we'll get out to traffic before they notice we've left."

Bund complied.

The engine startup sounded like a bellowing elephant in Nina's ears, but her mother, watching the front of their house, didn't twitch.

The car pulled out and swung around, pulled away, accelerating.

"A man just ran onto our front steps," Grace said. "Very square. I believe it might be the man who shot you, Mr. Mackenzie. The major. Looking for our license plates?"

"Too far away," Mackenzie said.

He turned his face back towards Nina and this time caught her eyes. That stare! Against her better judgment, her entire body wanted to grind into his.

"Lean closer," he whispered under the rumbling sway of the car.

She felt her face go hot, but complied, wetting her lips. But he turned his face a little to the side and put his lips by her right ear. Then he whispered so quietly that she and she alone could hear.

"He'll already know the license plate, and he'll keep coming, Nina. After me. After Janine. I need to get her to safety, and I need to find whatever it is Tom took from these people so I can give it back."

"You never told me Tom—"

"Shh. He did. I thought there was an outside chance he hid it in your parent's house, but I found nothing there. Didn't really think I would. Because I *know* where he took it. And the one good thing is that the place is so remote, so...improbable, that I can take Janine there to hunt for it and they'll never find us. But I'm not going to be able to manage the trip by myself. Not in this condition."

Nina's eyes locked onto Janine's, dark and wide where she lay curled in the wheel well. And despite Mackenzie's charismatic energy, she knew craziness when she heard it. "No. Let me take her. We split up. Maybe they'll follow you, maybe they won't, but it'll be easier for us to hide without a bleeding, shot man raising questions."

He heard a moan from Mackenzie that might have been a whispered, "Bitch."

"What did you call me?" she hissed.

Mackenzie closed his eyes and shook his head. "She goes just with you, you'll both be dead in a day. Two at most. I can't allow that."

"You can't 'allow'? What kind of macho bullshit is that?"

"I won't let you take her."

"And how are you going to stop me?"

Without warning his hand had shot to her wrist, clutching it like a vise. She bared her teeth and moved to strike his bandaged chest but he did something to the wrist that shot pain like jagged nails up her arm, all the way to her core and she cried out. Her mother spun from the front seat, lips pursed, then turned back to the front again.

Panting, face covered with sweat, Richard released her. "Here's the deal: you tell us where to go, where to sleep tonight. If we make it through noon tomorrow with no one on our tail, I'll give you Janine and I'll...disappear. Bleed out in a ditch somewhere. Whatever. And maybe someday they'll stop chasing you."

Ignore his self-pity and threats. Stay on point. "Noon tomorrow."

"But if they find us before then, you admit you need me, and you come along, help me get Janine where I think we need to go. To find what we need to end this."

She let her breasts press down against him for a moment, her belly, her groin. Letting him know she could do this to him because *she* was in control.

She had the power.

When she felt his penis respond, she smiled nastily into his face and nodded. "Deal."

"So where we going?" Bund grunted from the front. "Cop cars everywhere. It's like they're trying to shut down the city."

Nina raised herself up to sitting in front of Mackenzie's prostrate legs, and told him.

~~~~

Ten minutes later, grinding his teeth, Castinages dropped back to the park across the way from the Tauredaux home and watched a small bat climbing up and down a fir tree, ducking his head against the dark bark like he thought he was some kind of woodpecker.

Castinages's commo squawked and he got the report from his men that he'd been expecting.

Decoy. Diversion.

Which meant the blocky car he'd seen rushing off into the night with no lights had been the real escape.

He trusted that his watchers would have the license plate and the operation's FBI mole would be able to get a 10-16 on it fast, but damn it, that made three times now that Mackenzie had slipped through his fingers. And this last time the man had to be half-dead.

Castinages scowled a moment, then found himself chuckling. Coughing. Damn. Okay. Mackenzie was good. It was time to stop underestimating him.

"Back to Alpha Base," he snapped into his commo and disconnected. He coughed again, hard, then thumped his own chest to stop. Pulling his knife from his ankle sheath, he stepped quickly over to the cedar tree the small bat was still crawling up and down. One quick stab and Castinages impaled the little insect-eater on his knife.

He watched it wiggle for a moment, then stop. Castinages pulled the knife out and flicked it off onto the dirt, twigs, and needles.

He went to join his men.

11

CHESTER BUND DROVE THEM NORTH on the I-95, circumnavigated Baltimore, and went off the interstate when slowing cars suggested a roadblock ahead. They found a motel just over the state line into Pennsylvania and crashed for a few hours.

Richard noted the police car cruising slowly by just after sunup, the officer inside it squinting at the license plate number. Richard said nothing.

Ten minutes later, though, he'd rousted Nina and Janine and slipped the two of them out the bathroom window. He himself wouldn't fit, so he crept out the front, slipping sideways into the shadows for a slow circle around to meet them. A dark, chain link fence ran along the back of the motel and blocked the way out behind the motel office. Richard made Nina scale it, helped Janine over, then followed, his chest wound screaming its protest.

When they were across the highway and hidden behind a backhoe that sat silent on a half-started construction site, Richard had Nina and Janine spy on the motel front.

He, meanwhile, did a shadow walk behind the fast food stops and gas stations on that side of the highway until he reached the used car dealership he'd found in the phone book the night before. Crazy Curly's. Banging on the owner's window with a wad of cash got the man out of bed and onto the lot, where Richard picked out a 1981 green Chevy panel van with a second row of seats and just under 160,000 miles on the odometer. Richard figured the van could double as sleeping accommodations if needed.

As he was sweating over the ownership forms and limiting the questions by painfully pulling cash out of his backpack, the a.m. news came on the dealership office's T.V.

"...took a disturbing turn last night as the murdered woman's mother and sister both disappeared from their Georgetown house. Possibly connected is the reported disappearance of their neighbor, Alfred Hays, whose wife claims he drove off in the middle of the night and never returned.

"F.B.I. investigators covering the Mackenzie murders, house bombing, and possible child abduction nine days ago in Bethesda, Maryland, will not speculate whether the same group or individuals are involved in these disappearances."

The picture switched to a briefing room where the man at the podium, identified by subtitles as the Director of the F.B.I.'s National Security Division (Odd. Richard thought the NSD had been basically suborned by Homeland Security after 2005.), was holding forth with a face so pained he looked like he was having a gastric attack.

Nothing he said sounded honest. Vague reference to terrorist groups, but none had taken responsibility taken for the attack. No notes delivered. No communications. No leads. Nothing.

"Hey, you done?"

Richard nodded and handed over the forms and cash.

"Good, cause I don't want you bleeding on my desk here."

Richard looked down and saw the blood staining the red polo shirt he'd worn since last night. And his breathing felt harder. The bandage was probably drying out and letting air leak into his chest cavity, compressing his lung. He needed to punch in a needle to let the air out as soon as possible. And to redo the bandage with some plastic wrap.

Painfully scooping up the keys to their new van, he drove back to the rear of the construction lot. Parking out of sight of the highway, he slunk weakly around the pit to find Janine sleeping with her head in Nina's lap. Nina herself was peeking, face contorted in rage, around the corner of the backhoe, as a cadre of military men marched her mother and mother's lover out of the motel and began turning the motel room inside out.

But Richard barely glanced at the soldiers. Them he understood. It was Nina who fascinated him—this fascinating blend of beautiful, smart grit undercut by foolish arrogance.

One minute she hated him, the next she seemed trying to seduce him. While, if he'd had a sound body and the courage of a masochist, he'd be drinking her up right now, reaching for her waist, burying his nose into her hair.

"Bastards," she hissed now.

"Your...mother will be...okay," Richard said, kneeling beside her. He felt his chest racing and his breath harder to draw in. "She's...too connected...to just disappear. And she...doesn't know anything. That'll be obvious."

"How did they find us?"

"License plates. Bund's credit card when...we bought gas. Descriptions. A thousand eyes. You make any cell phone calls?"

She opened her mouth angrily, then closed it. "I called my office. Told them I needed to extend my leave a week or two. Probably screwed my chances at partnership."

"Ditch the...phone. Smash it."

She bared her teeth at him, obviously hearing his breathing difficulty because she was looking him up and down. "Fine. Okay. What if we went just on cash, maybe over to Ohio or something?"

So you could just take Janine and run? "How much...cash do you have?"

"One stop at a bank machine..."

"Net you a thousand...if you're limit's that high." He wasn't about to tell her about the nearly forty-five thousand dollars in emergency funds he'd stashed in his backpack when he'd first come back Stateside. They were going to need all of that for the next part of this trip, whether she stuck with him or not. "Look...they're close now. If they can...run the Pennsylvania cops, what's to stop them from doing Ohio...or North Dakota...Texas...Florida...Nevada? Whoever's doing this... Jesus."

"But you still think you can get us out of the country," she said. "To Tom's hiding place."

"I know I can."

"What if I told you that I know where the thing is that Tom took?"

"What?"

He saw her face was flushed, still angry probably from how her mother was being treated, but also something more. A prideful excitement. "What's the one thing that Janine has with her everywhere?"

"Her sense of humor?" He gasped a little, short of breath.

"Her stuffed armadillo!"

"Snuffles."

"Right!"

"Good thinking. Only I've already...slit it open once, then...re-sewed it. But go ahead. Knock yourself out."

Her face fell. "It wasn't there."

"I've told you where I think it is."

"Okay. How do we get there?"

In short gasps, and omitting a few key details, he told her.

~~~~

A couple scary hours later, just south of Stroudsburg, Pennsylvania, Nina watched Mackenzie sit on a rock off to the side of the deserted road, struggle his shirt off, and douse with rubbing alcohol the sharp end of a honking big hypodermic needle he'd had Nina steal for him from a medical clinic. Plus a rubber tube with a three-way valve he'd described to her.

Oh, the Gervais partners would love this. Nina was now a thief, as well as a fugitive. Just because Mackenzie was having a little trouble breathing.

Okay, a lot of trouble breathing.

Even after he'd changed the dressing over his wound to a fancy Saran Wrap affair, he sounded like he was drowning.

Damn it! What were they all caught up in here? Tommy had stolen something and smuggled it up to a hidey-hole in Canada. A hidey-hole that Richard Mackenzie knew all about. Like they'd done this kind of thing before? Stolen things. Pissed off dangerous people. Had Marie-Ange known? And should Nina still be looking for a way *out* of this arrangement?

Breath wheezing loudly, Mackenzie bit down into a thick stick and carefully felt up his ribs on his right side until his fingers were almost in line with his nipple. He placed the tip of the needle there, wrapped both hands around it, tensed, and gave Nina a crazed look. Nina looked away.

A sickening grunt. A hiss. A gasp and longer breath than she'd heard in a while.

Nina knew she should go to him now. Help him. But an ugly part of her hoped that maybe he'd just died from what he'd done. Then her conundrum would be solved, wouldn't it? She'd take Janine and...and...what exactly? Become fugitives? Turn herself and Janine in?

By the time she'd finally turned to check on him, he was sitting upright, shirt still off, needle stuck into his chest with medical tape all around it to hold it in place, and the tube with its three-way valve screwed onto the end of it. Mackenzie looked better than he had all day. The color was back in his face. He looked like he was actually breathing again.

God, he was a good-looking man.

Stop that.

As she watched, he peeled off the flapping Saran wrap bandages he'd fixed on the wound higher up on his chest.

"What are you doing?" Nina said.

"Stitches," he said. "Don't trust the bandages to hold, and I can't keep the hypodermic in forever." He held up the thick thread and sewing needle he'd had her pick up in the drugstore along with the emergency medical kit.

Oh, just shoot me now.

Nina turned away quickly and squatted behind the Chevy van, making herself *not* think of him sticking a sewing needle in and out of his own flesh. What sort of man could stab himself in a chest then stitch his own wound?

A soldier.

A criminal.

You're a criminal now too.

No, I'm *fighting* crime.

Defiantly, she returned to her own assigned task—the license plates. Using a screwdriver and a pair of navy blue and black markers, she began making the CHR into OHR, 3507 into 3687. Not properly dented out. Clear fakes if you looked closely. But the plates were old, battered, covered with grime. And hopefully no one would look too closely.

"*Unhh!*" Mackenzie grunted.

Janine appeared at Nina's side, her eyes wide and blinking hard as she gripped her elbows.

"Why don't you look at this?" Nina said to draw her attention to the plates. "Uncle Richard will be just fine."

And if he's not?

~~~~

Castinages was only ninety minutes behind them when he found the stop they'd made at a Pantry convenience store to buy a sewing kit. Getting a quiet APB out on the green Chevy van had been easy enough, but Castinages doubted Mackenzie would stick with the license plates, or even that vehicle. The Pantry stop had been a lucky hit. Sheer grunt detective work, and Castinages hated that shit. It was slow. It was unreliable.

And there were at least five different routes north from here. Castinages was sure that's why Mackenzie had chosen this place for supplies.

Fuck. He slammed out of the store and pulled out a cigarette. Choke One watched him as he lit up, inhaled, then coughed up a mouthful of pebbly phlegm which he spat onto the parking lot asphalt.

"He's...going to sew him*self* up, Major?"

Castinages nodded and stared up at the clouds scudding across the morning sky. "And I'm betting he'll head north. Canada boy's going home."

"Do we follow, Sir?"

Castinages took a long inhale and fought to not cough as his lungs felt like they were eating him up inside. Assets: a core team of six Green Berets stateside who were loyal firstly to him, a secret CIA contact who could manipulate the local police forces if need be, and the untried political clout of his partner-in-crime whom Castinages by habit thought of only as the Politician. The Politician *claimed* to have deals set up with the mob, the Russians, and the Taliban.

But only if Castinages pulled together his end of the deal and recovered what had been stolen.

Castinages exhaled and threw down the cigarette. "Choke Two stays with me. Five and six head for the border crossings. You, Three, and Four spread north from here. Check the local medical clinics for robberies and gunshot wounds. Constant contact."

"Sir? That's a lot of country."

"You have a problem, Sergeant?"

"No, Sir. It's just..."

"I'll be feeding you information, son. You're the hounds. We got nets out there to trap the fox for you. Worst-case scenario we go to the little shithole he grew up in. Foxes always run to home." Castinages coughed, thumped his chest and coughed again, feeling it clench his whole chest again and throb in his broken nose. He growled it loose.

"Sir?"

"Move your ass!"

12

Crossing the 49th parallel
Atlantic Ocean

Every roll of the lobster boat under Richard's feet was another memory sweeping over him. The gray afternoon, gray waves sloshing the hull, the throaty roar of the ancient Iveco diesel engines—they made him feel eighteen again; they gave his legs strength where he should have collapsed long ago.

It was the real reason they were going where they were. One of them.

Another was the ocean border crossing. At night. But it was a good ten-hour trip all the way around and up the Nova Scotia coast, and this one he couldn't just hand over to Nina.

In a perverse way, the fast sutures he'd given himself helped. They blazed and prickled with pain whenever he bent or twisted. His insides there kept flaring into a punching fists of pain, too. His heart raced. Maybe the rubbing alcohol he'd used to sterilize the needle and wound hadn't been enough. Even with the Neosporin applied afterwards. Infection then. Real bad.

Still better than coffee, though, right?

He jerked his head as a wave of suffocating weakness tested the idea. He reached up under his black windbreaker and shirt to open the valve on the hypodermic still taped into his chest. Another hiss of air and he could breathe again.

He closed the valve and tried to blink himself back to full consciousness.

He couldn't give up! Not when he had both a little girl and a beautiful woman counting on him. They were both below decks now that the accumulated stress of the flight had finally knocked Janine out. Nina was watching over her.

Nina.

Still hadn't figured her out. The way she'd conceded his leadership, assumed the care of Janine, then taken over the driving of the beater van he'd bought for them in Pennsylvania. It was like she was biding her time, waiting to see if in fact he *did* know how they were going to settle this and make Janine safe again.

Because she sure as hell didn't trust him. Every look she gave him was equivocal. The two times he'd hesitated in deciding which road to take, he'd seen her nostrils flare and her body tense like she was ready to take control, change their course, do things her way.

So now Richard never wavered. She'd only follow certainty? Fine, he was Mr. Certainty. And God help them all if he was...*ungh.*

He swayed as a bigger wave of darkness washed over him and the wheel turned. The boat, the comically-named *Santa Maria*, roared and swung. The head-high stack of lobster traps that covered the deck behind the cabin creaked creaking and clacked in their tie-downs. A tall wave hit them broadside and sent a briny splash up over the closed-in wheel cabin's window.

Richard jolted himself upright and clutched the steering wheel tighter, swung them back around.

Eighteen again. Right.

Better than caffeine. Right.

A thumping sound down to his right him told him his racy piloting hadn't gone unnoticed.

Her. Nina. She came up from the small, forward cabin below decks and he was stunned how, even through the fog of his fatigue and pain, his blood stirred. Silly, of course, since she wore one of the heavy rain slickers he'd bought off the same old-timer who'd sold them the boat. To even see she was a woman under that took far more imagination than he'd ever had in his life.

And balls.

Because he wasn't really the Mr. Certainty that seemed to turn her on. He was just a fisherman who'd trained up to be a swabby, then a signals man, a Special Forces Grunt. Good at listening to bad guys and killing. Better at following orders than giving them. The chances of Nina, once she figured him out, wanting to do a little skin-to-skin were about as...*unh*...likely as Richard trying to save the world.

Just survive. Protect those closest to you.

"Are you all right?"

"Hit a big wave," he said.

She searched his face, bit down some smart-ass retort, and said nothing. Just like she'd said nothing when he'd negotiated the trade of their van and produced a wad of cash besides to buy this scow. She'd watched him check it out, fill the gas tank, check the engine, plot their course. She saw things and learned fast. Probably already figured she knew enough to pilot them to safety if he collapsed.

He was almost tempted to let her try. The failure might knock down her arrogance enough, make her human enough that... What? What was he thinking?

She looked away from him, and Richard took a shuddering breath, realizing he'd been holding it while she'd studied him. Then he saw she was staring out through the window, across the wallowing gray of the early evening waves and socked-in sky. Did she see the bad storm coming up? He hoped not.

"How long until we get there?" she asked.

"First landfall in two hours, maybe three."

"Based on what?"

She'd moved in right beside him so he could feel her heat even through her rain slicker. The sexual power of her that seemed to steam out of the dampness of her hair. It made him want to sag suddenly, turn over the steering wheel to her as he had with the van. Lie down.

He gave himself an internal shake and blinked his eyes hard. She *didn't* know the sea. They'd never make landfall if he lost consciousness. "I knew someone who made this run a lot."

"Who?"

"Just a guy." *A drunk old bastard.* "He wasn't a great respecter of duties and the big companies and government trying to control the fish trade in Nova Scotia."

"He was a...fish runner?"

"Sometimes." *When he was sober enough. And not getting me to do it for him.* Richard shook his head. It had been so long he'd consciously *not* thought of his father that he'd forgotten how the memories hurt. Which was good. He could use the pain. Replay memories of all his prize moments in Afghanistan. Right. Anything to keep awake and sharp.

"How?" Nina said.

"What?"

"I mean why don't they stop us?"

"Too much ocean," he lied. "Friendly border. You don't check out of or into one of the approved ports of entry and you basically disappear."

In fact he had no idea what increases in naval security the authorities might have implemented since he'd gone overseas. For all he knew they had the entire coastline blanketed with radar. But the storm would help. And he knew there was no other way. He believed what he'd told Nina, that Major Castinages and whoever he was working for would find them anywhere in the U.S., eventually. But in Canada, he could make Janine disappear. Just as Tommy, he was sure, had gone there to make whatever he'd stolen disappear.

Stolen. The fact of it wanted to rise up again and grate at him with questions about what his brother had done, who he'd become. But all of that was as unanswerable as his childhood right now. All he had was the promise to keep Janine safe.

And Nina?

Her hip was pressed against his now, the warm smell of her steaming around him, making it hard to concentrate.

On a pretense of reaching over to tap the compass, he stepped away from her and asked, "Janine okay?"

"Sleeping." She moved back against him, unconsciously it seemed, like a child seeking comfort. But she was no child, he was no parent, and her closeness seriously distracted him from the pain he was using to stay upright. He subtly nudged her backwards. She pressed in harder.

Finally he growled, "Back off."

When she did, in flustered embarrassment, then anger, he looked away before he could apologize.

"We're going to need an inventory of everything onboard," he said. "Help us to sell this scow when we dock. Paper and pen here." He pulled them from the dash beside the wheel. "Best to do it while there's still light."

She took the paper and pen, hesitated, then just snapped an insolent salute, "Aye, aye, Sir," and left.

When the forward hatch door had closed behind her, Richard's breath came back in a rush with the *real* pain. Physical pain. It was like she'd been a magic anesthetic while she was there. Pulling him off course despite his best efforts. Dulling his mind.

Dangerous.

He straightened at the wheel and bumped the throttle up a notch to outrun the storm.

Yes, dangerous. You focused on the unattainable and you got screwed. That was life. Best to focus on realities. Find whatever Tommy had taken for what Richard kept telling himself was probably some noble, if stupid, reason.

Then find a way to give it back. Broker some kind of deal, give up whatever he had to give up to make sure Janine survived. Hang onto that little part of his life and his honor.

Focus, Mackenzie.

As your heart races to push around your skimpy oxygen supply.

Focus.

Get it done.

~~~~

Getting there.

They refueled and restocked in the tiny harbor of Rockeport, the southwestern tip of Nova Scotia, and Nina argued that they should abandon the boat and find a room for the night. They could get a car in the morning and drive the rest of the way.

Richard managed a dizzy shake of his head. If they drove they'd have to go through Halifax. In the unlikely event their pursuers' reach stretched into Canada, there could be road checks.

"All the way up here?" Nina said. "Isn't that a bit paranoid?"

"I assume they hadn't yet twigged onto Tommy when he came up here. But if they had, they might have tracked him."

"All the way to where we're going?"

"Not likely. He would have known."

"Because..."

"You'll know when you see the place."

So began another eight-hour trip up the Nova Scotia coast. In the dark. Through the rain Richard had been outrunning all afternoon across the Bay.

It caught them at just past ten p.m., thudding across the wheel deck window like a wet slap from God. All line-of-sight vanished. Nina panicked beside him, saying insisting they had to shut down, pull for shore. She wasn't reassured when he told her he'd been piloting by instruments only—compass and sonar—for the last hour already.

"Are you insane? Feverish?" She put a quick hand to his forehead, which would have been almost pleasurable if she hadn't been using it to just prove her point.

"Columbus's ships," he said, clutching the wheel a little tighter in case she tried to pry him off it. "What were their names?"

"What?"

"Christopher Columbus. Sailed across the ocean. First person to discover America, right? But he made it here and back again. What were his ships called?"

She pursed her lips at him. Such pretty lips. He wondered what it would be like to kiss those lips. Sink into them...

"The *Nina*..."

"Ha! You!"

"...the *Pinta*, and the *Santa Maria*."

"See? We're piloting the *Santa Maria*! We can't lose!"

"The *Santa Maria* ran aground somewhere," she said. "Columbus had to abandon it."

"It didn't sink, though, did it."

The timing of the wind hitting the wheel house hard enough to crack a side window could have been better. A seam of water appeared there as the rain hammered the glass, trying to get in. Richard spun the bow a little more windward with a tight grin, thankful that at least the adrenaline was keeping him awake.

"Richard..."

She'd made the switch to his first name at last. "We'll make it," he said over the rain noise. "Why don't you go check on Janine again."

"If you're..."

He looked at her. God, she was a beautiful, tall woman. Her mahogany hair had gone dark, big, and frizzy in the ocean air, like a wild woman. A selkie of Orkney Island legend. And her skin, ghostly pale in the running lights of the cabin, seemed almost luminous, begging to be touched. His hand would just fit around the side of her jaw, his thumb up to her broad cheekbone. And those lips again, not overlarge but inviting. Longing.

Richard blinked hard. The drugs, the blood and oxygen loss. He was forgetting everything he'd worked through about this earlier. *Focus.*

"I'm...just thinking that the storm might scare her. It beats like a drum on the decks, echoes around down there something fierce."

She held his eyes a second longer and he couldn't tell if the shudder that ran through him was from her gaze or the double-props clearing the water for a moment in a wave trough.

Then she turned and ducked down the stairs that led below decks. Leaving him alone and struggling to stay upright, conscious, focused.

Hours to go.

Simple.
Get there.
Then he'd kiss the woman, reason be damned.
That fantasy kept him going.

13

A STORM!

When Janine finally jerked awake, huge thumping noises of waves were crashing over the cabin. Then the boat lurched, turned and suddenly dropped sideways like it was sliding down a hill.

Janine screamed.

The boat bottomed and rose, swinging around sickeningly like no one was steering. Like Janine was all alone! Like they'd all left her and—

Whump! The boat thudded down and slid the other way.

Everything cracked and rattled and thumped as it changed directions at the bottom again, rose, and *dropped out from under her!* She screamed and suddenly Auntie was there, clinging onto her, looking horrible herself.

Then the boat switched directions again, Janine's stomach suddenly couldn't take any more, and she spewed all over the bed. Auntie cleaned it up and found a fishy-smelling bucket just in time for Janine to barf into it, and again as the boat slurped side to side. And again, until all that came up was stingy boogers. But her stomach kept wanting to keep barfing.

Then the boat thumped down sideways and she screamed again.

And Auntie Nina barfed too, in the same bucket, which was just gross.

"Oh, that's just gross," Nina called over the racket as she wiped her mouth. She looked at Janine, and even though Janine wasn't sure why, they both burst into giggles.

"Giggles!" Auntie Nina yelled. "Giggles and screams! That's a start, right?"

Then the boat lurched and Janine screamed again. And Nina almost lost hold of the bucket and swore. And a drawer full of knives and forks that had burst its latch and been sliding in and out, suddenly shot out completely and jangled all over the floor around Janine's feet.

No fun. *No fun!* Why couldn't Uncle Richard be here and let Auntie Nina steer? Was Uncle Richard gonna die? He'd been so weak ever since Nina's house. And breathed funny. And gasped a lot. And slept so much.

And—the boat lurched and she clung to Auntie Nina and screamed again—where were they going? Would her mommy and daddy be there? Did Uncle Richard wake them up those times he went off without her? Did he hide them someplace special, like with God in a secret cave?

Auntie Nina had opened her rain coat and Janine dug her face inside it, remembering her mother desperately. *Please, Mommy? I know you were hurt really bad. I know. But that's okay. You and Daddy always said it's okay to be hurt for a while, but then you've got to be a big girl, right? Then you've got to come back.*

And she wants to call out for her mommy and daddy, or even for Uncle Richard, but she can't. Her tongue won't let her. Her tongue keeps telling her she mustn't. She *mustn't.*

The boat crashes down sideways again and she screams again into Auntie Nina chest.

~~~~

No, she wasn't going to puke again, Nina thought.

Yes, she was.

Was not...

Somewhere in the middle of Nina's fight to hold onto whatever was left in her stomach, Mackenzie finally broke them free of the blowing storm, and roared them into a small fishing town with a crooked, out-jutting wharf. It was dead of night now, but Nina did what Richard ordered and staggered off the *Santa Maria*, managed to rouse a bluff-looking young man from the nearest house, and brought him stumbling out in a heavy sweater and rain slicker, boots, still pulling up his pants.

A muttered conversation with Mackenzie in the steady rain, and the youth took off through the town only to return twenty minutes later in a coughing pickup with a fat woman who looked maybe fifty. The youth's mother?

More mutters, of which Nina only caught a gutturally-accented something that sounded like "...sa'only troying..." while she straightened Janine's clothes and made sure they'd brought all their traveling clothes and supplies out of the boat. It sat in two little piles on the drumming wood—Mackenzie's backpack and two other plastic bags. Everything getting soaked.

Finally Mackenzie walked over to them.

God, he looked so pale and haggard. None of the jungle cat remained. Or even of the fierce man who'd bitten into that thick stick back near Stroudsburg to stab a needle into his chest while Nina kept Janine away and tried not to pass out herself. Now he was struggling just to keep his head up.

Nina knew she probably looked as bad or worse. Her breath stank. Her hair was frizzed out like the night itself. Her eyes couldn't look as bad as Mackenzie's sunken sockets, but they felt it.

And she was angry that she cared at all. Angry that a part of her still wanted him to think she'd "weathered" it okay.

"I got us wheels," Mackenzie said through the rain. "Partial payment for the boat. The rest...we discuss another time."

He suddenly stumbled and she caught his arm to steady him.

He pointed to the pickup. "You have to drive."

"You think?" Then Nina saw he was barely holding on and fought the fear that caused in her. For him, strangely enough. "We need to find you a hospital."

"No!"

"What? You think even up here...?"

"Yes!" And there it was. Under the collapsed exterior Mackenzie still had that indomitable determination. Stronger than any man's she'd ever known, even Pops, or François Gervais. Seductively easy to latch onto. And it wasn't that Nina was looking for someone to lean on or follow or anything stupidly feminine like that. It was just...seductive. Irritating and chauvinistic at times, yes. But seductive. And maybe the whole reason she was still with him on this crazy trip, Janine and the omniscient bad guys aside, was a simple desire to understand why that was.

But he still needed a doctor.

"Where we're going," he said, seeming to understand she wasn't giving in on this one, "there's a doc I know. Who'll treat me. Keep it quiet. Now let's go."

After a final pause just to establish it was *her* choice, she nodded and told Janine to pick up one of the plastic bags. Then Nina hoisted the other and Mackenzie's backpack, and walked with Janine to the truck. Mackenzie limped after them.

The pickup's interior was torn and cracked, smelling of rotten fish and machine oil. Enough to make Nina's stomach roll even though there was nothing left in there to come out.

As Mackenzie squanked open the passenger door and climbed up inside with a huff, closing the door after him, Nina realized that he stank too. A rotten, sweet smell like Coke and melted chocolate bars under a movie theater seat. Was his wound infected?

Before she could bring herself to ask to see it, he'd buckled himself in with the simple lap belt, no shoulder restraint, and started fumbling about for the middle belt for Janine. Nina pushed his hands away, startled by their coldness, and tugged out the belt from where it was buried in the seat crack.

"Head...for the 105," Mackenzie mumbled and pointed. "That way. You go north, left at...unh...Whycocomagh. F-follow signs to Inverness."

"That's where we're going? Inverness?"

He shook his head painfully as she started up the truck and pulled out. With a whumpf, he slumped against the rumbling door and closed his eyes. "Mackie's Cove. Turn-off...at a little bridge. Moose head on sign. About thirty miles. Come out of...woods. See it. To the right a hill. Driveway. That's Doc Klein. Friend."

He mumbled something else that Nina couldn't catch as she maneuvered her way up the twisting road out of the village. But she heard his breathing go thin and raspy. Janine, who had finally started to recover from the hours of cooped-up screaming and puking with Nina, tugged at Nina's arm on the steering wheel.

Harder.

Nina shot a glance at her, then to where she was trying to shake Mackenzie awake. He wasn't moving.

In a panic, Nina pulled over to the side of the road and skidded to a stop. She fumbled up under his jacket and shirt to find the valve on the hypodermic needle he'd stuck in and explained about. She opened the valve and heard a short hiss. Closed it. He didn't revive. And Nina had the vertiginous sensation of being abandoned, something she hadn't felt since her father had walked out on the family while she was in high school.

It wasn't so much that the land was strange. Sure, it was pitch black out, the middle of the night, in a foreign land where she was sure of none of the rules, none of the distances, times, languages even. But she'd left home pretty early. And she'd traveled in her job. She wasn't some inflexible stick-in-the-mud.

It was just...everything. Okay, the foreign land, the unknown killers chasing them, the little girl who'd gone completely mute again, the mystery around what Tom Mackenzie had done, the things Richard Mackenzie wasn't telling her, the fact Richard Mackenzie might be *dying* on her here...

"Damn it, Mackenzie," she muttered and jammed the truck back into gear. "You live and I'm going to kill you for getting me into this."

~~~~

Richard swam in and out of consciousness. Through the rumble and thick smells of the pickup's cab, he could feel Janine's skinny little body beside his.

And beyond her body, a woman's body with a man's strength of will—Nina. A man's will, yet a woman's...what? Need? He'd felt it call to him. Like her body, all wrapped in heavy clothes and a rain slicker, called to him. Said *Here I am. Touch me. Hold me. Wrap me up. Be with me.*

Okay, he was hallucinating now. Swimming in and out of consciousness just like...

A jolt as the truck hit a pothole shook him back into consciousness.

He was flying through the night with a little girl and love goddess. He was light as a bird. He was...

Blackness.

14
Ethan Allen border crossing
Vermont

W HERE?" said The Politician's voice on the phone.
    Castinages stood in the blank-walled immigration offices at the Ethan Allen border crossing to Canada and stared out at the window at the uninspiring wall of highway and stubby evergreens. "I believe they're headed north, into Quebec," Castinages replied.

"You don't know."

"I don't know the sun will rise tomorrow, but I believe it will."

"The sun has a predictable timetable, Major. What's the timetable for Mackenzie's apprehension?"

"Three days. An hour. It depends, to some extent, on the path our prey takes."

"Which means it could be a week. Three weeks. Never."

"No."

"No?"

"He's wounded. At some point he'll need treatment. If he gets it south of the border, we'll know within the hour. If he attempts to cross the border, we'll know sooner."

There was a long pause, then The Politician spoke again. "At eight-forty last night, a fisherman in the small fishing village of Starboard , Maine, reported the sale of his lobster boat to a family of three—a man, woman, and young girl. The girl was apparently mute. Her father had some kind of serious chest injury. The buyers paid with cash and a van but refused to sign any papers. They motored out of port that same night."

Castinages ground his teeth together, trying to figure what resources

The Politician was pulling on besides Castinages. Had to be the NSA. Almost certainly unauthorized or Castinages wouldn't still be in this game. It gave him the balls to snap, "When did you get this intel?"

"Mackenzie and the girl may have passed across the maritime boundary and be in Canada already, true?"

"This morning? Last night?"

"It's not surprising, is it, that they took a boat—"

"I did my part."

"—given his naval background."

"I fucking risked my men, got the package to you, then *you* fucked up. Your end. Not mine."

"However it happened, Major, the package is out there. And if Mackenzie finds it, or has it already, and decides to turn it over to the authorities or media, all our plans go sideways. Not to mention you, Major, getting exposed as a criminal, possibly a traitor to your country."

Castinages laughed so hard it turned to a choking cough. "I'm dying and I got no family to mourn me. You think I give a fuck about any of that?"

"Yes. About all of it. It's why we chose you."

Castinages closed his jaw hard.

"Well?"

"We need to meet. I want to know specifics on the agreements you've got lined up. Call it getting me 'invested' or some such bullshit."

"The clock is ticking, Major."

"It's okay. I understand Mackenzie. I know where he's going."

"And if he moves on before you reach him? Or turns over the package?"

"He won't. Guarantee it."

"Why?"

"He'll want to talk to us first. And I'll bet he's doing some heavy sorting out stuff now too—who to trust. Who's family. Kind of like our issues. We gonna meet?"

There was a pause, then, "Come back to DC, Major. I think it's time."

15

Mackie's Cove
Cape Breton Island, Nova Scotia
Canada

*N*EVER RETURN.
Dhachaigh?

No. This is not my home.

When Richard finally wobbled up towards consciousness, he was in a bed his sick body somehow remembered—narrow metal frame with a middle sagging like a hammock. Hot. A fly buzzed lazily somewhere. He squinted, blinded by the light, to see a thickly-painted window frame to his left, faded floral wallpaper, and...someone sitting on his bed.

Woman?

Things tumbled back in a rush. Nina? He blinked and tried to open his eyes more fully.

Not Nina. Oh God, he knew her, though.

He closed his eyes and saw her clearer in his memory. The woman's hair was as red as Janine's, worn wild and free. Eyes gray-green. Skin always milky pale with eyelashes and brows almost transparent. Arms smooth and strong. All bosom and hips with a tiny waist. Like a Marie-Ange on steroids. A pale wolverine.

He squinted open his eyes again and her eyes raked his. She was seated just below his bent arm—intravenous drip there—and shifted her skirted hip against him through the thin blanket.

"Coming up, are you?" she said.

It came out in the distinctive sounds of his childhood. Half west Scotland, west Ireland, part Newfoundland. *Combing ope, are yeh?*

He looked out the bright window to confirm it. Saw a piece of the long, sloping, sunlit hills he knew ran down to the town and ocean. *Dhachaigh.* Home.

"Angie," he croaked.

"Don't talk. Doc says you're sick. Been under a day and a half. Need to just lie there a while."

"Janine and Nina, the woman who was..."

He let it trail off as she shifted and he saw behind her, leaning against the door, the tall slim figure who was his present life as much as Angie was his past. But even as his heart leapt, Richard instinctively shut down his face because Nina's eyes were cold as ice. They narrowed as her gaze met his.

His present was maybe not so great.

"They'll be staying with me now," Angie lilted. Evangeline Neal. "As me cousin and her child. From the States. No one'll know different."

"And me?"

"Here with the doctor. This is the bedroom his son used to stay in, you know. Back when he'd still visit."

"Eli doesn't visit anymore?"

Angie held his eyes steadily, but he felt her hiding at the same time. "The place has changed since you left, Richard. Full of poison."

Before she could elaborate, Doc Klein himself bustled in, shooed Angie away from the bedside, and took her place.

God, he'd aged! Still the proper little German Jew, though he'd shaved his last fringe of head hair and trimmed his beard down to a white goatee. But it was around his eyes, all the wrinkles there, that Richard saw a world of disappointments.

Less bloating, though, than Richard remembered. Less drinking?

Doc Klein gave him a crooked smile like he knew Richard's thoughts. He looked at his watch while he put his fingers on Richard's wrist to take his pulse.

"I thought I heard talking up here, *ja?* How is my war hero?"

"Pretty fried, Doc. What'd you do to me?"

Klein waved his hand with a tch'ing sound. "Put in a proper chest tube. Re-opened your wound to clean up, remove necrotic material, dead tissue, and close it properly. I pumped you full of fluids and dosed you with antibiotics which you will need to continue for two weeks. The bullet must remain inside until you get x-rays."

"So I'm basically lucky to be alive."

"Still the master of understatement, I see. Yes, Richard, you should have died shortly after you were shot, or at least passed out and lapsed into hypoxia. As it was, you finally succumbed to shock, which in itself can be fatal." He'd pulled out a black blood-pressure cuff and reached over Richard's body to Velcro it around his non-IV'd arm. Pumped it up as Richard spoke.

"Then I guess I owe you a bundle. My health insurance cover it?"

Again the crooked smile. "I'm retired, so no. You can maybe buy me a dinner later." Klein released the pressure in the cuff. Watched the pulse.

"Retired?"

"It's a long story." He dropped Richard's wrist and unstrapped the cuff.

Richard tried to sit and felt blackness wash over him. He lay back down, breathing heavily. He forced himself to keep his eyes open so he wouldn't pass out. "Doesn't look like I'll be going anywhere..."

"A few days," Klein said.

"Nina must have questions."

"I have told her she may not ask them until you are stronger. In the meantime, she said to tell you that she called a friend of her mother and discovered her mother was apparently released from custody, but was somewhat shaken up. She and her boyfriend have apparently gone on holiday down in Palm Beach. So?"

"So what?" Richard said, relieved that Nina had at least not called her family home directly. He hoped. They'd surely have the phones bugged.

"So talk to me. Tell me where you have been. Why you were foolish enough to return. How you got shot and this poor woman's parents arrested. Entertain an old man."

"Doc!" called Angie from where he'd shooed her. "Yer getting pushy. And it's almost ten. Can I take my charges and leave now?"

"Hm? Oh, yes. Go. I need to check his wound now anyway."

Angie collected Nina, who had still said nothing, and the two women headed outside, calling Janine as they did. Richard wanted to stop them, find out what had happened, but he was distracted by Klein half-unwrapping Richard's wound dressing to examine it. Yuck. The thing looked hacked to hell, all purple and stitched. And Klein's slightest touch send deep spears of pain shooting through his chest, making it scary to breathe in.

Richard's forehead burst with sweat. He grunted and Klein nodded.

"Healing fine, I think. Though you should really have gone to the hospital in Sydney. Or anywhere else."

Richard started to laugh but stopped at the pain.

"Can you tell me what happened?" Klein said.

Richard closed his eyes. "Some of it." He opened them. "The woman and kid who came with me—are they going to be all right with Angie? As in—no one outside Mackie's Cove knows they're here?"

Klein hesitated a moment before saying, "You know this village has never shared much with outsiders. But with you in the picture... I don't know. You must walk softly."

"Tell me," said Richard.

Klein began, but was cut off by Nina's terrified scream.

~~~~

They surrounded them from three or more directions as soon as Nina, Janine, and Angie Neal stepped away from the house—a group of thugs in sweaty tee-shirts and cotton work shirts over them, all unbuttoned, some stuffed in, some not, two thugs wearing ball caps with bills facing backwards.

The one who'd made Nina scream by suddenly being right *there* was mid-twenties, with a long grizzled visage and a knobby nose. His dark hair stuck out every which way like it hadn't been washed in a few days. His dark gaze slid over her and Janine, making Nina reach down to touch the girl's head where she clung to Nina's leg. The man looked at Evangeline Neal. Back to Nina.

Were they with the men who'd been chasing them?

No.

How do you know?

Their breath stinks and they don't carry weapons.

Maybe they're just *hired* by the bad guys then. Because anybody who could have found them at that motel in Pennsylvania could sure as hell track them down here. Mackenzie had brought them back to his home town, for Christ's sake!

Nina felt a bump from behind and turned to see the big-gutted one had stepped up close to crowd her.

"Back off!" she snapped and drove an elbow hard into the man's gut.

~~~~

"Help me up," Richard grunted at Doc Klein, but the doctor looked frozen.

With a grunt at the lancing pain, Richard rolled off his bed without him and almost collapsed at the dizziness and weakness in his legs. Then Klein was there supporting him and trying to ease him back to bed.

"I'll...I'll go check," the old man said.

But Richard shook his head. "The window. Let me at least *see*, Nathan."

So Klein walked him over and Richard saw...

~~~~

"Do it!" the long-face man snapped. "Give 'er room!"

The fat tough, groaning and bent over, backed away from Nina. But she could still smell him. She could smell all five of them. Fish guts and body odor. If these were the best locals the bad guys could hire, then maybe—

Long-Face poked her so fast and hard on her sternum that Nina stumbled. "And don't *you* be getting ugly!" he said.

Then he turned lean over the shorter Evangeline Neal. "He's alive, then?"

Evangeline—"Angie" to Mackenzie—nodded so that her chin ended up higher than it was before, the lower lip out. "He is."

"And them?" The man nodded his jaw back towards Nina and Janine.

"My cousin from New York. And her little girl, Janine. I never told you about them?"

"Your cousin—Mackenzie's girlfriend? Wouldn't that just do it, eh? He's got a nerve."

Nina's already-pounding heart still managed to step up a notch and urge her forward. But the fat thug behind her stepped forward again and Nina suddenly remembered Janine as the girl hugged her leg tight. She stopped.

Wait a minute. The long-face man with halitosis was shaking his head angrily at Angie. And the obviousness of his jealousy finally sank in. These weren't hired by the bad guys at all. They were just besotted local boys. This was all about Angie, not Nina or Janine.

Just as coming here had been?

"You!" she called to Long-Face so that he looked up at her.

The fat thug stepped right up behind her to intimidate her again and she faked another elbow to his gut before stepping back solidly onto his shin with her free leg. He yowled and staggered back. The others blinked in surprise.

"By Jayzus," Long-Face swore finally and stepped towards her.

"Dougan!" Angie snapped. "Stop right there."

"Or what?"

"Or I'll crunch your little balls off."

Long-Face Dougan looked back at her with a mix of fear, loathing, and something else, but he took one exaggerated step backwards over the dirt. "It's not right what you're doing, Angie."

"And what am I doing?" Coy.

The redhead had crossed her arms under her substantial chest as she said it and Nina noted all five of the men looked that way like their eyes had fishhooks in them. It made Nina want to vomit.

Then to make matters worse, Richard came limping out the door with Doc Klein right behind him. And Mr. Macho Special Forces carried a shotgun loosely in his right hand.

"Dougan Smither," he said.

"Mackenzie."

"And Billy Cuddy," Richard went on, nodding to the fat one behind Nina. Then, to each of the other toughs in turn, "Gord Keen, Rob Dundas. You, I don't know."

"Andre Beaufort," Angie supplied.

"You gentlemen wanted to discuss something specific with the ladies?"

"By Jayzus," Dougan swore again, but it was now a surly apology. He slunk backwards a few steps as he said it. "Heard you'd died, Mackenzie."

"Nope." He swung the shotgun back and forth slowly. "Just back for a visit."

"On the QT," added Angie, with a hard look at Dougan.

Nina thought Dougan would laugh at the pseudo-military jargon, but the younger man pursed his lips and nodded like his woman had just invoked a sacred obligation of some sort.

Nina couldn't keep all the social dynamics straight here, but did know she was still shaking with the after-effects of her adrenaline. And she had a frightened little girl as her charge amidst a bunch of rough men and a gun.

"I want to go now," Nina piped up. "Angie Neal was showing my daughter and I where we'll be staying while we're here. If you *gentlemen* don't mind."

Dougan and his buddies blinked so obviously it would have been funny if Nina wasn't dealing with ragged nerves and a sudden, profound sense of loneliness. It was just her taking care of Janine now, wasn't it. Because Richard Mackenzie was caught up in his own little games here with Angie and the rest. Like Tom had been caught up? Was this really where Tom had come to hide the thing he took?

For some reason the last thought was even more alienating than everything else. Even Nina's college sweetheart, who'd married her sister, was a mystery to her. This whole place, these people. Nina didn't fit in.

"Billy. Gord. Rob. Andy. Let 'em go," Dougan said.

He stepped to one side but Richard shook his head. "No, I think it would be better if you all left first. I'll be walking the ladies down myself later on."

Dougan stuck out his lower lip but finally nodded, gestured to the others and headed down the hill on the dirt footpath path that wound down the hill from Doc Klein's house, sometimes paralleling the road, sometimes not.

"Going to the pub, most likely," Angie said, watching them go.

"Not to church, anyway," Doc Klein said. "People here don't do that anymore."

Nina said nothing. She rested her hand on Janine's head and stared stonily at Mackenzie, who stared silently down the hill at the departing men.

When the men had crossed the highway into the town of Mackie Cove itself and were out of sight of the house, Mackenzie swayed and swung the rifle down to use as a cane. Doc Stein ran to him and wrapped one of Mackenzie's arms over the slim doctor's shoulders.

"He does that a lot," Nina said.

"What?" said Angie.

"Faints just when you're getting ready to tear a strip off him."

Angie gave a grudging chuckle. "So do we wait for him, then, or go down ourselves?"

Doc Klein made to help Mackenzie back into the house but the big strong soldier (so *not*) stopped him and turned towards Nina.

"Neither," croaked Mackenzie suddenly. Doc Klein was trying to help him back to the house, but Mackenzie was pushing him away. "Not until I tell you something."

Nina pursed her lips and waited. He crooked a finger at her to come closer so it was just him and her and Janine.

"What?" she said when she was barely a foot from his face, Janine still hanging onto her leg. It drove her crazy that this close to him she wanted more than anything to reach out and support him, to feel his body supported against hers as she'd almost gotten used to in the Chevy van and the boat.

"This place," he said. "I didn't tell you I grew up here because I knew you'd worry they'd find us because of that."

"What? Me worry?"

He broke into a slow smile. "Uh-hunh. But I need to tell you they won't find us. Not as long as we lie low and don't tick off more of the neighbors."

"Because they're stupid? They won't figure obvious places you might go?"

"This isn't one of them."

"The place where you grew up isn't one of them."

"No."

His certainty was really starting to bug her. "Why?"

He told her.

16
coffee shop
Washington, DC

Hᴇ ᴅɪᴅɴ'ᴛ ɢʀᴏᴡ ᴜᴘ ɪɴ ᴛʜᴇ ᴛᴏᴡɴ ᴏɴ ʜɪs ᴘᴀssᴘᴏʀᴛ or the one in his military papers," said the intense man in Washington, DC and adjusted his glasses. The movement wasn't meant to intimidate or prevaricate, but simply to give the man time to gather his thoughts. Castinages had hired him before to provide local intel and analysis. He was using him now to give him ammunition to take in for his meeting later with The Politician.

"How do you know?" Castinages prodded.

"No one in either place has ever heard of him."

"How is that possible?"

"Circumstances and the desire and intellect to use them."

The man hunched forward in the restaurant bench seat and slid the salt shaker back and forth between his pudgy fingers with great precision. The two men had a booth in an old-fashioned joint on 10th St. NW, just north of the J. Edgar Hoover Building. They were an unlikely-looking pair, a true Mutt and Jeff. Except that intel-man Mutt was not so skinny, while the shorter Jeff, aka Special Forces Major Misha Castinages, was a wall of muscle.

The kitchen clatter alone was enough to cover their talk.

But that talk hadn't yet given Castinages what he needed for his meeting this afternoon. He shifted about in his one expensive civilian suit, a three hundred dollar job he'd had custom-made during a furlough in Hong Kong. He'd worn it today with the idea he might not be as conspicuous either here or later, meeting with The Politician. He'd also hoped he might sweet-talk The Politician's female liaison into seeing him privately later on this evening, but she'd refused to meet with him. Bitch.

"Explain," he said now. "What circumstance?"

The other man's hand stopped with the salt shaker and he raised his eyes, surprised at the rough edge to his former war buddy's voice.

"Richard Mackenzie's father, Strachan, was a dual citizen and itinerant fisherman before he got married. He followed the work around. Apparently he got a girl pregnant during one of his jobs south of the border."

"So Mackenzie's got two American parents."

"Which gives him—"

"Dual citizenship. Right. Got it." Mackenzie hadn't mentioned *that* in their little heart-to-heart.

The salt shaker began moving back and forth again. "Their mother, Mary, actually gave birth to Richard north of the border, in a small town in New Brunswick. They moved north back to Canada shortly thereafter to a small town in Quebec, but kept skipping back and forth. Managed to be south of the border for the birth of Richard's younger brother."

Castinages grabbed the salt shaker and clacked it down hard beside the wall. "Where did they grow up?"

"Well that is where a second set of circumstances come into play," continued the man, unperturbed. Thinking through every word, the peckerhead. It's why, Castinages knew, the man had left the military for more cerebral government spy work. Also why his career had stalled in his new line, too. It made him malleable for someone who knew what to offer. Who needed him as an independent ace-in-the-hole on this operation, so Castinages wasn't dependent on The Politician's resources.

"Richard Mackenzie's parents stopped filing income tax statements. And Richard Mackenzie's school records do not exist."

Castinages scowled. "Meaning..."

"Back in the eighties and nineties, various small schools in Canada were less than fastidious in their record keeping. Some didn't keep good records of their students. Many were slow to computerize them. The joint elementary/secondary school in the little Quebec town where Mackenzie claims to have lived burned down in 1999 before they had placed their student records in Canada's national computer database. All the records, both computer and paper, were lost. It was to this school and a falsely-implanted record in the recreated database that Mackenzie sent all schooling queries during his navy applications.

"The address he listed as his place of residence was an abandoned house that had sat unoccupied for years. He had a standing mail-redirect to a post office box listed to the military mail drop service for soldiers serving away from home."

Castinages's scowl deepened. "What about his brother?"

"His life apparently began at the age of thirteen in a boarding school in Montreal. The nuns there give the same false childhood home for him that his brother listed."

"So *no* one knows where Mackenzie grew up?"

The smaller man's left hand shot out and grabbed the salt shaker like he couldn't help it and began moving it back and forth again. "Someone somewhere knows, but we can hardly go from town to town, asking."

"There has to be records. A driver's license. Something."

"You think you know how to search better than me? I'm tapped into the F.B.I. search as well. I can assure you that they want to find him almost as much as you do."

"For the girl."

"Of course."

"Shit."

Castinages leaned his bulk forwards over the table, wishing could reach out and wrap his hands around his old friend's flabby neck.

"If we don't get him," Castinages growled, "and get him *first*, then this whole mission is FUBAR. I get screwed. The whole operation in the Middle East gets screwed."

"Not that you've told me how or why..."

"And I'm not going to because you don't need to know. But you do know you're going down with me if I go, right? Tapes of all our meetings." He tapped his right breast pocket.

The other man stopped sliding the salt shaker and visibly blanched. "You'd be on the tapes too."

Castinages laughed. "Like I'd care at that point."

"Tapes can be faked."

"You think your bosses won't be able to put together what you've done?"

There was a long pause while the other man stared at Castinages. Then he adjusted his glasses and dropped his eyes to the table. Finally he said, "Maybe Mackenzie senior registered a mortgage. Maybe Richard Mackenzie blabbed to friends he had in the Canadian navy."

"Now you're thinking."

"We'll find him."

"And find Tom Mackenzie's 'Deep Throat.'" The Politician didn't seem overly concerned about how Tom Mackenzie had gotten all his intel to start with, which made no sense, which meant The Politician had some reason for keeping him in the dark on that score.

"I'm close, but I have to be careful. It slows things down when you don't want to leave traces of your inquiries."

Castinages pushed back from the table and slid himself out as the waitress arrived with their bill. "Just move faster, partner. For both of them. Or I'll be the *nicest* thing you've got chasing your ass."

He stalked out of the restaurant, leaving Senior Cryptographic Analyst Leonard Junk, aka "Special Agent" Leonard Junk to smile weakly at their waitress and pay for the coffees.

17
Mackie's Cove
Cape Breton Island, Canada

NINA SAW NOTHING OF RICHARD the rest of that day or the next morning as they helped Angie clean and organize her small house for guests. Despite Richard's wheezing explanation of how his family had "fallen off the grid" when he was a boy, and how he'd used that to hide Tom's and his roots as a young man, Nina was still furious with him.

He'd lied to her. By omission, maybe, but he'd lied.

She wiped a hand over her sweaty brow. What else had he not told her? Already two different sets of people had come to the door and mumbled some excuse or other to Angie so they could walk into the cramped living room and meet her house guests. And when Nina shook their hands, the narrow, dark look in their eyes didn't hold welcome. More...what? Loathing? Fear?

They casually asked Angie about Mackenzie then, and nodded gravely when she told them of his injuries. When they left the house, Nina saw them each glance up the hill. But only quickly. Like something bad might happen to them if they were caught doing it.

What the hell had Richard Mackenzie done to these people before he'd left town?

Janine tugged on her sleeve. She looked and the little girl pointed out the dusty bedroom window at the hill.

"After lunch," Nina said with grim resolve. "First help me put these away."

When she finished transferring the meager collection of hers and Janine's clothes to the old wooden dresser and tiny closet, Nina looked around and nodded. They'd have room here.

The Neal house, which sat on the ocean side of a road that ran down from the highway, was a simple box like the others around it. Two stories, shake and shingle, painted blue with white trim. (Others were painted yellow or pink.) And only Angie lived here now. Her mother had passed away two years before.

Janine saw something outside and suddenly tore out of the room and down the narrow staircase. Nina ran after her, but stopped when she saw Janine digging into an old sandbox in the backyard. She was picking twigs and grass out of it with great concentration.

"Don't leave there without letting me know!" Nina called.

"She's a quiet one," Angie Neal said from where she was scrubbing the kitchen vinyl on her hands and knees.

"Yes." Nina frowned. Richard hadn't told her how much she could say. She felt muzzled, which was stupid. "Janine went silent when her father was killed. Tom Mackenzie. You knew him, didn't you?"

"Hmph." Angie didn't look up.

Nina walked to stand in the kitchen doorway. "He came back here a while ago? Do you know where he stayed while he was here?"

Angie halted for just a second and spat, "You think I spends me time tracking everyone who comes in or out of this town!"

It was so obviously a deflection that Nina had no answer for it. But she wasn't just going to back off either. "Doc Klein told me *you* had a younger brother."

"He'll be back. Soon's he finds there's no work anywheres."

"He's in Toronto?"

"It's a big, cold place."

Like all big cities? "What did he do here? Before he left?"

Angie paused and sat back on her heels, rubber-gloved hands on her hips. "Some fishing. Collecting unemployment, mostly. Hoping like the others the mine'll open back up again."

"There's a mine nearby? Coal mine?"

"Closed."

"What about you?"

Angie's face went red. "You think I'm closed up, too? No one'll mine me anymore?"

"No, I...I meant where do you work?"

"Oh." The redhead ran her tongue around the inside of her full mouth as she did like she was clearing a bad taste. "I work at the pub by the road. The Saint Ninian."

"Did Tommy spend much time there when he came back to visit?"

Angie regarded her stonily and Nina finally just shrugged.

"Fine," Nina said, and there was a long moment of silence.

Finally Angie said, "You, then. What d'you do?"

"When I'm not being your cousin from New York?"

Angie Neal waited, gloved hands still on hips.

"I work with an urban planner out in California. We help communities who are transitioning, densifying, adding suburbs." She might as well have been throwing words at a brick wall. "Or ecological studies. You know, when there's a land-use shift, new regulations..."

The pub woman's face remained a focused blank until it was clear Nina had finished. Then she nodded. "Pays good?"

"For San Francisco?" Nina snorted and saw Janine jump from where she'd been standing in the doorway, watching her and Angie. "Gets me a room with a view."

"No house."

"Nuh-unh."

"Richard tell you about his house here? Where he grew up?"

Nina's focus snapped fully to Angie. "No. He didn't."

"It's because he don't have one. Used to be on the south edge of town, down near the shore. An old thing, in bad repair. Just afore he died, like he knows what's coming, Richard's father burns it down. He says, 'If me sons won't live here, no one else will.'"

"When...did Richard's father die?"

Angie did a final swipe of the floor with her sponge, then plunked it into her bucket and stood. "Ask Richard that. And ask him why he didn't come back for the funeral. Tommy did."

"That's when Tom..."

"Ask him."

~~~~

Doc Klein telephoned just after Nina, Janine, and Angie had finished a simple lunch of baloney sandwiches and canned soup, and spoke to Nina. He said that even though Richard had come out of his minor surgery successfully, he would need a full week of recovery time. Preferably with no visitors to excite him.

The call broke through Nina's mask of patience and she swore as she hung up the phone. Of course she turned to see the mute, hopeful face of Janine watching her.

And the much colder eyes of Evangeline Neal. "He's not coming to rescue you, then?"

"Doc Klein says he needs a full week of rest."

"Does he now."

Oh, please, Nina thought at her. Just shut up. Maybe act like little Janine Mackenzie, who screamed and giggled in the middle of a terrifying storm but otherwise made no sounds at all.

While Nina herself went slowly mad. Yes, there had been honest-to-God men with guns making it necessary they go into hiding, but this... Baloney sandwiches! And for all her scholarship, Nina had never been good with either junk food or inactivity. Sitting around here, watched by everyone, treated like a romantic rival by the town floozie... God, it would make her pop!

The least she could do was scope out where Tom might have hidden what he stole when he came here for the last time, for his father's funeral.

"I'm going for a walk around town," she said. "Janine?"

In answer, Janine ran upstairs, but she returned a minute later with her stuffed armadillo and held out her other hand to Nina.

~~~~

Janine skipped a little as she walked along the road beside the highway with the giggle-auntie, Nina. She kicked at stones and looked down to the great wide ocean on her right, the funny hodge-podge of box houses running down the hill towards it, the docks and boats down there, a white church steeple way off on a kind of a cliff ahead.

It was like a fairy land. So bright. Everything was so clear, wasn't it.

She half-turned to Auntie Nina, wanting to say it, just like she would have before...

Before...

Before...

"What is it, Janine?"

Janine realized she'd stopped walking and was trembling all over. Breathing hard. Her skin was cold even with that bright sun beating down on her. Even with Snuffles tucked up so hard under her chin that her throat hurt. But she couldn't *see* anything, exactly. She couldn't *feel* anything. And she was saying nothing!

"Janine?"

Auntie Nina's hands were on her arms and Auntie Nina was kneeling down in front of her just and talking to her just like Uncle Richard had when Janine had been up in the tree. *I won't move this time. I won't go see this time. I promise. I promise.*

"Janine, it's okay. It's just you and me out here. I mean, there are other people, but no one trying to hurt us now. And Uncle Richard says they won't find us here. He says we're safe. Okay? Janine?"

I won't move. I won't make a sound.

There was a long pause where Auntie Nina didn't talk either. Then she started to sniff the air like a dog. Sniff sniff! Sniff sniff!

"Do you smell that?"

Janine wanted to ask what, but she knew she couldn't. She looked at Auntie Nina, though. Just a quick look. That had to be all right.

"Pie," Auntie Nina said. And the way she said it made Janine think it must be the most amazing pie in the world.

Sniff sniff! "Cherry pie? Blueberry? I'm not sure. Do you know?"

One sniff had to be okay. So Janine wiggled her nose a little, then breathed in. *Sniff.* And again, *sniff.* She turned her head a bit. Yes. Blueberry. Mixed with the hot salty smell that came up from the ocean and raced softly along the highway here like it was going to keep going forever.

Janine even thought she could tell what direction the blueberry pie smell was coming from.

"I think so too," said Auntie Nina. "Can you guide us there, do you think? Or do shall we just stay here and smell it?"

Stay here? She looked at Auntie Nina with pleading eyes. The lunch hadn't been that good. And the Angie lady hadn't served dessert.

"Well my nose isn't so good. If we follow it, we'll be wandering for days."

So Janine began walking again. It was *necessary.*

~~~~

The next day, Nina took another walk with Janine through town. This time she was more aware of her surroundings, not dawdling, not relaxed. She headed straight for the bakery.

It was closed. Of course. Sunday. But she couldn't help feeling it was because of her. Because after buying the pie yesterday and eating half of right there in the shop with Janine, she'd managed to get the baker talking.

"They calls me Crumpet," he'd said with a broad grin as he watched Janine dig into her piece of pie with the fork he'd found for her. "Crumpet Davies."

Nina had smiled. "I like it. You lived here long?"

"Me whole life."

"So you knew the Mackenzie boys, Richard and Tommy?"

Crumpet's pudgy face darkened and he went back to unloading his fresh-baked rolls behind the counter. "I knew them."

"Richard was about your age?"

The baker shook his head. "Tommy. We hung out. Drove around together. But he was messed up, eh. He and his brother. Dead cold liars about everything. Don't believe him."

"Don't believe Richard, you mean. Tommy's dead, you know."

"Oh yeah. We know. We all know."

"And Richard's still trying to find out why. Something to do with this place, he thinks. With Tommy's visit here. You know anything about that? You see Tommy when he was here?"

"Go away."

"What?"

"Go on! Take the pie with you. Just go!"

And it had only been then that Nina noticed one of the thugs from up on the hill outside Doc Klein's place, the fat one. He'd hung just outside the door of the bakery, watching Nina and Janine. Watched them when they left, too, but hadn't followed Nina as she'd hurried Janine back to Angie's.

Today, Sunday, back at the bakery, she'd hoped to apologize to Crumpet and try to be a little subtler in the way she asked questions. Instead, she just knelt and put the cleaned plate and fork he'd loaned Janine on the bakery's doorstep.

Sunday.

In DC half of Georgetown town would be very publicly going to church. Here no steeple bells chimed. Few people were outside. Those who were pretended not to see Nina and Janine. Even the children playing in their yards or running down the gravel paths between them, if they saw Janine, ran the other way.

It really was like Angie had said to Mackenzie when he'd first woken up here two days ago—this town had gone sour. Sick. Something was eating at it and Nina couldn't help but think they were blaming it all on her and Richard

Mackenzie.

Hurrying on across the top of the town, she and Janine reached the church to find it deserted. Its white, clapboard sides were peeling white paint. Two of its windows were cracked. The insides looked dusty and ill-used.

Such a shame, because an early morning service here would see the sun rise over the eastern ocean. An evening service would feel the hush as it blazed down in the west. And there was even a quaint little cemetery that stretched towards the edge of the cliff.

"You think we'll find your Uncle Richard's daddy there?" Nina asked Janine.

The little girl looked alarmed and Nina laughed. "I mean his gravestone, Janine. Just the stone."

Before she and Janine could start searching, though, Janine tugged on her arm and pointed. There in the distance, limping slowly down the path from Doc Klein's house, almost to Angie's, was a figure that could only be Richard Mackenzie, broad shouldered and perfect even seen from here. Even limping.

Janine tugged again and Nina nodded, her heart skipping. She took Janine's hand and they began hurrying back to meet him.

~~~~

"...be making blueberry grunt for dessert tonight," Angie was saying as Nina and Janine crept down the hill to avoid alerting Mackenzie to their presence.

Not they need have bothered. Angie had taken off her rubber gloves, pulled her wiry hair back on either side with a soft comb. Yet somehow she hadn't managed to change into any starchier clothing. She had on only her high-riding jean cutoffs and the ripped, low-neck tee-shirt from earlier that was so worn you could see her brassiere through it.

Floozy.

And Richard, like all the thugs up around the doc's house the day before, was transfixed by it. He'd stopped in front of her, almost mid-stride, it looked like. His square jaw and cheeks looked hollow, but he'd shaved and washed up. His curly chestnut hair glinted in the sun. Given the heat of the day, he was wearing just his jeans and tee-shirt above his ever-present combat boots. And if his hard-muscled body had been wasted by his injury, Nina couldn't see it. His biceps bulged out below the cuffs of his tee-shirt like a statement of intent.

What a... At least Tom had always undercut his good looks with an easy, self-deprecating humor..

Dead cold liars.

Had Tom been? Was Richard? It didn't fit with Nina's impressions, but there was obviously *some*thing about this place and their childhood that neither Mackenzie had wanted the world to know.

Nina stepped closer and said, "There's also the leftover blueberry pie that Crumpet Davies sold us."

Richard Mackenzie spun around, then winced in pain and looked down, breathing hard. But had there been a light in his eyes when he saw her? No, when he saw Janine. He'd probably been desperate to make sure his niece was all right.

"For the grunt, I picked the berries myself," Angie said. "Up the hills. Good crop this year."

Mackenzie looked up at Nina again, his face broken out in a sweat. "You met Crumpet Davies?"

Nina nodded.

"And how many others?" He shot an accusing look at Angie. "How much exploring have you done?"

For a second Nina was tempted to tell him she'd gone through the entire town, knocking on doors. But she finally just told him the truth—that she and Janine had only done two short walks so far. Almost no one had been willing to speak with them. Even Angie here, who'd deflected every question about Tommy's last visit with an "Ask Richard."

The barmaid snorted and leaned forwards and to run a finger suggestively down Mackenzie's shoulder. "Tonight," she said. "You come by and I'll tell you everything it is you want to know about Tommy's visit."

Nina gritted her teeth as Mackenzie responded the only way he could. He turned to her with his own smile and said, "We'll see, Angie Neal." And damn it if Nina didn't hear a little of the odd Cape Breton lilt in his voice when he said it. Like he was *flirting* with the woman?

Just because he needed the information? Not likely. Not given the way he'd looked at her earlier. The way every man up on that hill by Doc Klein's house had looked at her.

"But I've got another favor to ask first," Mackenzie said.

"Yes?" Almost a purr.

"I need to acquaint Nina with the town, give her a head's-up on things to watch out for if she's to go exploring on her own. Could you look after Janine for a few hours while I take Nina out walking?"

Angie's face blanched and Nina could hear the screech in it as she said, "Take *her* out for a walk?"

"If you could look after Janine," Mackenzie said. "And if Janine's comfortable staying with you, of course."

With a change in mood so fast Nina almost felt her neck snap, Angie smiled her full lips widely and swiveled around to take in Janine's hesitant little form hiding beside Nina's legs.

Nina's own heart squeezed as the little girl, who'd been so alive on their trip out to the church, now clutched her stuffed armadillo closer to her and stuck a thumb in her mouth like a girl some three years younger.

"You know what?" Angie said to Janine, with surprising warmth in her voice. She squatted down in front of her, looking suddenly so motherly that Nina flushed at her own inadequacies. "Your little animal there? What's his name?"

"Snuffles," Mackenzie replied before Nina could.

"Your little Snuffles," Angie went on. "Did you notice he's got a few boo-boos?"

Nina saw Janine frown and hesitantly hold Snuffles out from her body to examine him. Snuffle was indeed ripped in places. Maybe where Mackenzie had inexpertly sewn him back up. Maybe from the rough bathing he'd undergone with Nina's mother.

"I bet you and me, we could fix him right up. A little magic needle and thread, he'd be good as new."

Janine still looked hesitant, but wanting it, Nina could tell.

"And maybe," Angie continued, "when we're done, you'll even help me choose the very best blueberries to put in the dessert for tonight. You know how you check?"

Janine shook her head.

Angie covered half her mouth like she was whispering just for Janine to hear. "You have to gobble a few."

When Janine finally got that, her tight little mouth smiled wide around her thumb.

"Shall we go and fix Snuffles first, then?"

Janine nodded gravely and took Angie's extended hand. As the red-haired woman stood and started back to the house with her, Angie turned once, caught Richard's eye and smiled. "You go have a good time," she said.

"Right."

Mackenzie almost sighed it, drooling. Nina wanted to slap him. Or Angie. Both of them. "Now *there's* a mother," she drawled.

Mackenzie's head snapped up. "What?"

"Well our story's supposed to be that I'm the mother, but what's your first action? Peeling Janine away from me."

He frowned, "Yes," and the uncharacteristically soft expression that had been on his face vanished like a steel door had swung shut over it.

Nina kicked herself but just pressed harder. "And why didn't you just ask Angie right then what she knew about Tommy's trip? Maybe she knows exactly what it was he stole from the bad guys. Maybe she's hiding it for him."

"She would have hinted at that specifically to make sure I come back for dinner," he said arrogantly. "No, anything she knows, she's going to have to have some time to think about."

"Hence our walk."

"No."

"No?"

"The walk's for you. If you're going to go off half-cocked asking questions, you need to know some things first."

It made Nina's face burn. "Like the fact you and Tom were *personae non grata* when you left here? That you were known as liars and troublemakers?"

"Really." He gave her a wry little smile which, on him, was almost like laughing in her face.

"That's what Crumpet Davies told me."

"Crumpet. I see."

"We bought a pie from him. He was being friendly."

"No doubt."

Nina tossed back her hair. Why did every conversation with him have to turn into a sparring match? And why did each one get her so...excited?

The revelation made her face burn again and she ducked it, busying herself with tugging her hair back into the ponytail it had mostly come out of.

"You think Crumpet was lying to us?" she said.

"Did he tell you if Tommy he left something here for me? Or why Tom and I left Mackie's Cove in the first place? Or how my father or mother died? Anything?"

For a second Nina was tempted to lie again, but finally she shook her head. "No."

"You had all day yesterday, and this morning. These are simple questions."

"No." Said blankly. Two could play at that game.

He missed it completely. "No. Because you're strangers. You'll get from them only what they want you to get. Hell, even I am going to be treated like a stranger by most of them. Just the way it is. But at least I can give you the lay of the land so you might start to sense when they're lying or hiding something."

"For when I'm off searching on my own."

He worked his jaw around, obviously struggling with whether to bust her down on that. But finally he nodded. "Or with me. Yes."

With me. The suggestion of intimacy in the words was probably totally unintentional, but it still shivered through Nina so hard she had to grit her teeth to stop any outward reaction.

"Okay," she said.

"Then let's go." Mackenzie pointed down the winding road in the direction of the docks.

18
Falls Church
Virginia

T HIS IS IT, BIG GUY," said Denise D'Alvay and walked, with her conscious
ass-twitch, in through the doors of the low-rise industrial building.

Castinages narrowed his eyes to slits under the canopy of maple trees
outside, looked left and right, then followed. He still had Mackenzie's SIG
225 in a new waistband holster around his back as a kind of mission charm,
as well as his own more-dependable Glock in a shoulder band. Both were
adequately concealed under his suit jacket, where he'd assumed they'd stay
for this meeting.

Now he wasn't so sure.

Because this meeting place was bogus. Something stank. And when
D'Alvay drew up short just outside a nondescript office door, linoleum floor,
his internal bullshit meter went crazy.

Why? D'Alvay stood watching him with her usual half-smile twisting
her mouth. Same one she always gave him when hanging off his arm for The
Politician, giving him orders, delivering messages. Mid-twenties, with a body
and attitude that screamed *Tie me up, baby*

But she wasn't moving to go through the door herself.

"Go ahead," he said.

She shook her head. "Uh-unh. You're the one wanted to confirm the
deal with the mob. This is all you."

"Your boss isn't in there."

"My 'boss' thought that meeting Gregor Lechenko would be more
motivating."

Russian mob. By all accounts a growing power in the U.S. elections scene, but also with strong ties back in Russia and its neighboring state, most importantly Tajikistan, on the northern border of Afghanistan.

"Fuck me," Castinages said.

"Not today," she said, must have seen something twitch in his face, and laughed. "I mean that Lechenko doesn't seem inclined to kill you. More, to just enhance your motivation and focus."

"I'll enhance *his* motivation out my ass."

"Oh, be still my beating heart. Misha, you play tough with these guys and your time with us will be even briefer than it's already going to be."

He gave her a long, steady look then. A look that had brought his Choke Force team of stone cold fighters to absolute attention under heavy fire more than once. This time it only produced D'Alvay's maddening half smile.

"Just a friendly meeting, Misha," D'Alvay said. "So you understand the stakes."

Then she knocked on the door for him, it opened, and a rail-thin man Misha thought looked familiar from the private "security" teams that had been operating in Iraq for over a decade now motioned him in.

~~~~

Mackie's Cove
Cape Breton Island, Canada

He couldn't help it, with Nina beside him, Richard felt like his eyes were more open than they had been in days.

His chest still ached where Doc Klein had operated and sewn him up; Doc's own words were *Bist meshugah?* (Are you crazy?) when he'd told him he was getting out of bed today. But as he limped along, this tiny fishing village where he'd grown up had the hyper-reality of a mission target. Everything was crisp, definite. He could smell the brine in each breeze, hear the splashing clunks of boats down by the wharf and clicking of a clothesline as someone brought in their hung laundry. He tasted the dust the sun raised off the parched grass, the slurp of someone emptying a cooked crab shell for early lunch.

And Nina's temper? Well, he couldn't really figure that out. The stress of their flight to get to this place? Not getting along with Angie? Fear over what Crumpet Davies had told her? Annoyance with him? There were times, with women, when you just had to pretend you understood and let it roll off your shoulders.

Like he had to let his hopeless attraction to this tall, leggy woman roll off. Forget his fantasies onboard the scow that had gotten them here. The mission, finding and retrieving whatever Tommy had hidden, was going to be difficult enough without adding that complication into it.

"We're going all the way down to the docks?" she asked suddenly.

"Yes."

"To see your childhood house? The burned one?"

"No. That's...not important."

"Then what?"

"The docks. You need a basic understanding of the people who live here."

"Oh, I'm getting a feel for them."

"I doubt it."

She turned to him with the flashing eyes again, and walked faster, as if knowing how much it was going to hurt him to keep up.

But jumping Joseph on a stick, he wished he *could* keep up!

Because look at her. Even after their nonstop escape up the eastern seaboard, avoiding every toll road and monitor point, then riding that wallowing scow through the storm, jouncing through the rough inner island roads to get here, she still looked like she was modeling those hot pants and peach-colored cotton blouse for some fashion magazine.

The long neck, the long legs, the unconscious grace she had every time she turned to look at him or stop and gaze out over the ocean they were nearing.

Richard half-wished she *was* some uneducated bimbo model. Or a shop girl. Even a pogue, running supplies for the troops. Then she'd be down around his educational level and he could just "roll her" as his old Navy bunkmate Goober used to call it. No interference with mission then; just a perk.

"Should I sit down and wait for you?" she called back at him.

"Funny!"

"Well?"

She'd swept on ahead around a curve on the road past where old Albert Gunny used to live. Their shouts had made heads stick out of windows on either side, looking at him, silently studying him and Nina. Claire Coleman. Gordie Chute. A young girl he didn't recognize, probably born since he'd left. Neighbors from his childhood. Strangers now.

"Go on ahead!" he called, then smiled and nodded to the people who'd recognized him.

No one nodded back. No one said hello.

Yeah, that confirmed the chill Doc had warned him about. The bitterness that Richard would feel, a deep hurt that he'd be the focus of.

A hurt from what? Richard had asked. *Economic failure?*

Mostly that, yes.

But there's been the alcoholic's twitch in Doc's eye as he'd said it. He'd been lying or hiding something. Another mystery here beyond the one of Tommy's theft. Or connected to it?

Resisting looking to the left to the house at the far end of the beach road that he knew from Tommy was now a charred wreck, he caught up with Nina right down on the stony black sand itself. The beach dove sharply down into the water almost the whole way along here. Not a draw for swimming tourists, but good for boats.

Nina was walking north past the line of weather-beaten storage shacks that hunched a ways back from the shoreline. When she reached the long wharf that ran along the shore and out in a fat tee shape, she hopped out and strode out along it, displaying those gorgeous long legs to anyone looking down from the village, and stopping at each moored vessel and pausing as if trying to figure it out.

Richard hurried after her. On the port side heading out, a rusted-looking huge tub of a fish trawler wallowed almost level with the deck of the wharf. High tide. To starboard, two thirty-six foot longliners that should have been out on the ocean. Close in was someone's new-looking pleasure sloop, tourist class. Visitor, obviously. Pulled up on the shore, far over near the tuck shop, were a twenty-foot open vessel and a line of four small dories looking all the world like a resort's line of paddle-boats for rent. Two tarped-over boats, one a longliner, were moored over by the second dock and boathouse near the Shatter Rocks. Those rocks, cause of not a few wrecks in years past, thrust out the north side of the cove like the little harbor had been made by a God with a giant sand scoop.

At least all the lobster boats were out. Somebody was actually working today.

Richard saw Nina pass a grizzled old man going over one of the newer-looking longliners fifteen yards out on the wharf, just short of the gas refill tank. When the man turned, his profile revealed, droopy lips, a pronounced hump on his back and a lumpy skull. Richard grinned. It was Clive McGee, still smoking like a fiend.

"Hey, Mac!" Richard called, hurrying out on the boards.

Nina stopped and looked back. McGee himself squinted at Richard, then grinned, puffed hard on his cigarette, then pushed himself up as straight as his crooked body could go, climbed off the boat, and stuck out a calloused hand. "Heard you was back."

Richard shook, impressed as always by the working fisherman's grip. Even if Clive McGee's hair had gone white and his face become a rubber mask of wrinkles, McGee had been a big-trawler fisherman most of his life and still had the strength to show for it. He'd moved to Mackie Cove because of a woman who looked past his deformities. He'd married her and took to managing the wharf and starting a small trucking operation that ran the fishermen's catch down to the processing plants in Canso and, when those were shut down, all the way to Sydney. His wife, Magda, had died shortly before Richard had left. Richard wondered if the trucks still ran.

"Aye, Skipper," Richard said now.

"Heard you got a woman and girl in tow. Angie's cousin from New York." McGee nodded approvingly to Nina, who promptly turned away.

"That's a tale," Richard said, deciding instantly that the truth would be better than the story Doc and Angie had come up with. With McGee spreading the news, it might even garner them some sympathy and help with his and Nina's acceptance for the time they were here. "They're in-laws actually. Tommy's wife's sister and Tommy's little girl."

McGee's rubber face fell and his mouth formed an "o" that almost dropped his cigarette. "Heard about that, the shooting. You vanishing."

"Yeah. They targeted Tommy's whole family and the government's involved somehow. We're hiding out until they come clean about exactly what happened."

"Ah." Puff, puff.

Whatever their private beef with Richard or Tommy, one thing Cape Bretoners understood was government tricks and lying low. Richard suspected that this part of the story would get suitably inflated by the time it made it through all the shops and Ninian's Pub.

"So...the boats, then." Richard pointed at the idle longliners and half-unconsciously found himself slipping back into the dialect. "Noonis and Smithers are the longliners, if I remembers right. Why ain't they out working?"

McGee's face screwed up and he took his cigarette out of his mouth, flicked it into the water. "Oh, the bye's are working, awright. But down in Canso. Couple up in Bell Côte. At the fish plants as are left, pickup crew, some doing tourist runs. Mostly just lobster men out now. Due back soon.

I'm helping t'others find buyers for their boats."

"Dougan Smithers?"

McGee's eyes took on a crafty look and Richard noted that Nina had drifted back close to them, pretending to be examining the boat McGee had been working on.

"Doc said to watch out for him especially," Richard elaborated.

"Cause he's going with Angie now, did you know?"

"Yeah. Little young, isn't he?"

"Aye."

"Loves her or something?"

"Or something."

"And her him?"

McGee cackled and coughed. "Aye, there's the real question, eh? Especially with you back in town."

Nina spun towards them and the effect of her sunlit face close up made McGee blink too, Richard noted. "What does he mean by that? 'Especially with you back in town?'"

"Just a sister-in-law, is she?" McGee said to Richard and cackled and coughed again, longer this time, until Richard thumped him on the back.

"Gotta stop smoking, Mac."

"Trying. Trying."

"You're not going to answer it, are you," said Nina.

"Later, maybe," Richard said. "Mac, can I ask you a quick question?"

The fisherman grew suddenly wary and ducked his head. "Things I can't say. You know that, Richie." And added in a mutter Richard wasn't sure he was supposed to hear, "For all that you ought ter know."

For a long moment Richard paused wondering how hard to push. But the other fishermen down the dock were looking at them, as was Nina, jutting her long neck forward so obviously he was tempted to give her a backwards shove.

"Just this, Mac," he said. "Tommy came back up here for my father's funeral, right?"

Mac nodded, cringing.

"Did Tommy...do anything unusual? Speak to anyone in a secretive way? Go someplace he wouldn't normally go?"

Mac raised his face, with the look that this obviously wasn't what he'd expected. Which dashed Richard's hopes that he knew anything. But then Mac thought long and hard, rubbing his chin with his callused fingers. He finally shrugged. "He spent some time with Angie. Took out the *Mary-Hester*. Talked with just about everyone. Had a grand time of it, cause it was just him, you know. He didn't bring his family. It was just like old times."

"But not with me here," Richard couldn't help saying, and he saw Mac's face fall again.

"No. Not with you here."

"Why?"

Mac stared at him a long time. Then he took the cigarette out of his droopy lips and threw it onto the wet metal grating of the dock. Ground it out with his boot. "You stay here a time and you'll figure it, Richie. But I can't tell you."

It took Richard all his willpower to keep his face even because the feelings of anger and hurt that raged through him were otherworldly. He'd felt nothing like them since...well probably since he'd left this place long ago and put it all behind him.

"Okay. Okay, Mac." He looked around. "The *Mary-Hester*. Where is she?"

Mac grinned carefully. "I own her now. Bought her from your da." He nodded at the tarp-covered boats. "Doing some work on her. Take her out in a few days, if you want."

Richard nodded, feeling another surge of feeling push up in his throat. "Thanks, Mac."

"And now," Richard said, suddenly acutely aware of Nina's heat at his right arm, "I've got the rest of town to show Miss Tauredaux. We're going up the hill, that way, now. If your legs are up to it, Nina. No taxis here."

He almost laughed at the piercing look she shot him. Like her glares could hurt him more than Mac just had? Instead he just winked at Mac so she could see, then turned and set off down the dock towards the hill.

It wasn't until they were halfway up, past Clive McGee's house and empty truck yard, that his bones seemed to grind together and all of Richard's earlier resentment and hurt at the dock began to feel like nothing compared to the simple trial of acute chest pain.

~~~~

Nina could hear Richard struggling in the changing thud of his steps behind her, his labored breathing. But after his performance on the docks, she'd be damned if she was going to slow down or coddle him. He was the professional soldier. He was one who'd *knew* this town.

As they approached the highway, though, she glanced back and felt her face blanch in sympathetic agony. The man looked like he was about to pass out. His face was pasty white. He winced with every step.

Goddamn him!

She spun and grabbed him by both or his thick, tanned arms, and pushed him backwards towards a large rock that sat just off the gravel shoulder of the road. He let her, and let her push him down to sitting, which showed just how bad off he was.

"You need to lie down?" she asked.

He shook his head. "Just...some fruit juice or something. Sorry. The gas station over there."

"Money?"

"Wallet. My back pocket."

And because he made no move to get it, Nina had to lean in, smelling his masculine heat, his hot breath, to tug it free of his jeans.

Worried that he might pass out on her, and feeling a little shaky herself suddenly, she half-ran to the station and bought not only two orange juices, but a pair of sandwiches and two chocolate bars. Her own stomach was growling. They'd walked right through lunch time. That explained her own shakiness. That's all it was.

Richard was still upright when she got back, though he'd slid to the ground to lean back against the rock, face to the road so he could watch her coming. His eyes lighted up at the juice and food. She sat cross-legged before him on a swept smooth spot of hard-pack and handed them to him.

He finished both with measured precision. Like army rations. Or navy?

Aye, Skipper.

His breathing and color were better, but as Nina watched, he closed his eyes, still wincing a little at whatever pain his wound was giving him. How could someone who seemed so incredibly competent one minute, so badly gauge their physical capacities the next?

"You cloud my judgment," he said, as if reading her mind.

"I do?" She finished off the last bit of her chocolate. Licked her fingers. "How so?"

But with his eyes still closed, Richard merely shook his head. As if he'd said something he shouldn't. As if he'd almost been admitting he was getting attracted to her, obsessed by her. Something like that. Anything like that.

With most men she would have just relished this revelation and filed it away as information she could use to help her gain her objectives. But here and now, it gave her a funny, tight feeling in her throat. As did having him momentarily weak before her like this.

Not good. She'd long ago given up feeling vulnerable with a man. Right around the time Tommy betrayed and dumped her, in fact. And here was another Mackenzie, and here she was...

She forced herself back by remembering the conversation at the dock, and the way Mackenzie and all the other men had been grabbed so thoroughly by the crass charms of Miss Cape Breton Big Boobs. And how this whole thing was either about saving Janine or saving his own ass. It had nothing to do with Nina. Not even to do with some noble purpose, like finding out *why* Marie-Ange and Tom were killed. No, Richard Mackenzie was just focused on survival. He'd said as much. It made her angry at him all over again. Good.

Nina pushed herself up to standing in front of him.

"So should I walk back and get the truck? Drive you back to Doc Klein's?"

Again he shook his head. He opened his eyes and found hers. "Sit beside me."

"Why?" She kicked at the dust.

"Just sit. Please."

So she did. Finding a spot on the dry grass two feet away, she started to draw her knees up to her chest like a kid, then forced them down and folded her legs to the side. Like a lady should. Like the future president of her own consulting firm would.

"What do you see?" Richard said.

She snorted and looked back and forth along the highway, such as it was out here on the north edge of town. Two narrow lanes of hot, dusty asphalt with crumbling borders. Scrub on either side. No cars.

"I see the top border of Mackie Cove that I walked with Janine—a gas station, a few houses, the edge of Crumpet's bakery, and across from it the famous Saint Ninian's Pub..."

"It is."

"Further along that way is the abandoned church and the cemetery where I think I'd find your father and mother's graves if I look hard enough. Right?"

A look of anger flashed across Richard's wan face, then was gone. "Only what you see. What do you see?"

"Closed off. Okay." She turned her head. "In the other direction, and across the road, and for miles and miles and miles in any direction—nothing at all. Trees, dirt, grass. And, oh yeah, in that direction," she jerked her thumb behind her, "the ocean."

"For a lot of people here, this town is their whole lives."

"It's a bad design."

"Pardon me?"

"It's hodge-podge. And I get the impression it's dying. That was the real point of going to the docks, right? Show me how poor everyone is? How hopeless."

Richard gave a pained smile. "My, you're compassionate."

Nina's face burned. "Look, Mister. It's *you* who got out of here fast as you could when you were young, right? Made sure no one knew where you came from? You never planned to come back, did you."

"Not because of the *place*."

"The people?"

"Some of them."

"Your father." She waited, then shook her head angrily. "Fine. The people. The people shape the place and are shaped by the place. You can't separate them."

"They teach you that in university?"

She narrowed her eyes at him, hearing something sharp in the tone. But she ploughed on anyway. "My job teaches me that. My life experience teaches me that. It's why I left Washington. It's why soldiers coming back from places like Iraq and Afghanistan should be put through some massive kind of social detox before they try to live normal lives with civilians again."

"Soldiers like me."

"Well you have to admit you don't exactly relate to other people in normal ways. Which suggests to me you probably saw things that—"

"You know *nothing* about," he snapped.

With a grunt of angry pain, he leaned forward and pushed himself up to his feet.

Nina jumped up beside him. "I just meant—"

"That you have an opinion on everything! I asked you to look. Not comment. Not judge. Just *look*. Seek to understand. Because if you're going to get people to talk to you, you have to know what they care about, who they are, why they should want to help you. Do you know any of that? *Any* of it?"

"What do you mean?"

His eyes blazed at her so fiercely that for a minute she thought he was just going to turn around and limp away, be rid of her for good. And she wouldn't deserve it, of course. But she was a woman, and women weren't supposed to be smart or speak their minds or be as competent as men. She'd faced that her whole life. You were pushy as a man and it was healthy ambition; you pushed as a woman and you were an aggressive bitch.

Which was the real reason Tom had chosen Marie-Ange, and the only reason she wasn't yet a partner at Gervais Planners. But for some stupid reason she'd figured Mr. Super-soldier here could take it.

Apparently not.

Except that, as suddenly as he'd blown up, Mackenzie seemed to change his mind and stuck out a hand to help her up. She ignored the hand and stood herself.

"There are times," Richard said quietly, "when you've got to gather intel in an area that may be hostile. And there are techniques, some of them sophisticated but most of them not, for blending in and getting people on your side."

She almost laughed at his military intensity. This was his hometown! Where he'd grown up!

But she couldn't argue with the fact he knew the place and people better than her, so she just locked her mouth closed and nodded.

"Okay," he said. "Getting back to it—if want to blend into a place, first understand it. How do people make their livings? What do they care about? What makes them happy? What makes them afraid."

"Which is why you showed me the docks," she blurted.

"That's part of it."

"Why does almost everyone here hate you?"

He froze, staring at her and working his jaw. Such a strong jaw. Nina felt the sun beating down on her head. She should have worn sunscreen. She was going to burn and peel right here in front of him while he figured out how to whip whatever was left off her bones.. *Speak* already!

Finally he nodded. "I don't think they all hate me. More like they resent me. And they're afraid of me a little."

"Why?"

"I left. I got Tommy out, then I left too."

"Like Angie's younger brother left."

"Yes. Except he'll probably come crawling back and everyone will welcome him, slap him on the back, love him to bits, because he'll have proved what they've always known and feared."

"Which is what?"

"You can't make it out there. Cape Bretoners, all Maritimers maybe, have got to stay here. Prettiest damn poorhouse in North America."

He looked up, squinching his face at the sun, hiding his feelings and... something more?.

"What else?" she said.

"Hm?"

She longed to reach out and take his strong face in both her hands, draw his attention to her with a touch, feel him press that wounded, hard-muscled chest against hers... She steeled herself against it.

"There's more to why they're uncomfortable with you," she said quickly. "Something to do with your father. Or Angie Neal?"

He grimaced. "Both."

"Are you going to tell me? Or are you going to leave it as a landmine for me to trip over sometime?"

He considered her long and hard. "I might tell you. Eventually. When I trust you a bit more."

It sent a shiver through her from her scalp to the base of her spine, making her gasp. What was that? Excitement that he might trust her more? That he might do other things with her when he did? And what? She was going to now do everything in her power, go all sappy and soft or evil and manipulative to help him get there?

God. He thought *she* clouded *his* judgment? A week ago she was bucking for partnership in San Francisco's premiere urban planning group. Today she was grieving her sister and trying to figure out how to befriend hick fishermen and their wives in butthole Canada.

With a wounded Special Forces soldier as her coach.

What was wrong with this picture?

A family van roared by them on the highway, just five feet or so from Richard's back, heading north. The dust blew up around him and little stones flew past his legs, nicking hers.

"Come on," he said, jerking his head vaguely in the direction the van had gone. "Another important part of town to show you."

"A place with answers?"

"Maybe. About you more than anything."

"What the hell does that mean?"

"Consider it a kind of a test."

Then he was limping across the road and Nina had to hurry to catch up to him.

19

Falls Church
Virginia

"WHAT YOU DON'T SEEM TO COMPREHEND, Comrade Castinages, is that this little 'operation' you have begun is not something you can just walk away from."

The speaker, Gregor Lechenko, ground out the second full cigarette he'd smoked through since Castinages had been ushered into the fifteen-by-twenty, windowless room. The room contained a chair where Lechenko sat, a table with a clear bottle Castinages guessed was vodka, a cigarette package of Export A's, an overflowing cheap ashtray, and a palm-sized digital recorder that was not turned on. Behind Lechenko stood two bodyguards. One was the rail-thin merc Castinages knew from his long-ago time in Iraq. The other was a bulkier blond who might have matched Castinages's own weight class, though he was considerably taller. Both bodyguards were dressed in nondescript military garb and carried assault rifles aimed at Castinages.

"Why do you think I want to walk away from it?" Castinages said.

Lechenko curled his scarred upper lip and switched on the recorder in playback mode.

"...if Mackenzie finds it, or has it already, and decides to turn it over to the authorities or media, all our plans go sideways. Not to mention you, Major, getting exposed as a criminal, possibly a traitor to your country."

[Catinages laughs so hard he coughs.] "I'm dying and I got no family to mourn me. You think I give a fuck about any of that?"

Lechenko switched the recorder off again.

Castinages grinned. "You're bugging all our calls?"

Lechenko shrugged, but it didn't touch his face. "I keep track of my assets."

"Assets. Right." He couldn't help eyeing the cigarettes, shit brand they were, until finally Lechenko leaned back and waved two fingers at them.

"Please."

Castinages reached for them with his left hand. The blond bodyguard suddenly stepped forward and clamped a hand over Castinages's extended forearm.

Without even a grunt, Castinages jerked the arm sideways across the table and simultaneously hammered his right fist into the blond's face so the boy's nose shattered with an eggshell crunch. And Castinages was already spinning out of the way as the gun butt from the merc swept past his left temple.

A second later he stood behind the blood-streaming blond with the boy's assault rifle raised up in a stand-off with both the merc and Lechenko. The Russian mob boss looked bored, but his heavy-duty HK Tactical, with sound suppressor, was casually aimed at Castinages's face.

"Smoking is so bad for us," drawled Lechenko.

"Ain't it just," Castinages said.

"Laurie..." Lechenko set down his gun and waved away the merc's. "Take Pavel out of here and get him cleaned up. I would like to discuss some things with Major Castinages in private."

Without even looking at Castinages, the rail-thin merc took the blond bodyguard off his hands and helped him stagger out the door, closing it behind them. Castinages laid the assault rifle on the ground.

"The woman and child that Mackenzie saved at Abdul Adeeb's compound," Lechenko said. "Do you know where they are now?"

"They're the ninth and tenth wives of an isolated tribal chieftain in northern Pakistan. I sold them to him myself. Arch stone of the jihad."

"But did you know that this chieftain's wives help him tend his own opium harvest and the older ones talk with the wives of those who carry this opium south? And that they, in turn talk with their husbands, who may talk with their dealers in Iran and into India and Eastern Europe? Who knows what information might be passed from Abdul Adeeb's wife to the broader world, yes? It is as if she can whisper into the ears of Interpol or the Queen of England, yes? What is the saying your country came up with—everyone is separated from everyone else by only six degrees of separation. Even in Northern Pakistan."

"Fuck," Castinages muttered at his shoes. "Did she...?"

"She and her daughter are dead. The man and girl who may actually have what she could have talked about are not. And for someone from a nothing country like Canada, this man, this Richard Mackenzie, seems to know many powerful people. *One* degree of separation. I do not like this."

Fuck fuck fuck, what had he been thinking when he hadn't just killed Adeeb's bitches himself? That he owed Mackenzie for saving his life in that raid? That saving the bitches somehow paid that back?

Well, that was all done with now, wasn't it. If Castinages wanted to make a difference, it was by aligning himself with the powers who could do so and helping them out with services only he could provide.

He looked up. "When I get it back, the package, can you guarantee it's going to end things in Afghanistan? Let us win the *long* game?"

This time when Lashnikov's upper lip curled back, it was a pained smile, with the man's washed-out eyes fully engaged. "There are no guarantees, Major. Only plans and forces and—what's the word?—'waves' that we can see coming. But if the package, or even news about it, is released, the waves that are now sloshing about in Afghanistan will drown us all."

"Okay."

"Okay? You are now 'invested'?"

"Yeah."

"Good." Lechenko stood up. The meeting was over.

Castinages cleared his throat and ran a hand over his buzzed hair to smooth it.

Lechenko laughed. "She is not waiting outside the door for you, Major. Would you like me to give you her schedule, so you know where you can find her next?"

Castinages shrugged. "Bitches."

"Yes."

~~~~

Mackie's Cove
Cape Breton Island, Canada

The dark cave, north of Mackie's Cove, sloped down from inside a dark, boarded-up factory building that Richard Mackenzie had broken them into. Nina felt turned-around in here but figured the tunnel went into the hill the building was built up against, or below the highway. It breathed dirty gas up at Nina, cold and dank. Threatening. But when she stepped back, she hit the end blocks of the black cross-ties that ran down into the pit, a light railroad track running on top.

"We're *not* going down there," Nina said.

"Just a minute." There was some rustling and clanking about, things dropping, then Richard came back to her, carrying with both hands what looked in the darkness to be an old, unlit kerosene lantern. He sloshed it back and forth and smiled. She could barely see his teeth.

"You're kidding."

"No electricity any more. No battery lights around. But Bingo told me once they always kept some of these near the entrance just for emergencies."

"Bingo?"

"One of my dad's old friends." He'd taken off the glass and was fiddling with the wick in the darkness, screwing it down lower, presumably to touch whatever gas or kerosene still remained in the base. And the smell of kerosene mixed with the other dirty gas smell to start Nina's heart thudding.

"Don't!" she said, grabbing his hand as he came up with a cigarette lighter from somewhere.

"What?"

"Don't you smell the gas? What if it...you know...explodes?"

He didn't move for a moment, then grinned at her in the darkness. "Low probability there's enough methane, but okay. Good thinking."

With a quick tug, he freed his hand from her grip and reached into his jeans again, coming out with something that looked like a lumpy cigar. He clicked it and light shot out the end.

"You bastard!" Nina said. "You have a flashlight!"

"I do. Come on."

And he set off down the hard-packed slope beside the tracks. Rather than stand lost in the dark, Nina hurried after him. As she caught up and matched his pace, she started to ask him what they were doing, but he shushed her and pointed. An old, abandoned mine cart lay on the tracks before them. All metal, it was slim at the bottom, broad at top. In the light of Richard's flashlight, she saw it was filled with all kinds of junk—discarded gas cans, paper, coal. Almost like some disgruntled miner had once planned to start a fire and blow the mine up.

"Keep going," Richard said and led her around it.

After a good five minutes of walking downslope, with the air getting noticeably chill and the roof lower and lower so that even Nina had to stoop and walk along like some kind of ape, they came to a fork in the road. Richard shone the flashlight straight ahead where the tracks plunged into more darkness, then left where the tracks didn't go. It looked like a side-cave, walled off with tight wooden slats. The crusted-over outline of a door made out of the same slats started a foot off the floor on the left side. Its handle looked rusted shut.

Without the sound of their feet to distract her, Nina gulped and forced herself to breathe. The darkness, the rocks all around, felt like they were pushing down on her, squeezing out all noise, making the air thick, the methane smell stronger, the space smaller. She had to go back. She had to.

No, damn it!

Yes.

As if sensing she was close to breaking, Richard whispered, "The first coal vein was here. Back in the 1800s sometime. They drilled and blasted their way down. They had pit ponies living down here to haul the coal. They used little kids as young as ten or eleven. Post one of them by the gas-blocking door here to wait in the dark for six hours until the men came back. He was the alarm if things went bad."

He banged on the rusted old latch a few times and knocked it free. Then he shouldered open the slatted door and Nina recoiled at the dank, truly gassy smell that breathed out of the deserted tunnel. Like the throat of hell.

Richard caught her look and shuddered the door closed again.

"Later, with longwall mining, better wages, they brought down the rails and carts. But it was still like digging into your grave every day. You all right?"

"I...huh..." Nina gasped and steadied herself on his arm. Her chest felt like someone was squeezing it with both hands. "I can't stay down here."

"Okay."

He covered her hand with his, shone the light back the way they'd come, and led her back up. It wasn't until they'd cleared the building completely and were standing on the hill above it, looking down on its narrow top floor and sprawling heap of factory going down the hill that Nina could figure the direction of the mine shaft and the direction they'd walked.

"It goes...under the water," said Nina.

"That's why we didn't take an elevator down. It's a different kind of pit."

"You took me under the water." The feeling of claustrophobia she'd felt in by the door of the turnoff underground rushed back to her and she put a hand to her throat.

"Yes."

"Why?"

Richard turned his square jaw upwards towards the sun. "The mine here shut down in '92. Cost overruns, problems with flooding. The last Cape Breton mine, over in Prince, shut down in 2001. And with the fisheries almost dead, the fish stocks dying off, that's like ripping the heart and lungs out of small centers like Mackie's Cove."

"And they're *still* too scared to find new lives somewhere else?"

"Scared? Maybe." Richard lowered his chin and turned to look at her, his eyes full of sun. "But you just went down into that pit a little way, for maybe twenty minutes. I want you to think what it takes to face going down into a place like that every day for eight, ten, hours so you can feed your family. Or head out on *top* of an ocean that has the kind of storms we came through all the time, and that keeps giving less and less fish. Or waiting at home for the men and boys who've gone down or out on the waves, wondering if this is the day their luck runs out."

Despite being manipulated into it, Nina couldn't help but shiver at both scenarios.

"That's what the people of Mackie's Cove have done most of their lives," Richard said. "Think about it as we go around asking them questions. They deserve your respect."

~~~~

Respect? It was the first thought in her mind when Richard walked her back to Angie Neal's house. Because Angie saw them coming down the dirt path from the highway and came out to meet them as they crossed the narrow blacktop in front of her house.

She was still dressed in her jean cut-offs and see-through tee-shirt. Nina wondered what a miner working a long shift or a fisherman back from fifteen hours out on the cold ocean would feel walking into the pub where Angie was serving. Like she was the just desserts? Or...unattainable?

Unattainable because she was spoken for by Richard Mackenzie—tall, strong, don't mess with him.

Then Mackenzie leaves. Dougan Smither tries to move in. Tries year after year. The faithful Mackie's Cove boy courts the local barmaid and even takes a job that involves a daily long commute out of town to show he's worthy. And ever so slowly, after years and years, Evangeline Neal gives up on her desperate hope that Richard Mackenzie will return and she actually lets Smither come near. Maybe lets him into her bed. Even half-listens when he proposes marriage, whispers he'll take her far away from Mackie's Cove if that's what she wants. At least as soon as Angie's mother dies.

Then Mackenzie comes back.

Nina shook herself. God, she'd been a fool not to see it all at once. And it was with someone here that Tom had left whatever it was he'd stolen. Did Richard Mackenzie honestly think anyone here was going to help him? Not Smither or his friends certainly. Doc, yes. (But presumably Mackenzie had already questioned him and gotten nothing.) Maybe that funny guy at the docks, Clive McGee. (Except that it seemed he'd already told all he was willing to tell.)

Which left Angie. How much further into this mess would Mackenzie go to get Angie to talk to him?

Nina caught herself looking at Mackenzie's strong, tan neck and shook herself out of a ridiculous state of jealousy. As if Nina honestly had any intentions beyond poking through Mackenzie's infuriating mask of indifference. But she didn't want him to get his little head ruling his actions here either. He'd already claimed that Nina made it hard for him to think clearly. Well Nina felt like a piker in a granny's bonnet compared to Angie Neal.

On cue, Angie gave Mackenzie a smile you could have melted butter on and said, "We got Snuffles all fixed, made the blueberry grunt, and put little Janine down for a nap. And have you thought about coming over for dinner later?"

"If it's to talk about Tommy, I'd like to, but..."

Nina burned inside to hear the subtle lilt that had crept back into Mackenzie's voice.

"We'd make it early. Four-thirty. I've got to work at six."

"I can't, Angie. The walk—it just about killed me. I guess Doc was right about it being a little early for me to be up and about. But right now, maybe."

"Now," Angie repeated. She glanced at Nina and back to Richard, clearly struggling not to gnash her teeth. *Good.* "All right. While Nina goes up to get the truck maybe so she can drive you back to Doc's."

Nina stepped forward. "Wait a—"

"Good idea," Mackenzie said, and the pallor on his face cut off Nina's further objections.

Okay, it was right for Nina to worry. But what could happen, really, with

Mackenzie in this state? It wasn't like Angie was going to drag him into the bedroom and demand conjugal favors in exchange for information, was it?

As she stepped back, Mackenzie nodded gratefully and walked to Angie's front stoop. Sat.

But as Nina turned to head up the hill, she caught Angie's victorious smile watching her go and felt sick all over again. Because Angie might not be able to get much physical action out of Mackenzie right now, but promises? Stupid words that would make the whole situation here untenable at best?

Nina decided she'd better jog.

~~~~

Richard's entire right side felt on fire and his whole body exhausted as he leaned back against Angie's front door.

Strange how the minute his focus shifted off Nina Tauredaux and her maddening challenges, all the pain came back three times as strong. Doc was going to kill him if Richard hadn't done enough damage to manage that on his own.

"You want a lemonade or...anything?"

Angie hovered right in front of him, subtly sticking her chest out at him. Her lower lip. Pouting. What, exactly did she expect him to do with her in the ten minutes it would take Nina to get back here? Even if he'd wanted to. And what did he expect to learn?

Richard cleared his throat. "So...Tommy came back here for the funeral."

"An' you should have been here."

"He told me about it. About how my da died fighting over a gambling debt and almost no one showed up to mourn him."

"But you should have."

"Did Tommy tell you anything about what he'd been doing?"

"That he'd married. That he had a child. And of course that he wished he'd never left Mackie's Cove for all the fine education and money and living that he'd done since."

"Did he bring anything with him that he might have left behind? A large box? Bags?"

"No." She was still weaving in front of him in the sunlight. Her hair blazed red in the sunshine. Anyone in the neighboring houses could see them if they just looked out their windows. What would they think? What did *he* think? He remembered so much that was centered on this woman.

From the time she was just a playmate in school to...later. So much.

"Did he spend time with anyone here in particular?" he said quickly.

"Me. Dougan and his buddies. Gordon Chute. The minister who came up from Inverness for the burial."

"Name of the minister?"

"Blackon? Blackton? Something."

"How long was Tom here?"

"Came on a Wednesday and left on a Sunday."

"And he didn't leave anything with you to give to me?"

"Only this." And she was suddenly on her knees on the stoop beside him, holding his shoulder lightly and pressing her soft body into his, her lips onto his. He could feel her breasts crushing into his own chest, mixing sharp pain with erotic pleasure so intensely that he thought he'd be warped forevermore. And her lips! Her hot breath!

While seeing her had set off gauzy memories, the kiss set off explosions. His sixteenth summer. His mother still alive. His father off on a big commercial boat run to earn ready cash. And Angie, eager and eighteen, the object of all his horny teen desires, suddenly gives herself to him for three amazing weeks. They kiss and laugh and touch, explore. Then he loses his virginity to her on the deck of his father's boat, way out on the ocean, rocking in the waves with the sun so hot on his back he gets a burn that lasts for weeks.

And her body! He sees it milky smooth and freckled in the sunlight. Her breasts already huge pillows with dusky pink areolas and nipples. Her red hair spread out around her head on the blanket he's spread on the deck...

Unhhh!

Richard pulled back from her kiss with difficulty, fully aware of the hard erection he'd sprung in his jeans.

As was she. She ran a finger lightly around his lower lip and smiled with hooded eyes. "Oh, how I've missed that, Richie. Yes, I have."

Richard shook his head, hard, willing himself strong enough to stand up, but feeling his upper chest shriek in pain when he tried to move. "Angie," he said. He fell back against the door, looking around to see if they've been watched. "Don't. I...understand you're with Dougan Smither now."

The smile was still there but she stood up, smoothing down her clothes, showing him her body had only grown more magnificent with age. "He thinks so."

"You're not?"

"D'you want me to be?"

"Angie..." Richard grunted a bit at the pain in his side and shifted positions. "You know we're just here a while. You know that, right?"

"You says you'll only be gone a while when you left here. Nine years is a long while."

"I never said that."

"With your eyes, with your lips, you promised."

He hadn't! The time frames were wrong. He'd been sixteen. They'd been together three weeks before his father had returned. And after that... After that he'd wanted her, but it had never worked out. His father worked him, then his mother died and things fell apart. He quit school. Worked all the time...

"Shit. Angie... Doc tells me Dougan's got good prospects. Just made foreman at the fish plant. A real leader with the men here."

"Never get yourself cornered, do you." She gave a long sigh and turned from him, brushing back her blazing hair. "Was it on account of Tommy and me?"

"What?"

"That you left."

That day... Tommy's face all bloody. Smashed up. His father yelling in the background. Drunk. Raving. The memory threatened to turn into the screaming Hadjis in Afghanistan, explosions, or the terrorists in Maryland shooting Marie-Ange and Tommy. Richard snapped a mental door shut on all of it.

"I left because of Tommy, yes," he said. "And others. Not because of you." Not exactly.

There was a long pause, during which Angie turned and scrutinized him. And he saw the lines around her eyes for the first time. He knew she was the same age as him, but the weather and the hard life out here had aged her more. In a good way, actually. They'd given her more character than he remembered.

"You don't even know what the people of the town here said about you, do you?" Angie said. "About why you sent Tommy away to Quebec for his high school? What they said about me?"

"What did they say?"

After another long look, her eyes suddenly welled up and she shook her head. "You keep asking around about Tommy and you'll find out about that, sure. And when you do, you come talk to me, okay? Get my side of it."

Richard frowned, but before he could press her on it, she walked around the house to the side door. He heard the screen door slap closed behind her when she went in.

20

S HE WAS GOING TO POP. It was happening again and Nina was going to pop if she didn't get out of here. She could *not* be cooped up like this.

After she'd brought Richard back from their little hike around town and his talk with Angie, Doc Klein had basically forbidden her presence for five days to prevent a relapse. Richard needed bedrest.

Which meant no joint exploring—of either the town or each other.

Not that Nina had just sat back and twiddled her thumbs. With Janine along, both out of necessity and as a door opener, she'd set out to meet all of Mackie's Cove over the last three days. Top to bottom. One house at a time. Even Dougan and company. And took along a notebook to record and memorize names. Crumpet Davies, Dougan Smither, Billy Cuddy, Rob Dundas, Andre Beaufort, Claire Coleman, Gordon Chute, Clive McGee, Jovie McAllister, Foster Gill... Nobody other than Clive was warm to them, but no one spat in their faces either. It was a start.

She also found the gravestones of Mackenzie's mother and father, the latter bearing a strange inscription that she copied down in her name notebook and took back to find Angie having a frowning heart-to-heart with Dougan Smither, back early from work at the fish plant.

But Nina still got Angie to translate the inscription.

M'athair! Seall, a chinne-dhaonna. My father! Look closely on it.

Angie shrugged. "I'm guessing it was Tommy chose and paid for it. Like a last kick at the old bugger."

"Meaning?"

"It's a Gaelic thumping," grumped Dougan. "Like—don't be a drunken asshole or you'll end up like this one."

Progress. But then, as if upset at her initiative, Thursday morning brought black clouds and so much rain that all the dirt road and paths turned to mud. It forced Nina to stay in Angie's home with Janine and play patty-cake, hide-and-seek, eye spy, and anything else Nina could think of that might distract Janine just enough that the little girl might actually let her guard down and *speak*. Like she'd screamed. Like she'd giggled.

Speak, damn it.

Nothing.

And just before dinner, after she'd left Janine alone for a nap, she came in to find the kid building a "house" for Snuffles in the wet bathtub...out of an entire roll of toilet paper and Angie Neal's makeup kit. Nina screeched, grabbed Janine's arm, felt instant guilt at the Janine's soundless terror, and dropped the arm. Babbled apologies. Went to reach for Janine's face to kiss it better and slipped and hit her own head on side of the tub.

Goddamn it!

She rubbed the lump on the side of her forehead now as she sat in the kitchen and watched Angie sweep the floor. Enviously. Was that how mothers coped? Distracted themselves with things like sweeping or learning names or games, anything to avoid simple worrying about your child. Nina wasn't good at that. It wasn't her place. It wasn't what she was meant to do, to be.

"Is there any place around here with internet access?"

Nina's question finally got Angie Neal to turn and look at her. "Internet?"

"It's not a dirty word."

"Are we boring you, then?" said Angie. She'd been in such a foul mood since whatever she and Richard had talked about. Easy to avoid when Nina and Janine had been out most of the day. Hard to take this morning.

"You don't bore me."

"You're sure? Because the pub has a TV. And Sydney, on the other side of the Island..."

A sudden clacking sound announced Janine scooting into the kitchen under the table, wordlessly pushing an old wooden choo-choo train she'd found with her free hand; the other hand clutched the sewn-up Snuffles, still sporting tiny bits of wet toilet paper. Without warning, Janine rammed her choo-choo into Nina's ankle.

"Ouch!"

Janine looked up, scared for the second time that morning, as Nina grabbed her ankle and squeezed her eyes shut, willing away the pain.

"No!" she snapped. "Run the train around, but not into people. And not into walls or furniture either. Got it?"

Nina opened her eyes to see Janine nod slowly, a mini-Marie-Ange with red hair, tears in her eyes. Then she quickly turned the choo-choo around on the floor and pushed it out on her hands and knees, back the way she'd come.

"There might be one place," Angie said. There *moight*.

Nina whipped her head around. "For the internet? Where?"

"What d'you want to use it for, then?"

"What do I want it for? You really want to know?" Nina found her voice rising as she spoke faster and faster over the drumming sound of the rain outside. "To see what they're saying about me and Richard and Janine, or about what Tommy might have taken. To see if they're still looking for us. To see if they've got any leads on the terrorists who killed my sister. To read something other than the *Cape Bretoner*. To get more news than television sound bites. I want chat groups, conspiracy bulletin boards, people I know, my web-based e-mail account that tells me what they're doing in my company! I want my life back!"

Angie stared at her for a long moment, then said, "Oh," and went back to sweeping, looking thoughtful.

"So?" Nina's body was thrumming. She wanted to jump up and grab Angie's broom from her hands like Angie was the stubborn little girl now. "*So?*"

"Clive McGee used to have it, though he's not running trucks no more."

"Clive McGee."

"Purple house. North end of town. Side the mine's at."

"I know where he lives."

Nina sat stunned, the thrumming all moved to her head. She stood. "Thank you. Angie."

"It's pouring rain."

"I know, but if I...were to go right now, and it might take a while, would you be able to...?"

"Watch Janine? Until seven, I would. On one condition."

Here it came at last.

Angie stopped sweeping, leaned the broom against the sink, and ran both hands up to sweep back her sweat and wiry hair. "We got a little party at the pub a week Friday. Calls it a *céilidh*. You hear of them?"

Kay-lee? Nina shook her head.

"Bit of dancing, singing, storytelling, drinking. But me boss put me in charge of organizing it this time round. You think you could help me do it?"

Nina blinked. "Help you organize..."

"Got a fiddler and his band to call down from Inverness, special food to order in, a storyteller or two to rustle up. Boss wants there to be some kind of decorations this time. Advertising around the town. Like we're all fancy. Maybe get some tourists to come down. And there's you and Richard, of course."

"And Janine?"

"Kids'll be there for some of it, sure. After, maybe you hire the other kids in town to watch her.

Babysitters? The idea sent both a terrified chill through Nina and an almost suffocating thrill. After only five days of nearly full-time childcare—wait, more like eight if you counted from the time Richard brought her to the Tauredaux home and then took off to get shot—she was almost set to explode. She loved Janine dearly, but her silence, the constant reminder of Nina's shortcomings as surrogate mother...

"I... Sure. That sounds like fun. Something I actually know how to do."

Angie frowned at her. "It's not planning a city."

"No, no. But before that, before school, I moved out west, I used to help my mother plan parties. Big parties for all these DC movers and shakers. I'd be on the phone with caterers, following up with guests lists..." She stopped at Angie's glare. "Sorry. Childhood memories. Making me babble. I'm nervous. Yes, I'd love to help."

"Good. Then you go find Clive McGee, see if he's got your internet. I'll look after Janine."

There'd been no "Thank you," Nina noted as she watched Angie leave the kitchen to track down Janine. But it was still a potential thaw of the ice between them.

About time. Nina squinted out the kitchen window at the rain and thought she could actually see some blue sky moving their way.

It was about time.

~~~~

He had to tell her.

Thursday afternoon, while Doc Klein slept, Richard watched the rain peter out, then slipped out of the house again to do his slow descent to the town. He watched, as he had the last two times, for the telltale sweep of thick brown hair over tall shoulders. His heart beat faster when he thought he saw her between the houses, halfway down the winding paths to the docks.

If it was her, he could call out to her right now. Tell her right now. Accept however she reacted and make plans to move on.

But then the figure bent down over two playing children, obviously her own. Not Nina, for all her reported wanderings around the town.

Richard hissed out his held breath.

He crossed the highway in a wide northern sweep, ducked between the spinning whirligigs in the Tavish's yard, and cut through the high stickle grass surrounding the back of Clive McGee's double truck garage (empty now) to approach the north side of the purple monstrosity Clive called home.

Clive had built it all when his three-vehicle trucking business was turning a decent profit, covering Cape Breton's east coast from Port Hood all the way up to Chéticamps. It was the bent little man's way of saying *Look out, world! I'm here!*

Only "here" was Mackie's Cove. "Here" was barely a wart on Canada's butt.

Richard banged on the back door. He heard a shuffling sound inside but no one came to the door. He banged again.

"Hey, Mac!"

This time there was not only shuffling but voices. An argument, it sounded like, with a woman. He thought Clive had said that since Cheryl died he didn't have visitors. So who, Richard wondered, as he leaned against the outside door jamb to wipe his brow and catch his breath, could have—

The door was yanked open and a rain-frizzed, damp-shirted Nina stepped out at him so fast he almost collapsed backwards.

"'Has to stay in bed,' hunh?" she spat at him. "'Needs a good week to recover.' So I grit my teeth and try to do what you said, get to know the people of the town, treat them with respect, while also playing mother to Janine, something I'm not particularly suited to, and what are *you* doing this whole time?"

"Actually...um..." God in heaven how his fantasies had shifted. As a teen it had all been about Angie and her precociously huge boobs. Then life, the war, the deadness, and now this—danger and desire all rolled together in an arrogant package of low-cut designer jeans that he had no control over.

"Don't you give me that look! What is that look? You lied to me! You said you'd bring me in on your investigation, let me look with you for whatever it was your brother stole. Instead you sneak down here without telling me. Looking for hints about what was taken, aren't you? Seeing if Tom left messages."

She fumed, bare arms crossed over her chest, waiting for him to deny it.

"Yes," he said.

"What?"

"Yes. And Janine?"

"With Angie," she sputtered, then turned from him to McGee, opening and closing her mouth as the old man shrugged an *I told you so*, and grinned widely. But Richard wasn't grinning. He was keeping his face carefully blank, forestalling the moment when he told her how little he'd found. That maybe he was wrong about Tommy hiding stuff here. That his whole escape plan was useless.

"You told Clive to not let me on the net!" Nina said.

"In case you snuck down here. I didn't know if you knew how to hide your tracks, set up re-routers so no one could track your IP address."

She glared at him. "I wasn't going to *e-mail* people."

"Chat boards. Google queries. You don't think the government can monitor you through those? Like they can't follow your credit card use?"

Nina opened her mouth to protest. Closed it again. Her lips were red and she didn't look like she was wearing lipstick. Or almost any makeup, for that matter. And these were the last things he should be thinking about, especially now. He steeled himself.

And still stalled.

"Nina, I started in signals intelligence. Besides working with all sorts of cool bugging equipment that could listen to conversations even through solid metal doors, we did a lot of internet stuff. I *did* send e-mails and collect replies from dead drops."

She stared. "Well?"

Just like that. No nonsense. "Can I come inside maybe so we don't share it with the whole town?"

"You expecting me to scream?"

Maybe. "No."

Nina held his gaze another second, then looked around at the truck yard, the neighboring house, the road going past them from the docks up to the highway. She finally nodded her head and let him up the steps past her. But she poked him on his wounded right side as he went, making him wince. He shot her a look and received a smile of satisfaction in return.

Clive led them through his narrow back hall to the kitchen with its steel-ribbed table where, for his bachelor satisfaction, he'd also set up his computer and television set. Ash trays everywhere, many of them full. "Less to clean if it's all in here, eh," he'd told Richard. Clive cleared two ashtrays from the table then lifted the small T.V. off as well so there was room for Richard and Nina to settle.

"I can't believe Doc could lie to my face like that," Nina muttered as she leaned back in her chair.

Clive started making them some ginseng tea, his rubbery lips twitching like he wanted to laugh.

"Not a lie," said Richard. "He really did order me to stay in bed until Friday. I just don't follow his orders and he pretends he doesn't know."

Clive broke in. "Cause the doc, he's like the powerful Oz, eh? Knows everything."

"No," said Richard. "Unfortunately."

Nina gave him her burning look again, turning from him to Clive, then back to Richard again until Richard couldn't keep it in and let a half-smile slip out. Which made her eyebrows come down even tighter.

"You know when you do that..." he began, then stopped himself.

"What?"

She'd leaned forwards over the table at him, sticking out her full lower lip. Her thick, damp hair frizzed down around her head, held back only by a hair band. Her mahogany eyes matched the hair so perfectly that with the tight green top it was like she was a woodland creature. The red highlights in her hair? Fire. Richard had been playing with fire this whole time. He should have left her back in DC. Maybe the Major would have just questioned her and let her go. And Richard would have taken Janine and...passed out before he got anywhere.

"We made it up here because of you," Richard said.

A flash of what might have been disappointment flashed across her face, then of closer looking. "You're about to tell me something bad. What? They found us? How?"

"No. They haven't found us. But..."

He was interrupted by the whistle of the teakettle Clive had put on. The humped fisherman-cum-trucker went to it, pulled it off the stove, and poured into a teapot, humming softly as he pressed the teabags back and forth to pretend he wasn't listening to everything with great interest.

"But what?" Nina said.

"I... No one's stepped forward to claim responsibility and there've been no more attacks. Anywhere. On anyone."

"So it wasn't a terrorist attack."

"Yet it was staged to look like one."

He saw Nina look down to her left, remembering something. "Politics."

"What? To scare people?"

"Or anger them. Keep the heat on the Middle East."

For a second Richard considered it, tried to put it together with Tommy telling him to spy on the Choke Force team, with Tommy calling Richard back for protection, and Tommy's behavior once Richard was there. And with Tommy stealing something from them, whoever "they" were.

Heroin, Richard had thought at first, but that was so pedestrian. And the government had already done that, the CIA had, in Vietnam. They'd bought and sold the stuff without ever feeling the need to bring it back stateside or involve the Russians.

Damning political intel? Photos, video, something that would destabilize one or more of the governments over there. Except that they couldn't *get* more unstable, and the US forces couldn't *be* more despised.

A bomb? Nuclear warhead? Possible, if some Afghan warlord had gotten hold of one and tried to what? Smuggle it to Pakistan? Iran? The U.S.? But that would mean rogue military, not government sanctioned, some kind of weird terrorist exercise. And how the hell would Tommy have been able to recognize it, much less steal it? He'd been investigating elections fraud, not nuclear holocaust. It just didn't fit.

"I think it's a diversion," Richard said.

"From what?"

"I don't know." He put both his hands, palms up, on the table between them. "Which is the fundamental problem here, Nina. I don't know much of anything except that Tom found out something, stole something, a highly-decorated Major is involved plus some higher ups, and they're chasing me and Janine because they think we have whatever it is Tommy took."

"So—"

"Let me finish. I brought Janine here, got you to help us come here, because Tommy told me as he was dying that I'd find what he took if I went 'home' and this was the only place I could figure he meant. Especially since he'd just been here for our father's funeral."

"Which you didn't attend."

Richard dropped his head and clenched his teeth, then fought off the automatic anger. It wasn't relevant. Not for this discussion. Or was it? He raised his head and frowned as he met her eyes, still keeping his hands out. Didn't she understand what this cost him?

"It's possible," he said, "that Tom sent me here because of that. Some kind of final encouragement to heal our family wounds or something. He was always more into that than me."

"What...? Never mind." Nina was looking at him seriously. "You're telling me you're not sure we're in the right place to find what Tom took."

"If there is a right place. If he actually hid it somewhere other than his house, his 'home' which blew up."

"No. He wouldn't have left it when he ran."

"I didn't think so."

"But now..."

"Listen! We've been here a week now, looking, and the bad guys haven't tracked us down *so far*."

"But..."

"But neither has anyone in Mackie's Cove come to see me about anything Tom left for me, messages or otherwise. Nothing."

"You haven't been easily accessible. Maybe they're afraid." She paused. "Shy?"

"Everyone knows I'm back, and Tom wouldn't have left something like this to someone 'shy'. Or afraid. He'd have left it with Doc, maybe Clive, someone he trusted to look after it. But he didn't, so we might have some hard choices to make here about..."

"No, wait!" Nina grabbed his hands just as he'd almost reached the limit of leaving himself this exposed. Her warm, smooth strength around his fingers sent a deep shock down to the pit of his being and he frowned to cover it.

"What?"

"Tommy was a joker, wasn't he?" said Nina and she seemed to be ferociously willing him into her own recollections. "A game player. Liked tricks. Did he ever play them on you?"

A snorting giggle from Clive over by the stove confirmed how closely the old sailor had been listening.

"So if he was going to leave something for you, wouldn't he expect you to search for it? At least *try*? He could have hidden it in your father's burned-down house, or someplace you two used to play as kids, or...or..."

"My father's boat."

"What?"

"Clive? You said you'd bought it off him."

The hunched sailor suddenly bent almost double as he dug into his trouser pocket, then straightened with a key in his hand.

"Wondered when you'd get around to that," he said. "Take her far offshore so you can look in private, I'm thinking. Pry bars, hammer and nails by the door, long as you put her back together before you're back. You want some of this tea before you go?"

~~~~

Nina hummed with nervous excitement as they passed Mackie's Cove's main wharf and walked to the tarped-over longliner on the dock by Shatter Rocks. It was low tide and the covered boat rocked a good six feet below the level of the dock.

"I could take her out myself," he said.

"Don't be silly. There's no storm this time, and the boat's got to be better than the one we came in on. Right?"

He smiled. "Oh, you got that right."

Mackenzie set down Clive's tools and jumped down to the boat, began pulling off the tarps, and Nina gasped a bit in relief. The *Mary-Hester* wasn't just better; it was beautiful. It looked recently fiberglassed with a bright blue and white hull that cut deeper into the water than the scow they'd ridden here on. Nina smelled salted wood and polish.

But even more exciting was the way Mackenzie seemed to light up as he talked about it. About "her." Like she was some kind of thoroughbred.

"Thirty-nine feet long," he sang up to Nina. "High-curved bow. Windowed wheel-room in the foredeck. You see how her wide, flat hindquarters are open on top and hollow inside? That's how you know she's a "Novi", a Nova Scotian. Makes them light and buoyant. Gives them a big hold for the catch—cod, turbot, capelin, shrimp, lobsters..."

And he was throwing the tarps up onto the dock, chasing up the dock ladder after them and folding them quickly. He was a jungle cat again. His arm muscles bulged. His body moved with that scary but exciting precision that belied the wound he'd received, the infection, the surgery.

Because of the boat? Or because Nina had given him hope that he could find the object of their quest here?

Either way it caused a delicious little flutter in Nina's belly that she was pretty sure wasn't just fear of going out on the water again.

Mackenzie was back down on the boat, running his hands inside the lower lip of the gunwales. Finding nothing, he stepped to what looked like a thigh-high set of steel boxes taking up the whole last four feet of the rear. He lifted the hinged lids on each toward, looked inside, then let the lids fall shut.

"Not there?" Nina said.

"Nope." But he flashed her such a wide smile that the fluttering in her belly had full lift off.

He spun back up to the boxed-in wheelhouse up front, opened it with the key Clive McGee had given him, and turned back to her.

"You know my father tried trawling with her once? Used a Danish seine we hooked up amidships here." He pointed to a set of filled-and-painted-over holes in the center of the boat just behind the covered deck and down the sides, grinning at the foolishness of it. Then his grin faltered.

"What?" Nina asked.

"Nothing. Bring down the tools." He ducked into the wheelhouse, but not before she saw the pain in his eyes. The sweet and the bitter obviously danced together for Mackenzie here.

She scooped up Clive's tools and climbed down the ladder to the boat. Her last foot had just touched the deck when, with a throaty roar, the boat lurched to life.

Nina stumbled and swore. Mackenzie turned to her with his smile again so broad that she barely recognized him. And for just a second he was Tom, young and carefree and loving Nina against all reason. Touching her face. Nibbling her ear. Convincing her she was more than just a brilliant mind. She was a body. She was *fun*.

"Cast us off!" Mackenzie called over the sputtering roar of the engine.

Nina grabbed onto the side gunwale. "How?"

"You have to climb up and unwrap the ropes from the cleats, front and back!"

She hesitated but he'd looked away from her, checking something, obviously expecting her to handle it. The boat was thrumming and popping now. Idling. Waiting.

Okay, then.

Pursing her lips, Nina sprang up the ladder as fast as she'd watched him do, found the ropes and tugged and swore at them until they came free. Each one got tossed grandly onto the *Mary Hester*, then Nina scrambled down again and ran around the wheelhouse to climb out onto the upsloped bow of the boat.

The *Mary-Hester* wove under her, bobbing slowly away from the dock, making her running shoes slip on the slick surface. Nina dropped to her knees and quickly tied the loosed rope around a set of cleats near the window.

Then Mackenzie chugged them into gear so that the boat jerked and shuddered under her. Started moving away from the wharf, out to sea.

Nina's eyes shot wide and she glared over her shoulder at Mackenzie's grinning face. He waved at her from behind the window. *Come on back.*

Inching a slow turn around, she reached and got hold of the wheelhouse cover with one hand, then two. Pulled herself cautiously to her feet. Gripped it tightly with each new handhold as she worked her way around the narrow gunwale to drop into the open rear.

She was breathing hard, her heart racing a thousand beats a minute, her face sweating and red, her legs suddenly like jelly.

As the *Mary-Hester* gleefully puttered out of the shelter of Mackie's Cove and headed to the open blue.

~~~~

God, I've missed this, Richard thought.

But there was something else dancing inside him too. The prospect of finding whatever Tommy had taken? Maybe. Maybe. But he doubted it, because if Tom had hidden it here it would have been easy to find or he would have left a clue. No. The dance inside him came from the feeling that for just two hours he was stepping back to a simpler time, or a time outside of time, a place away from the staring eyes of Mackie's Cove, away from the pressures of hiding and searching, a place to just *be.*

With Nina.

There was a sudden increase in the sound of wind, roaring motor, hull thumping over waves as the wheelhouse door opened behind him and he looked back to see Nina had finally found enough of her sea legs to enter.

"How far are we going?" she said.

He reached a leg back past her and kicked the wheelhouse door closed. "Near shore."

Nina squinted back at the coast where he doubted she could even pick out Mackie's Cove. It was already just a narrow, dark strip of land.

"What does that mean? Near shore?"

"Inside the two-hundred mile limit. Maybe thirty miles out. Half way to Newfoundland, 'the Rock.'"

"And we need to go this far out because...?"

"Still too many boats in this close. They'll see us and swing in."

"I see." She shifted to her other foot, turned around to look back at the shoreline again, went to the side window, drummed her hands on the ledge and tried to look bored. Richard fought hard to keep his eyes off her finely shaped rear and the shape of her back through her tight tee-shirt. The impossible attraction she held for him was proof that this was another world, a brief detour from reality.

She turned back to him. "This is probably far enough."

"You think so?" Richard smiled and tapped up the throttle just a bit to make the engine growl and surge them ahead. Nina jumped and her eyes went wide.

"What are you doing?"

He laughed. "I don't know how you survived our trip through the storm."

"I was too busy throwing up to scream. Much."

"But you grew up near the Potomac River."

"Never went on it. Not once."

"But you moved to San Francisco. Lots of water there. You still never...?"

She brushed back her hair with her hands. No hair band today, though, he'd noted gratefully, and her hair looked wilder than he'd almost ever seen it. It was exciting.

"I go to the beach sometimes. I swim. I play."

"You play?"

She shot him fierce look. "I do know how."

"Who with?"

"Hm?"

"Who do you play with?'

"With...friends. From work. From my kick-boxing class. From a political group I'm with."

"The group?"

She hesitated. "The Young Republicans."

"*Young* Republicans." He laughed because he could see how tense she was about it. How serious it was for her. "What? You want to change the world?"

"Don't you?" she shot back. "Isn't that why you went into the military?"

"Yeah, right."

And he wanted to laugh again, except that she was looking at him so intently, staring at him like she was measuring him, judging him. And for an instant the old defensive anger flared up in him. *She thought she was so superior?* Except even that misplaced arrogance of hers just seemed to goose his desire. Made him want to cut the engines and grab her.

And a part of him said, *Why not?*

"Because you *should* want to change the world," she burst out. "Do what's right. It's our responsibility. Like when we find whatever it was Tom took from these people. What if it's something they're not supposed to have? What if it's proof of something awful they've done? Something so damning they killed him and Marie-Ange to get it back. This is someone in our *government* doing this!"

"*Your* government."

"Your brother's government. And yours! You said you have dual citizenship, right?"

"Yes, but—"

"And these are the people who killed your brother and my sister! You're going to just let them get away with it? If you find what Tom left you, and it actually proves something about his murderer, you're just going to hand it back to them?"

"Jesus, no," Richard said. "I'm going to negotiate with them first. I'm going to get some guarantees that Janine will be safe, and that I will, and you. *Then* I hand it back to them. It's called being a realist."

"Or a coward."

"Right. Of course."

He jerked the steering wheel right, then left, and the *Mary-Hester* did a great wallowing swerve. Nina stumbled back from him before she grabbed the dash and held on.

"Just shut up, Nina."

"Oh, I get it." She was sticking out her lower jaw now. Breathing hard. "That's it. Fear. That's the real reason you're not stopping this boat. You're afraid we might find something and you might have to do something about it."

"You think that's why I'm not stopping?"

"Isn't it?"

"You want me to..."

A scree of gulls and movement to his left made Richard look around and see another boat off to their starboard, hauling in a catch. In frustration, he swung away and opened the throttle all the way, so that the sound of the 60 series GM engine thrummed louder than the roar of spray around the hull.

Nina gripped his arm as the deck tilted slightly and he felt himself burning inside at her touch. Especially because she wasn't letting go.

The ocean stretched gray-blue around them again. Just them and it. The sky. The sea air. His memories. Youth.

And then, even though a tiny sensible part of him was shouting that this was stupid and he'd regret it the moment it was done, he lowered their speed to a slow cruise, locked the steering wheel, and turned to grab Nina by both her arms.

21

near the Capitol Building
Washington, DC
Same time

FROM THE SHADOW OF A BROAD SYCAMORE TREE, Castinages watched
Denise d'Alvay walk out of the west side of the Capitol building. Another
guy who was her age, skinny, with a bad suit, walked beside her, and the
two of them talked as they bumped their rolling, thick briefcases down the
shallow Capitol steps. Like a couple of paper-pushing lawyers. Like a couple
of sycophantic bullshitting junior interns.

It made Castinages want to snarl. The phoniness of it.

There was a time, before Rwanda, before Iraq, before Afghanistan,
when Castinages's dreams of advancement would have had him running for
national office. To get up there and make decisions that affected the world.
All that power. The money. The smug, scrubbed righteousness.

But that was before he discovered what true change required. It meant
looking at what people *wanted* and who they fucking *were*. Because when
you had young men with ancient weapons willing to run screaming to their
deaths for a bullshit jihad, or kids blowing themselves up, or mothers blowing
opium smoke into the faces of their starving kids to calm them down, then all
the cocksucking words and promises in the world weren't going to fix things.

And if d'Alvay still believed in those games? Then Castinages was so
wrong about her that he wanted to puke. His skin itched. It was all he could
do to stop himself from running out and tearing her papers away from her to
scatter them all over this white stone descent.

But then d'Alvay and the punk kid hit the bottom of the stairs and
separated. The kid walked north, d'Alvay south. And twenty paces along,

149

Castinages fell silently into step behind her.

"Denise," Castinages croaked out and coughed. Cleared his throat.

Denise d'Alvay stopped, turned slowly, and gave Castinages a cool look, up and down.

After three days of fleshing out leads on Richard Mackenzie, including tracing his late brother's flight to Montreal and the car he'd rented there, Castinages had finally figured he had enough to justify making contact again. So he'd showered, shaved, splashed on cologne, and put back on the suit that his tailor and friends all assured him made his freakishly muscular frame look simply square. He'd never be a smooth political type, but Denise didn't really want that type of phoniness. Couldn't.

"Major," d'Alvay said.

"Can I...walk you to lunch? Talk about developments?"

She stood stock still, obviously considering whether he was a threat or on the level. Her eyes flicked around quickly. What? Wondering how much she could afford to be seen with him? They'd already played at being a couple once, but that had just been to get him in the door of the Tauredaux home following the funeral so he could see a possible place Mackenzie might come to hide. Afterwards she'd dropped him like a steaming turd. Only seen him again on orders to take him to see Gregor Lechenko. Like he was just a job to her.

Was that all he was?

"All right," she said. Her voice held no enthusiasm. Her face was unreadable.

Without asking him or suggesting a place, she set off brusquely in the direction she'd been walking, crossed Independence Avenue and told him to wait while she dragged her briefcase behind her into the Rayburn House office building. Five minutes later she was back, without the briefcase, and set off up C Street with Castinages loping to keep up.

They ended up at a small place on 3rd Avenue. A pub more than a restaurant. Despite DC's smoking ban, the place smelled like an old ash tray, enough to get him coughing again. Grimy plastic wood. Dirty brass rails. Fake greenery. The tube television up on a rack was tuned to fucking Anderson Cooper, though only about twenty-five percent of the room could see the set anyway.

"The food is terrible, too," d'Alvay said, watching his reaction. "And the drinks are overpriced."

Cough. "So no one comes here."

"Not more than once."

"Got it." And he did. She either didn't want to be seen with him or wanted to drive him off by taking him to a dive that showed what she thought of him.

"Find us a table," she said. "I want to freshen up."

Without waiting for his assent, she strutted away from him and vanished down a dark, small hallway which presumably held the washrooms.

Castinages shrugged so hard the air shifted and got the attention of the joint's only visible waiter, a skinny dude with bad acne. The boy waved him to a table over by the back near the washrooms hallway. Castinages grimaced and bulled through the crowd to reach it. Sat. Had a mini-coughing fit that had him spitting dark phlegm into his napkin.

Waited.

Pimple boy brought menus and water. Castinages ordered a Coors for himself, house white for d'Alvay. She had class. Women with class always drank white wine.

The drinks showed up in another five minutes, by which time Castinages finally wondered if he'd been stood up. Maybe d'Alvay had slipped out the back. Maybe she'd done something even sneakier like setting a decoy and walking right by him without him seeing. Just to tweak his nose. Piss him off.

Another five minutes.

Well fuck her. Castinages nodded his scowl forward. The beer was gone. He'd drunk her wine too. Like he'd told Lechenko, she was a bitch.

If she hadn't wanted to go with him, she could have just said it. If she were a man in his command, he'd bust her down for this. If she were a man *outside* his command, he'd stalk her and hurt her real bad.

As it was...

Bitch!

She even knew about his condition. Told him so when she'd first contacted him on behalf of The Politician. Knew he only had eight months or so at the outside. Knew everything about him. Knew he didn't mess with women much. Had to know that, for reasons he didn't completely understand, she drove him crazy.

And without being fully conscious of a plan, Castinages had pushed himself back from the table and edged his bulk down the narrow hallway into the stink from the bathrooms. The sweet, acrid smell of pot mixed with everything else. He coughed and kicked open the men's room door as he passed and saw it was just a single room—a sink and a toilet.

The lady's room door was closed. He grabbed and twisted the knob. Locked.

He gave a single, hard-fisted knock. "Denise?"

No answer, but under the muted clatter from the main dining room behind him, he heard a snick of the door unlocking.

Castinages engulfed the knob with his big hand, turned, and pushed it open, stepping in.

D'Alvay was there, leaning back against the sink basin. Her suit jacket lay folded over the closed toilet seat lid. She sneered dreamily at him and took another drag of her joint. Blew it into his face. Offered him the joint.

He suppressed a cough and shook his head.

"Close the door," she said. "And lock it."

When he did, she hiked up her skirt and he saw she'd already taken off her panties. Her hair was shaved to a narrow patch around her cunt. His cock sprang up faster than it had a right to at his age. Damn near ripped through his suit pants.

"Time for a special op, hunh?" she said. She lowered her chin and looked up at him through the hair falling around her face.

All Castinages managed was a grunting cough as he struggled out of his suit jacket and dropped his pants.

Every op was special. This one, though, had long ago jumped all the previous guidelines of his life so he wasn't sure he'd call it an op so much as a necessary jihad. For the first time he could remember since the police came to the door of his childhood home in Brightmoor, Detroit, his knees felt weak and he truly understood what it was to be desperate. His stomach rolled. He felt dizzy-sick from the neck up.

None of which stopped him from stepping up and gripping the pale flesh of her thighs with his hammer fingers. Spreading them apart. Stepping in and finding her hot core with his own heat.

Oh, and when she looked down and saw what he was doing, her face lit up like a five year old?

Hoh-oh-oh-oh.

"You're...closer in age...to that Farthering kid at the Tauredaux party," he panted as he rubbed it up and down her slit. "He was watching you...the whole time."

"He watches everyone. And I'm only closer in human years."

"And what're you?"

"A bitch. What d'you think."

That was when his knees found some strength again and he pushed and wiggled his hardness into her. Not like a knife into flesh, but like a soldier into his sleeping bag. Like a child into his mother's skirts. Like a face into soft, freshly baked bread.

And while he knew he could never tell her, Castinages finally understood the real reason behind everything that he was going to do in the coming days.

Oh, yes.

22

The ocean off Mackie's Cove
Cape Breton Island

THERE IN THE CRAMPED CONFINES OF THE *MARY-HESTER*'S WHEELHOUSE, Mackenzie's hands clutched Nina's arms so she couldn't have moved if she'd wanted to.

And despite all her talk about finding what Tom had stolen, she'd somehow known *this* was the real reason for the trip. The throbbing engine and rushing water had filled the air with it, this heat between them.

Even so, her mouth half-opened to tell Richard off for grabbing her. Tom had never grabbed her. Tom had sweet-talked her, seduced her, made her feel funny and sexy and brilliant, like him. Then he'd oh-so-slowly touched her face, her jaw, lifted it to his.

But Tom's approach had never gotten her heart absolutely trip-hammering like this either.

Nina could feel the blood pounding in her neck as Richard dropped his lips there, kissing and nuzzling like an insistent animal, drawing in her scent.

And her face was so hot. Her chest—her heart was suddenly too big for it. And her legs... Were they wobbly from the deck's tilt and roll over the waves?

Richard's mouth burned on her skin! Worked its way up! Over her chin. She felt his hot breath around her lips. She couldn't see, she realized, because she'd closed her eyes. She opened them now to see his face just inches from hers, his eyes locking hers with something in them as wild and limitless as the ocean all around.

Then one of the hands that had been clutching her by the arms, released and went for the back of her head, her hair. Sank into the thickness there.

Pressed her inexorably an inch or two forwards as he rotated his face ever so subtly.

And the connection, two live plugs, hot, came together. Lip sliding on lip. A tongue. His. Then hers, answering. Slow-dancing with each other.

While all the while their eyes never shut, never left one another's.

Nina's chest swelled up as she sucked in air through her nose, unwilling to release his mouth. Richard's did too. His chest met hers, flattened her breasts.

His arm slid down from her head to the small of her back. He pushed there and Nina gasped as she was suddenly belly to belly, groin to groin with him. She could feel his hardness. Caused by her. *She* had done that. Somehow. Not intentionally. And yet...

A small groan escaped her lips and she closed her eyes, raised her hands up over his bulging, hot arms. She still had his tongue sliding against hers.

Then suddenly it was gone.

His lips too.

She opened her eyes to see him pulled back from her. His own face was red, his eyes still wild but struggling.

Nina leaned forward to engage again, but his hands rose to her ribs, holding her back from him.

"What?"

"This..." He cleared his throat. "This was a bad idea. The boat..." He gestured feebly at the steering wheel he'd locked in place.

"What about it?"

"You and I..." Another throat clear. For a tough Special Forces guy, he sure couldn't breathe easily. "We're not right for each other."

Nina snorted. The big belly laugh snort she'd inherited from her mother that was such a professional liability she'd even tried hypnotherapy to train it out of herself. But right now it was one hundred percent called for.

"'Not right for each other?' Come on. That's supposed to be *after* you bed me."

"Which would be a mistake. What with Janine and...the situation...what I have to do..."

"Because what you have to do is going to change," she said, drawing it out dramatically, "if we have a little nooky?"

"Nooky. Hunh."

Looking all the world like he'd just been insulted, Richard turned from her to the *Mary-Hester*'s steering wheel, unlocked it, and spun the boat in a slow turn. Then he cut the engine. It made the boat rock on the waves and Nina had to steady herself.

"What are you doing?" she said.

"What I came out here to do."

Nina sucked in a quick breath and took an involuntary step back. But her blood started pounding again. This was it, then, after all. He was going to ravish her out here on the open ocean where no one could see or hear her if she screamed.

Because she was going to scream. She licked her lips. Oh, yes. When she got this man's clothes off, licked every delectable inch of that hard body she'd been trying to keep her mind off. She was going to make *him* moan. And she had no doubt that he was going to make *her* scream.

Just the way she was, Tom had told her. A screamer. Part of never wanting to be put in a corner by anyone.

"Okay," she said. She spread her feet just a little, taking a wider stance in case he wanted to rush her. The air in the little wheel house was crackling and thick now. Close. None of the windows open.

"Outside," he said.

Kinky, but, "Okay."

She turned and opened the door behind her, half expecting Richard to rush her then, push her up against the wood and glass, and strip her down.

It didn't happen.

She opened the door and stepped out, him following. For a just a second it was even more breathtaking than stepping out of Doc Klein's house up on the hill back in Mackie's Cove had been. The air! God, if filled you up instantly. Seemed to clean you out. Replaced everything you'd had inside you with itself—the sea, the sun and wind and waves. Splash. The spray coming off the wave tops, tanging her tongue as she opened her mouth.

"Have a seat," Richard said from behind her.

She turned to him in surprise. She wasn't sure exactly what she'd been expecting, but not that. "Where?"

"The side. The hold covers. The deck. Pick one."

He sounded agitated, not turned on. Or maybe turned on and fighting to cover it? Because Nina had *felt* his hardness. He'd been there. He'd been ready. Even now the front of his jeans looked awfully big.

"Okay," she said again, and chose the rear hold covers as he started to pace. She put her hands behind her and arched her back, knowing how that made her smallish breasts pop forward in the tight tee she wore. He stopped, stared, then tore his eyes away in frustration.

"I want," he said at last, "to get some things straight between us."

"Oh, you did that," she said, pointedly looking at his crotch.

He blushed and shook his head angrily. "Exactly what I mean. That... mess in the wheelhouse is the sort of nonsense that could get us and Janine killed."

"You're not serious."

"I am. If we don't find something from Tommy here, on this boat, in Mackie's Cove itself, then we're going to have to make some hard choices. Do we stay? Do we run? Do we make Janine stay with Angie while you go home and I go back to DC?"

"You're not—"

"I *am* serious, Nina! Listen! If any of us stays in Mackie's Cove, we need them on our side. It looks a million miles from anywhere, but everyone still has phones. Clive McGee has the internet. People drive down to bigger cities every day for work."

"So?"

"So we make one real enemy there and it's no longer safe."

He'd been pacing again, shaking his hands as he said it, and now finally ended up in front of her, hands open in front of him. Almost begging. And Nina finally got it.

"You're worried that Angie's going to rat us out if you make love to me."

His face visibly blanched. "Maybe. But it's more that there are others in town who will lose respect for me if they see me falling for you."

Ouch. Nina fought not to slouch down and turn away. "Am I that much beneath you?"

"Beneath me?"

"I mean, I don't have big breasts. I don't know how to fish. I can't cook or keep house or parent worth a damn. Okay. And I'm tall. But I'm not ugly. I've fixed my eyes. I've fixed my skin. My hair. I've lost weight."

Her eyes were stinging now and she angrily shook her head but it didn't help much. They just kept on filling.

"So what do you *want* anyway?" she blurted. "What do I have to *do*?"

She focused hard on the deck beneath her runners, fighting to keep herself still, horrified by what she'd just done. It was immature, weak, helpless, everything she was *not*.

Except for right now.

There was no sound from Richard. No laughter, snickers. Disgust?

Horror? He'd already pointed out that she wasn't a suitable mate for him. (Faster than Tom had figured it out, she might add.) Was he just nodding now, filled with pity for this poor landlubber?

Still no sound.

At last unable to stand it, she raised her head and looked at him. He stood stock still, studying her. His eyebrows were pulled down and together. His whole face seemed painfully focused on figuring out what she'd just said. Or what she *was*.

"Well?" she choked.

"You don't...have to do anything," he said.

"What?"

"You're just fine."

"Ha!" Her eyes flooded with tears again and she furiously wiped them away. "'Just fine.' They can call me 'Just Fine Nina.' Sounds like a racing horse. One that always come second."

"This isn't a race."

"Oh yes it is!" Nina cried, jumping to her feet. "Everything is! Didn't your parents ever teach you that? It's a race to get the best marks! It's a race to join the right clubs! To meet the right people! And if you ever fall in love, you better damn well run fast and find a way to tie the fellow up because if you don't, some other girl—your sister maybe?—will be right there behind you, ready to snatch him away!"

Nina's saw his eyes go wide and slapped herself. "Oh, God, I can't believe I said that!"

She couldn't breathe. She felt like she'd just stripped herself naked before him and danced around in a crazy circle. Or puked on his shoes. Or picked her nose. Or...

"Ahhh!"

With nowhere else to run, she dashed past him and into the wheelhouse, pulling the door shut behind her and fumbling with the knob until she found the lock and locked herself in. Then she slumped down onto the floor with her back to the door and wrapped her arms around her legs to hide.

Of course, all he had to do, probably, was climb around the side and he could look in at her. Maybe slide open a window and crawl in. But Nina wasn't going to get up and check to see if the windows locked. There was only so much self-respect you could give up in one day.

And if Richard Mackenzie had any decency, any sympathy for the crazy and pathetic...

There was a light rapping on the door above her head.

"Nina?"

She pursed her lips closed and wiped at her eyes. She could not believe she had come to this. Could not believe it. With a second Mackenzie male, no less. Or maybe, of course. As if almost a decade of personal and career growth meant *nothing*.

"Nina." The voice had moved lower, like he was squatting down behind the thin door, talking to her through it like you might do to a little child. "I didn't know...about you and Tom?"

She heard the question in his voice and almost snorted. Men. You tell them something and they can't get it unless you spell it out for them.

"But...if you did once...have something for him," Richard's voice went on, "I'm not surprised. Tom was always smart and charming. He knew how to talk, how to how to wheel-and-deal, get people to love him. I just don't think he liked challenge in his relationships."

That did get a snort from Nina and she almost slapped herself for it. "What? You think I'm challenging?" she called through the door and was gratified to hear a chuckle.

"Yes. Most of the best people I've known, the ones with real grit and character, are a little difficult."

"Well you must be Mr. Grit himself, Mackenzie. You know that?"

"Oh yeah."

"Like you're not supposed to kiss a girl like that then pull back and tell her she's a tramp."

"A tramp? I didn't..." There was a long pause during which Nina held her tongue with difficulty. "I said that you and I didn't fit together. It wasn't because you were beneath me in any way shape or form. You hear me?"

She sniffed. "Not buying it. That sounds too much like, 'Oh, honey it's not *you*, it's *me*.' And other such bullshit."

She heard him mutter something unintelligible and suddenly there was the sound of a key in the lock above her head. Before she could fully push up to her feet, the door jerked open behind her and Richard caught her as she fell backwards out of the wheel room.

He spun her around, Nina still off-balance, so that her back was to the open door. Then closed as he kicked it shut behind her and pushed her up against it.

His hands went to either side of her face and held her head firmly. His own head darted in and he kissed her hot and full on the lips, stopping only after she unwillingly felt herself starting to respond.

This time when he stepped back from her, his eyes were full of anger and purpose.

"Now go back there and sit down!" he ordered. "I have some things to say!"

"Bastard," she muttered. But his eyes had reverted back to that dangerous look that didn't allow for serious challenge so she raised her chin a little and walked over to sit, cleaning her eyes and nose as she went.

When she'd resumed her seat on the hatch cover, Richard squatted in front of her and knitted his fingers together.

"Now I want you to listen really hard because I'm only going to say this once and you'll never hear it from me again. You listening?"

She nodded and he started to talk.

23

"WHAT I AM," Richard said slowly, trying hard to get this right after he'd screwed up so badly, "is a straightforward guy who started life as a fisherman and managed to use that skill to get into the navy, then the Canadian Special Forces, the JTF2. That's all.

"I never went to college. I never studied 'city densities' or stuff like that unless it related to my mission to take hostages or blow things up. Usually the latter.

"And the people back there in Mackie's Cove know that about me. A lot of them don't like me particularly—we can get into all the reasons why some other time—but they understand who I am and accept that. It's why they're grudgingly letting us sink into the life of the place. They understand me. I'm from here. And they see you as just someone I'm protecting. They get that."

He raised a hand to keep Nina from interrupting. He had to get through all of this, he knew, before she'd understand. If she was able to understand.

"If I start up with you, though, they either have to think I'm just screwing you, which isn't the sort of thing I do. Or they have to think that Richard Mackenzie was actually canoodling with a university trained, DC-raised blue-blood who looks like a Hollywood movie star. And that's about as—what's the word?—*dissonant* a scenario as the Mackie's Cove mind could imagine.

"You get it? It was bad enough that I left Mackie's Cove. At least if I come back here pretty much unchanged, we can fit in for a while.

"If I come back this whole other person they don't understand, that *I* don't understand, we're going to be ostracized, shut out, and you can bet your last American dollar that someone going down to the fish plants in Canso is going to blab about it, connect it to the stories in the news, take it upon themselves to do their civic duty and report us somehow.

"That can't happen. For our sakes. For Janine's.

"Do you understand?"

He stopped, closed his mouth and swallowed dryly, unaccustomed to speeches. And a little scared too. By himself as much as anything. He'd always prided himself as being clear-eyed about people and situations. It was what had gotten him and Tommy out of Mackie's Cove in one piece. It had saved him too many times to count in battles.

But here, today, he'd let his attraction to Nina turn him as delusional as a coke or heroin addict. He'd thought he could somehow hive off this one little trip from the rest of their lives, do with her what he'd been aching to do since he'd first laid eyes on her, and then just leave it alone.

Oh, yeah. Sure, stupid. Because even if, by some miracle, Nina could cross that bridge and then pretend nothing happened, Richard couldn't. Not with Nina.

Jesus, he was messed up.

A seagull had followed them from the other fishing boat, circling high overhead. It now concluded disgustedly that they weren't fishing after all and so let loose a stream of white poop that splatted near Richard's feet.

He jumped backwards. The seagull scree'd and flew off. Nina laughed.

"Birdshit," she said. "Exactly."

"What?"

"'University-trained, blue-blood, movie star.' Right. The fact is I'm difficult, tall, and deep down you just don't like me."

Richard's jaw dropped. Then he closed it and silently both cursed and thanked his brother for the awful number he had done on this amazing woman's head.

"You know what?" he said. "You're right. Deep down I think I just don't like you and we'll leave it at that, all right?"

She held his eyes and he tried not to look away.

"I think I want you to just kiss me again to prove it," she said.

It sent an electric shiver of desire through Richard but he shook his head. "Not going to happen again."

"You sure?" she said shakily. She pushed herself up to standing before him and took one step forward. Her whole body looked like it was trembling. Like he could make her wrap herself around him with a single touch. *Heaven.* Or totally destroy her with the wrong word. *Holy God, Tom. If you were alive, I'd kill you right now.*

"Nina..." He swallowed hard. "I told you I'm a simple man. Don't press it."

"You said if people thought we were 'canoodling', they'd take it wrong. And the way you used the word suggested it was more than just fucking. Am I right?"

Richard winced and frowned. "That's right."

"It would be more like 'courting' or even 'falling in love', correct?"

She'd arched ever so slightly towards him so that a bad roll of the boat would make her fall into his arms. And Richard almost longed for that to happen. He'd take it as a sign. Just to feel all that smooth, strong skin again. Her beating heart.

Richard raised up a hand and put it, stiff-armed, on her shoulder.

"If you keep pushing me, Nina, you're going to get hurt. I'm not Tom. I don't play games like that."

"Yes you do. You kissed me, passionately, then you said that deep down you don't like me. I believe the kiss more than the words."

Shit. "Believe what you like, but get this: it's *not going to happen again.* Get it?"

He bored into her with her eyes the way he did with non-coms and enemies he wanted to silence rather than have to kill. She didn't even blink.

"Not going to happen while we're in Mackie's Cove," she said. "I got it."

Richard shook his head violently, then turned and went back into the wheel house. He had trouble getting the engines to start and slammed the heel of his hand into the dashboard. Kicked it hard. Realized he still had the steering lock on. Took it off and started the engine.

He throttled up and jerked the wheel around sharply to head back for Mackie's Cove, a place he was starting to hate all over again, for a whole new set of reasons.

~~~~

Fifteen or twenty minutes into the ride back, he felt, as much as saw, Nina came in to stand silently beside him. She held a hammer in one hand and a crowbar in the other.

"You already looked around in here, I assume."

He nodded.

"So which planks do I pry up to look for stuff?"

Richard looked at her solidly without saying anything.

"You imitating Janine?"

"We have to get her talking," Richard said finally. "Tom might have told her something."

"Oh, good idea. I'll have to try that. 'Get her talking.' Good plan. Now which planks do I pry up to look for stuff?"

"It's not here."

"Which ones? Or should I just start ripping at random?"

Richard stared out at the gunmetal waves. His emotional exhaustion had dulled most of his senses, and his hunger for dinner was clamoring for attention, but he still had the urge to shut her up with kisses. "If Tommy planted whatever it is onboard this boat, the place he hid it will be clearly marked somehow and easy to pry up without hurting anything else."

"Why? Some kind of fisherman's code? Protect the boat at all costs?"

"Tommy wasn't a fisherman. But he'd protect *this* boat."

"Because it was your father's."

"No, because... Just because."

She stared at him but thankfully didn't press. "Okay." Then she frostily turned away her fabulous figure which was now denied him and walked out of the wheelhouse. He glanced back through the wheelhouse door window and saw her slowly examining the gunwales and deck of the vessel inch by inch. Finally focusing on the painted over holes in the middle of the deck behind the wheelhouse and down the sides where the Mackenzies had once set up poles for skein trawling.

~~~~

He was stupid. Men were stupid. But in the middle of all that stupidity was someone pretty fabulous. Honest. Brave. Committed to doing the right thing whether he knew it or not.

If he could just get his super-soldier head out of his super-soldier ass.

Play along. Play along.

And what kind of marking would Tom make to show he'd hidden something? Let's see. Nine years ago, when he'd been hiding his affections for Marie-Ange from Nina, the tell-tale sign had been...no sex?

Hm. Well *that* was everywhere on this boat. For now, she'd check these supposedly abandoned-and-covered holes for trawling. She set about banging and scraping at the first one. Because one way or another, she had to find this stupid cause for murder and get her and, *Richard* Mackenzie—

no just *Richard*—out of this backwater and into a place where he wasn't so scared to…um…kiss her good.

Shiver.

~~~~

This time, after *Richard* returned the boat key and tools to Clive and spent some time explaining that he'd fix all the fruitless holes Nina had made in the deck, he walked Nina back towards Angie's, then stopped a block away and said he was going to cut straight up and around the top of town, back to Doc Klein's.

"We don't even know how big this thing is, do we," Nina said, knowing it sounded stupid but unwilling to let him go. "It could be…a microdot planted under Janine's skin."

At least it broke his stolid countenance. He smiled at her. "Like something out of *Mission Impossible*?"

"Well?"

"Sure. But if it's that small, we might as well give up now." He stopped. Shook his head. "No. Tommy would have told me that. It's got to be something that we'll know when we see it. And I honestly still think it's here in Mackie's Cove. I just can't figure out how Tom expects us to find it if he didn't leave a clue with someone."

"Or we just haven't asked enough people yet."

"Maybe."

Richard turned to go.

"Did you know," Nina said quickly, "that anytime I can't find Janine for a while it's usually because she's by the window or in the back yard, staring up the hill towards Doc Klein's house?"

The flicker of deep concern, then something almost like rage flitted over his face and he muttered, "Not this time."

O-o-okay. Another cryptic connection to the past. Not critical to getting them out of here, but Nina was obviously going to have to solve the mystery of the Mackenzies in Mackie's Cove as well if she was ever going to really unlock Richard.

At least she'd figured out one part of on the way back here.

"The *Mary-Hester*," she said. "That was your mother's name, wasn't it. And why you don't think Tom would ever have done anything to hurt that boat."

Richard nodded, holding her gaze.

"Did you father truly love her?"

"Everyone in this town loved her."

"Why?"

Richard pursed his lips and his eyes bored into her. "Because she was a simple woman of good cheer, Nina. That's all she was. That's all anyone expected of her and it was enough. And if she'd lived, I probably never would have left Mackie's Cove. I'd have stayed a simple fisherman. Simple and good. Owned a house. Raised a family."

"With Angie?"

His eyes flicked away, tellingly, then back. "Maybe."

"I don't believe you."

He frowned. "You don't believe I'd marry Angie?"

"Nope. And I don't believe you would have stayed. I don't believe you could have. Even with your mother here."

"You didn't know my mother."

"No." Nina found herself smiling wistfully and tilting her head. "But I think I know you, just a little. You're bigger than Mackie's Cove."

He laughed uncomfortably. "Right."

"No, you are. Despite what you say about everyone's courage here and your simplicity, you're the one who got your brother out, right? And left yourself. You saw the world. You, not them."

"I guess that makes *you* too big for Washington, DC"

"Just too big for my parents' house."

He had no answer for that and finally just said, "I'll come by and see Janine more." Then he waved and walked away.

Nina watched his receding form for a long minute before she whispered, "I'm not letting you get away, you know."

She turned and made her way to the winding road that ran up past Angie's place. Inside, she found Angie bustling about in a panic, throwing dinner together and gasping when she saw Nina come in. She looked pointedly at the kitchen clock, which said six-forty-five.

"Just give me some numbers to call for the *ceilidh* and go, Angie," Nina said. "Janine and I will manage on our own."

Angie threw a spiral notebook on the table and dashed out the door. Nina grimaced and picked it up. "Now," she said, "we'll see what we can do."

24
Turkey Run restricted area
northwest of CIA Headquarters
Langley, Virginia
Sunday

WITH A ROAR, Castinages surged out of the muddy bank of the Potomac and shot Paz Gomez with two marking Simunitions rounds, one in the face and one in the chest.

"You're down, soldier!" he shouted, then sprinted east across the riverbank and into the trees before the two others of his team still in the DC area broke tree cover to find him.

It took them just under two minutes, but it took Castinages a full five minutes to pin them down and "kill" them.

Good. Better, at least.

Like everything in this op was going better now that he'd burst his mental cherry by finally nailing Denise. Shit, that woman. Drove him crazy twenty ways to hell and back and was going to cut his remaining months in half if they kept on like they were. But Castinages didn't fucking care. She'd opened things up somehow. The universe was finally unfolding like it was supposed to.

He slicked the mud out of his eyes and nose and bent over in a racking cough for a moment, training rifle down at his side. His three men calmly watched, waited, and snapped to attention when he straightened.

"All right, crunchies," he rasped. "Listen up. You're all marked and dead, but today that means you get to go out and try to do better this time. And do you fuckheads know *why* you're going to do better this time?"

It was Burton who answered. "Because we're the best, Sir!"

Castinages walked up to him and looked up into the man's bruised face. Castinages was shorter than Burton by at least eight inches, older than him by two decades, and heavier by at least forty pounds. But the forty pounds were solid muscle, and the decades were experience.

"Fuck, soldier. You ain't the best. Mackenzie took out you and Gomez when he was nearly dead, and he didn't even feel the need to kill you. What does that say?"

"Sir?"

"It says he's a damn sight better than you. Hell, maybe better than me. But we're still going to take him down. Do you know why?"

"Because...he's protecting civilians. Slows him down. Sir!"

"That's right, soldier. And because he thinks he's safe. But your fellow GBs have found the direction Mackenzie's brother drove when he left Montreal for his father's funeral. And that led us to the boat Mackenzie and his civilians snuck across the border in. So we expect them to locate him very soon. Then they come home and we go in. Will you be ready?"

The tall Special Forces soldier, who was one of only five Castinages had privately recruited over the years for a farewell bang just like this one, raised his chin with more determination than smarts.

"Yes, Sir! Papa."

Castinages grimaced, wondering just how that Choke Force handle had spread back Stateside. But he could handle it. He fully expected these new "children" of his would be able to take a surprised, handicapped Mackenzie with no casualties.

Only trick was going to be retrieving The Politician's package from Mackenzie before Castinages and kids put him down for good.

"Then Search and Subdue on 120 count. Same quadrants. Go."

~~~~

Mackie's Cove and surrounding area
Cape Breton Island

I *think* we're safe, Snuffles. That's why I leave you alone sometimes now.

Cause Uncle Richard is talking to us again and he's not so scared. He even smiles now sometimes. Mostly when he sees Auntie Nina. Mostly when she's not looking. It's funny.

And yesterday? When I left you here? Uncle Richard took me on a walk.

First we got groceries for the Doc guy. Then we did like Auntie Nina. We went up to people's houses and got them to let us in so Uncle Richard could ask them stuff. But with Uncle Richard, I got to play spy! He told me to go and snoop while he distractored them. I didn't know what I was s'posed to find because Uncle Richard didn't tell me. But it was fun.

And then we got to watch him fix Doc's upstairs sink, and his sticky doors, and his washing machine.

Uncle Richard's good at fixing stuff. But I don't think Auntie Nina should marry him. Cause *I'm* going to when I grow up.

I want to tell him that. And tell him what Daddy told me about you.

I *want* to, but I *can't.* Cause...cause...it's scary. *You* know. You saw what happened. Don't talk don't talk *don't talk!* See? I told you, Snuffles! I told you!

... Mommy? ... Daddy? ...

What? I am too not crying. I'm trying to *talk.* And I will.

You wait and see.

~~~~

Monday, just before noon, Richard finished re-tarring a leaky part of Doc's roof and stopped for lunch. Sipping a can of beer, he stood at Doc's front door and wondered if he should take another walk down to visit Janine, maybe catch a glimpse or two of Nina. Or whether he should finally face the south road of Mackie's Cove, where his father's (and Richard's, Tommy's, their mother's) old house sat as a blackened husk.

Tommy wouldn't really have left whatever he'd stolen there, would he?

Take Janine home, Richie.

Richard felt the sweat trickling off his forehead and it wasn't all from the sun and labor. His heart was beating fast as he contemplated the obvious. Tommy hadn't meant home as in Mackie's Cove. No. He meant home as in the actual physical house where the Mackenzie boys had grown up.

And it was only Richard's stubborn fear of the ghosts he'd feel lingering in the burned walls that had kept him from exploring it. What would he see if he went down there? What would he remember? Smacks and cries? Mumbled apologies that never made things right? Or deadly, deadly silence. The silence he'd walked in on his coming back from his first long trip from home.

Richard shook it off. His hands were balled tightly, his jaw clenched. He forced himself to release them and take a deep breath.

Yes, he had to go check out the house.

Right after lunch.

Well...right after he drove the pickup north to Chéticamp to get some lumber to rebuild Doc's back porch.

~~~~

"You know who you look lak?" said the man loading Richard's bought lumber into the truck. "Dis man Strachan Mackenzie. Use to come up here for de lumber sometime."

"Really."

"*Oui.* But he die, I think, *hien?*"

Richard nodded. "I heard. Bad heart."

"Yes." The grizzled yard-man grinned. "*En les gosses,* eh. Too much of de boom boom."

"If you say so."

~~~~

And after he got back and unloaded the lumber, he still didn't go down to the burned house.

He decided Doc needed more groceries if Richard was going to be having Janine visiting up here for lunch sometimes. So down he went down to the small general store, dead center of town on the highway, right next to Ninian's Pub.

And despite the fact he'd been trying to copy Nina in visiting the people of Mackie's Cove one by one, he again got the freeze. The store owners Jovie and June McAlister looked up when he walked in then conspicuously turned their heads like they smelled something bad.

Fine. He grabbed one of the little hand carts from near the door and wandered through the paltry collection of fresh vegetables and meat, buying enough for some salads and chili he could make for the doc, and finger food for Janine.

Then he felt the hot whoosh of air as the door opened behind him. Richard saw Jovie's face light up like a baby's, while June rolled her eyes and poked him.

Amused, Richard turned to see who in town had become so golden since he'd left.

"Oh! Richard!"

It was Nina, but not the carefully demure Nina who'd passed off Janine to him the last two days. This Nina wore a bright peasant skirt in a blue-and-red floral with matching button-down top that somehow brought out her eyes. She'd let her hair go as wild as it had been on the *Mary-Hester* and she wore no makeup, just the glow of an outdoors tan.

But the real glow was in her expression and attitude. Not a trace of the self-righteous or whiny socialite. She stood so comfortably in the doorway with a bright red canvas handbag over the crook of her arm, a raised flip-book and pen, she looked like she owned the place.

Holding up a finger to Richard, she said, "Jovie! We're doing the *Kelligrews Soiree* theme after all. So we're going to want samples of just about everything in the song—cherry wine, pig's feet, skip the cat's meat, dumplings boiled in a sheet, jowls—" She looked up from her list and grinned. "I'm told they should be mackerel jowls, given where we are."

Richard listened in stunned bemusement as she listed another eight foods Richard thought had probably been written into the song only to sound outrageous. But Nina looked so happy and fierce that he found himself nodding along with Jovie.

June, who'd been wiping the counter with a rag while Nina went on, now stopped and wiped her hands. "You know it's a Newfie song, d'you dear? Different island."

"So I have been told," Nina said with a smile. Easy. Like it was a private joke between them.

"Are you trying to change us, then?"

"Just making it lively. *Out on the Mira* didn't mention food."

"But there's still dancing," Jovie said, eyebrows raised.

"Of course," said Nina. "I'm bringing Morag Maclean and her family in from East Margaree to help with the dances, and Ashley MacIsaac will be making a special appearance."

June and Jovie looked at one another then back at her. "But he's a big star!" they said together.

"Who's home for a vacation," Nina said. "And was open to a party invite."

"All down at our little Ninian's?" said June, jerking her chin towards where the pub sat just north of them.

"With overflow outside as long as it doesn't rain." Nina quickly stepped back to the door and knocked on the wooden doorframe.

"Well then," said June. "Well then."

Jovie said, "I guess I'll need that list of yours again, Nina." Which Nina answered by ripping the page off the front of her flip-pad and walking it over to him.

He looked sadly down at it. "No drinks?"

"Ah, Jovie," Nina said with a fair imitation of a Cape Breton lilt, "and how would Ninian's be making a profit if it couldn't liquor people up in grand Gaelic fashion?"

Jovie still looked sad but June laughed and hit him with her dust cloth. Then she stuck it out of sight beneath the checkout counter and smiled at Nina.

"You know, Nina-from-away," she said, "I dare say it'll be the first *ceilidh* that I wouldn't miss for a world of Sundays."

Nina flipped her notebook closed and winked. "I'm counting on it, Mrs. June McAlister."

Then she turned like she'd completely forgotten Richard was there, and flounced out of the shop.

Richard stared down at his nearly-full hand basket, then out at Nina, disappearing along the road, turning south down through town. Making a quick decision, he walked to the checkout and laid his basket down. "If you'd bag that and hold it for me, June," he said, "I'd appreciate it. I'll be back to pay shortly."

Then, not staying even long enough to catch June's withering glare, he ran out the door to catch Nina.

He caught her standing in front of Foster and Gwen Gill's house just down the winding street towards the docks, the same one they'd taken on that first walk together. Nina was glancing at a sheet she had that was covered with blue pen handwriting, not all her own.

As Richard approached, she quickly stuffed the sheet into her red carry bag, and knocked on the door.

Gwen opened it, with her daughter Loren, a teenager now but sadly as lumpen as her mother, right behind.

"Mrs. Gill? Gwen? I'm Nina Tauredaux. You know, Nina-from-away. Staying down at Angie Neal's house with my niece for a while."

"Yuh?" Gwen Gill stared past Nina at Richard and her beady eyes grew to little points behind great squinted folds of flesh.

"Gwen!" Nina said to pull back her attention. "The *ceilidh*. This Friday night."

"I knows about it."

"Oh, I doubt that. This is going to be *the* event of the summer, let me tell you." She ran quickly through much of what she'd told the McAlisters, then turned to Loren, whose dour face had lit up considerably when Nina had mentioned Ashley MacIsaac.

"There's also some boys driving into town from Baddeck Academy," Nina said. "That's where you go to school, isn't it, Loren? Grade ten? Someone named Greg asked me to make sure you knew he'd be there."

Gwen Gill's mouth dropped open and she turned to stare at her daughter, whose face was flushing beet red. For a second, Richard almost thought the girl looked...charming.

Nina was thrusting a sheet she'd pulled from her red carry-bag into Gwen Gill's hand and closing Gwen's pudgy fingers around it with her own hands so that Nina was holding the woman's hand in both of hers, further disconcerting the woman.

"You'll all have a good time," Nina urged. "I promise. You make that husband of yours come too, okay? It's probably high time he took you out dancing, isn't it."

And Richard had another shock as he saw tears glisten in the corners of Gwen Gill's eyes.

After one more squeeze, Nina said goodbye and turned to walk off the step and on to the next house. Richard ran quickly to intercept her before she reached it.

"What was that?" he asked her.

She stopped on a lumpy knob of asphalt, edging the side of the windy road down, and regarded him with amusement. He had to fight to stop himself from darting his head forward to kiss her sun-warmed smile. She just looked so...fresh. Smelled like sweet honeysuckle.

"I'm helping Angie with this week's *ceilidh*," she said.

"Helping? Or taking over?"

"Her boss gave her the responsibility and she passed it on to me. She still gets veto power."

"If she knows what you're doing." *Kiss her.*

"I give her reports."

"About Ashley MacIsaac coming and the Macleans from East Margaree, I'm sure." *Grab her and kiss her.*

"And the theme."

"Right. The Newfoundland one. Burl Ives, right?" *Grab her and—
Damn it, keep it in your pants, Mackenzie!*

She laughed. "Burl Ives did a version? I don't know. Angie was just singing it in the house one day and Janine started following her around, swinging her head and arms in rhythm. I got her to sing the whole thing to me. Then I had to ask around to understand it! Do *you* know what birch rine, tar twine, and cavalances are?"

Richard caught himself watching her lips and mentally slapped himself. "Speaking of Janine..."

"Lili Anstruther, thirteen years old, is over babysitting, with Angie still there. And Dougan. It's a practice run for Friday, so Janine can get used to her."

"Why didn't you just call me?"

"Because I expect you to be at the *ceilidh*."

"Do you."

"Have you interrogated everyone in town? Been through all their houses?"

"No."

"Then you need to be at the *ceilidh*, making friends, fitting in. That's what we're supposed to do as long as we're here, right?"

It was a challenge. She was sticking out her lower lip at him like she dared him to bite it. Or kiss it. But she wouldn't initiate it because she'd promised. She'd just push at *him* to break the rules, damn it.

"I also suggested we keep a low profile," he said.

"No, you didn't actually. Might have implied it, maybe..."

"So."

"So this is more important," she said sweetly. "Did you know Mackie's Cove hasn't had a really big *ceilidh* here in over two months?"

"Poor babies."

"The local fiddler, a woman named Rosaleen Kincade, got breast cancer and her family shipped her down to Halifax for treatment. I got the Macleans from East Margaree to convince a man they usually work with, Liam Killin and his partner, Kerr Sherlock, to come play for us."

"Very impressive. I'm sure they'll be telling stories about you for miles around. Exactly what we want when we're trying to hide out."

"You really think so?"

"I really do."

"I don't. I think they're much too busy telling stories about you."

Richard frowned, a sudden bad feeling in the pit of his stomach. "What stories?"

She cocked her head and gave him a mean smile. "Well they can't be true. Because surely you would have told me yourself. Prepared me."

"What. Stories. And who'd you hear them from?"

"I heard the reason you left Mackie's Cove, the reason you ran off and joined the navy, wasn't because of itchy feet. It was a lover's quarrel. You and Angie. And Tommy makes three."

"Par—" It fully sunk in. "*Tommy?*"

"Sad, really, how she went from the older son to the younger."

Something in Nina's tone had become harsher, jabbing, like she wanted to wound. And he *was* wounded. Angry and bleeding inside. But not from Nina. From whatever sick person in town was telling lies about his family.

"Who said it?"

Nina's eyes dropped for a second and she looked away. "I don't think I can tell you that."

"Because they're lying to you."

Her eyes whipped back to his, but her electricity only pumped his anger up higher.

"Well?" he demanded.

"You kicked your brother out of the house. Made him leave town. Against your father's wishes."

"I kicked him out? My father's wishes?" Richard snapped his jaw closed like he had to hold in the hammering of his heart, the pressure in his head. It was like all the years he'd been away were nothing. He was eighteen again, barely a man, and his world had just gone down the toilet. "Is that what they told you? Was it Dougan Smither?"

"Not Dougan. And not just one person."

"More than one." Richard's jaw snapped shut again. And if it opened he would surely scorch the ground, kill whoever was in his path. And it was Nina in his path.

"Six different people."

"*Mo chreach!*" Richard burst out in Gaelic. His mother's single curse. The one she used when she thought no one heard her. "Do you know how old Tommy was when I supposedly 'sent him away'? He was fourteen! I'd just turned eighteen. Angie was Twenty. So you've got six different people telling you that Angie was fucking my brother when he was barely out of elementary school?"

Her face had gone pale before him, but Richard was so caught up in his rage he couldn't stop now even if she begged him.

"I didn't say—" she tried.

"Yes! You did! From the older to the younger! Assuming Angie was the love of my life! Like everyone in this town assumed! Building lifetimes out of one summer, less than one *month* we were actually together when I was sixteen! Everything else it fantasy! It's making up a soap opera to fill boring little lives! Looking for the...the thrills because they can't find them in their own lives! *That's* what you're buying into?"

Finally he shut his mouth again, glaring, knowing he'd said something stupid but still buzzing with all these people of his hometown turning on him like this. Twisting his past. Blaming him for their sickness.

They could all *ith mo chach!* His father's favorite.

Nina had taken a step back from him and was looking back and forth at the houses on either side of her as if deciding which one to bolt to.

No one was opening the doors of either house, though. And Richard wished they would. He truly did. Because what he'd tell *them*... Well, let's say he'd give them more fuel for the well-stoked little blaze they had going about him and his.

God*damn* it!

Nina planted her feet and stared back at him, her eyes wide. "Are you going to hit me?"

"*What?*"

Her gaze flicked down to his hands and Richard realized they were half-raised, balled so tightly the knuckles where white.

"I..." He forced them open, snarled at them to open. Shook them out. Then he turned away from her and ran his hands over his face. Took some deep breaths.

When he turned back to her, he'd pretty much regained control, though his insides still burned like he'd eaten a caseload of hot chili peppers. And he still couldn't meet her eyes. Didn't want to see what was in them right now.

"There are not many things," he said slowly, staring hard at the scrub grass and dirt that edged the road, "that can put me over the edge. But lies about my brother and father..."

"Did you send Tom away?" Nina asked bluntly and Richard felt it thud into him. The woman never stopped.

"I did. For his own protection."

"From you?"

Richard jerked his chin up, almost losing it, remembering Tom dying in his arms. "Not from me."

"From...your father?"

He looked away from her. "How many people are you going to speak to personally about this Friday?"

"You didn't answer me."

"How many?"

"If I answer you, will you answer me?"

He could feel her holding him with her eyes. God, it was like her hands were on his face—hot and soft, the sun-warmed lips and hair close to his, making his stay, making him tell her whether he wanted to or not. Was this how weak he'd been when he was eighteen? How had he ever survived?

Because there were some moments too harsh to ever bring up again. Like Tom's death. Like Tom's near-death so many years earlier. A foreshadowing. Near death. Temporary rescue.

Oh God. Oh God.

Gritting his teeth hard, he shook his head and down the hill to where a burned-out husk of a house was waiting for him. "I left my basket of groceries with the McAlisters, but I don't think I'm going back for them right now. If you see them, apologize for me, would you? I think I'd just spit in their faces."

Without waiting to hear her response, he strode down the path between the houses, heading for the beach road.

~~~~

Nina watched him go then dropped her red carry bag to the blacktop and almost collapsed herself like a wobbly pile of jelly.

Richard Mackenzie had been this close to physically losing it, something she hadn't thought was possible. A simple, straightforward man? She didn't think so!

But she'd kept pushing at him anyway, wanting more from him, needing to know what it was that made him tick at the basic level.

"Great game," she murmured. "Poke tiger with stick."

And she seriously questioned for the first time whether something was wrong with *her*. Why did she feel compelled to break him? Why Richard Mackenzie? Because he was Tom's big brother? Or because he was dangerous. Unattainable. A challenge like every other challenge she'd faced and beaten since Tom.

Which begged the question of whether she'd only helped him run with Janine from DC because of the danger. The challenge.

No, Stupid. There'd been men with guns. There'd been Janine to protect. *Ye-e-e-s. More danger. All connected to Richard.*

Taking a deep breath, she shook it off, *and* the memory of him kissing her on his boat three days ago. He'd explained why that was never going to work. She'd stubbornly decided it would. Maybe that decision had been a mistake. Maybe she really should just back off.

Except that the mere thought of not seeing him again made her throat clench inside.

Okay, too much. You're running in circles, Nina.

She clenched her fists to regain her balance and focused on the few things that lay clear before her. She'd been the one to convince Richard to stay in Mackie's Cove and search longer for something Tom had left for them. But there'd been nothing. No clues. No hints from anyone.

And despite what she'd said about the *ceilidh* being a chance for him to fit in more, it seemed ultimately hopeless. Richard was right. If Tom had left something here, they should have found it by now.

Which meant that the *ceilidh*, which really should be a lot of fun, might also be their farewell celebration. Or just hers and Richard's? Nina gathered, from hints Angie had dropped, that Richard had already discussed with her the possibility of disguising Janine and keeping her here, as Angie's daughter, while he and Nina left again.

Nina wasn't sure she could stand that, but maybe it was best? Like maybe Richard would also send Nina home to San Francisco because she wasn't specifically targeted and he certainly wouldn't need her any more. She'd just slow him down.

Damn it, Tom. If you really did take something important and hide it here, you've done a damn poor job of leaving clues anywhere.

And just in case you're listening up there, does my vow to personally invite every single person in Mackie's Cove to this *ceilidh* make a diff? Or is just grand irony my last role here is the one my mother's been playing her whole life?

Nina scooped up her red bag, turned, and walked with rubber legs to the next door on her list.

~~~~

Richard spat on the stony dirt. This was it?

The Mackenzie family house, up about a fifty yards from the high-tide mark, was on the north end of the shoreline road, long past where the pavement ran. It butted up against the steep scoop of bluff on top of which sat the old church and cemetery.

Like all the town's dead had threatened to slide down on their heads his entire childhood and he'd never noticed.

Now his childhood home was just black timbers. The west side had collapsed and taken most of the roof down with it. The second floor was a few blackened joists. And as Richard picked his way in, over mounds of black wood, plastic, brick, steel, he saw that the pipe that once rose off the potbelly stove had fallen with the wood supports around it.

He imagined he could still smell the stink of the gasoline his father his father must have poured everywhere, that he could smell the stink of his father splashing it around (probably drunk out of his mind) and throwing on lit match after match until it caught.

Went up like them Roman candles, a neighbor had said. *Fwoof!*

Richard reached the middle of what had been the kitchen, the largest room downstairs, and stood, taking it in. Here was where his mother had once made him breakfast in the mornings. Here his drunken father had later beaten Tommy to within an inch of his life.

And here had been that silence the afternoon he'd come home from his first long trip. Tommy sitting there. Their hung-over father slumped there...

No signs. No clever little Tommy markers or arrangement of the garbage. It wasn't here.

"So that's it, Tom?" he said to the tipped-over potbelly stove. "Was this just a 'make peace with it all' trip after all? Would you be that stupid with your last words? Because the men looking for us, Major Castinages in particular, isn't big into self-actualization. He'll want back what you took."

Richard kicked a black boulder with his boot and it exploded, being mostly ash. "*Where it it?*"

25

FRIDAY MORNING, Angie Neal delivered the invitation to Richard at Doc Klein's house.

Richard had been outside Doc's upstairs bathroom window, re-shingling the final part of Doc's roof that needed repairs. He felt good about it too, because emotionally he'd finally given up hope of an easy ending for him and Janine and Nina. Which fit his world view better. No easy answers. Make tough choices and live with them.

He'd do that tonight, right after Nina had enjoyed the big party she'd put together. It was the soldier's way. It was Richard Mackenzie's way.

Then the doorbell rang. And someone banged on the door. Louder. Louder still, until it was obvious Doc had stepped out somewhere and wouldn't be answering.

Richard slid inside and tromped downstairs.

He opened the inside door and pushed open the screen door to find Angie standing there in a modest, striped summer dress that covered her shoulders and didn't even snug in at the waist.

But her eyes weren't modest. They ran appraisingly up and down Richard's sweaty body. It made him feel even more undressed than he already was, wearing just his jean shorts and combat boots.

"Well, then," Angie sighed. "Was it you I heard singing? I used to love your singing."

"Is everything okay with Janine?" Richard said. "With Nina?"

"Not them I'm here about, is it."

"Angie, I already told you that—"

"I'm inviting you to the *ceilidh*, Richie. You ken? Nina was going to come and invite you and Doc personally, but it seems something you did a day or

180

two back scared her so bad she couldn't. You scared young Loren Gill too. She was watching from her bedroom window."

"Yeah, that fits." Watching him. Judging him. He wouldn't be sorry to leave this place again. "Now the whole town's talking about it, I bet."

She tilted her head, picking up some of his strange mood. "No. No, Loren just whispered it to me when she came by the pub for her father. On account of you used my name. You said something about me 'fucking' your younger brother. That's how she put it."

He laughed roughly. "What I said was, it wasn't very likely, you being twenty at the time, and him fourteen."

"Any more likely than me fucking you...at the time."

He nodded. "That's right."

"Why is that? Was that? Can you tell me?"

"Are you asking about then or now?"

She paused. "Both."

"You've got Dougan."

"And you know I'd drop him like that, were you just to give me the sign."

She'd moved closer on the step to him as she said it so that Richard could feel the heat from her, smell the fruity perfume she wore. And even in her modest sun dress, what man in his right mind wouldn't have been drawn to her Botticelli figure? Her red hair, pulled back in bun, was like a corona of fire around her head. Her face was worn with wrinkles around her eyes and mouth not from frowns but from smiles. Laughter. And knowingness that soaked every movement of her limbs and torso.

But it still annoyed him when his body started to respond. Then he was annoyed at his annoyance. Exactly what *was* stopping him? Loyalty? To whom? The town? Nina? That was stupid because he was out of here tomorrow and so was she...separate from him and the target on his back.

But the flash of Nina's face, her touch, still shot through him and he stepped back.

Disappointment washed over Angie's face until she looked down his front, up again, and her eyes were filled with challenge.

"You won't tell me why?"

"Angie..."

"That's okay, Richie. That's okay." Then she reached out a sinuous hand and laid her palm against his sweaty chest before he could stop her. He was sure she could hear his heart race, damn it. It just wasn't for her exactly.

She said, "You're coming to the *celidh* tonight, though, aren't you? You and Doc both."

Her hand was still on him. He was still hard. "We'll...show up."

She smiled wolfishly and stepped back, withdrawing her hand. "Good, then. I'll be seeing you there. And I'd bring a dish or two of your own food. I don't think folks'll much like the stuff Nina's bringing in."

"Jowls and cavalances?"

"Cat meat. Pig's feet."

"Dumplings boiled in a sheet."

"Crazy stuff."

"Indeed. I'll have Doc bring some of his potato salad."

"And maybe I'll have something for you, Richie Mackenzie. Something so good you'll wonder how you've lived so many years and never tried it."

With a last smile and twitch of her hips, Angie Neal turned and walked back down the hill.

~~~~

Inside the house, Richard went to the kitchen and stopped, shocked to see Doc Klein sitting there, eating the last few crumbs of the night-before's apple pie.

"You were here the whole time?" Richard said.

"Hanging on every word." Doc daintily touched his napkin to his mouth and goatee. "You and her—better than some of the new soaps, *ja*?"

"Dirty old man."

"No. Just lonely. The Torah does not allow us to be dirty."

"Only drunk?"

Doc shook his head. "Not since Tommy died. You've been here. You have seen."

"Yeah, I have. But the soaps?"

"I watch them to learn about human behavior. How else could I know that what Evangeline just did was offer to sleep with you?"

"Experience, Doc. You and Sarah."

"I think not. Our courtship was dignified."

"Oh, come on." Richard walked to the sink and began washing his hands with dish soap and cold water. "You're saying not once in your thirty-plus years together did she ever push herself up against you or grab you and pull you into bed?"

Doc looked at him and, embarrassingly, the old man's eyes began to well up. "There was once."

"Hey, look..." Richard turned off the tap, opened the cupboard under the sink, and dried his hands on the dish towel.

"It was a hospital bed. The last week she was alive."

Richard held up a hand, but the doc kept speaking, as if he needed Richard to know. Needed *somebody* to know. "My little *bubbeleh* had shrunk down to less than a hundred pounds. The chemotherapy. She could not eat. She could not sit up." Doc's eyes tracked the ceiling. "After visiting a former patient who was also in the hospital, I went up to my Sarah's private room on the third floor."

He paused for a second. Richard made no sound. Doc continued.

"She looked like a child in the bed, all curled up in the white sheets. Bald head, smooth like an egg. Her face—it was tight over her bones. But she still looked better than she had in weeks. And when she saw me, she smiled. She struggled up to sitting and let the sheets...drop away. She had taken off her hospital gown and was naked. She held out her hands to me. She winked. She said, 'You close that door and come over here to me, Nathan.'"

He closed his mouth and stared at a fixed point, far away.

"Did you go to her?" Richard finally asked.

Doc smiled and looked at him. "I did. I locked the door. I stripped off my clothes. I did not even fold them. I crawled into that hard bed with her. And we made love for the very last time."

Richard let the moment settle, then said, "Wow."

"So why are you not grabbing these opportunities while you can, my friend?"

"You mean with Angie?" Richard laughed and turned back to the sink, turning on the tap to splash his face and slap some water on the back of his neck. "I'd hardly put that opportunity in the same class as Sarah's request."

"I was not talking about with Evangeline."

~~~~

The door creaked gleefully and Nina looked up from brushing out Janine's hair for the hour or two the little girl would be at the party.

"He's coming," Angie said and strutted by her to the bathroom.

As the prime organizers, Nina and Angie had been back and forth to Ninian's all day to oversee the final setup, welcome the musicians, drive about for last minute supplies, and help stow the "Kelligrew" appetizers in the rear bar fridges. Because the weather was cooperating, they'd gotten Angie's boss to hook speakers up outside the pub as well. Then they'd strung multi-colored streamers from the telephone and other poles, and swept the side deck and hard-packed dirt-and-grass of the parking area for dancing. Out-of-towners would just have to park on the streets and walk, like almost every single person in Mackie's Cove would be doing. It would be worth it.

The only question mark had been the two men up on the hill. And suddenly Nina felt sick that she'd been too chicken to go ask. But the amount of emotional investment she had in this party was too much, the stakes ridiculously high for all of them.

She'd needed to maintain her distance.

A grunt from Janine made her almost drop her brush, except that she realized she'd been tugging hard at Janine's hair and not paying attention.

"Sorry, hon," she said and Janine wrinkled her nose at her in a question.

"Just...distracted," she answered. "Let's finish getting ready. Big party. Food. Music. Then you get to play with Lili until she takes you back here and puts you to bed. 'Kay?"

Janine wrapped her arms around Nina's neck and, for the first ever time, gave her a big smoochy kiss.

Nina's eyes welled up. Oh, Janine. Oh, Marie-Ange. Against all odds, we'll get some answers tonight. I believe it. I do. Then everything will be as right as it can be.

She put away the brush, grabbed her bag, and took Janine's hand to walk to Ninian's.

26

Quality Inn, 31st Street
Washington, DC

IN THE SOUPY AIR OF THE LIME GREEN HOTEL ROOM, not far from Washington Circle, Castinages raised his butt off the bed to meet the downward thrust of Denise d'Alvay, straddled over his middle. She arched back to grab the bed sheets and pumped her tight ass up and down even harder.

"Unh," Castinages grunted, feeling the pain in his chest, using his thumb to work her sex. "Yeah. Come on, babe. Come on come on come on."

Finally, with a guttural screech, she did, shaking like a crazy banshee.

"Fuck yeah," Castinages said and threw her to the bed beside him while she still shook. He spread her and plunged back in, pumping his own oak-like hips between her legs and slapping her already-red face back and forth until it made him build like an M72 rocket launcher and he went off in bone-grinding spasms.

When he was done, he rolled off her, coughed into his pillow so hard his gut hurt, then looked up at the ceiling, panting. Sweat dripped down his face and trickled from under his armpits. From hers too, he knew. From her whole tight little body. So clean, so precise in everything she did. It made him want to bury his head into his pillow again and weep.

Instead he rolled to the edge of the bed and reached down to his trousers, crumpled on the floor. Pulled out his rolling papers and tobacco—the heavy, flue-cured, Zimbabwe brand that always took him back to the cardamom-flavored coffee, low couches and endless political gossiping in Baghdad's Beirahdi Cafe. He propped himself half up against the headboard and licked and rolled a smoke.

"Me," d'Alvay said, so he rolled her one too.

He lit both of them. She took a drag and then broke into a racking cough.

She passed back the cigarette, waving her hand in front of her face. "Holy fuck, that's awful."

Castinages took a long, exaggerated drag then stubbed both his smoke and hers out on the lacquered bedside table. He held in the urge to hack his own lungs out again as he did so.

Then he felt d'Alvay running a hand over the bullet and shrapnel scars that covered his body from the scalp on down.

"You like taking risks," she said as he turned back to her.

"If the objective's worth it."

"Like me?"

He laughed. "You're a perk, bitch. I'm retrieving this thing for the money I get, nothing else."

"I don't believe you." she said. "I did at first. All that shit about needing a retirement fund while there was still time to spend it."

He coughed and took another long drag of his cigarette. "Eight months tops."

"Oh, I know. I pulled your medical chart, remember? I just don't think that's all of it."

"Women shouldn't think," he growled and rolled to his side to tweak her nipples back to attention.

She moaned and shoved her small breasts up at his fingers, then slapped his hand away. "You're a true believer," she accused with a bright glint in her eye. "Despite all those layers of flint, you saw stuff over there that got to you, didn't you? What was it? The addicts like your mom? Or the suicides like your dad?"

"Will the right answer get me more pussy?"

She gave him a heavy-lidded smile. "It might."

"Well in that case—"

His cell phone rang.

Castinages swung his legs over the edge to grab it out of his crumpled trousers, and flipped it open.

"It's paying off," said Junk's flabby voice, low and rushed. "He's up here somewhere but you have to let me handle it. Pull your boys back."

Castinages stood up. "Deep Throat?"

"I've got stuff on him too, actually, but I'm talking Mackenzie right now. I'm up in Canada. I took vacation time and flew into Halifax this morning."

Fucking hell. Junk had more balls than he'd thought. "Give."

"I found out the target was a maritime boy, small-time fisherman like his father, probably Nova Scotia. Something about the type of boat he used."

"That's it? We knew that," said Castinages. Then he looked over at d'Alvay watching him and rethought the voice. He could not sound remotely weak or ineffective. He had no illusions that d'Alvay would cut him the same slack he cut her. Whatever his motivations, he was still just candy for her—good for as long as he was good.

"No," Junk was pleading. "Your boys found the boat he used to reach the east shore of Cape Breton Island. My intel makes it small towns only. Fishing towns. And there just aren't that many up here. But they're closed little communities. They take the right touch from someone who doesn't stand out. It's why I'm here and you've got to call off your boys. Do it, Misha."

"You're sure on this?"

"There's also a boat registry I'm trying, and only so many fish processing plants still in operation. I sent ahead pictures of Mackenzie, the woman, and the girl to the local television and newspapers hitting today. It'll break any time."

Castinages turned his back to d'Alvay and spoke quietly into the phone. "Listen, Len. When you locate his home, he's going to be there. *Don't* move in before I fly the rest of my team to join you. You got that?"

There was silence on the other end of the line.

"Is there a problem?" Castinages said.

"You've got draw back your boys until I find him, Misha. He's never seen me, and even the Tauredaux woman only met me briefly. She won't recognize me with my different hair and clothes, different context. But Mackenzie will spot your soldiers by smell alone. He'll vanish. You know it. Let me go in alone."

Castinages chewed the air a moment. "Done."

"Then I'll call you when I find him."

"Good hunting."

Castinages ended the call and immediately did as he'd agreed with a second phone call, curt and coded. Then he shut his phone and tossed it onto his crumpled pants. When he turned back to the sheets, his heart and pecker leapt to see d'Alvay still lying there, nude.

She smiled at him with a dark glint in her eyes. "Leonard Junk, NSA," she said.

"No such agency. No such person."

D'Alvay laughed. "You men and your secrets. Always think you're a step ahead of everyone else. Well, that's okay, long as you get results. C'mere, true believer."

He stepped close to the bed and she rolled to her side to grab his penis, making it swell again far sooner than it had any right to. But like this op, when it was time for insertion, it was time.

Her smile widened and she licked her lips.

"Round two," she said.

27
The ceilidh
Mackie's Cove
Cape Breton Island

WHEN RICHARD AND DOC KLEIN SHOWED UP AT NINIAN'S AT SIX, Doc carrying a large bowl of potato salad and Richard with two bottles of Sprite, they had to push through crowds who'd already spilled out the front door and all over what looked like an improvised dance floor along the side of the building.

In fact the band had set up outside for the time being, their lead man sawing on an amped fiddle over thumping drums and electric bass guitar.

Richard and Doc grinned but kept pushing into the pub itself. All the tables had been pushed back to the walls and covered with food and drink. A set of low risers along the side wall was obviously where the band would go later. Kids ran between people's legs, playing tag. A group of teens Richard didn't recognize, though he suspected he'd remember their younger faces if he stared long enough, were huddled by the side door, staring out it at the band and crowds, whispering and giggling shyly.

And where was—

"Ah, you came, then!"

It was Angie, wearing a more form-fitting cotton top that bared her freckled shoulders and showed off her great sweep of wiry red hair and ample bosom. She grabbed Doc's potato salad from him and gave the old man a loud kiss on the cheek for his trouble. Doc grinned.

"Food and drink's all over there!" Angie called over the crowd noise and band. She waved her chin towards one of the tables set up kitty corner to the bar. "Drop your food and come back and find me!"

Richard gave a noncommittal nod. Doc had already been grabbed by an older couple who looked familiar, but Richard couldn't remember their names. He hoisted his pop bottles and worked his way through the crowd to plop them onto the table beside some large pitchers of some kind of fruit punch. The Ninian's bartender, cleaning out beer mugs behind the bar, looked over at him and grinned.

A sudden tugging on the back of Richard's pants made him turn around and look down, and his face split in a smile.

"Hello, little girl," he said to Janine.

He touched her hair lightly and she wrapped her arms around his leg like he might vanish on her.

"She's missed you," said a contralto voice that sent shivers through him. "The last two days were tough."

Nina shook her head at him, stepping close so they didn't have to yell. "It's okay."

They stood there awkwardly for a moment, taking each other in. God, she looked...edible. As sun-kissed as she'd been three days ago, she had her shoulder-length hair gelled back a bit on the sides to emphasize the fine bone structure of her cheeks. And her neck, long and slender. Shoulders covered only by a set of spaghetti straps from her pale pink top. Below it was a crepe-style summer skirt, long and light, with pockets in the front. And a pair of open-toed sandals with a small heel that she certainly didn't need for height, but which made her the length of her legs just delectable.

"*You* found some shoes too," she blurted.

Richard waggled his feet with a wry smile. "Drove down to Port Hood. Got the pants. Shoes. Didn't want to step on anyone's feet in my boots."

"So you're planning to dance."

"It's a *ceilidh*. That's what you do at these things. Dance and sing. Everyone does. They don't let you leave until you've performed."

Nina blanched. "You're kidding."

"Angie didn't tell you that?"

The emotions running across Nina's face looked like twenty shades of horror and her eyes darted around, probably trying to find Angie.

"The dancing's not that hard," Richard said.

"I know!" she said, still looking about wildly. "I got Morag to coach me a little this afternoon. And I can make speeches until the cows come home. But I don't sing. I've never sung. I sound like a constipated frog." Her gaze snapped back to him. "Do *you* sing?"

He smiled slowly and ran his hand gently over Janine's hair. "If someone asks me."

A teenaged girl with braces appeared suddenly at Nina's elbow. "I'm sorry I'm late, Ms. Tauredaux. I'll watch Janine now. That is, if she...uh..."

The girl pointed at Janine, who still clung to Richard's leg. But as if she'd decided she'd shown Richard the requisite affection, she pushed off and grabbed the girl's hand. Together the two ran outside to where most of the people were dancing the kind of Scottish line dances Richard had grown up with.

"She seems like a good kid," Richard said, watching her go. "Lili Anstruther, right?"

"Came highly recommended. Angie asked around for me."

"You and Angie getting along then?" He cast a sidelong glance at her and saw her face run a gamut of emotions again. She'd become so much more open since being here. As if Mackie's Cove, for all its secrets and hidden bile, had still somehow worn off the Washington and San Francisco masks. It had let the real Nina Tauredaux shine through.

And after this party he was going to have to rip her away from it. Send her back to a more guarded life whether she wanted it or not. Was that a good thing or bad?

"What Angie and I have," Nina said now, "our relationship, it's... complicated. I think we've reached a kind of truce."

"What were the terms?"

Nina blushed and looked down. "Unspoken, but simple really. I just have to step back and let her..."

"Richie!" He turned to see Angie weaving back in through the still-crowded front door. "You didn't come and find me! You have to come dance!"

"...do that kind of thing," Nina finished so quietly Richard wasn't sure he was supposed to hear.

But he didn't have time to confirm it because Angie had him by the hand and was dragging him out the side door of Ninian, the direction that Janine had dragged Lili only moments before. He looked back at Nina with an elaborate shrug, surprised to find himself actually relishing the feel of the music, the beat and drive of a fiddle in a double jig, the sudden crush of people all around him as he passed through the door.

Then they were out and the crowd had formed a circle in a space bounded by streamers strung between the Ninian's walls, two telephone poles, and an old sailing mast driven into the ground and held straight with sandbags. Just left of it, the band had set up on a single, long, deep riser. On it the lead fiddler was sawing away fit to start a fire.

Younger kids ran back and forth across the beaten dirt of the parking lot-cum-dance area. Teens shrieked and twirled to the rhythmic clapping of their parents. And even Janine was in there, hand in hand with Lili, running and twirling. Janine might be mute but she had a smile so huge Richard swore he could hear her laughing.

It made his eyes water suddenly and he started clapping with the rest to mask it.

Then Angie at his right side, wrapped her arms around him from the side, under both his arms, and squeezed him with such open affection he almost fell over. But as he regained his balance, she still hung on, looking up at him with her ruddy face flushed, her eyes bright.

"Angie...?"

"Dance with me!" she said.

He looked around and saw people looking their way now, even as they clapped on the children.

"I said *dance* with me!" She tried tugging him out among the children.

Now a bunch of the clappers had turned towards him, still clapping, their eyes bright, too. Laughing? Gloating? Well, he thought with a sudden bubble of laughter inside, to hell with them! I'm gone tomorrow. I dance tonight!

So he stumbled out onto the dance circle with Angie. Without so much as a nod, he swung her alongside his right hip and she lifted her arm to him. Then, just as if there were a line of women on one side and men on the other, they boldly jigged in a straight line, Richard spinning Angie from his right over to his left, then back again, "stripping the willow" as all the kids used to do so many Saturday nights ago.

Like riding a bike. You never forgot.

And by the time they reached the far side, two straight lines had formed in their wake, men on the right, women on the left. Richard spun Angie around at the far side, stepped stylishly back onto the end of the men's line, she to the women's, and a second couple came jigging and spinning their way down as the band slipped into a "The Jig o' Slurs" and parents slipped forward to gather up their children.

Looking to his left, Richard wasn't at all surprised to see Doc Klein there, clapping and sidestepping the men's line along with Richard.

"Rescuing me, were you?" Richard said to him over the commotion.

"I think you might be doing that yourself, my son."

Richard looked left and right now and wondered if it were true. Nobody was scowling at him now any more. And even those still laughing seemed to be laughing *with* him. At least it felt that way. It felt, foolishly and ironically, in this raucous group of all ages he was mentally saying goodbye to, like he was finally home.

He savored the sensation because it was better than it ever had been when he'd actually lived here.

Then he was at the top of the line again, and the band had swung into a "Pride of Erin" waltz. The line broke up, the couples joined up, and they were swinging in quick steps and swishes.

And even Angie's lush waist under his hand felt like home. A home that might have been. So much so that Richard let himself look into her eyes as they swung about. They were still bright. Tipsy maybe. Just happy? Richard had never been able to read her well. Maybe that was real reason they'd never made it past that one glorious summer together. That and the thousand other things wrong with his life back then.

A tap on his shoulder made him turn. Dougan Smither, his long, skinny face, freshly razor-shaved with all the little nicks and scrapes to prove it, stood there with his face red. Dougan's right hand stabbed out behind him, telling his buddies to stay back.

He needn't have bothered. Richard was done with his splash into what might have been. He gracefully released Angie, did a little bow, and hopped quickly away for the door going back into Ninian's.

Doc Klein, waltzing by with old Mrs. Cumberland, gave him a dignified wink and whirled on.

Then Richard was in, and it was considerably calmer here now that the dancing was on outside.

A short boy who looked maybe eleven or twelve, sniffed beside Richard elbow to catch his attention.

"Me mum says you're a bastard," the boy said.

"Does she now?"

"Says you run your own brother out of town and give your dad a heart attack."

"I heard there was a rumor like that around. D'you believe it?"

The kid looked at him like he was daft. "Me mum says."

"Ah."

~~~~

Nina paused in the doorway of the pub's back room where she'd gone to bring out more Kelligrew surprises. She'd heard the exchange and caught Richard's barely discernible wince.

What struck her most was that no one else around him saw it. The boy who was looking him dead in the eyes didn't. Nor the woman Nina vaguely identified as the boy's mother, in part because she was flushing beet red as she watched the exchange. Nor even Doc Klein, who'd just that moment followed Richard in and was casting smiles from Richard to Nina in the doorway behind him.

Why didn't they see? Because he hid it from them, of course. Trying to spare them. Trying to fit in. But why could *she* now see the pain? It was so clear to her.

Richard caught Doc Klein's gaze and half-turned to catch her staring at him.

"Yummy treats," she said lamely and raised her tray.

It held two enormous plates of guinea fowl. They were, said the little tent cards she was going to prop up before them, prepared in two different ways—boiled in a gumbo, and roasted and served cold.

Motioning the men to follow her, she swooped her tray over to the long table she'd set up to one side with a white table cloth. There she unloaded it beside two rather lumpy looking tureens filled with suet and raisin puddings that had been boiled inside cloth bags—"boiled duff" and "cold duff." Other tent cards fronted non-food items such as "birch rind" (birch bark) and "crackey's teeth" (teeth from a yappy dog, provided in good faith by an old man named Mr. Higgins who lived with his daughter and kept all sorts of odd things in their woodshed).

"Well?" Nina said. She held her breath.

Richard was lost in bemusement, reading the entire eight verses of *Kelligrew's Soiree* that Nina had printed out in flowery letters on a large banner hung over the table.

Doc Klein sniffed one dish after another in horror. "If anyone actually tries these..."

Which apparently prompted Richard to do exactly that, grabbing up some guinea fowl with a napkin and fingers and taking a large bite. He swallowed.

"Not bad," he said.

"Savage," sniffed Doc.

"No," Richard said, "*savage* would be eating those." He pointed at the mackerel jowls at the far end.

"Or that." Doc Klein pointed at the pickled pigs' feet.

"Oink," Richard said.

"Hey!" Nina cried, tag-teamed and overwhelmed.

Richard turned to her. "Join us for some of Doc's potato salad?"

"It's a little early."

Doc snorted and Richard said, "If you wait until the first round of dancing's done, you'll have to fight like a dog to get anything."

"Especially my potato salad," Doc said.

Nina's face felt hot for no reason she could name. "Can I...can I get Janine?"

"Of course."

She nodded and slipped away, light-headed. All the heat of the day, the preparations, finally having things come together. And knowing everything was coming to an end.

But I can see things in Richard Mackenzie that no one else does!

Except Angie Neal? Angie was waltzing, none-too-happily it seemed, with her young boyfriend Dougan. The long-faced one. The one who knew Gaelic curses. The one who'd tried to bully Angie and Nina almost the first day Nina arrived here.

For a second, Nina almost felt sorry for Angie.

Then she scooted through the onlookers to track down Janine and her babysitter. She found them fifteen yards away, rolling down a grassy slope with a passel of other kids. Herding them up, she got them back inside just as the waltz ended, the band declared a break, and the hordes descended on the food and drink.

Luckily Doc Klein and Richard had piled up plates and drinks for all of them and, after a little awkward shuffling, they all made it outside, to a picnic table beyond the *ceilidh* dance area.

Janine chose a spot beside Doc Klein, who was instantly transformed into his kindly grandfather persona. But was that alcohol Nina smelled on his breath? Couldn't be. Lili squeezed in beside Janine. Which of course left Richard and Nina beside each other. To talk about...nothing.

Nina vaguely heard Doc Klein telling Lili and Janine about how he'd arrived here in the mid-eighties...*and Richard's black-cottoned thigh touched her bare one.* The coal mine had still been open then...*as Richard's short-*

sleeved shoulder moved inches from her sleeveless one. The fishing...*his square jaw chewing food.* The people...*his breathing. The light musk of his sweat. He moved; she moved.*

They were synching, she knew, both consciously and unconsciously, but so profoundly that she felt like she was becoming one with him. They reached to brush away a fly at the same time, caught each other's eyes, and smiled. A wonderful, buzzing, anticipation.

"Now your Uncle *Richard*..." Doc Klein reached across the table and pushed Richard's shoulder. "When he was just eleven years old, not much older than you, little Janine, do you know what his father did?"

Janine, big-eyed, shook her head. Richard almost imperceptibly dropped his and Nina felt a dark tension shoot through him.

"He took him out on the *Mary-Hester* as a crew hand. Do you know what that means?"

Janine shook her head again. Richard shut his eyes.

"It meant that Richard was expected to make sure the longliner's automatic baiter worked smoothly, scooping up the little bits of bait and flowing out into the water. Then he had to help pull each fish off each hook when they pulled the line up, and toss it into the hold. It cut his young hands almost to ribbons."

Nina interjected, "Didn't they wear gloves?"

"Oh, some did. But not Strachan Mackenzie's boy. He was a tough one, *ja?*"

Richard raised his head, but this time his face truly was blank and Nina couldn't read it. "My mother and father were both very proud of me when I got home."

"After dinner, his mother brought him to see me. I had a nurse, then, helping. My wife. She called me in to see the cut-up hands of this skinny little boy."

"She thought I'd been whipped," Richard murmured and Nina heard a slip of pain in it. She looked at Doc. Should he go on? Didn't he see what he was doing?

Apparently not, because he continued with gusto. "I thought he'd been whipped too! Until I got close enough to his hands to smell them. Phew!"

"That...was cruel," Nina said.

But her words broke Richard's mask, not into anguish but surprise. "Cruel? No. It was...harsh. But that night, coming home to see my mother, was probably the proudest single moment of my life. I learned you can do anything, weather anything, if you've got the will to."

"And you stuck with it," Nina said.

"With what?"

"Fishing."

"There wasn't a lot else."

"There was the pit," Doc Klein offered.. "Coal mining."

Richard laughed bitterly. "A fine option."

"Did Tom fish?"

Richard's jaw tightened and again Nina had the impression only she saw it, though Janine's ears had pricked up. "I didn't let Tom fish. I kept him in school."

"Until you kicked him out of town."

Richard's eyes flashed at her, then he looked at Janine and away. Nina wanted to grab him and snap, *So I'm as bad as Doc. But we've only got tonight! Tell me what happened, damn it!*

Doc Klein finally answered for Richard. "Ach. What's this *meshugas* that you listen to, Nina? Where do you think Tommy went? A boarding school. And who do you think paid for this by dropping out of school to take over your father's boat? Richard. He got Tommy out of town so the boy could *be* someone."

"He couldn't be someone here?" Nina said and Doc Klein rubbed his jaw hard, looking like he desperately needed another drink.

"Oh, come on!" Nina said, slapping down her fork. "It was because of their father, right? Tom was in danger. But why him? Why not Richard? What aren't you telling me, either of you?"

28

RICHARD BUNCHED HIS ARMS UP UNDER THE PICNIC TABLE. What was he not *telling* her?

How about that he'd rather be anywhere with her right now other than in this dumpy parking lot discussing Tommy in front of Tom's only daughter. Jesus, Nina! This was supposed to be a send-off, not a frigging inquisition!

"Well?" she said and he whirled on her.

She was saved by a burst of music and applause as the band started reforming itself on the outside riser. A trio of young teenaged girls, led by Loren Gill, were suddenly at the left side of the table too, staring at Richard.

"Yes?" he said carefully.

"Um, Lili told us that someone told her that you used to sing at every *ceilidh*," Loren said.

"A lot of people did."

"But always you."

Richard grimaced. "Only when my mother was around," he lied. "Sorry." Then, with sudden inspiration, "But Nina here—I think she invited Ashley MacIsaac, didn't she? Has he shown up?"

"Not yet," Nina said stonily. "And you told me you *always* sang at these things."

Relentless. He held her eyes for a second but couldn't tell if that was fury, curiosity, or what glittering deep inside there. Not as easy to read as he'd thought.

He turned back to the trio of teens. "Maybe later, I will."

All three girls smiled and giggled with release. "Okay!" They turned and ran back to the growing circle, the sound of the fiddlers and bass guitarist warming up. The drummer. The edge of the highway bounding Ninian's on the east seemed even more choked with parked cars since the last time Richard had looked. Out-of-towners still arriving. It was only going to get worse.

"Oh, come on," Richard sighed at Nina and swung his legs out from under the picnic table.

"What?" she said.

"A walk. You and me. Answers to all your questions. At least all the answers I have."

Something in his resignation must have registered because he saw a quick look of fear dart over her face. But she nodded, stood, then glanced at her watch, the sun getting low across the western sky, and Janine. "Lili?"

Janine shook her head furiously and pointed at Richard, but he shook his head back at her. "Won't be singing in the first round, hon. That means way too late for you. You need sleep."

She was blinking furiously at him.

He laughed. "Maybe get Lili to sing you to sleep, okay? Lili, do you know any songs?"

The girl looked embarrassed. "A few."

"They help Janine sleep."

Nina looked at him. "They do?"

Richard shrugged and suddenly felt guilt ripping his chest over dumping Nina with the main childcare and not sharing that. And if Janine stayed here with Angie, would Angie sing to Janine? Would she ever play tag with her? Would she respect Janine's fear of closed-in spaces? Would it ever be safe for Richard to come back for her?

Nina nodded at Lili. "We'll be back about eleven."

"Huh!" snorted Doc Klein, daintily picking crumbs off his sporty waistcoat.

"When things quiet down," Nina amended.

Then Lili and Janine were gone and he was walking Nina over to a thin part of the circle.

"I thought we were going for a walk."

"In a minute," he whispered and made her stop.

Because sure enough, at that very moment, old Morag Bran stepped up onto the band's low riser, her loose-fleshed arms wide and face upturned to the dying sun like she was summoning the Gaelic gods of song themselves.

And as the fiddles began softly behind her, she threw her croaky old voice into a rendition of a traditional Cape Breton song that grabbed Richard by the heart and jerked him back and forth with every word.

When she hit the chorus about being just a rock in the stream, he foolishly found his arm around Nina beside him, swaying her as everyone in the crowd swayed, adding their voices, knowing the lyrics, knowing the soul of it.

And the packed dirt under their feet was right. And the ocean breeze that chose that moment to blow up through the town and whirl people's hair. And he could smell the chicken and garlic on people's breath. He felt their warmth. He felt again that elusive strum deep inside that sang 'home.'

Until the song ended.

He released Nina, embarrassed, trying to ignore the shine in her eyes, and joined into the enthusiastic applause.

The next singer swept forward. None other than Jovie McAlister, running a hand back over his balding head and whispering to the band.

"You know what he's going to sing?" Nina said.

Richard rolled his eyes, feigning cynicism again. "After that? Oh, probably 'Out on the Mira.' Or 'Farewell to Nova Scotia.' Or '*Oran do cheap breatuinn*.' The other big three. The good stuff only comes later, after people have more juice in them."

"You mean when they're drunk."

"Exactly."

"Is that when you sing?"

"That's when I sing. Doc too, maybe."

"Pagh! Never!" said Doc Klein, who'd come up behind them. "I don't drink anymore. I don't sing anymore! But I wouldn't miss *you* doing it for the world."

"When?" said Nina.

Richard glanced at the sky then around the circle. "Couple hours."

"So now we walk? I'll have to find my bag. I brought other shoes."

"You all right here by yourself, Doc?"

"Go. Go."

So after Nina had changed footwear, they did, Richard leading Nina down through the town one last time...

29

A LMOST A QUARTER MILE SOUTH OF NINIAN'S, a vintage blue Crown Vic
pulled off to the side of the road behind the other cars still arriving.

The doughy-looking driver adjusted his glasses then turned off the engine and climbed out.

For a minute or two, NSA cryptoanalyst Leonard Junk just stood there, agog. He could make out the lights and noise even from here. This was *not* the sort of place Richard Mackenzie would hide out. And finding him had been too easy. Too fast.

Yet the shopkeeper down in Port Hood had been sure in fingering the photo. And the story rang true.

The man who'd come into the little shoe store that afternoon had been wearing what looked like combat boots. He'd needed nice shoes for a party, but wouldn't say where the party was. He'd paid in cash. He'd just laughed when the shopkeeper asked his name.

"And he moved out on the street like some kind of ninja guy, eh? There one second, then just kind of gone."

Sounded like Mackenzie all right.

One way to find out.

Shrugging off his own discomfort with crowds, Junk pushed up his glasses again, hitched up his pants, and began walking towards the cacophony of music and babble.

30

THIS TIME WHEN THEY REACHED THE BEACH ROAD, Nina now wearing her familiar running shoes which added their own quirky sexiness to her ensemble, Richard took her south to the burned-out husk at the very end.

He stopped to stand in front of it in the dying light with his hands in his pockets, his mind sliding away from her as he remembered everything about this place one last time.

"This is where you grew up?" Nina said softly beside him.

He nodded.

"Did you hear about it? The way your father died?"

He dragged himself up from it to look at her. "What version did you get? His heart finally burst from missing his sons? He ran himself into debt and the loan sharks got him? He tried stealing his boat back from Clive and popped his valves?"

"Which is true?"

"Who knows. Who cares. He torched his house. He was obviously ready to go, one way or another."

"Harsh."

"You think?"

Before she could answer, he nodded towards the ocean and set out again, trusting Nina to follow. She did.

When they reached the shore, they wandered along the beach, to the rocky northern end where the *Mary-Hester* was moored. The boat looked so solid in the calm water that Richard let himself calm down, too. He pointed out the misty tendrils coming off the gunmetal water as the sun sank into the horizon. The feeling of heaviness in the air.

"Fog's moving in," Richard said. "Air's chilling fast. We'll be socked-in."

Nina shivered and he almost stepped closer to wrap his arms around her, do what Doc had told him to—take advantage of this chance while he had it. But the feelings driving him now weren't lust. They were deeper. And he couldn't be like Doc—put his whole heart out there when he knew it was going to get ripped apart tomorrow. Any more than he could suddenly become the crusading superhero Nina seemed to want. He was just a survivalist at heart. Looking out for himself and his own.

And damn it, Nina wasn't his and wasn't going to be. This night was to... make that okay for both of them.

As if reading his mind, Nina shivered again and stepped further away from him. "You promised to tell me everything."

"Right. I did. Just..." What did it matter? It was just information. A final gift he could give her. "Tell you what. I'll give you my story if you give me more of yours first."

"More?" Nina turned to him in the dimming light and he could see her blush. "Than what? All I've told you is what I do for work and that my sister stole your brother from me"

"And...you grew up with a nanny and a mother who wanted you to be a politician. You were a straight-A student in elementary and high school. A bit overweight. An intellectual snob. You went to Harvard University. Must have lost weight there to get Tommy's attention. You went out with him for a while but then your sister showed up and stole him away from you. So you graduated and fled west to San Francisco. You landed a good job in urban planning, moved up fast, but haven't made a lot of friends because you're working all the time. That's why, when your sister called, you decided having a family might not be such a bad thing after all and you came back to patch things up. Only it was too late."

He cut himself off, with an internal kick in the shins. "Sorry. But is that about right?"

Her blush was even more intense now. "You're good. What *don't* you know about me?"

"Why you let Marie-Ange take Tom away from you."

Nina snorted. "You're kidding, right? You met my sister."

"I did. And I've met you. And Tom wasn't as shallow as I said. He knew quality. He wouldn't have ditched you if you'd really wanted him."

Something almost shifty slid across her features before becoming the anger of denial. "My father," she said. "Would have thought he knew quality, too. But he still left my mother. Found younger women who admired him for what he had. A series of younger women, in fact."

"That's what you did? Left Tommy for a series of younger women?"

She stared at him for a second before her scowl cracked and she poked his chest—the good side. "You're missing the point, smart stuff. I was relating to my mother. And if you ever tell her I actually did that..."

"Highly unlikely."

"Point taken," she said.

"And I won't even raise the fact you didn't answer my question."

They both dropped into silence and stared out over the water that had become a dark misty blur as the fog rolled in.

"It's dark enough now," she said. "Tell me about your father."

And it *was* dark enough. Richard could still hear the *ceilidh* up the hill, clear sky behind its lights, but down here on the beach it was like they were being swallowed into another world. A good place for invoking ghosts.

"My father," he said carefully, "was *not* a cool guy. Nobody ever gave him a thing in life, except for my mother, whom he loved...completely. And when she died of breast cancer, he basically fell apart."

"Became a drunk."

"Not really. That's Doc's bag. My dad got drunk a lot, but it was more that—his whole attitude towards life plunged six feet under. At eighteen I dropped out of school and took over the fishing boat. I supported the family."

"And sent Tom away."

"Yes." Richard swallowed fog and tasted its bitterness. "My father and Tom never got along. He was always threatening to throw Tom out. One day I got home late from unloading the *Mary-Hester* with my crew, came in, and found my father beating on Tommy. Blood everywhere. My father kept shouting that Tommy was a treacherous, oversexed bastard who couldn't keep his dick in his pants."

"But..." Nina frowned heavily as Richard struggled to lower his breathing again. "You said you sent Tom away when he was fourteen. Why did your father think...?"

"Because he was stupid! Mentally screwed up. And Tommy did have a way with the girls. You know that. Little charmer. Who knows, maybe he *was* screwing one of the local girls. Not like that would be a surprise in a place like Mackie's Cove. Not a lot else for the kids to do, exactly, was there?"

"And that's when..."

"That's when I decided Tommy had to go away. That's right. 'Kicked him out of the house,' as they say around town."

"Not because you were jealous of him and Angie."

"He was fourteen!" Richard grabbed his hair with one hand and pulled, knowing even through his protests that now *he* was being stupid. Tommy at fourteen was enough of a little love devil he could have charmed anyone. Even Angie Neal.

"Did *you* love Angie?"

"No! No, wait. For three weeks, I might have. I told you about that. I was sixteen. I lost my virginity with her. Not hers, I might add. Mine. But still...okay. Big deal at the time. But after that... I lost a mother, my dad hit bottom, I started working on the boat thirteen hours a day and trying to hold everything together. And after Tommy left? Then it was just me and my da, who'd become basically useless and never fished anymore. The town turned against me. All I did was work and dream about getting *out* of here. That's it. No women in the picture. Nothing from here, at least. Angie included. So if I looked at her and she thought my intensity was somehow... If I danced and she took it as a promise..."

His hands were palm-up claws in the air in front of him. God. *Had* he led her on somehow?

"That wasn't my fault!"

Nina suddenly put a hand on his outstretched forearm, burning, thrilling, and hurting him all at once. Because now she knew. Like he did. That it *had* been Angie and little Tommy, and maybe... An even uglier thought occurred to him about why his father had been wailing on Tommy.

And, oh God, it all suddenly made such awful sense.

He pulled away from Nina and found himself clutching his chest. But not from the still-sore bullet wound. No, this hurt was inside him. The childhood he'd tried so hard abandon, yet obviously couldn't let go of. It was like the Gaelic sense of a fatal flaw. *Mo chreach!* Literally: My ruin! Somehow he and Tommy had taken too long to get out, and the forces that had ripped apart his family had fully settled on them. Richard had fought it by getting Tommy away, fought it when he'd left and plunged into fighting halfway around the world. But it still found Tommy down in Maryland. And it was once again chasing Richard and anyone close enough to him to get sucked in.

My doom. *Mo chreach!*

"It's all right, Richard." Nina again. "It's all right."

"No," he said raggedly. "It's not."

He couldn't even explain it in a way that would sound like anything other than a lame justification for splitting them up tomorrow.

"Richard..."

Or could he?

All light was gone from the ocean and the fog had rolled heavy around them like wet cotton batting. It smelled of salty tears and lonely nights. Just as it should.

He took a last deep breath of it. "I've got a song for you," he said. "Shall we go back up?"

~~~~

Back at the *ceilidh*, Nina felt the anticipation.

Everyone had moved inside Ninian's. Hot. Sweaty. Listening as intensely as Nina, because Richard said the song he was going to sing was one he'd written himself, not long after he'd left Cape Breton to join the navy.

He had center stage, sitting on a stool with a guitar like a classic troubadour. But as his fingers began picking out a repeating riff on the twelve-string, Nina swore it charged the room with magic. She could feel it shiver through her skin.

He opened his mouth to sing, mournfully like the night wind, but clear and true, with an accent like he'd never left this island at all.

When you're all alone on the ocean,
a fisherman and his crew,
every one of you knows that the people at home
are all counting on you.
And your mamma lied!
You're the poorest poor there is.
But you've got your pride!
It's beaten into your goddamn skin.
So you keep on working,
trying,
sweating,
dying.
God, you're a Cape Breton boy.

Friend's dad is killed in a mine shaft.
Blown up with his own damn fuse.
All he leaves behind is a messed-up mind

and the feeling that it's just no use.
And your mamma lied!
You're the poorest poor there is.
But you've got your pride!
It's beaten into your goddamn skin.
So you keep on working,
trying,
sweating,
dying.
God, you're a Cape Breton boy.

So you hug the beauty around you—
sea-bound coast, mountains, streams,
then you pack up each part,
store it deep in your heart.
You'll remember it in your dreams.
Cause your mamma lied!
You're the poorest poor there is.
But you've got your pride!
It's beaten into your god-damn skin!
So you keep on working,
trying,
sweating,
dying.
Anywhere in the world...
God, you're *still* a Cape Breton boy.

When Richard finished, there was a long moment of silence. Nina's own mouth was dry and her heart hammered hot in her throat. He was telling her something. Talking to *her.*

She took a shuddering gasp of air and realized she'd been holding her breath. But she didn't feel foolish about it, because at that moment the rest of the crowd also seemed to come to its senses and broke into raucous applause.

She looked around at them all, clapping and stomping their feet. Didn't they hear the pain in the song? Or were they responding because they *did*? Because they understood it at a bone-deep level that she was just scratching the surface of?

She looked back to Richard and found him staring at her, those burning eyes demanding something from her. What? Recognition? Understanding?

She nodded to him, shaken. Because all at once she *did* understand. Apart from anything else the song was saying, it was a goodbye. To her. Maybe to Janine as well.

And she wanted to run up to him and scream *No!* She'd been thinking that way, too, but *No!* Because just like she'd veered in and out of honesty with him—exposing herself on the boat, but only one part of herself, playing games—he was starting to let her see who *he* really was. That was more important than he could possibly know to someone raised in the school of how to put on a good public face.

She screwed up her courage and walked forward.

But Richard, who'd just returned the borrowed guitar to a band member and hopped off the riser, was suddenly tackled face-to-chest by Cape Breton's red-haired answer to Marilyn Monroe. Angie! She dragged herself more upright by his arms, grabbed his face with both hands, and planted a convincing smooch right on his kisser.

Nina stumbled to a halt. She felt faint.

So did Richard, from the look of it. When Angie released him, he took a shaky step backwards and almost tripped against the riser, knocking over the mike stand Liam Kilin had replanted there. Richard stumbled up onto the stage. Angie went after him.

The crowd surged forward around Nina for a better view.

Oh, Richard, no...

"Quite a party you throw here, Ms. Tauredaux," said a mocking voice by her elbow and she turned to see the handsome, grizzled face of man she mostly knew from CD covers. He wore dark glasses, though the Ninian's interior wasn't that bright. No one else seemed to have spotted him.

"Mr. MacIsaac. You came."

"And by the looks of things, it's absolutely the last thing on your mind, right?"

"Pretty much."

"Yer boyfriend."

"No. Maybe?"

"Good looking." He gave her a large wink.

She blushed and knew she should be doing more as the official *ceilidh* organizer, welcoming the fiddling superstar, thanking him for dropping by, asking him if he'd play for them later on.

But it was all meaningless beside Angie kissing Richard. Him responding.

Was he responding? *Had* he responded? Was this somehow about him deciding they were going to leave? That everything was over? It was wrong. So wrong.

"Go on," said the fiddler. "Deal with him. I'm just here to have fun."

Nina nodded gratefully, touched his arm, then turned and began fighting her way to the stage where Richard was turning around and around to keep the circling Angie in front of him. The crowds had crowded right to riser, laughing and cheering. Shouts of "Again!" "Get 'im, Angie!"

With a grunt, Nina made the front, but someone suddenly grabbed her arm from behind. Doc Klein! "Let him sort it," he slurred.

"What?"

Doc's face was red, his eyes bloodshot, lips loose. He'd been drinking! Like he knew Richard was going to leave. That everything was coming apart again.

She tried to rip her arm free, but Doc held on fiercely.

Angie had meanwhile gone in for the kill and Richard was holding her back with both arms. She was almost wriggled out of her dress to get close to him. Her red face strained. "Come on, Richie," she said. "Just a little. All the times you wanted to. All the times I did. Come on, Cape Breton boy. I'm yours. You know I am. You know. You *know* I am. An' I'll prove it!"

"An-*gie!* An-*gie!*" the crowd began chanting.

"Come on, Richie!" She grabbed one of his hands and dragged it down to her breast.

"*Gahhh!*"

It was Dougan Smither, bursting out of the crowd onto the stage. He laid his hands on either side of her shoulders and ripped her backwards from Richard. She went stumbling backwards and might have hit her head except that Dougan never traveled alone. The big fat one of his buddies, Billy Cuddy, had suddenly stepped up and caught her. Held her. She tried to struggle up and began spitting out a string of expletives.

Dougan wasn't listening. His own face was red to bursting and now *he* was slapping at Richard's outstretched arms, spitting at him as he tried to get in closer.

"Dougan, don't do this," Richard said.

"Outside, you prick! You fish-sucking bastard!"

"You don't—"

"Out*side!*"

He took a lunging swing at Richard, who turned to catch it on his shoulder. But the other three stooges Nina had met that one time up on the hill were now up on the stage too. They were at his back and sides, reaching in to shove him as he held Dougan back.

Richard glanced at them, at all the others crowded near them in the tight space, and finally nodded. "Okay. Outside."

No! Nina saw some of the faces around her filled with fear, but most with a barely-concealed lust for blood. MacIsaac had faded back into a corner, grinning Cheshire-like at the whole affair. He caught Nina's eye and nodded her towards the side door.

But she could barely move in the crowd. Dougan's thugs had grabbed Richard's arms and quickstepped him to the door, the crowd parting to let them through. Then the crowd surged to follow, jamming up and shouting and shoving at the door.

Nina shook off Doc Klein's hand and the old man blinked and released like he'd forgotten she was there.

She cut to the right and managed to slip out the side door of Ninian's, running hard towards the front so she could maybe...

Too late.

A thick ring of people had already formed on the far side of the highway past the cars parked there. It was a big open space of scrub grass with a broken-down picket fence along the northern side, guarding a small miner's museum.

The ring hooted and shoved as Nina plunged in. It was mostly men and women from Mackie's Cove, but also outsiders she didn't recognize. Not that it mattered. Backlit by the pub and shadowed by the rising fog, they all looked like ghouls. Or zombies. Inhuman.

Except for Richard and Dougan in the middle of the ring. And the ugly set faces of Dougan's friends.

Richard was still playing peacemaker as Dougan circled him, fists clenched.

"Come on, Dougan. You don't want to fight me. Angie's yours. You know that. We all know that. This was just a blast from the past. Too much to drink. You can't get upset over too much to drink can you? Come on..."

And so intent was he on calming the red-faced Dougan that he didn't see Dougan's buddy—Rob? Andre?—slide behind him and step in to give him a shove forward.

Off-balance, Richard stumbled and caught a right-handed wallop with his mouth.

Nina screamed and clawed her way forwards. Got through! She ran at Dougan.

He spun, punched, and it was like her cheek had hit a metal post going full tilt. Nina's head snapped back and she staggered sideways, no one catching her as she fell face first.

Everything blurred.

Her ears too? For surely that roar, like something from a bull or lion, couldn't be happening here. She forced her hands under her and lifted her face from the dirt. Got her elbows under her and couldn't go further.

Throbbing face. Spinning world.

But as she blinked over and over and raised her head, and at last her eyes cleared enough to see Richard had not gone down like her. He'd gone deadly.

His left hand yanked Dougan Smither sideways to him while Richard's right foot blurred up into Dougan's bent-over torso again and again like some kind of machine piston. Nina could hear the air being kicked out of the younger man. *Oof! Oof! Oof!*

Then the man who'd shoved Richard at Dougan a few moments before ran at him from behind. Richard swung his elbow back and clopped the man's forehead. Like that—*Clop!* Bone on bone. The man staggered and Richard spun a snap kick to the man's gut that doubled him over. One more pile driver down across the opponent's face and the man collapsed.

Another stooge ran in. Richard turned and yelled as he drove two stiff punches into him—one in the face, one in the chest. *Thud. Thud.* The man dropped like a sack of rocks.

Dougan staggered upright to swing at Richard again and Richard drove a roaring hammer blow into his face with the sound of crunching bone. Blood spurted from Dougan's nose as he fell.

Richard pivoted then, hunched and slow, shaking blood from his hand and slurping it off his own lower lip. "Come on, Andre. You and Billy want some?"

But Andre Beaufort, the new guy who hadn't even known Richard in the old days, shook his head and backed away. Billy, holding a stunned-looking Angie Neal, didn't even shake his head. He just stared from the fallen Dougan to his other two crumpled friends, and back to Dougan.

Richard sucked up the blood from his lip again. Nina could almost taste it with him. Salty. Metallic. She smelled the bitter sweetness of it. Felt his joy of violence and *hurting.*

Then he turned to her.

And maybe she should have been horrified by the blood and violence. If she'd been Marie-Ange she would have fainted. If she'd been the weak or silly Nina from either boat ride with Richard, she would have blanched and gone sick.

But the woman Nina was starting to recognize as the real her rejoiced in Richard's victory. Because he'd fought back. Because he wasn't just giving in to the world like Nina's father had done. Like Tom had done. Like too many—

No!

There. Right there. Standing in the murky-lit mists directly behind Richard, was a face that shouldn't have been. Chunky and pudding-faced. Pock-marked skin. Glasses. Wearing a bad suit.

He'd approached her after Tom and Marie-Ange's funeral in DC, claiming to be FBI. But the F.B.I. had never heard of him. Then he'd freaked out at the sight of Major Castinges. Given her a business card. Disappeared.

Now he was here. Wearing different clothes and glasses. Hair done funny. But it was him.

Leonard Junk.

Nina felt her breathing stop as the man seemed to be avoiding her eyes. Then he looked back over his shoulder which, if you cleared out the crowd and mist, was a direct line to Angie's house, where Lili was babysitting Janine.

"Nina?" Richard stepped forward and crouched in front of her, obscuring her view

She swayed right on her elbows to see around him. Gone. Like a snake. A desperate snake in the dirt.

"Nina, I—"

She couldn't see him. He wasn't there. Gone. Gone after Janine. Gone to get guns. While Nina just lay here?

No. No-no-no-no-no-no-no...

Wrenching herself mostly free of her shock, she scrambled her knees and feet under her, leapt up and tried to speak, but found that any movement of her jaw sent pain like a stabbing knife through it. She desperately pushed Richard hard to the side, and *ran*.

~~~~

Oh, God. What had he done?

Richard hung his head as Nina ran from him. The horror on her face!

And when he looked up, her horror and loathing on everyone's face here.

He was no longer the returned Mackie's Cove son. He was other. He was evil. A Cape Breton boy, maybe forever. But he was no longer a Mackie's Cove boy, was he. Not after this. Maybe not since he'd left the first time, and all his efforts here had just the doom that—

"What—have—you—*done?*" said Doc Klein's angry voice to one side.

Richard rose tiredly to face him. Doc was obviously been drinking more heavily than Richard had noticed, and maybe got seriously into it while he was off with Nina. Because now he wove back and forth as he faced Richard in the midst of the frightened, dissolving circle. But his gaze, fixed on Richard, was fierce and focused.

"Richard, what have *done* here? Do you want to be your father? Strike out at everything around you? Destroy it. Destroy everything. Everyone. Where is Nina?"

"Gone. She ran off."

"Of course. Of course she has!"

"I need to go and find her." He turned.

"What are you thinking! Stop! These people you hurt. You must help them now."

Richard looked about him. Dougan was still breathing. So was Gord Keen. Richard stepped to Rob Dundas's side and toed him. The man groaned. "They'll live," he said coldly.

"Of course they will," Doc said. "But they need medical attention and I am not in any shape to do it." He held out a shaking hand.

"They'll live with or without medical attention, Doc. You know that. They're just a bunch of hoods who bit off more than they could chew. And, unlike me, they're true sons of this town. Let Mackie's Cove take care of its own."

Again he started to walk away. But this time Doc Klein staggered quickly forward to stand in front of him. "It's not *them* I'm concerned about, boy. It's you."

"Bleed for someone else, Doc. I'm a soldier. We kill and walk away all the time."

"But not *this* time. Not *here.*"

"Especially, here, Doc. This place has done nothing but spit on and kick me since I've been back. Since before I left, in fact." He threw his gaze out to crowd still dissolving into the fog plus the ones still hanging around watch the aftermath. "Isn't that right, people? I never had a chance here, did I? Me,

Nina, even Janine. You were going to kick us all out, weren't you? Or call the cops on us? Right?"

"No, Richie!" Angie wailed, bawling now, mascara running as she struggled again to free herself from Billy's hold.

"Richard..." said Doc.

He spun back to him. "Doc, don't push it. I appreciate what you've done for me, but bad stuff is following me around and I need to make it stop. I need to go to one of the two people here I have a real responsibility to. I need to make sure she's okay and then—"

"She won't love a man who just ignores another man's pain!"

Richard stopped. Not because he wanted Nina to love him, he told himself. Not entirely. But because, in that brief second, he saw himself all at once and with startling clarity through her eyes. And his own. He saw himself dragging Afghan wounded to safety during Taliban attacks, saving Abdul Adeeb's wife and daughter, trying to save Tommy for the last time. Doom and all. That was him. Warrior, yes. But not only that.

Whatever this fucked up town thought of him.

"Okay," he said quietly. "Hey!" he called out to the people still hanging around in the fog. "We need some help here! Have to get these three to the hospital at Inverness!"

Then he went and knelt beside Dougan Smither first.

Soothing Nina would just have to wait.

31

NINA'S HEART WAS RACING SO FAST she could feel her blood pound in her cheek and jaw where Dougan had punched her. It drove her feet faster and faster down the path to Angie Neal's house.

Forget the *ceilidh*. Forget Ashley MacIsaac, who must be wondering what sort of insanity infected the waters down here in Mackie's Cove.

The house suddenly loomed out of the fog before her, her and Richard's truck still parked beside it. Nina stumbled to a careful creep, circling it to see if Junk or others were already there.

Her heart still pounded. She had to save Janine. Save Lili too, for that matter. Had to get them both out of the house and take them...where? To safety! Which was where? With Richard! Oh, yes. She'd get them back to Ninian's, find Richard, then...then...drive out of town!

A clanking sound behind her made her spin around. Nothing there. Or was there? Visibility was ridiculous. She could see maybe ten feet. Dull lights gleamed through the fog from other houses. Even the music from the *ceilidh* had turned to nothing but murmurs and voices, the sound of cars pulling out and honking their way carefully down the highway.

But no sound from Angie's house. Did Junk even know where they were staying? Or had he gone up the hill for Doc's place first?

She snuck up the front door and opened it a crack. Heard the muted sound of the T.V. on in the living room.

"Lili," she whispered harshly, forcing herself to open her just enough. And again. "Lili!"

The T.V. shut off and the teen appeared, yawning like she'd been asleep, smiling, and checking the time. "You're early."

"Janine?"

"Upstairs. She was really good. She— What happened?"

Nina didn't answer. She was already halfway upstairs and down the narrow hall to the narrow room beside Nina's own. Stopped in the doorway. Janine was there, tucked under her puffy tick with her red curls around her face, snoring softly. It was the only sound, other than screaming and that one fit of giggles, Nina had ever heard her make.

"Ms. Tauredaux? You look scared. And your face..."

Nina touched her swelling cheek—*ouch!*—and looked back into the hallway where Lili stood nervously rubbing her thumbs and forefingers together.

"No one came in?" Nina said, speaking through the knife of pain jabbing in behind her teeth. "No one knocked on the door while I was gone? No faces at the window?"

"No." Lili's rubbing was harder now. She was scared. Well so was Nina. Despite the pain, she was starting to babble and couldn't stop herself.

"Okay. Help me gather up a change of clothes for Janine and put it in the truck. Then Janine. I'll drive you back to your parent's house. *Carefully*, because there's no shoulder strap except for the driver. No accidents. Everyone safe, okay?"

"I...I can walk."

"No!" Nina took a deep breath and forced herself calm. "Just...do as I ask, Lili, and everything will be all right."

But she didn't believe it any more than Lili, as the babysitter hurried to scoop up Janine's day clothes. That face she'd seen... It wasn't the fog or her being punched. Nina knew what she'd seen.

Tired of waiting for Lili, she scooped up Janine and ran for the stairs.

~~~~

Richard was nowhere in sight when Nina pulled up out front of Ninian's.

People still ghosted in and out of the fog on the field across from the building, but the *ceilidh* was obviously over. The cars had been cleared from that side of the roadway and Nina saw Doc Klein leaning over one of the thugs Richard knocked down. The rest of the crowd still seemed in slow dispersal mode. Cars pulled out and crept off. Junk could have been in any of them. He could be hiding just inside the lit doors of Ninian's. He could be leading in an attack group right now.

Or Richard had seen Junk and run! Or Junk had already killed him!

Heart thudding, Nina double-parked and left Janine and Lili in the tuck. "Wait right here!" she ordered. Then she jumped out and ran towards Doc. Whatever it was, she had to know.

Before she was within ten feet, though, Richard's cat-like form slid out of the fog on the hill side of the field and loped towards Doc, each arm carrying a large doctor bag.

"Richard!" Nina called out and her voice cracked.

Richard dropped the bags beside Doc and looked up. She couldn't read his expression, but it wasn't joy. More like worry. Did he know? Could he know and not have come after her?

Then she decided she didn't care, because the swelling in her heart at seeing him alive was almost too much to bear. She abandoned all pretense of grace and ran at him, throwing her arms around his neck and driving him back a step.

"I thought you were gone!" she choked into his neck.

"I...was getting Doc's medical kits. We've called an ambulance. Dougan and the others..."

"Let 'em die! I mean, no. Of course not! But..."

Then she was kissing him, feeling him wince at the pain from his cut lip and not caring as her arms wrapped around his strength, and her lips and tongue pressed into his mouth, his warmth and caring, his *life.*

His arms finally wrapped around her body too, pulling her hard against him almost as if he'd been just as afraid for her, which actually—

She jerked herself back. "Junk!"

"What?"

"Leonard Junk! The guy in DC who claimed to be FBI but wasn't. He's here! I saw him! I got the truck and Janine's stuff. We have to get out of here!"

"Leonard Junk?"

"Come *on!*" She stepped back, pulling on his arm. He wasn't coming. He was staring intently at her. "You don't believe me?"

Richard lowered his eyes. "Nina, this has been a crazy night. Noise, lights, fog, fighting. Lots of people we don't know showed up. Lots of faces."

"I know what I saw."

He raised his eyes and met hers with that same burn she remembered from the first time they met. Only now it was familiar. Something she did not want to lose—either physically or by losing his respect.

"I know what I saw."

"Okay. We'll look for him...after the ambulance shows up and we get these boys bundled off the hospital."

"Can't Doc just...?"

"He can do the external soft tissue stuff, but I broke a few bones, Nina. Might have ruptured a kidney or two. And your own face..."

Still the stare, like he was expecting something again. Always expecting more of her somehow. And somehow, she kept finding it. "I'm fine, and they got what they deserved, Richard. But for all that, I'm glad you're helping them now. It's the right thing to do."

And strangely, saying that, seeing him smile in response, made everything seem suddenly all right again. It even made her question whether she really had seen Leonard Junk, because after all, nothing had happened. That was the reality. No one had attacked. And like Richard said, there'd been all that fog, she'd just been hit hard, there'd been all those people she didn't know...

He'd been looking down to his right, smiling. Now he looked back at her. "That kiss..."

"I know we said we wouldn't..."

"...was one damn fine kiss, woman. Makes me rethink everything I was going to talk with you about tonight."

Nina's breath came out in a rush. "I know. I know what you were going to say. We've failed in our mission here. Haven't found what Tom stole."

"Or even *what* he stole."

"Or why, or who, or just about anything. Total disaster there. And we failed to win over your hometown..."

"Which, to be fair, might have been an impossible task, given the things I've been discovering about my past."

"You mean Tommy."

"And my father, yes. You know, I'd always wondered about what sent him over the edge with Tommy that day. And I don't think it was just finding Tommy had been screwing Angie. I think it's the fact that, when he found that out, *he'd* been screwing her too. Right, Doc?"

Nina looked down at the same time as Richard to see Doc frozen over the boy he'd just finished bandaging up. There was no hiding the fact he'd heard everything she and Richard had said. And while Nina waited for an answer, she quickly looked around to see if Angie was still there. But she wasn't. She'd been taken inside somewhere, thank God.

"That was...a long time ago," Doc said, not looking up at them. But he painfully rose from his knees, picked up his bags, and staggered over to the next of Richard's victims. Nina and Richard followed, and stopped beside him when he knelt and began cleaning this next boy's wounds.

"It's her life, Doc," Richard said quietly. "Angie's. But how long did it keep going after I sent Tommy away?"

There was a long time of silence while Doc just worked on his patient, but finally he answered, "It ended then, I think. Your father tried over and over. Others in the town had to lock him up once or twice to keep him from bothering her."

"And what? Made a pact to never tell me about any of it?"

Nina could feel Richard's tension and pain. And she could hardly wrap her own head around it. How could such a small place close together like that against one of their own? Shut him out about what was happening with his own family? How could his own *family* have shut him out that way? And she'd thought DC politics were bad.

"Answer me, Doc," Richard snapped and kicked the dirt beside the old man. "Answer me!"

Doc finally gave a long sigh and stood with difficulty to face Nina and Richard. His eyes were bloodshot, but they were fully focused now. "They were all afraid of you, Richard. Afraid of what you would do. I was afraid. They are still afraid."

"That what? I'm going to kick their butts?"

Doc glanced behind him at the young man he'd just bandaged, Rob Dundas. And at the others. "What you did tonight will not have helped that."

Richard pursed his lips and looked away from Doc, but Nina knew he was doing the same thing she was—looking around at the Mackie's Cove people in the crowd, seeing them watching him, trying to figure out if the look in their eyes was disgust, fear, hatred, or all of the above.

Before they could share with each other what they saw, the sound of a siren cut through the night and the flashing light of an ambulance cut through the fog, rolling cautiously down the highway and pulling off onto the field with the milling people.

"If you will excuse me," Doc Klein said. "I have one last boy to attend to. Maybe you can direct the medics to the first two?"

He walked off without waiting for an answer, leaving Nina and Richard staring after him. Then Nina felt a shift in Richard, an exhalation that told her he would once more do what needed to be done, however much he might want to hide or just take off.

"Oh my gosh," Nina said. "Lili and Janine! I'm parked over there, in front of Ninian's. I have to take care of Lili, and... You really think I was wrong about Leonard Junk?"

He nodded and forced a smile. Just for her, she knew. Not for anything else here. "I think after tonight, someone here is going to talk and we'll have about a day to get out of here. But I don't think anyone south of the border has found us yet, no. If they had, they'd have already used all the confusion here and our separation this last half hour to attack. I would have."

"Okay, then." She hesitated, rocking towards him and away.

"You need to get going." He also wasn't moving.

Finally she stepped in quickly and kissed him, lingering after it with her lips barely an inch from his. "I think I love you," she breathed.

Then she quickly turned and darted back to the car before he could say anything to ruin it.

~~~~

Leonard Junk, formerly 2nd Lieutenant Junk of the 3rd Infantry Division during Operation Desert Storm, now a cryptographics specialist with the NSA and supposedly moonlighting as a serf to former army buddy Misha Castinages, raised a bottle of Alexander Keith's Premium Lager and went for the deeper game. He clinked bottles with Herb Gunny, Robert "Crumpet" Davies, and Jovie McAlister.

"Well, he scared the shit out of *me*," Junk said before taking a swig which was in fact ninety percent blocked with his tongue.

"An' you don't know the why of you should," burbled McAlister, nodding his bald head. "I mean you should don't...you...why scared."

The other three men squinted at him over the upturned packing crate in the back of Davies's bakery. The yeasty smell of day-old baking gave a flat backdrop to the beer and hard liquor they'd brought over from Saint Ninian's Pub, but obviously didn't help cut the effects. All but Junk were well past anything resembling sobriety.

Junk banged on the crate to wake them up. "*Why?*"

McAlister spilled sideways out of his chair and Gunny jumped, but Davies poked a fat finger back at Junk. "Yer not from here!"

"Right!" said Gunny.

"Tha'ss right!" said McAlister. "My wife, she hates you people!"

"But I know things!" Junk insisted, careful to slur a bit. "My cousin, wife drove him home, 's from the States. Recognized that girl with him. That Nina

Tore-ee-doh. Big shot. On the news all the time. You know who she is?"

"Who?"

"Who?"

"Wha—?"

"Well I won' tell you!" Junk thunked his still-full beer bottle onto the crate. "You guys don' truss me. I don' truss you."

"Well I don' tuss you...either," said McAlister.

"Oh, if you knew though..." Junk said.

"Well Mother Mary full of piss," moaned Gunny, and waved his skinny arms over his head. "*I'll* tell him then."

"No, me," said Davies.

"The whole thing," said Gunny. "About his mother. Everything."

"Go ahead!" said Davies.

"Yeah. Everthing!" said McAlister.

So Gunny grabbed the edge of the upturned crate and began to talk.

32

AWKWARD. Wasn't that the catch phrase of the decade?
Usually used when one person of a couple feels something radically different than the other person in the couple.

Except this time, thought Richard as he helped Doc collect his dishes from Ninian's to walk home, it wasn't that he felt something a lot different than what Nina had expressed. It was just that he didn't believe her. There was something a bit...slippery in Nina's emotional makeup. And the circumstances they were in, the sort of things she'd just seen him do and learned about his past, were all a little too much and too sudden even for him.

He didn't trust her response to it.

Especially walking around in the midst of so much mistrust. Doc called it fear, but it didn't look that way. Every woman he passed both in and out of Ninian's, drunk or sober, drew back like he stank. Every man nearly snarled at him, would have bristled if they'd had visible fur down their backs.

And while he was tempted to call some of them on it, like the men he'd played with as a kid or their mothers, he ultimately kept his mouth closed and just walked out of Ninian's with Doc. He used his flashlight to see the old man home, then returned to Ninian's in the foggy darkness, moving stealthily and covering the entire length of the town on the other side of the highway from it.

He believed what he'd said about no one from Washington showing up in Mackie's Cove before tomorrow afternoon at the earliest, but it didn't hurt to scout. And there was just enough craziness tonight already that it couldn't hurt to get a sense of any other mischief afoot as well.

He slipped across the road and began ducking from shadow to shadow.

~~~~

Janine lay curled up and shivering in her bed.

Auntie Nina was scary tonight. First dashing around and carrying her out of here. Telling her and Lili to be quiet and *Stay here!* Just like Uncle Richard had done before... Before...

Then coming back to the truck like all smiley and talky-talky. Happy and giggly, but nervous too, kind of.

Then mad like bees when they got back here and saw Angie.

But maybe that was cause Angie was drunken. Real bad. Angie's face was all smeary and she kept wiping her nose and crying. And Auntie Nina just said get out of the way and took Janine upstairs and put her back to bed.

But Janine couldn't sleep. Not when so much was going on. Janine didn't know what, but there was this kind of tight feeling in the air she remembered from when she was running and hiding with Uncle Richard. But Uncle Richard usually slept beside her and sang to her when she was scared. And Auntie Nina didn't. And...and Janine was scared now.

Throwing back her covers, she slipped out of bed, opened the door as quiet as she could, and crept to the top of the stairs to listen to what Angie and Auntie Nina were talking about.

~~~~

The phone rang and Nina, still dressed in her summer dress and running shoes and sitting in a kitchen chair with a half-drunk cup of lukewarm tea before her, looked over at the counter where Angie was leaning. Leaning, crying, sniffling, making excuses, rambling, lapsing into a stuporous silence.

"You want to take this one?" Nina said.

Angie looked blearily at her, nodded as the phone rang again, and took it off its wall cradle. She listened then held it towards Nina. After a brief hesitation, Nina reached out and took it.

"What?" she said into the phone.

The voice that came back was male, throaty and slurred. "Slut. Yer a honkin great slut."

"Well you're a pucker-mouth asshole," Nina said and handed the phone back to Angie, who hung it up. "I love the irony here."

"What's ir'ny?" Angie said miserably.

"How many phone calls is that now? How many different people? And they can't come up with any variety?"

"What's ir-o-ny?"

Nina stared hard at Angie. "That they're calling *me* slut."

Angie stared back at her, finally got it, took a great phlegmy sniff, and dissolved into tears again. "It weren't like that. Never like that. Never in a million years of Sundays, either with Tommy or Strachan. Just...just...so unfair to me you're being. That you're all being. No one knows what we were to each other. No one—"

"Shut up!"

Angie's head jerked up and she sloppily wiped at her tears. "In my own home you're telling me—"

"Just shut up, Angie," Nina said again and got out of her chair, pacing to the window, then the back door, looking out into the night for Richard, dying inside over the fact that she'd told him she *loved* him and he wasn't here. He hadn't come to her. Why hadn't he come?

"You know it was Richard who started it," Angie said, sucking her chin into her chest with a great hurt expression.

"Tonight? Or are you talking about when he was sixteen years old and you 'made him into a man?'" She put all the sarcasm she could stuff into that last expression and it still rankled her more than it possibly could Angie. "Don't even answer that."

One-fifteen a.m. Where *was* he?

Out of patience finally, she strode to the phone. She was just going to call him at Doc's and find out. But the phone rang even as she reached for it. She picked it up.

Drawling male voice she vaguely recognized. "Just get out of town you—"

"Fuck off!" she said and hung up.

"If you want me to," said a voice from outside their locked door.

"Richard!"

Nina ran to the door and threw it open. She could feel the blood rushing to her face, her heart beating over one-eighty. Her hands actually tingled. And when he looked up, changed into all-black clothes like some kind of ninja, his lip cleaned off, his eyes sparkling in the light from the kitchen, he smiled and Nina could have fainted dead away.

But that wasn't her, obviously. So instead she forced a stern expression on her face and said, "So where've you been?"

He held a finger to his lips. "Scouting around. Looking for your mysterious Junk man."

"And?"

"Nothing. And if he'd really been there last night, I'm sure we would have seen something by now—Castinages, law enforcement, something. There's nothing. But the town itself... I've never seen it this riled up, even after I shipped Tommy out. Something's...happened out there. I've been trying to figure out if it's dangerous."

"There's phone calls. Obscene. Mostly calling me a slut."

"Calling *you* a slut?"

"That's what I said."

"Makes no sense."

"They saw me kiss you."

It jerked his gaze back to hers. "Yes. About that... Can I come in?"

Nina was hit by a sudden fit of insecurity, and blurted, "First..." She reached forward and grabbed his face with both hands. Then she drew him forward and met his lips with hers in a kiss. This time she made it slow and sensuous, brushing her lips over his first, moistening them with a full-on pressure, pulling back, then going in again, parting his lips with hers and finding his tongue.

And as he responded in kind, she could feel the shiver run from her neck all the way down her spine, so strong it shook her knees and his arms went out to steady her.

"Now," she breathed, pulling back. "Come in."

He did, immediately saw the tear-streaked Angie leaning back against the kitchen counter with her arms folded over her chest, and seemed to have a minor coughing fit. "A-Angie! I thought you'd be in bed."

"Why?" Angie said. "So she could have you all ter herself? You don't think you need to think about the little one?"

Angie nodded to the stairs through the door to the right and Nina turned with Richard to see Janine, thumb in her mouth like a baby, Snuffles under that arm, staring at them both with wide eyes. She suddenly ran forward and wrapped her arms around Richard's leg. Then Nina's leg. Then Richard's.

The phone rang.

Richard held up a hand, detached Janine from his leg, and strode over to pick it up. He held it tight to his ear, his face in tight concentration, holding it past when Nina was sure the caller had spewed whatever it was they were going to spew.

Then he said, "Bernie Tavish? Does Flo know what you're doing?"

A grim smile flitted across his face and he hung up. "There's one who won't be calling back."

"But how many people are there in this town?" Nina said.

Richard looked down. "Good point." He went over to the phone and disconnected it. Then he turned back to Nina and Janine. "Now why don't you two go up and get some sleep. I'm going to stay down here tonight just in case." He winked at Janine. "Scare off any bogeymen."

As Nina's heart sank, Angie looked from her to Richard and grinned suddenly. "Ha!"

Richard cut her smile in half with a look Nina hoped never came her way. "Go clean yourself up and get to bed, Angie. Sleep it off. We'll talk in the morning."

Chastened and still obviously inebriated, Angie bit her lips and nodded, shuffling past Nina and upstairs, stumbling on the steps as she climbed.

"We've got to run again tomorrow, don't we," said Nina.

"Yes," said Richard. "But together."

"That's a start."

~~~~

Leonard Junk watched Bernie Tavish come stumbling, red-faced back to the living room where Junk and Bernie's wife sat in the darkness. Junk had insisted they kill the lights when he thought he'd seen Mackenzie's dark form sliding around between the houses north of them.

"He knows," Bernie said, collapsing on the couch beside Flo. "He was there. He knows it were me." He looked with wide eyes at Junk. "D'you think he'll come after me now?"

Junk pushed up his glasses. "I don't think he needs to. I think he's so sure he's going to ruin you all that he doesn't want to do anything to threaten that. *She* would have told him that. She knows how to do the maximum hurt."

"To think," said Flow with her hands to her mouth, "I let her come into my living room with that child. She sat right where you're sitting. Lying to my face."

"You're good people, Flo, you and Bernie. It's why I had to warn you all about this."

"An' God bless yer for it, Lenny. So you'll stay here tonight? Only got the couch."

Junk inclined his head. "Long's it's no trouble to you folks. I'm...probably not too good for the drive back to Port Hood tonight."

Both Tavishes laughed, got him his blanket and pillow, and finally bade him goodnight.

When all was quiet, he pulled out his cell phone, stepped outside to find clearing skies, and, after waving the phone around a bit, managed to get a one bar signal. Enough.

Dial. Click-click. Ring. Ring. Ring. Connect.

Denise d'Alvay's voice, whispering and breathing hard like she'd had to scramble for her phone and race it to somewhere private. "Better be absolute tit-puckering good news at this hour, Junk."

"I found him. Him and the girl and the girlfriend."

"Okay, that gets me hot. Where?"

"Little fishing village called Mackie's Cove on the west coast of Cape Breton Island."

"The package? Who knows?"

"No one around here, apparently. And I searched both places they're staying. Means they've got it hidden somewhere here. I've started some flushing moves to get them to go for it before they run."

"When?"

"Tomorrow morning, I think."

"Castinages?"

"You want me to bring him in right away?"

There was a pause as d'Alvay obviously considered. Junk pictured her sitting naked on a closed toilet lid, the bathroom door locked, Misha lying sprawled and fucked to total collapse on her bed just outside, oblivious to how the real game was played. Which was smart men like Junk figuring things out, making money deals on the side to the highest bidder, then delivering the real goods. Sexual slavery was for idiots. That's why Junk had gotten married ten years ago—so he'd never have to deal with sex again.

"Call him first thing tomorrow," d'Alvay said at last. "Much as I'm coming to respect your tracking skills, Leonard..."

"It's Misha with the muscles."

"And guns. And backup. Just don't let Mackenzie leave before you get there."

Junk smiled in the cold breeze off the ocean. "Oh, I think I can arrange a few things to slow them up."

33

Nina woke up with her body zinging, but it took her a few seconds of watching the sunbeams dance dust motes towards her wall to remember why. She threw off her covers. She'd slept in! She couldn't believe she'd slept in!

She ran downstairs in her light nightgown to find Richard sipping a cup of coffee as he stared out the kitchen window. Janine had already finished a bowl of cereal and was down on the floor with a puzzle that one of the Mackie's Cove mothers had brought over earlier that week. Angie was nowhere to be seen.

Richard turned when he heard Nina and his eyes raked over her in such a carnal way that she hung in the doorway of the kitchen feeling stark naked and excited.

"Morning," he said.

"Did you sleep?"

He shook his head and rubbed the stubble on his chin. Just that movement, the bend of his arm, the shift of his strong shoulders, sent a thrum of anticipation through her body.

"I did think about sneaking upstairs to wake you up," he said.

Nina blushed furiously and shivered. "Why didn't you?"

"Things to do first."

First, she noted he said. "Like what?"

"Billy Cuddy came by early, quietly. Told me Dougan wanted to see me up in the hospital in Inverness."

Nina's hand instinctively reached for her bruised right cheek. It had already started turning yellow and orange last night before bed. "So what?"

"He said it's about what's happened after he was knocked down last night. About what might happen today."

The sexual tension seemed to evaporate instantly. "You said we had to leave today."

"Before the town breaks on us, yeah. But if what Dougan's got relates to that, I have to know."

"How long?"

"Half hour drive, maybe. Half hour visit, depending. I should be back before eleven. If you could get yours and Janine's things all packed by the time I'm back..."

"I will."

"Also..." He looked down, then out the kitchen window again. "I'd stay close to the house today. Maybe even inside. I'd attribute most of what happened last night to the drinking and the fight. People got excited. This morning they'll have slept it off. But I don't trust them anymore. So play it safe, okay?"

A part of Nina automatically flared up at the chauvinism. Despite the voices on the phone last night. Despite the face they couldn't trust everyone in town to cover for them anymore. Because a part of this town was still the people who'd loaned things to her for the *ceilidh*, who'd trusted her promise to return them when it was over. And even if they had shown themselves of weak character, Nina wasn't. She'd promised.

"I'll stay close," she lied.

He nodded, set down the coffee cup and started towards her, his eyes again taking in her entire form through her nightgown and Nina's whole body again shivering in anticipation.

But then he stopped and swayed a bit, obviously struggling.

"Oh, come on," Nina said. "Just a kiss."

"I...couldn't stop there. Not anymore. And seeing Dougan's important. Urgent, even."

Nina's own breath was suddenly so high in her chest she could hardly breathe. "Then you'd better go immediately, Lieutenant Mackenzie, or I'm not going to let you."

"I will."

"And this is just a rain check."

"Oh yeah."

He turned and almost ran out the door.

~~~~

Inverness
Cape Breton Island

Damn but the air was clear this morning, Richard thought as he drove north. The last of the fog along the shoreline was burning off. The air was crystal. Fresh. Yes, there was a rising chop of ocean waves further out and dark clouds well over to the east, but for this moment, this trip north to Inverness, the world was perfect.

Then he arrived at the town, the hospital. He parked and hurried inside.

And even here things seemed extraordinary. He strode through new-smelling halls, on squeak-free linoleum, thinking how much Doc would have enjoyed working in a place like this. Not the hum of the latest CAT and MRI scanners you'd get in a big city hospital, but all a hundred years ahead of anything in Mackie's Cove or most of the Island.

The front desk had told him Room 84. He slowed as he approached it, mentally rechecking that he was right in his soul about what he'd done. Excessive force? Perhaps. But Dougan had started it and his friends had played dirty.

And Nina said it was right.

That shouldn't really have made a difference, but somehow it made all the difference in the world.

He entered to see Dougan Smither, the room's sole occupant, lying in a bed with his entire torso wrapped in a cast. Both of his eyes were a puffy purple. Bandages wrapped around his head, clumping like a tent over his nose. As Richard walked in, Smither was drinking in little gaspy sips from a straw attached to a clear plastic canister of ice water that he held daintily beside his torso cast. The long-faced man looked frail and shriveled, all the bluster and fight sucked out of him.

Rather than recoil at the sight of Richard, though, his bruised face split in a wide grin that showed a blackened tooth.

"Um...Dougan," Richard said, halting a good four feet from the bed and nodding.

Smither just kept on grinning. "Nina's back at Angie's?"

"Yes."

Smither tried to nod, then winced and thought better of it. "I worried, you know," he said.

"About what?"

"You and Angie, eh?"

"There's nothing between Angie and me."

"Yeah. I know that now. After the fight."

What? Richard had literally kicked some sense into him? "How do you know?"

Dougan sipped his water and grinned again. "The *reason* you fought, eh? Wouldn't fight. Wouldn't fight. I punch her"—he mimed it weakly—"and you suddenly go all...*Ha! Hee! Hai!* And Billy told me about the kiss afterwards too, eh."

It took a beat before Richard absorbed it all. "Hunh," he said, met Dougan's eyes, and nodded.

Dougan rested his canister of ice water against his torso cast and stuck out his right hand towards Richard. Richard walked forward and took it. The two men of Mackie's Cove shook.

And that, apparently, was that. Except it wasn't really why Richard had come.

"The other guys?" Richard asked. "Billy? Gord? Rob? And who was it... Andre?"

"I don't know," Smither said. "Gord's out, I think. Rob's down the hall. Mostly scrapes and bruises. They teach you all them moves in the Navy, eh?"

"Some there. Some in other training."

"Jesus. Pay good?"

"Decent."

"Think they'd take me?"

Richard regarded him long and hard until Smither smiled. "Yeah. Angie." He looked at the ceiling. "Angie'd go with me, now her ma's passed on, you think?"

"Maybe. Dougan, what was it you wanted to tell me about what's happening in Mackie's Cove?"

"Right." He dropped his gaze but still didn't meet Richard's eyes. "It's something that happened last night. Everyone suddenly finding out you knew, eh? That you'd found out somehow. Only I know you didn't, cause... Well, it's about your mother."

Richard tensed. "My mother?"

"She was... Well you know that me and Billy, Rob, Gord—we all loved your mother when we was kids."

"So?"

"An' when your da had that string of bad luck when you was seventeen..."

"You mean gambling away all our catch money down in Maine."

Dougan ducked his head. "Yeah. And then he was getting drunk so much, you finally did a big catch and run it south yerself. Cold snap. You remember?"

Back at Mackie's Cove, Richard comes off the boat feeling good. His hands and face are frozen, but he's paid the crew off just like a real man, and still brought home money in his pockets. But when he gets to the house, something's wrong. It's so quiet. His da is in one chair, staring at the wall. Tommy's in another, staring at the floor. And in this house that's still lantern lit, no lanterns are on. Only one candle guttering like they've been too scared to light more. And where's his mother?

"I remember," Richard said.

"An' they told you your ma went out walking and slipped into the water, didn't they. That's how she caught pneumonia and died."

"What *happened*, Dougan?" Richard's guts were twisting. After last night he hadn't thought there could be any more family secrets. He thought he'd heard the worst he could hear. He'd obviously been wrong.

Dougan took another sip of water then put his head back on his pillow hard and closed his eyes like he was reliving it. "I was ten, yer brother just thirteen. And your da was a big man, you know. Even drunk. An' I don't know exactly why or how, but he kicked your mother out of the house one night when you was gone down south. Cold night."

"But—"

"Thing was, I think everyone around was scareder of your father than they even are of you now. He was meaner. Especially drunk."

It hit Richard with such stunning, obvious clarity that he couldn't understand why he'd never thought it before. Never imagined. "He locked her out and no one else let her in," he said slowly.

Dougan nodded and Richard saw his eyes were open, red and leaking, even though Richard couldn't bring himself to feel anything. Not yet. Not until he heard it all.

"She pounded on me own father's door," Dougan said. "We didn't let her in. She went from door to door because she was just in her nightie, with no shoes, and the wind was howling something fierce. I could hear her gasping over it. Like evil spirits coming in."

"What about Clive? Doc?"

Dougan shook his head. "Clive weren't moved to town yet. I don't think your ma ever made it up the hill to Doc's. Tommy and a few of us found her shivering and blue under a boat by the shore the next morning. Took her in when your da went out. But she was bad off, like. Just got worse after. An' when she died, everyone in town met up about it. An' we all swore each other t' secrecy. Even Tommy, though he were crying hard. Cause we knew you was coming home. An' we thought you'd kill your da. Maybe kill a few of us too."

The silence in that room. The absolute silence in the house. "Ma?" Richard calls out. And no one answers. No one.

"You killed her then," Richard said at last. "The whole town."

"Y-yes," Dougan snuffled.

"And *you*," said a sudden voice at the door behind him, "found out about it, Richard Mackenzie, didn't you. It's why you finally came back to Mackie's Cove."

Richard whirled to see a pudding-faced man in glasses gazing at him with a pompous little smile. Richard had seen him before. And had Nina's description. This was Leonard Junk, affiliation unknown. He had a .44 Magnum raised and pointed at Richard's chest. Impossible to miss at this range.

"What are you talking about?" Richard said.

"He's been telling everyone you're back here to gather evidence," said Dougan miserably from his bed, "of what the town did. Going t' bring us all to trial for murder or some such. Or sue us out of all our homes."

"That's insane!" Richard said.

"Then why," said Leonard Junk calmly, "have you hired one of the brightest, best connected, *cruelest* trial lawyers of America to come up here with you to help you build your case?"

"A trial lawyer...?"

"Seen her on all the best talk shows. That's what I've shared with everyone. Told them about the way she's taken on towns like this before and ruined them, shut them down, driven everyone out for the sins of their past."

"You bastard," Richard said as he finally saw where the lies were leading.

"I think they now hate Nina almost as much as they hate you, Richard. And here you've left her all alone, smack in the middle of them."

34

Mackie's Cove
Cape Breton Island

ANOTHER BEAUTIFUL DAY IN PARADISE, Nina thought as she took Janine's hand and stepped out Angie's front door. Too bad about the snakes.

And too bad they had to move on, as well. Because in the short time she'd been here, she realized, Nina had truly grown to love the ocean freshness of the air, the way it was always blowing, the way it carried the constant background surf of the sea, the occasional cry of a gull.

It was a little cool today for her summer dress, but she'd wanted to look her best. Put together, like nothing the town had done to her last night could shake her.

Janine tugged on her hand and pointed down towards the ocean where the ground shoreline was still vaguely steaming. They'd been to the beach there a few times this week. Janine loved looking for shells among the stones.

"Maybe later if there's time, sweetie," Nina said. "Duty first."

So saying, she set off with Janine for Ninian's. But every person she met en route...

She stuck her head into Jovie and June's general store to ask if they'd seen Angie this morning and got "We're just closing," from June at the front counter. Jovie, over by the dairy fridge, busied himself with some sort of inventory count and wouldn't look at her.

"It's Saturday. Nine a.m.," Nina said.

"An' you're wondering if we're losing money, is that it?" June snapped.

"I'm...just trying to be neighborly."

"Don't make me laugh, you. We're not dumb as you think."

"Is there something I said?"

"Go on!"

"The fact I kissed Richard? I'm dangerous by association? You know it was Dougan who attacked *him*. Three to one."

"An' the three's all in hospital, them."

Jovie finished at the dairy fridge and stepped over in front of Nina, and she could see from his bloodshot eyes how hung over he was. Before she could joke about it, though, he said. "Take Janine and go, Nina." Hard and cold.

"Your voice," Nina said. "You wouldn't have called me at Angie's last night, would you, Jovie?"

He didn't answer, but the twitch in his eyes made a hard lump of ice drop straight through her chest. "Oh," she said. "Oh, I can't believe it."

She turned and pulled Janine out of the store as quickly as she could walk.

At Ninian's, Angus-the-bartender finally came down from his apartment above the bar to open the door for her so she could collect the *ceilidh* decorations she'd promised to return. Angus was even gruffer than Jovie had been.

And when Nina returned the fancy lace tablecloth to Helena May and the box of crackey's teeth to Mr. Higgins, both simply took them and her thanks without a word and closed the door in her face.

Clive McGee, her one hope to explain why this town had gone suddenly crazy sour, wasn't home. Nina was sorely tempted to follow Richard's admonition and just go back to Angie's. She could go inside, lock the doors, pack their things, then maybe hide behind a couch until Richard returned.

So not.

With a defiant jerk of her chin, she decided to take Janine down to the docks for some beach play time, maybe find Clive there.

But Clive wasn't there. And the five men who were, off work from the packing plant and getting extra pay by mending nets and jawing together down on the main wharf, fell silent when they saw her and Janine coming.

"I'm looking for Clive McGee!" she called out and climbed onto the wharf. She even sank to flicking her hair back with her fingers, trying for the oh-so-effective innocence Marie-Ange had always managed.

The men looked away, working the nets spread over their laps like Nina wasn't there.

Janine ran up to the youngest of them, an older teen who looked vaguely familiar from the *ceilidh*—maybe he'd even danced with Janine there—and tugged on his sleeve.

Without looking he shook off her hand so roughly that Janine ran back to Nina with fear in her eyes.

Nina scooped her up and pursed her lips at the men. "You men, whatever you think's going on, should be ashamed of yourselves!"

She turned and stomped back towards the road up.

But for all her bravado, Nina was feeling the first real glimmers of fear. Because whatever had driven the Mackie's Cove men to make coarse phone calls to her last night wasn't gone. And it was more widespread than Nina had wanted to believe. As if the entire town as one had decided to turn against her.

Why?

Then even that didn't matter so much, because, by some unspoken signal, all the men from the docks suddenly dropped what they were doing and started to follow them.

Nina clutched Janine's hand tightly and walked faster, cutting off the side road to go up the steeper paths directly between the houses. She could feel her veins starting to course with adrenaline. Would these fishermen attack them? Surely not in broad daylight. Not in the middle of town.

"Oh my God," she breathed, and stopped dead.

Ahead, clustered around the front of Angie's house, with dark clouds far behind them in the distance, was a mob that looked like it included most of the rest of the town. They glared down at her as she started to walk again. Jovie and June, the Mortons, the lumpen Gwen Gill with her husband and daughter, Gord Keen and Rob Dundas, old Mr. Gallagher, Drew Boyle and his wife, Connor Irvine, Helena May... All of them her friends, she'd believed, welcoming her so completely just yesterday afternoon, trusting and supporting her.

Until the *ceilidh* fell apart and...what?

Angie came suddenly running around the side of the crowd, her face bloodshot but apologetic, not harsh. "I don't believe it," she told Nina fiercely. "What they're saying about you. But...let me take Janine, okay? Just to be safe?"

Safe? *Safe?* Nina's body full of adrenaline now—skin tight, narrow visual field, heart beating hard. "Take her," she whispered. To the rest of the mob she called out, "Just what is it you all think you're doing here?"

~~~~

"It's very simple," explained Junk where he sat in the rattling passenger seat of the truck, still aiming the gun. But Richard wasn't listening much. He was blasting them southward at nearly eight-five mph, along a highway made for sixty. The truck hummed and rattled like it was coming apart, engine whining high and scary.

"You see," said Junk louder, "I'm 'Deep Throat'. I was the one who got your brother into this."

Richard didn't take his eyes off the road, but snarled, "Bullshit."

"'I saw a flock of gulls today.' 'Better birds than bombs.'"

"Still bullshit. My brother's phone was tapped."

"Probably. But it's still true. Ask yourself why your good friend the Major isn't already here rounding up prisoners or just shooting you point-blank to wipe out an inconvenience."

"Because he hasn't found what Tom stole from them."

"Them?"

"Whoever the fuck it is you're working for."

There was a long silence while Richard took a few sharper turns in the road, the tires squealing as he refused to slow down. He was *not* going to be too late this time. Not this time.

"You were going to run again today, weren't you?" Junk said, adjusting his glasses with his free hand and wiping a thin line of sweat off his forehead.

"That why you did this? Spread lies to get the town to keep us here?"

"Let's just say it was leverage. More interesting than simply threatening you with a gun. It also ensured you didn't have any surprise allies."

"For what?"

Another left turn, with a car on it coming the other direction so he couldn't hug the inside. Richard cursed and took his foot off the brake to slow going in. Just past mid-turn, he jammed his foot down again to roar this rattling bucket into whatever speed she still had in her.

The swerve as he steered out of the turn a little fast, whipped Junk sideways into him and Richard was tempted to slam an elbow into the man's ear for good measure.

Instead, he repeated, "Leverage for what?"

"You've got the package your brother stole, or know where it is. I can save you and Nina from death by mob. I think we should trade."

"What about your masters?"

"Oh, I'll tell them where you are eventually. They'll show up and find you gone. What could I do?"

"Only one problem," said Richard.

"What's that?"

Richard suddenly slammed on the brakes so that his passenger, who had only a lap belt with no shoulder restraint, was thrown forward to crack his head against the dash. Both his glasses and his gun tumbled into the foot well.

Richard swerved to a complete halt at the side of the road, flung himself at the groggy, fumbling, Leonard Junk, and pinned him up against the inside passenger window of the truck. Then he frisked him from top to bottom. He scooped out a box of Winchester rounds from Junk's right jacket pocket. Hollow points. God*damn*. He put the box in the driver's side foot well. Junk's wallet was in his left rear pants pocket. Richard opened it to read Junk's NSA badge and wonder if it was real or a fake. Then, while Junk was still coming back from his bang, Richard reached down between his legs and retrieved the Magnum from where it had dropped. The gun wasn't as accurate as Richard's SIG, but the hollow points certainly gave it stopping power.

He checked. It was fully loaded. Six shots.

"This and you are going to go and save Nina now, you piece of bugshit."

Richard roared back onto the road and accelerated until the pickup truck was again wailing along the highway like a speared bull.

"And then what?" moaned Junk, reaching about for his glasses that Richard had left in the rattling foot well. "Major Castinages...unh...will be on the way. There's only...one or two roads out of here. How do you think you're going to escape?

"You said you haven't called them yet."

"I lied."

"Sure you did. Now shut up and pray Nina and Janine are still okay when we get there."

~~~~

Before anyone in the mob in front of the house answered Nina, she was suddenly shoved forward from behind.

The same young fisherboy who'd thrown off Janine earlier was sneering at her. His older companions stood on either side, as if challenging her to shove back. Nina looked from them to the crowd that now peeled back a little to surround her.

Helena May, a woman who lived with her parents and had taken some real convincing to come to the *ceilidh*, stepped forwards and said, "You know, I liked the fact you were tall."

"And that you didn't put on airs," said another woman Nina hadn't met. Standing behind Andre Beaufort. His wife? Girlfriend?

"And not that pretty!" belted out Gwen Gill. "S'why we figured you for okay. S'why I let my daughter talk to you. Why we all did."

Now Herb Gunny. "But you were faking us, eh? Using us and spying on us.!" He spat on the ground, dancing back from the spittle because it was dribbling down to his shoes.

"Faking?" Nina said. "I don't..."

"We know about you!" one of the younger men behind her said. "What you do."

"I'm an urban planner. So? I never hid the—"

"Liar!" Someone else. Nina didn't see who.

"And I'm the sister of Tom Mackenzie's wife!" Nina said. "Doesn't that count for—"

"Yer lying again!" someone spat. "Yer Richard's whore lawyer!"

"Bought and paid for!"

"Scum sucking bottom feeder!"

"Money pig!"

"Shyster!"

"Slut!"

"Can't believe he brought you here. Can't believe he thought we'd never find out. Like we was stupid. Like we was *trash* he could get talking while you was just taking down names and figuring out who owned what!"

That seemed to finally rev up the parts of the mob that had been holding back, so that Nina, with growing panic, saw that even old Mrs. Cumberland was nodding along with the comments that were getting ruder and coarser by the second. Building. Even as they closed the circle completely around her so that Nina had to start turning in circles to keep track of what was saying what, who might still be on her side.

Then something wet hit her on the temple and she looked up, thinking it might have been a seagull. A second glob of spittle hit her other temple, thicker, running down in chunks.

Nina blinked, not comprehending, not believing. She wiped her cheek and saw a row of people spitting now, jeering and spitting. It hit her on the chin and nose and forehead. Her eyes.

"God *damn* it!" she shouted, wiping her fingers through the spittle and flinging it back at them. "You all *stop* it! Whoever's told you this about me is *lying!*"

"Yer the liar," said the kid fisherman, suddenly behind her. He squeezed her ass through her dress.

"You little sonofabitch!" She spun around and slapped him across the face, then whipped up her hands before her like claws and bared her teeth at the rest. "Who's *teaching* him that? What bastard here has him as a son? What bitch? Come on! Come out here right now and face me! You? You? How about you!"

And for a second it seemed to stun them, drive them all back. But only for a moment. Then someone yelled, "You see? You *see?*" And someone reached in and shoved her from the side. She stumbled and another set of hands hit her on the small of her back. Then on the front. Rough hands squeezed her breasts as they shoved.

She yelled and struck out herself with a straight punch she'd learned in kickboxing. Felt it connect with a satisfying thud.

But then someone kicked her bare shins with hard boots. The pain! It felt like they'd peeled off half her leg! She staggered in a wave of sick and clutched her stomach. She was going to fall. Right here. Right now. And they'd be on top of her. They'd kick her. Break her.

She was going to fall...

A throaty roar and sound of skidding tires stopped her, made her plant her feet and stay up. Then a crack so loud it felt like the sky broke made the people around her peel back.

Then...oh God...Richard was there. He strode towards her through the parting crowd with a huge smoking revolver held up in front of him and the look of steel in his eyes that scorched anyone trying to get in his way.

"I'm...I'm sorry, Richard," Nina gasped. "I...should have..."

He reached her and ran a hand down one side of her spit-covered face, but didn't set down the gun. Instead he stepped in front of her, aimed the gun squarely at where Herb Gunny's was starting to sneer. Richard calmly half-pulled the trigger of the revolver so it made an audible click and Gunny froze.

"Now I understand that a bunch of you have been foolish enough to believe the lies of a man named Leonard Junk!" Richard said. He looked sideways over his shoulder, where Nina saw their truck on the road, both doors open, and Richard swore quietly. Junk was gone.

"*You* call them lies, asshole!" called a voice that Nina recognized as Gord Keen, one of the men Richard had thrashed the night before. Obviously not hard enough. He came pushing out through the mob now. "He told us you were Special Forces! Yer like a professional killer!"

"That's irrelevant!" Richard said, swinging the gun barrel towards him.

"It's true, though!" said Keen.

"And you let Tommy die!" wailed June McAlister. "I didn't want to believe it, but it's true, isn't it? You stood back and let them kill your own brother!"

"Not what happened!" said Richard.

"No?" jumped in Keen. "I say you were jealous of him! Y'already kicked him out of town! Beat up your da! Left town and never came back! Why should we believe *you*?"

The mob was shifting forward again, re-finding their ugly. Nina ducked her face towards one shoulder then the other, wiping desperately at the remaining spittle on her cheeks, forehead, nose, and neck. She couldn't let them get at her again. Couldn't. Couldn't.

"Yeah, Mackenzie!" someone shouted. "Kill Tommy, then come back here for the rest of us, eh? And you bring this lawyer slut right—"

Kee-rack! The honking big revolver, fired straight up.

As the crowd pulled back a little, Nina saw, through her shivering, that a bunch of other faces had arrived from the direction of the highway. Doc Klein, marching down with Clive McGee, the latter carrying a black shotgun. Billy Cuddy was helping Dougan Smither, then Rob Dundas, out of Cuddy's little Yaris and Dougan was calling out, "Leave him alone!" and trying to wave the crowd apart the way Richard had done.

It didn't work, but Richard didn't seem to care! And even through her dry-mouthed fear, Nina got it. It had to be just Richard. His stand. His showdown with the town.

"You want the truth?" he said. "Then let's talk about truth!"

He waved the gun out at the crowd. "I just learned from Dougan—*just now*—about what happened when my mother died! How's that for truth! Something every goddamn one of you here knew and didn't tell me! How's that! And if this woman *was* a lawyer and collecting evidence for a trial, then it would only be justice, wouldn't it! *Cibé a rachaidh timpeall, tiocfaidh sé timpeall freisin!* Whatever goes around, comes around!"

He spun back to Nina. "But this woman, she's not part of your Gaelic karma. She's only here, surprise surprise, for the reason she *said* she was here for—to protect her niece, who also happens to be *my* niece. And for that you spit on her, and kick and shove her. You are the biggest set of goddamned cowards."

Like her sister had called herself, Nina remembered. Like Nina, in so many ways had been, thought she'd left behind. Was again. This minute. Barely holding on.

Richard, glaring, had lowered the big revolver so it hung by his side.

"*You're* no peach, big man!" someone yelled from the crowd, careful not to show themself.

"Fine! Let's talk about me!" Richard actually put the gun down on the ground and opened his arms wide in front of him. Nina stepped shakily up to his side. She would support whatever he was about to do, even if the mob went crazy again and attacked.

"I had a drunk father," Richard said, "who basically killed my mother, with all of your help. Then he laid around all day, picking fights, scaring everyone. Then he somehow managed to screw my first girlfriend, only to find she was also screwing my baby brother. So he beat Tommy to a pulp and blamed me for it when I sent Tommy away to a boarding school. Made my life hell, as did all of you, until I finally got out too. That about cover it?"

Nina gasped that he'd said it so baldly and her hands shook harder. Heads turned in the crowd. Eyes shot towards the front of the Neal house where Angie still stood with her hands holding Janine's shoulders. The barmaid stuck out her chin.

"But do you know why?" hissed Rob Dundas, hopping forward like a runty toad. "You know *why* all of that happened, Richie?"

"Because this town is cursed."

"No. It's because *you* are. You and your 'Do the right thing' Boy Scout bullshit. Everyone around you feels like nothing. And everywhere you go, you got violence and stuff. Like this Junk guy." Dundas did a hopping circle, looking out over everyone in the mob. "You want to tell us why he did all this? Why he hates you so much?"

Richard suddenly shut his mouth Nina felt it ripple through his body.

"You cracked one of my ribs, Richie," Rob Dundas said, quieter now. "Coulda killed me. Dougan's all 'Let's accept him now', but that's only cause Dougan wants Angie back. I say you're a danger to this town. You fight someone now and they end up in the hospital. You wave around a gun. *You* bring in someone who's tricky enough to fool all of us. You accuse us all of killing your ma."

Nina saw the words roll through the mob in a wave, evoking equal parts fear, anger, and determination.

"So you're saying what, Rob? You want me to go?" Richard looked around at the rest of them. "You all want me to go?"

"Not just you, Richie," said Rob. "Her too. However she is. And the little girl."

Richard said nothing. Nina saw him look from face to face. When he made it to Doc and Clive McGee, with Dougan and Billy beside them, Doc shook his head definitely and pointed at the ground. *You stay!*

But then his head turned back to face the front of the Neal house, where Angie, red-faced but not backing down, still stood with Janine. Richard reached sideways to find Nina's hand. Held it lightly.

"We'll be out by mid-afternoon," he said.

"Back to DC?" Rob asked.

"Junk put you up to that question?" Richard said. "It's none of your business and never will be."

"Why not leave right now, then?" Rob said.

Right now? Nina began to quake harder so that her whole body shook. Right *now?* Running again like the had from DC to here? People after them? Right *now?*

~~~~

Richard felt Nina start to shake violently and instinctively understood. She was going into emotional shock. Like he himself was already there, he felt so black and empty inside.

He could take it. But if they started running right now, before he helped Nina through it, he feared he'd lose her for good. There was tempered strong and there was broken, and he couldn't chance Nina ending up on the wrong side of that.

And Janine?

His gaze flicked to the wide-eyed little girl standing on the doorstep beside Angie. Silent as always. Accusing? Loving? Needing? God, Richard couldn't even tell and he knew that made him a wretched surrogate parent.

But he was all she had right now. Like he was all Nina had.

Make the hard choice.

Releasing Nina's hand, Richard leaned down sideways and snatched up the big, silver six shooter. He aimed it point-blank at the still-combative face of Dundas.

"I've got things to do, Rob. Get the fuck out of my face."

As Dundas did, fading back in stumbles and steps, and the rest of the mob dissolved in all directions, he heard Nina release a shuddering breath so deep it almost turned into a sob. Then another. Another. And for a moment Richard worried she wouldn't be able to stop.

But then she visibly reached deep for the strength that Richard knew she had and managed to get a grip on it. Barely. He had to get her away from here for a time. Just the two of them. But Janine...

"Wh-what you have to do," Nina said. "Can I help?"

"Yes." God, it was hard to look at her. Her eyes had gone from their usual intensely *present* hazel, to a distant, unfocused glaze. "You and Janine both."

Without waiting for Nina to fully catch on, he stepped towards Doc Klein, Clive McGee, and Dougan and waved them close. Conferred. Then he walked to the robust, quivering form of Evangeline Neal.

"I told you, didn't I, Richie?" she said as he approached. "I says, 'When you find out, come talk to me. Get my side of it.'"

Richard just stared at her.

Then he dropped to his knees before his niece and the girl flung herself around his neck, hugging as tightly as her skinny arms would let her. And for just a second, that big empty lack inside him felt like it might not be as empty as he thought. He put his own arms around her too. Tiny, like children everywhere. But more. This one was Tommy's flesh and blood. This one was the one Richard had sworn to save. This one was the wide-eyed kid who still managed to make him laugh even though she'd refused to do it with words.

This was Janine.

Richard returned the hug more gently and murmured, "It's okay, precious. I want you to change into something warmer and grab some fresh clothes, okay? Maybe your whole suitcase. And Snuffles. We're going on a boat ride to a fancy place to wash up."

He stood and called back for Nina, essentially telling her the same thing. She gave him a look of blurry confusion, but didn't argue.

As Nina vanished upstairs behind Janine, Angie poked Richard on the shoulder and he turned to see her crossing her arms over her chest, her face red and streaked with tears.

"That's it, ain't it," she spat. "You're taking them and not coming back. Not telling them. Just leaving."

"That's right."

"And what about me?" She rocked forward at him, squeezing up her bosom, her plump face more strained than he'd ever seen, her face turning as red as her hair.

"You'll get by."

"Ha. I'll get by, he says. Thanks to you, I'll *rot* here. You and your promises, leading me on. Making me look after your woman. Look after your wee girl."

"Stop it."

Suddenly she was on him, grabbing him and pulling herself against him, soft and desperate. "You can't go, Richie! You can't leave me again! Not after all this! We belong together, you and me! You always said—"

Richard broke her grip with a grunt and pushed her back against the door, bringing his face close to her to speak low and intense. "I came back only because my brother sent me, Angie. That's it. And you... Forget my mother. Forget your lies. Did I ever tell you how long it took Tommy's kidneys to heal up after my father got through with him? Or how, after I got him settled in Montreal, he woke screaming at night, calling for me? How I kept feeling his blood on my hands and chest for years after?"

Her face blanched and she looked around at Doc and the rest watching her. Helena May, Gwen Gill, and some other women were still there too. They didn't even pretend to look away.

"You-you can't..."

"Hush!" Richard commanded. "I have a little girl and a woman now who've actually been treated worse than you, believe it or not. You will let me lead them gently out of here because you *owe* me that much. You—owe—me."

Then he stepped slowly back from her, leaving her still red-face and breathing hard. But she said nothing as he turned to Clive. "You sure you're okay with me taking the *Mary Hester*? And your shotgun?"

A snort. "'Course."

Doc stepped up to him. "I'm sorry it had to end like this, *mein freund*."

Richard looked down. "I swore when I left here to join the Armed Forces that I'd never come back, but I think I somehow knew I would. Just to get the truth. Which I did. So that's a good thing."

Doc nodded. Dougan, looking miserable, hadn't stepped forward.

"You're going to take care of them?" Doc said, nodding at the stairs as Janine came bouncing downstairs wearing a jacket Richard had picked up for her in Inverness the previous week, plus a canvas bag she'd found somewhere, stuffed with her clothes. And behind her, Nina, tentative, still a little dazed, but dressed now in old jeans and a plum turtleneck sweater she probably got from Angie. So beautiful. She and Janine made Richard's heart ache a hundred different ways.

"So!" she said with forced brightness when she saw him. That inner toughness again. "Where are we going?"

He smiled. "To Clive's, while I get my own stuff from Doc's. Then I take you both to a place where I never thought we'd go. I think you're finally ready."

She raised her eyebrows in question.

35

Just south of Chéticamp
Cape Breton Island

RICHARD, NINA, AND JANINE STOOD on the rear deck of the *Mary-Hester.* Clive's shotgun, was stowed out of sight under the dash in the wheelhouse and the *Mary-Hester* itself lay dead calm on a sea gone the color of hammered-out pewter.

It meant a big blow was coming, Richard knew. They needed to be finished here before then.

"It's a got a kick," he explained as he helped Nina raise the .44 Magnum up between her two hands, made her plant her feet shoulder-width apart, and sight down the long barrel. "Particularly if you've never fired a gun before. Have you?"

Nina shook her head dully, but when she raised her head, there was just a flicker of her old self returning in her eyes. And when they met his, for just a minute the black void in his heart where Mackie's Cove had once been didn't seem so empty. She trusted him. The hell she'd gone through back in Mackie's Cove had shaken her, made her lose herself a little, but she trusted him to lead her back. That was special.

And Janine reaching out to grab the leg of his jeans? That too. Near perftect.

"Okay," he went on. "If someone runs at you suddenly, you won't have time to react, even if they're thirty or forty feet away. Don't bother. Cut and run. But if you can get them in your sights *first*, make sure you brace yourself. Then breathe out and squeeze, don't jerk, the trigger. Try it."

He stood off to the side and let her aim across the water. Squeeze...
Blam!

The revolver kicked back and Nina yelped, almost dropping it. She turned to him with her nostrils flared, her eyes bright. Definitely coming back.

Richard just nodded back out to the ocean, and threw out one of the empty cans of Sprite he'd found under the seat of the truck. It splashed down maybe ten yards out. Then he took her revolver, ejected the spent cartridge and put in a fresh one.

"You've got six rounds. See if you can hit the can. I'll show you how to reload when you're done. Janine, you come with me."

They both did as asked, Janine following Richard went back to the cabin where he'd stored both Clive's shotgun and a 9 mm pistol he'd cadged off Doc. He considered briefly prepping her on all three weapons. Maybe even showing Janine the basics of the 9 mm. He smiled wryly down at the girl. Hm. Maybe that could wait a few years. Like...twenty.

But Nina had to know. If anything happened to Richard, it would be up to her to save herself and Janine.

He lifted Janine up onto the side counter in the wheelhouse and dragged over the map. "You want to see where we are right now?" he said.

She nodded, bright eyed. All an adventure to her. But she still made no sound.

After Nina's fifth *blam!*, she shrieked and Richard darted back outside, adrenaline racing. Nina was pumping the air with her right hand and whooping at the sky.

"I got it!" she crowed, her eyes streaming with tears. "Got the mother!"

Behind Richard, came a soft little, "Got it."

Richard whirled around to see Janine there, looking up at him seriously, and he couldn't help himself. "Did you say something?" he said.

She closed her mouth tighter than ever and shook her head. Had he just imagined it? He finally just nodded and turned back to Nina with a bubble in his chest. Janine speaking? Nina reclaiming her strength. If they could recover, damn it, he could too. Nina laughed roughly and pushed back her hair with her hands, as if she were conscious, suddenly, of not being fully clean. "You said we were going to clean up."

"There's a place just outside of Chéticamp," Richard said, "about twenty minutes north of here, where I stayed once. Decent bath, big towels. A woman and her pregnant daughter used to run the place. If they're both still there, the daughter's kid would be just about Janine's age now."

"And it's Sunday..."

"I'm hoping she might watch Janine while we clean up."

"'Clean up.' That's what we're going to call it?" Her voice shook a little. She understood the invitation.

But before turning back to the wheelhouse, Richard held out his hand for her gun, showed her how to release the barrel, eject the spent cartridges, and reload it. Then he handed it back.

"You're good. A natural. Keep practicing," he said. Then he turned to Janine, squatted down to her level and whispered, "You, too, sweetie. Talking is a *good* thing."

~~~~

Talking is a good thing.

That's what Uncle Richard said. But we don't believe him, do we, Snuffles. It's okay for him 'cause he's like sixty feet tall and can do anything. Even Auntie Nina—she shoots guns now. She looks wild and stronger than all those people who threw things at her.

And...and...together, they're like this extra bright thing. Like they spark when they touch, or something. Auntie goes all red. Uncle stops being worried.

It makes them stupid, though. Hunh? Like they forget bad guys are after us. They almost got Auntie Nina just like they got... They got...

C'mere, Snuffles.

Shhh.

~~~~

Riding the thumping roar of the open back deck with her gun hand high and her other hand holding Janine's, Nina wasn't sure if she was truly recovered from what had happened, but she did feel changed. And for the better, maybe. Like she'd been beaten, melted, and reforged. Like Rob Dundas said—you were around Richard long enough and you felt like nothing...*or you got stronger.*

Or maybe it was just that the sky had darkened and the wind had picked up. Though it wasn't yet noon, its chill ripped through her turtleneck sweater like she was naked. And every time she took a shot—every bit of debris on the ocean was a moving target—her nerves zinged. She almost bit her tongue twice. She got very good at firing without twitching at the recoil.

She stopped at last only because she was worried about using up too much ammunition.

When they made landfall at what looked like a private dock, Richard had her and Janine follow him up a pair of rickety wooden stairs. It mounted a rocky bluff to a wood-siding house that loomed out over the ocean with heavy eves and heavily-mullioned windows.

The rain started to fall and they ran for the front door. Knocked. On the second knock, the door opened to reveal a very wide, cross woman with dark, bluish hair that clung in small, tight curls to her scalp.

"*Qui m'achalle maintenant?* What are you? Why are you bother me?" she said, with pursed lips that demanded an answer.

"Madame, we need a room," Richard said with a smile. "*On a besoin d'un chambre.*"

Nina stared at him. Richard spoke French. Of course he did. What couldn't he do?

The woman's frown relaxed somewhat but she shook her head. "*Pas du chambre.* We have closing for de season."

"Just for the storm," Richard said, pointing back over his shoulder at the rain that was now coming down in sheets. Then he plunged into an earnest stream of French that, to Nina's ear, seemed a little cockeyed, squeezing off vowels and nasalizing words she thought she recognized from her own high-school studies.

But the old woman shot back with the same accent and Nina figured it had to be regional. The woman began gesticulating wildly and point around the yard, apparently demanding to know where their car was. Richard answered by pointing at the stairs down to the water and the woman insisted on hitching up her heavy corduroy pants and walking back there with him to see.

By the time they returned, both dripping wet in the rain, the old woman was laughing and patting Richard's arm, waving them both in.

"She remembers me now," Richard whispered as he passed. "Her daughter still lives with her but is on a trip to Halifax for work and she's babysitting the kid, a boy named Bruno. Without me even asking, she volunteered to babysit Janine downstairs as well, while *you* get the deepest, hottest, foamiest bath, you've ever had. Right after we all get some apple Acadian, made with phyllo pastry and vanilla sauce, and coffee. Meal in itself."

"Um. Janine gets coffee?" Nina said.

"Milk."

"Okay."

Her insides began quivering again, but not with the emotional shock and fear of earlier that morning. This was more anticipation. Because just this once, it seemed, everything was going exactly as Richard had planned for them. And she didn't have to think hard to figure out where his plans led.

Nina determinedly clamped down on her quivering and instead let her gaze sink into the strong lines of Richard's back and butt.

Okay, tough guy, she thought. *You'd better be planning what I think you're planning, because this time I'm not taking "no" for an answer.*

~~~~

The Cuddy residence
Mackie's Cove
Cape Breton Island

Intolerable, Leonard Junk thought. Execrable.

He'd managed to avoid the mob after escaping from Richard Mackenzie, and had even tracked his way back to the home of Billy Cuddy, who had apparently been one of Tommy's closer friends from his childhood. He'd slipped inside because these fisher folk never locked their doors, day or night. And he'd waited.

But now the big man and his wife, Elizabeth, were looking at Junk like he was some kind of child molester. Like they might, at any moment, sound some kind of alarm and have him hauled off and locked away. Not that Mackie's Cove had any sort of jail or police force. Maybe another good stoning?

"You lied to us," Billy said now, huffing and puffing like he needed to inhale the courage necessary to say it.

"Yes, I did," Junk snapped and pushed up his glasses. "Have you figured out why? Have *any* of you figured out why?" He looked pointedly at Elizabeth Cuddy, but she just blinked and shook her head.

Junk sighed. "It's like your Mr. Dundas said, why would I be here and make all this stuff up unless Richard had done something bad to get my attention. Well he has. He did. Actually his brother did. He stole from the Russian mob."

Billy and his wife looked at each other doubtfully.

"You doubt me? Little package like this?" Junk held his hands out to demonstrate. "Or a small sack about that size? You never saw Tommy carrying it? Or Richard?"

Again the Cuddies shook their heads.

"Then I suppose I'll just have to go to Angie Neal's, is it? And take the little girl. I really don't see any other way of forcing Richard to turn over the package peacefully. I can tell you the hit squad the Russians send will be far less genteel."

"Um...they're not. I mean, I don't think we can let you do that," Billy Cuddy said, shifting his bulk forward.

"Um...then maybe I'll have to show you who else in this town has Special Forces training, hm?" And Junk took one half-step back on the Cuddy's worn living room rug, sinking into one of the few stances he remembered from his old army hand-to-hand training.

It was enough to make Cuddy hesitate, which was all Junk had needed before he turned and ran.

Except that a puffing Gord Keen was suddenly in the back door and Junk, even putting on full brakes, slammed into him and bounced backwards. As did Keen, who blinked at him then nodded like everything seemed to make sense.

"Billy!" Cuddy said. "They're here," he blurted.

Junk frowned at him. "Who's here?"

"These people Dougan talked about. Richard's friends, you know? Four army types. One's a really big square guy. They're over at Angie's now, asking where Richard and the little girl took off to. And asking about you, Lenny."

Oh, shit, Junk thought. *Here we go.*

~~~~

Just south of Chéticamp
Cape Breton Island

The Acadian pastry dessert was, as Richard had promised her, delicious. Sweet, melting crispness on the outside, and a hot, tart, core. Even the coffee slid down perfectly, hot and strong.

Until Nina felt like her old self again. No, better. Stronger.

And getting hot in more ways than one.

She looked sideways to where Janine had just finished her own pastry and glass of milk and now mimicked Nina's sigh of contentment before looking up at her with a grin.

Which Nina returned, then shared with Richard, across the table from her.

And just like that, Margrette the innkeeper swished Janine out the door to a basement rec room where Margrette's grandson was already apparently vigorously fighting bad guys on some kind of T.V. game console.

"Time to go up," Richard said, jerking her attention back to him. "While they're involved and the tub's still hot." They'd both watched Margrette run up and down the stairs with hot kettles of water while they ate.

"You're sure we shouldn't wait for Margrette?"

"I'm sure."

No more Angie. No town opinion. No immediate danger. Nina stood, took his hand, and he led her up the stairs.

But even expecting something special, Nina gasped when the y reached the room at the end of the upstairs hall.

The bathroom was easily ten by twelve, with a huge, steaming, claw-footed steel tub taking up the far left corner. Bath bubbles wobbled in foot high mounds across the top of the water as Richard shut the bathroom door behind them and locked it. Then he walked to the bath and checked the water temperature. The candles burned in a row on the deep-set window sill, more on the mantle over the sink, on the stool beside the bathtub, on the floor in the right-hand corner. They threw flickering light up over the steamed-up glass and high ceiling. And some sort of scent. Jasmine? Lemon?

"I told her we're honeymooners," Richard said.

"With a child?"

Richard shrugged.

Nina reached down and tugged off her socks, one by one. Her feet were marked red from the cold and wet. "This is... Oh, shoot me now. I'll die happy." Crossing her arms down in front of her, she grabbed the bottom of the sweater top and pulled it up and over her head in one smooth motion.

She turned towards Richard in just her wet jeans and brassiere. The bra was simple and white, but also sheer and still wet, so her hard nipples were easy to see. She could feel them poking at the material. Every movement sent little tingles through them straight to her sex.

She dropped the sweater turtleneck on the chair by the wall and was gratified to see Richard's eyes raking slowly over every inch of her torso.

Those eyes weren't steel now. They were fire. Burning coals that somehow made her shiver.

"Well?" she said.

"Not planning to shoot you," Richard said, "exactly." He shed his own wet tee-shirt.

Nina gulped in pleasure. Damn, she'd seen this man's naked torso once or twice before, but only when it had been wounded and bloody or all wrapped up in bandages. Seeing it now, in the peak of health and free of anything but some pink puckers where his stitches had been, it was almost enough to make her want to run and call their company's city photographer. Catch the perfection. Preserve the hard, flat curves of his chest, the ridges of stomach muscle, the shoulders and arms. Nothing over-muscled or bound. Everything strong and deadly.

God, if he made love like he fought...

She was so wrapped up, she almost didn't notice him waiting. Then she smiled. It was her turn, right? With a casual flick of her fingers, she popped the top button on her jeans, unzipped them, and shimmied them down and off.

He followed suit with his until he stood before her in a set of leg-hugging boxers, his middle leg doing its best to press through them.

"Aw. He looks crowded," she said.

But it was her turn again. And even though she knew as a woman you were supposed to worry about your breasts, it was the one thing she'd never questioned. They'd been bigger when she was plump, but their shape when she finally discovered the pleasure of hard exercise, was just right.

At least she'd always thought so. Her lovers had told her so. But would *Richard* think so? Everything about him was...bigger than life.

"The bath's getting cold," he said.

"Um..."

"Do you want some help?"

"No." Good. Firm. Decided.

With a quick motion, Nina reached a hand back and flicked open the catch of her bra.

36

RICHARD TRIED TO SWALLOW but his mouth had gone dry, so he just fought to keep his face calm as he watched Nina slide the bra from her shoulders.

He could feel his blood pound through his muscles, urging him to act as she straightened up, staring him straight in the eyes.

Then, with what seemed like deliberate languor, she bent forward and slid her panties down and off. Richard had about four seconds to be mesmerized by the patch of curly dark hair between her legs before Nina stepped past him and into the bathtub.

He spun quickly to catch a glimpse of her perfect ass before she sank down.

Then she was down and under the bubbles up to her neck, her back to the faucet, looking up at him with a lascivious grin. "The bath's getting cold."

Nodding, dry-mouthed, he realized he'd crossed the point of no return with this woman a long time ago. Certainly from their first kiss. Maybe from the moment he'd dropped down from the tree in front of her, back in her mother's garden. Nina Tauredaux had slipped her irritating, arrogant, surprisingly tender and resilient self so deep under his skin that it had outlasted bullets and betrayals and even losing what felt like his entire history.

Now it was time for *him* to slide into *her*.

He quickly doffed his boxer shorts and stepped into the bath, facing her.

It was scalding hot and his mouth dropped open in surprise. Nina laughed, snorted, and threw some bubbles his way. "If you want to just stand like that, it's just fine." she said, ogling him.

But Richard decided that if she could handle the heat, he could too. He leaned over, gripped the edges of the tub, and slowly lowered himself down.

And...it wasn't so bad. His face flushed. His heart pounded. He just couldn't tell if it was the brutally hot water or the brutally beautiful woman sizing him up with such hunger in her eyes that he felt his shocked erection recovering double time.

Without warning, she slid quickly forward in the tub, feet and legs over his, stopping just short of hitting him. With her long torso, she was barely shorter than him and hardly had to tip her chin at all to bring her lips a whisper from his. Her breath brushed his face. He moved his own lips to—

She pulled back. Put her two hands on his chest.

"I'm going to wash you," she said, and gave the dirty smile again.

"Okay."

In fact, good. Because Christ, the moment he started moving on her, he wasn't going to be able to slow down. And if she was expecting some kind of smooth lover...

His erection bobbed only inches from where it so desperately wanted to go as Nina took a sponge from a rack on the wall, dipped it into the water, then used it to slowly wet his upper body and face. He raised his eyes to study the high ceiling rather than search for the swell of her breasts in the bubbles. Focus elsewhere. Tight control.

"Hey, Mackenzie. Look at me. Look into my eyes."

He did, and she massaged the soap over his neck and shoulders, carefully over his still-tender wound area and down his chest, under his arms, down his belly and below the water as he held his breath. Her hands wrapped around his erection, squeezing once. Found his balls and handled them gently.

He grit his teeth and concentrated so hard on the depths of her eyes, the dark brown beauty of them, that the indescribable pleasure/torture going on below the layer of bubbles and water could have been happening to another person.

He was *here*. In her eyes with her. In her soul.

~~~~

Damn, he was good, Nina thought, her mouth half-open.

His face, his eyes, his whole being was focused on her so intently she felt like she had that first day in the garden—like he could see right through her. No, *into* her. Like he was wrapped up inside her mind with her. Mind fucking.

But her fingers said his body wanted her at least as much. His huge erection was bobbing in her hands as she stroked it under the water. And when she fondled his balls, she felt shivers run through his body despite the heat of the water.

He really did want her. Despite her silliness at times, her stupidity that time on the boat, and the way his whole town had literally spat on her.

He wanted her.

That sent even more intense ripples of lust through her than the sight of his body. So that without even being aware of it, she lifted her hands away from his center and clear of the water. Up to his face, his beautiful, serious, intensely-focused face. She skimmed one set of fingers lightly over each cheek and tilted her own chin forwards and sideways.

He matched her motion and their lips met. And it was a slippery heat so attuned to the temperatures around them that Nina's whole body seemed to feel it. She closed her eyes as her mouth opened and their tongues met. Gentle. Exploring.

When they broke contact, it was only for an inch or two. She could feel his breath on her, hear him pant like he was still mind-fucking her. Still in her head.

Without opening her eyes, she whispered, "Touch me."

~~~~

The words shot through him like an order to *Go!* and Richard had to breathe deeply to contain it.

Slowly.

His hands could haul a fish line, tile a roof, kill a man. Now he slooshed them gently through the water to touch Nina's naked waist. The curves of it. But the hot water deadened the sensation too much and he moved his hands up, around her ribs, then clear of the water, spreading away the soap bubbles from the water and her breasts so that he could truly see her.

With a quickened breath, she spread her arms to support herself on the sides of the tub and arched backwards. It not only raised her fine tits clear of the water, red bullet nipples high and proud, but pushed her groin hard against Richard's erection.

And as his eyes drank in the sight of her, she ground against him, moving herself up and down along his shaft until he feared he'd explode right there.

"Wait," he grunted his last ounce of restraint. "You're on the pill?"

"Yes," she gasped without bothering to raise her head up to look at him.

Not stopping her hips either. "Oh, God, yes."

"Good."

He grabbed her hips still and drew his own back so the tip of his cock just touched her pussy lips.

Poised.

Nina quivered there, lifting her head finally to meet his gaze. Her breasts rose and fell in quick little jerks and Richard wished he could capture that look forever.

But then she braced most of her weight on her left arm so she could reach down with her right and grab him, guided him just inside.

Then she pushed forward over him and drove herself down.

~~~~

Onto him.

"Oh my God!" she panted, gripping the sides of the tub on either side of him. Then she rose up and plunged down again and her whole body felt like it was catching fire. It shot through her, through her legs and feet and toes, through her chest and arms and hands, her fingertips.

She rose and fell. Rose and fell. Until she wasn't even sure it was her doing it anymore. It had to be Richard somehow. His power. His hips. She was riding danger and death and the knife edge of life that she'd never quite made before.

The water splashed and sucked around them. A part of her saw it soaking the tile floor, heard her moans and yelps, and wondered how much of it was carrying downstairs. She didn't care.

Then a too-vigorous thrust lost the connection, she tried to reach down for it, and almost slipped headfirst into the metal side of the tub.

But Richard caught her. And in a violent tsunami of bubbly water, he somehow slid back from under her, got a leg out of the high-sided tub, and bodily pulled Nina out, dripping and gasping, to the cold floor.

A quick series of grabs and he'd spread four huge, pink bath towels down like a sheet.

"Down," he commanded, and she dropped, rolling onto her back and spreading her legs.

He followed but rolled her to her side and came in from the rear, driving his fingers down her front to the slick nub of her, to rub and spread and play as he thrust in, huge and needy, from behind.

"Oh, God. Oh, God," she panted, then shut up and just rode it, the waves and waves of heat burning her chest and face the rocketing from all over her body towards her clit, towards the sharp build of pressure and sensation making her world a fun house of *demand* and...and...

It hit in a wave that shuddered and shook her head to toe, rattling her bones, scouring her veins, making her dance like a spastic puppet and yelp sounds she couldn't bear to think she was making.

It went on and on, even as Richard somehow came out and flipped her back to her back, entering from her front now and thrusting like a madman until he, too, tightened and felt huge inside her.

He exploded in a profound, contained grunt of pleasure that just made her yodel louder.

Oh, *God* yes!

37

H E SAID, "You're really noisy when you make love, you know that?"
They were lying side-to-side on their backs on the bathroom floor,
Nina with a towel wrapped over her. She turned to look at Richard's blasé
profile and raised one corner of her mouth. "You think so? You should hear
me when you really get me going."

He chuckled and they lay without moving.

Then Nina gasped, swallowed it, and said, "You didn't say when I had
sex. You said when I 'make love.'"

The only sound was a last bubble crackling into nothingness in the tub.

"You said it." Nina blushed, suddenly feeling very naked.

"I did."

The blush became a slow-spreading warmth, a pleasant echo of the
incredible heat earlier. He'd admitted it. She wasn't going to push it. For now.

She saw Richard look to the window where the two candles were still
flickering their light.

"The storm's over," he said. "I think we blew it out."

She wasn't sure if he was serious until he turned to her and smiled. She
smiled back. More of that lovely afterglow warmth.

"We have to go back now," he said.

"This lifetime?"

"Janine."

"We're not going back to Mackie's Cove, are we. You never intended us
to. We're on the run again."

He nodded. "I'm that easy to read?"

"You brought your whole kit. Said intense goodbyes to Doc and Clive.
Yeah, I noticed. And you made sure Janine had Snuffles."

"Damn you're smart."

Nina gave a long sigh and snaked her fingers over to find his and entwine herself there. "Sure we don't have another ten or fifteen minutes to make love before we go fugitive again?"

"I'm sure," he said, letting her wording slip by as he rolled to his feet and stood looking down at her. "But we will find ways, from here on in. Just as long as you—"

He cut it off at the banging on the bathroom door.

"*Monsieur!* Richard!" called Margrette, slurring his name to *Ree-shard* but losing nothing in urgency. "Your friend from *le* Mackie's Cove! *Le docteur*! He calls you! There is shooting!"

~~~~

Richard lunged for the door, barely restraining himself long enough to wrap a towel around his waist and make sure Nina had one.

Then he threw the bolt and yanked open the door. Grabbed the wireless phone from their hostess.

The harsh breathing in it sounded desperate, choking.

"Doc?"

"Richard..." There was a thudding sound then Doc spoke again. "C-Castinages. He says to tell you he'll kill us if you don't come back."

"Kill who, Doc?"

"Already got Clive. He's..."

"Doc?"

There was a shuffling sound and a smoke-graveled voice Richard had somehow known he hadn't heard the last of came on the line. "You remember how twelve of us took out Abdul's entire compound, Mackenzie? And that was against trained soldiers."

Richard's whole body had gone cold and still. "Why did you shoot Clive?"

"We didn't shoot him, actually. Just yanked him out of his car and put him down. We're trying to keep a low profile here. An aura of threatening calm. The town doesn't mess with us and we don't mess with them, right?"

"So why grab the town doctor? Actually the retired town doctor."

Castinages laughed nastily over the phone line. "You mean the guy you were staying with here, the one you treated like a surrogate father? And I'm hurt in that, by the way. I thought *I* was your Pappa."

Junk. They had to have hooked up with Junk. In fact, it was probably him who'd called them in. Richard should have been running. If he'd been long gone, they'd never have reached him. They'd have had no reason to take anyone prisoner. They'd... Shit.

Nina was on his arm, squeezing it and looking at him with frightened eyes. He shook her away from him.

"What do you want?" he said to Castinages.

"You know what I want."

"I don't have it."

"I don't believe you."

"Then fuck you."

"And the people in this place start dying, one every thirty minutes."

Richard let a beat go past, letting that settle into the ether, sorting through the possible scenarios for one where everyone didn't die. None looked good.

Finally he lied, "Thirty minutes is too short. It'll take me a good forty to drive back there."

Another harsh laugh. "Bullshit. But I want you to boat back. On the same boat you left on, the *Mary-Hester*. Bring the kid. And the sister-in-law. And the package. Anything less, or you send down the Mounties, and people here start dying."

Survival scenarios. There had to be one.

Just boat away? Vanish? Take away Castinages's leverage?

Unacceptable. Castinages was crazy enough to kill people just to make his point, knowing Richard would find out, thinking he'd use it when he caught up to Richard the next time.

"You can't have the woman or the girl," he said finally. "They don't know anything and I'm not letting you execute them."

There was a pause. "All right. Just you. *Forty* minutes. With the package. Or I will kill everyone you care about in this town, then kill you, then hunt down your woman and the little girl."

"Mwahahaha."

"It's just the mission, Lieutenant. Your time is running."

The connection clicked off.

Richard handed the phone back to Margrette, then looked at Nina.

"Don't even say it," she said fiercely and pushed back her wet hair. "You don't have a hope going back by yourself. I'm coming with you. I drive the boat and I watch your back."

"You'd just get in the way."

"Bullshit. And don't tell me to run, either. He said he'd track me down, didn't he. Janine and I won't stand a chance on our own. You told me that yourself, remember? If there's a scenario where we come out alive, it's with me covering your back."

"I can't..."

"Then why did you teach me to shoot a gun?!"

Reading his mind.

Richard looked deep into her eyes like he'd done that very first day in the back yard of her parent's house after he'd dropped out of the dogwood tree with Janine. And he saw the same intoxicating strength there. Even after everything she'd been through. If anything, the fire and determination was even brighter.

Okay.

He turned to Margrette, who looked twice as frazzled as either Richard or Nina, even though she was dressed and they were still in towels. In Acadian French, he explained to her the situation and asked two things of her: 1) take Janine, her grandson, and herself into protective custody in Chéticamp; and 2) tell the authorities there what was happening in Mackie's Cove. Tell them in person, not over the phone.

Then he'd scooped up his jeans, fished out his wallet, and paid her for a night's accommodation before sending her out and starting to dress.

Nina, he was pleased to see, was way ahead of him.

~~~~

She should have told him earlier.

No, it had been the right time.

If he'd even gotten it. If he'd understood.

If *she* even understood what it meant.

She wished they'd had more time, that they could have talked about it. Another three hour crazy boat ride back to Maine would have been good. A long car ride.

Instead, all they'd had was a stressed-out, half-hour rush on the *Mary-Hester*, engine cranked to full, neither of them speaking much.

When Richard had sighted Mackie's Cove on what looked like a homogeneously gray and rocky coastline, he'd turned the helm over to Nina and prepared the guns. He now held the shotgun, barrel down by his leg, his windbreaker pockets heavy with shells. He'd stuffed a smaller revolver, "the

Glock", into his waistband. The .44 Magnum Nina had been practicing with sat on the humming steering console beside Nina's right hand.

"Will they meet us at the dock?" she said now.

"Probably. Less chance of us stirring up anyone else in the town."

They'd already gone over the basic plan—bluff about Tommy's package until Richard could confront Castinages directly, take him hostage, wait for the authorities.

Chances of that working? Slim to none, Richard had said.

Encouraging.

"Shatter Rock on the left there," he said now. "Slow down and go out to the middle of the break before you go in."

Which she did, the chop of the open ocean dropping to a wallowing thrumming as she passed the rocks on either side and suddenly saw the familiar beach. Not welcoming, but familiar. Only...something wasn't right.

"Not there to meet us," she said.

"No one there at all," Richard said tensely beside her as they roared closer. "No boats going in or out. No one working on the dock."

"You think they're all just...?"

He shook his head. "Speed up and head for the right of the main dock," Richard said.

"But what—?"

A rifle shot cracked and splintered the top of the wheelhouse, inches over the top of the window. Nina shoved down the throttle and spun the wheel so the boat swung right and then back as she course-corrected, picking up speed and racing headlong for the stony beach. Her heart was thrumming louder than the motor though. Pushing. Scared. Another shot and a bullet punched through the windshield with a crack that made Nina duck and scream, grabbing her cheek, pulling out a sliver of glass.

"Keep driving!" Richard said, pulling her up high enough to see the shore barreling closer. "They want us to turn!"

"Are we *going* to turn?" Nina shouted.

"Ten seconds!"

She was going to be sick, but Richard suddenly grabbed her arm and grinned. "Fear's normal. Actions count."

Then he jerked open the door of the wheelhouse.

"On my mark," he said, "swing the boat hard left, throw her into neutral, and let her drift! Got it?"

She nodded.

"Now!"

And as the boat swung with a whining protest just shy of the main wharf and its boats, Richard skidded the shotgun out through the wheelhouse door and leapt after it with his pistol up.

38

Mackie's Cove
One last time

A DARK FIGURE HALF-ROSE AT THE BEACHED DORIES. Richard spun and fired. The man's head rocked back. He staggered and dropped.

Another sprang from behind the fueling station on the main wharf. Richard shot him in the side and he stumbled into the water with a dull splash.

The third man, already out on the main wharf and aiming, was too far around and Richard threw himself down. Two shots whizzed over his head, one thunking into the *Mary-Hester*'s gunwales.

Richard jammed the pistol into his windbreaker pocket, snatched up the shotgun, scrabbled and popped up four feet down the gunwale with the shotgun. He fired as the man on the wharf swung his aim. The top left side of the man's head shredded in spray of red. His screams scared off a line of gulls that had been flying down to rest.

And Richard rolled again, clutching the shotgun, reloading. Up. Scan. Duck and roll again.

Where was his target? He could almost smell him.

Then Richard saw him, the unmistakable tank-like shape running along the shoreline, the man Richard knew had taken more men through impossible walls of opposition than almost any other living soldier. Misha Castinages.

The Major must have been on the Shatter Rock dock, ducking about, probably trying for the final shot. But then his men were taken out, his decoy play spoiled, and now Richard was too far away. The *Mary-Hester* was drifting sideways for the shore and the line of storage shacks with their one dead bad guy. Only three? Of course. Why would he need more than three? They were probably Special Forces or Rangers, SEALSs, who the hell knew? Richard couldn't count them definitively out yet.

But Castinages himself was the threat right now.

"What's happening?" Nina called from inside the wheelhouse.

Richard ducked and looked to see her sitting on the deck with her big Magnum up and ready to one side of her head, her eyes focused. What a woman. He held his fingers to his lips, then pointed to himself and to the shore. The *Mary-Hester* was going to run aground in about thirty seconds and he had to get out and moving. If he were Castinages and had lost his overwhelming advantage, his next step would be to fall back and...

"Hey, Mackenzie! You'll want to see this!" his former commander bellowed across the waves at him.

...use his hostages. Oh, shit.

The *Mary-Hester* ground out at that moment, coming to a shuddering stop, her stern swinging slowly to starboard. Which meant they'd be only about ten yards from shore, given the deep drop-off from the beach. Richard could splash to it in about ten seconds, keeping his guns dry enough to shoot, but he'd be an easy target in that time.

Better to throw the boat into reverse and race back to the wharf, spin his way in...

He doubted Castinages would give him the time.

Rising carefully, the wheelhouse between him and the shore, he saw the Major with a shape in front of him. A woman. A distinctive woman, all curves and blazing red hair. Angie.

Richard dropped back.

Why not Doc? Had the old man tried to run and gotten shot? Richard fought a flashback to his brother's house and forced himself to think. The real question was what had changed between when Castinages had called him and now? No more bargaining for Tommy's stolen "package." Which meant he somehow knew Richard didn't have it, or didn't care. Didn't care because? Because either he'd take it off Richard's dead body, or take it from whomever Richard had left it with.

If he'd figured out who Richard could have left it with.

Where Richard could have left it.

Janine.

Oh, goddamn it. Demanding Richard come back in the boat hadn't been to keep Nina and Janine from running in it. It was to give the Major *time* to get Janine. Maybe they'd already been on the way when he'd called. Faster by highway than water.

Richard called out, "That's it? That's all you got?"

"They got Janine!" Angie screamed from the beach. "She—"

Castinages silenced her with a thud of his gunstock, probably to her kidneys or maybe her neck. Keep her quiet but still standing.

"Bitch has about five seconds to live, Mackenzie!" the Major croaked. "I don't want you dead or you already would be! I want to talk! Negotiate a trade! You give us back what your brother took and I give you this hotty and the little girl! What do you say?"

The Major burst into a round of hard coughing.

Richard frowned. Was Castinages suddenly ready to bargain or was it a trick? And if it was just a trick to make Richard come out, what were his options?

None.

Richard ditched his shotgun, pulled out the Glock, stood, took a long aim at Castinages, who was bent sideways with one arm still wrapped around Angie's neck as he hacked his guts up.

Richard fired.

The bullet clipped the Major just over his ear at the back of his crew-cut head.

Angie screamed. Castinages grunted and staggered backwards with her, pulling her down on top of him. Angie screamed again. Wouldn't stop. Richard scanned the rest of the beach with the Glock. No one running to help, neither soldiers nor townsfolk. Had Margrette sent the cops or been taken first?

A movement back at the base of the wharf. The third soldier! Not dead. Out of the water and limping slowly back to help his commander.

"Reverse and take the boat back to the wharf," Richard hissed at Nina. "Keep your gun ready."

As she rose to put the boat into reverse, Richard stuffed all the ammo but the Magnum's into a plastic bag, then jumped over the side with it and his weapons held high. He saw Castinages push Angie off him as Richard hit the water.

No!

But the Major wasn't swiveling to aim at Richard as Richard fought for his footing on the hard-mud bottom. No, as Richard found his footing and began driving towards shore, Castinages dragged himself backwards, one arm clutching his rifle, his eyes seemingly unfocused. The Major got to his feet and staggered up the beach. Broke into a jagged run.

Richard swore and slooshed forward harder. By the time he splashed up on the beach, Castinages was gone and his third soldier had given up trying to catch him. Instead the man turned back towards Richard, pulled out a smaller gun from inside his body armor, and aimed it at Richard's head.

~~~~

Fucking...Mackenzie...

Castinages could hardly see straight. The blue and yellow block houses of this two-bit village swayed back and forth with each of his steps. They tilted and jolted alarmingly. Or was that him?

Buh-blam! Double shot. Came from the beach. Who? He thought his men were all dead. Should have brought more.

Misha was having trouble telling up from down, his feet from his hands. And his neck was soaked, his collar squishing. Blood. Brain matter? He ducked around the corner of the nearest house and leaned back against it, reaching back to rub his neck and draw back his hand, squint at it.

Just blood. Okay. He'd been here before. Too many times to count. Too many scars.

Secret was to keep moving. Bad guys were after him. Mackenzie. Bad guy? Son. Coulda been. Wanted to kill Castinages, though, didn't he? Blamed him for death of his brother. Sister-in-law. Having to run away.

Everything was spinning on him and it made it hard to figure his directions. All he knew was that he couldn't go down. Had to stay up. Keep moving. Armored Jeep back at the highway. Make the Jeep.

Terrified faces swam before him in little square windows. Town natives. Hiding inside. He waved his rifle at them and they ducked back from the glass.

The narrow road split before him. Which one to take? Had to go up. Knew that. Which one? Mackenzie had to be coming. Misha had to *move.*

"This way," said a flabby voice. Misha spun with his rifle.

Flabby voice, flabby man. Glasses. Pock-marked skin. Holding his own rifle.

"The doc got away but I've still got the girl. Come on."

Junk. It was Junk. Useless Junk. "Where?"

"Someplace I believe no one in this town ever goes anymore. Someplace dark and cut off. Unfortunately, the girl's a bit of a claustrophobe and we may need to move her. Come with me now. We'll go see."

Useless. No. S'posed to stay at the house. S'posed...

Misha jerked himself up from a near fall and nodded his head, steadied himself on Junk's outstretched arm. Not a lot of options. Had to make some.

Together the two men staggered up the left-hand dirt road.

~~~~

"Damn it!"

As Nina ran to him along the beach, her honking big revolver pointed high so she didn't shoot someone by accident, she heard Richard swear again as he pulled the soaking bad guy she'd tried to shoot and he *had* shot over by the driftwood, half-hidden. The man looked younger but as hard-muscled as Richard, even bleeding from his leg and head. Obviously dead.

Well too bad for him, Nina thought, gritting her teeth tightly.

Angie ran towards Nina then, her hands fluttering, face in a rictus of tears, and threw her arms around Nina.

"What? *What?*" Nina snapped, annoyed at suddenly being cast as some kind of Amazon.

"The guy, Junk!" Angie cried. "He's supposed to watch Doc and me and Janine! But Doc fights him! Janine runs! Junk knocks out Doc and goes after her! I comes down to warn you and—"

"The big guy grabbed you," Nina cut her off. "Yeah, we saw. Which way did Janine run?"

"I don't know! I don't!"

"You two stay here," Richard said coldly. "See if either of the other two guys I shot are still alive." He stuck the Glock into the pocket of his windbreaker and reloaded his still-smoking shotgun. "I'm going after Castinages."

39

TRACKING HAD NEVER BEEN RICHARD'S BEST SKILL, but when your quarry was staggering in rain-soaked mud *and* bleeding, it made things easier. The Major and his team might have been careful to come down on the rocks and grass, but now the Major's staggered boot prints stood out like flashing sings on the path going up.

A deviation off the path at the crossroads. A house with blood smeared on the siding. The Major had stopped here, and then...

Richard frowned and knelt down to run his fingers over the wet grass and mud. There was a second set here, someone helping Castinages. Dress shoes with hard heels. Richard could only think of one person in Mackie's Cove who'd have only dress shoes to wear out in the mud.

Junk. Damn it. He and the Major had hooked up again.

Richard looked up at a hissing sound and saw an open window across the road with a boy's face sticking out, *pss-sst*'ing at him. Then his mother pulled him back inside. Claire Coleman. He remembered riding the school bus with her. Silly girl, buck teeth, very loud. She looked much the same, just with more wrinkles, signs of a hard life. She drew her lips together tightly over her big teeth.

"You saw which way they went?" Richard said. "Tell me. They've got my niece. She's six years old. They'll kill her if I don't stop them."

After a second, she nodded in the direction of the gravel road, the one that ran up past McGee's.

Richard nodded and set off in that direction but he stopped when she called to him. He turned. "What?"

"He said..." Coleman stopped herself, held her fingers to her mouth like she used to do in school.

"Tell me."

"He said the girl was someplace dark and cut off where no one ever goes anymore. And that she was claustrophobic."

"The mine."

"I think so."

"He was telling you so," Richard said. "Telling me."

He began to run.

~~~~

"Ungh," Castinages groaned as Junk helped him up the narrow dirt road that ran north of Mackie's Cove, parallel to the highway, looping up then down to what looked like a half-collapsed factory building built against a steep hillside. "Did she talk?"

Junk shot him a surprised look, probably shocked that he was becoming coherent again. But whatever Mackenzie's shot had done seemed to have rattled his brain more than chunked a piece out. Even if Castinages was still dizzy and had the beginnings of a killer headache, at least he was starting to think straight again. A cold wind had picked up again. That helped.

"No," Junk said to answer his question. "She just whimpers and tries to scratch me when I come near."

"Where is she?"

"Inside."

Junk indicated the wood-slat door that had a combination padlock on the outside. But the walls, all wood, three stories at one end, up against the slope, and lower on the side that faced the ocean, looked like they'd break apart with a strong kick or two. Broken windows up top. A sick, gassy smell all around.

Junk stepped forward and twirled the lock back and forth until the lock opened. Castinages didn't even ask how he happened to be carrying combination locks in his car. Everyone had their obsessions.

"Come on," Junk called and walked into the dark interior.

Castinages turned slowly with his C8 rifle half-raised, but didn't see anyone following him. Just dust off the road and long, blowing grass. So far. He had no doubt that Mackenzie was coming. Castinages had been sloppy when he ran from the beach. He knew it. And part of him heard Junk blabbing to someone. Spelling it out.

So this factory would be where they had the final showdown. Fine. With Junk even nominally on his side and the girl as a hostage, Castinages had the advantage. But he wouldn't underestimate Mackenzie again. He needed to go in and give the place a quick once-over, figure the best shooting blinds.

So he did.

Just as he was getting a good sense of it, Junk called to him from the railing of the third floor. "He's coming!"

Castinages went to one of the wire-laced, grimy windows and looked out. It took him a moment, then he saw Mackenzie, slinking low and fast through the grass off the side of the road. He surely knew he'd be seen. He was just making himself harder to hit.

Castinages went to the first hole he'd poked through the wall, tracked Mackenzie's moving form and fired just ahead of him.

Mackenzie dropped flat but kept moving, obviously not intimidated. Castinages grinned. Good. Maybe he understood his commander had missed him on purpose. That he could still trade the package for the girl.

Of course Castinages would still have to kill Mackenzie and his girlfriend at the end of it, but at least the girl would live. For a while.

A sudden intense urge to cough his guts out swept through Castinages's chest and made the back of his head where Mackenzie had clipped him pound like hell. But he suppressed the cough and clenched his teeth at the pain and the swimmy feeling it gave him. He'd crawled out of an exploded Humvee with half his ass burned off a year ago, dragging two G.I.s out behind him. And he'd been fighting this damned lung cancer off for a year past his due-date. A little flesh wound wasn't going to stop him now.

Mackenzie had reached the end of the road, scanned the mine building, and raised himself up to make a dash for the westernmost door.

Castinages stuck out his rifle barrel again, took aim, and laid down a spatter of shots directly in front of him. Mackenzie dropped down flat again, scanning for the source, finding it, and firing back a round of high-powered buckshot that spattered the wall where Castinages hid. *Whoom!*

Castinages laughed and called out, "You ready to trade?!"

"Where is she?" Mackenzie called back.

"Up top! You throw me the package and I let her walk. Let you all just walk away, long as you stay up here in Canada."

"Show me she's okay!"

Castinages drew farther back in and waved at Junk up on the third floor. It was dark enough he wasn't sure he saw the return nod, but he heard the

N.S.A. analyst shuffling something towards a window.

"Look up at the third floor!" Castinages called out at Mackenzie.

~~~~

It's okay, Snuffles. It's okay. We're gonna be okay. Uncle Richard's coming to get us. He's going to kick these guys in their *wieners* and just let us...

Oh, no. What's smell-booger doing? I'm scared. I'm—

~~~~

Richard looked up as third floor window shattered. Then a small form, a little girl's body, was held out, dangling on the end of a short rope that had been tied tightly around her body. Leonard Junk no doubt held the upper end.

Janine's red hair whipped around her face in the wind as she wriggled like a fish on a hook. Her eyes blinked wide. Jesus, she still clutched her stuffed armadillo. Made not a peep.

Scared.

I know, honey. I know.

Promises to his brother. Promises to Janine. Singing her to sleep. Carrying her. Her his neck or leg. And her just starting to talk this morning on the boat. Just starting...

Options?

Again, none.

Richard laid down the shotgun and stood up slowly, his hands raised above his head. "Let's talk," he said, walking forwards.

"Freeze!" Castinages called. "Let me see the package."

"Pull the girl inside."

There was a pause, then a snapped order and Janine's dangling body was pulled up. Junk's glasses glinted in the high window as he pulled her in. Richard walked closer.

"Far enough! Toss me what Tommy stole or eat shit!"

Richard held his breath and slowly reached into his right windbreaker pocket where he'd shoved the 9 mm pistol. He could feel Castinages aiming at his forehead. And Richard knew he was going to die. No matter how fast he aimed, how fast he dove, Castinages would be faster.

But Richard had no choice. He started pulling out the Glock...

And a loud roar from his right let him dive to the ground as a capped Ford Super Duty, big as a frigging armored personnel carrier, thundered straight for him up the dirt road.

Past him. Heading for the mine structure.

Knowing somehow that it had to be Nina, Richard scrambled up to run behind it, shooting at the boards around Castinages's cover to alert whoever was driving where to go.

And Nina, or whoever it was, obviously saw, because the truck swerved that direction and drove headlong through it, shaking the entire structure so that Richard worried that the third floor, where Junk held Janine, might collapse down on top of them.

It didn't.

Then Richard was inside the building, through the opening made by the Super Duty, as Nina leapt out of the Super Duty's driver side with her little gun drawn in her hand. From the passenger side, scrambling with almost as much vigor, came Doc Klein and Clive and Rob Dundas, of all people. Reassembled, conscious again, armed, and spreading out around the front of their vehicle like they had to have seen done on some television show somewhere.

Sitting ducks if there had been anyone in the building to shoot back at them.

But Castinages was gone.

~~~~

Gahh!

Misha was running again. Stumbling again. Somehow that earlier shot to the head had done more than he'd thought. Slowed his ability distinguish sound. To make judgments. Something.

Because when the monster truck they'd driven up here had shown up, coming at him from the gravel road, his mind had short-circuited and he'd just watched until almost the last second, when he'd flung himself out of the way.

He'd been clipped and torn badly along his leg and side and back as he dove. He'd lost his gun, even his backup in his leg holster. Almost been knocked out.

But before the dust had cleared, he'd been up and running again.

Never stop moving!

The only direction away from the truck and the guns and people spilling from it, was down the railway track he'd seen before. Into the pitch black of the mine. Into the throat of the ocean. The depths of hell.

Forty steps in, following the track by feel alone and keeping his hands up in case the ceiling suddenly dropped invisibly in front of him, he collided with something metal and solid.

He stopped and scoped it out, breathing hard. Fighting down a need to cough as the coal gas swirled thickly around him.

A mine cart. Broader on top than on bottom. Filled with dusty garbage. No brake on. No motor. Just unhooked and left here. Squeaky but functional.

Don't stop moving!

Shut the fuck up. There were times when you had to stop. Had to think. Mackenzie would be coming for him, he had no doubt of that. He'd have to save his little niece first, of course, but he couldn't just let Castinages walk.

Any more than Misha could leave without Mackenzie. They had different objectives—Mackenzie a stupid short-term justice; Misha helping save a country—but both needed to kill the other to bring it home.

In the pitch darkness he turned back to the mine cart, exploring its contents by feel. Now what could he do with this shit and the stuff he still carried?

~~~~

Nina's entire body was vibrating like a high piano string, as taut as she'd been during her orgasm at Chéticamp with Richard.

But she felt in control as she flung herself out of the metal beast with her gun up. Her eyes scanned the dim cavern she'd crashed into, looking for guns through the clouds of dust, the falling dirt, for that one big man whom Richard had chased up here. *Me, Hulk!* Nina remembered thinking of him. Unstoppable. Richard had shot him and he'd still gotten away. Was still out there.

"Upstairs!" Richard was shouting in her ear. *Had* been shouting? How many times? Her gun was twitching back and forth, from shadow to shadow. And she kept blinking. So much dust.

"What?" she shouted back.

He grabbed her then, painfully pressing down her upraised gun and making her look at him. "Janine," he said, straight in her face. "You have to get Janine. She's up on the third floor. Junk's got her."

"We'll get her!" called Rob Dundas from her right somewhere. Nina still couldn't tear her eyes from the shadows, from thinking she saw shapes jumping there, aiming at her.

Then another voice called, rough and scratchy like the throat was half-torn out, and echoing like out of a deep hole. "Macke-e-enzie!"

Richard called past Nina's head, "Be careful on the stairs! Everything in here's unstable.

"We got it!" Rob Dundas called back.

"You get him, Richard." That was Doc.

"We'll get your girl!" Clive.

"Ri-i-i-ichard!" Like a long echo. Closer? "You know you wa-a-ant me! Come get me!"

"You stay here," Richard said and that finally snapped Nina back.

"Excuse me?" she said. She shook her head and truly saw him at last. He'd already slipped away from her, walking to the mouth of that dark tunnel he'd had the gall to walk her into before. She darted after him to catch him at the head of the mining cart tracks and grabbed his shirt, shaking off a cloud of dust and dirt. "Are you out of you gonad-driven *mind*?"

He stopped and spun towards her, eyes like steel again. "What?"

"Oh, please. You're going to go stalking down a dark mine tunnel after an armed madman built like King Kong? Get a grip."

"It doesn't end unless—"

"Then seal the motherfucker up inside this place! Bring it all down on his head! Lock the doors and call in the freaking police! I don't care! Just don't... Oh shit!"

She couldn't believe it. Even when Richard followed her gaze and saw it too.

Coming out of the pit, squealing like a banshee from hell, rushed a blazing fire that grew bigger by the second.

~~~~

Castinages!

Richard shoved Nina to one side and stepped to the other as the flaming mine cart reached and rushed between them, only to come to a thumping halt at a block just fifteen feet or so up the tracks.

What the—?

No! Richard realized a second too late how watching the cart had momentarily blinded him. He spun back towards the sound of running feet just in time to have the entire weight of Castinages hit him full on. It drove him backwards towards the cart, still stumbling on his feet but unable to stop.

He hit with a thud that nearly broke his back and snapped his head backwards in a horrible whiplash. But as Castinages reared off him to deliver a killing blow, Richard managed to roll to one side and drive a knee to the Major's side.

It was like hitting rock. Castinages spun on him with a roar and Richard saw how bloodied the man was. The entire right side of his head looked mauled. And his right arm and leg—torn and bloody, with flaps of clothing and flesh hanging loose together.

But the eyes were bright. The smile was the same ferocious one Richard had seen in the middle of that mission to take Abdul Adeeb's compound.

Castinages shot a left hook at him without telegraphing and Richard barely ducked. His guns? Gone. Somewhere in the crud on the floor. There! He'd somehow thrown the shotgun back up the tracks towards Nina!

Before he could go for it, though, Castinages's foot connected with the back of his leg, barely missing a crippling blow to the joint.

"Fucker!" Castinages shouted. "You don't give it up and the war over there *never* ends."

"I don't even know what...unh!" Richard's spin-kick back caught the man's gut, but almost got his own foot caught in the process. "..what it *is!*"

"Bullshit!" Castinages roared.

Richard hopped then ran at him, spinning sideways at the last second to slam an elbow at his jaw, so that Castinages stumbled against the burning cart, screamed and rolled around it to the side.

Then Richard was running towards the shotgun, tripping on the rails. Falling!

He looked up to see Castinages, his face lit in blazing shades of gore and soot. The Major had embraced one poker-hot side of the cart with his bare hands and chest and rocked it from its stop to roll it back towards Richard. Picking up speed. Driven by a locked-on force that refused to die or give up.

Move! Richard scooped up the shotgun and rolled to the side as the cart screamed by him. He jumped up, raising the shotgun before he realized that Castinages wasn't getting off. He was roaring, running alongside it and jerking about as the cart accelerated down the slope, but some part of Castinages had either welded to, or gotten snagged on, the cart's metal.

"Richard! Coal gas!" Nina shouted at him, and the reality of the rolling bomb Castinages had created finally dawned.

"Janine?" he called, turning to her.

Together they ran back towards the stair that Rob Dundas and the others had climbed to go after Janine, only to find the entire troupe of rescuers rushing down with stricken expressions.

No Janine. No Junk.

"He must have taken her out the top," Doc Klein coughed, staggering.

"Door up there was closed and locked!" said Rob Dundas.

Richard was about to push by them and climb, when a sonorous boom sounded from down in the bowels of the mine. Richard turned his head to see an enormous gout of flame roaring up the mouth of the tunnel towards them.

40

*T*HIS WAS TRUE HEAT, Nina would think later. But while it was happening, all she remembered was spinning to run up the stairs after Janine before Richard grabbed her, threw her over his shoulder and ran out through the debris-littered hole in the wall behind the others.

Until somehow they were all outside as the entire mine building seemed to light up like a Jack-o-lantern, blowing out its windows and loose boards, sending wired glass spraying through the air, fragments catching Nina's cheeks and forehead and arm as Richard stumbled and dropped her in the grass—a controlled fall.

And then...it was over.

The explosion, anyway. The entire crew crawled and scampered back from the building and southward almost to the line of trees that marked the rise out of Mackie's Cove. They finally turned and stood in the long, wet grass to watch the building breathe out a sudden whoof of flames. It shot up around the roof and back in before becoming Cape Breton's biggest bonfire and sending out wave after wave of heat. It burned against Nina's face, her hands, her chest, so it was hard to breathe.

But even so, she found herself looking around at the others and felt her chest catch completely. Janine? And Richard, where was...? She saw him, running in a wide arc around the outside of the burning building.

"Where's he going?" she said.

But it was obvious to everyone and no one answered. They just watched, with long, soot-blackened faces as Richard ran up the right side of the hill the mine building burned against, looking a like a stray piece of floating ash himself.

Then he was at the top, staggering back southwards from what must have been a terrible heat, turning and turning under the socked-in skies, seeking the lost child that was part of his life, of Nina's life. Junk could not just take this part of them away.

Then Richard's turning form stopped; took off down towards Mackie's Cove.

"He spotted her," Nina said and walking to the back of the bluff to look down towards the town herself.

"Should we...?" Rob Dundas said behind her and she guessed he'd been thinking of using their commandeered truck. But the vehicle the bad guys had brought to Mackie's Cove only to have Nina and her crew steal it and use it against them, was part of the bonfire now. Not usable anytime soon.

"There," said Doc beside her.

Nina followed his pointing arm and saw a dark boat of a car pull out from the side of the road just south of Mackie's Cove, roaring off in that direction. Towards the bridge to Nova Scotia proper, Nina knew. To a boat. To a plane. Something.

As she watched, Richard's distant form came running on a straight path to where the car had been. The figure staggered to a halt, took a few hesitant steps after the departed car, then stopped and stood there for a long minute. Not moving.

It was like Nina could hear his brain rushing through the options from here. Get the truck and give chase. Call the cops on the car. Call the border patrol, the airports, the government. Sure, Richard (and probably Nina) would go to jail for the murders on the beach and the one in the mine, but just maybe...

And tell them what?

Nina felt her insides shake and a great flood of tears begin welling upwards, but she pushed them down again. "Come on," she ordered the others, and began walking up to the highway that would take them to where Richard was, even as she saw Richard turn back and begin walking the highway towards them.

As they did, they heard sirens coming from the north and began passing a growing stream of people coming out of Mackie's Cove itself to check out the blaze. Nina shook her head at them as they gave her group a wide berth. *Now* they came out. Now that the police were here. Now that people were dead. Now that Janine was taken.

They met Richard at the same time as a particular, red-haired slut, last seen screaming on the beach, also arrived.

Angie looked nervously at Nina's soot-streaked face and found no comfort from Richard's, Doc's, Clive's, or Rob Dundas's either.

"We all talked together," she said quickly. "The town. Couple of the boys hid the bodies from the beach. Said it was just the two crazy men who grabbed your little girl and took her to the mine. Unless those two say different?"

Richard stared at her dully. "They won't be talking to the police anytime soon."

"That's what we figured, what with you going after them," Angie simpered.

"So you'll just cover it all up."

"We all agreed..."

"Because you're good at that. This town. Lots of practice."

At that, even Doc, Clive, and Rob hung their heads. They probably didn't see, like Nina did, just how close Richard was to cracking.

"He won't hurt her," Nina said to him. "He still thinks we've got what Tom stole from them. He or whoever he's working for will try to use her again to get it from us."

Richard's nodded at her, his face twisted into a horrible caricature of a smile. "You're probably right. Of course, since we still have no fucking clue what it was Tommy stole, or where he put it, maybe we should just give ourselves up now."

"Richard..." Doc said.

At that moment a series of cracking sounds rolled out over their heads and they turned as one to watch the glowing three-story ember shudder in the distance. In a series of exploding fires, the wall and ceiling supports gave out one after another, until only a series of tall spires stood. Then these fell as well, in a single enormous crash that shot sparks and chunks of flaming debris flying in all directions.

Richard hands flew out with them. With one heart-cracking sob, he suddenly dropped to his knees and beat the ground with his fists. "*Mo kreech,*" he moaned. And again, "*Mo kreech!*"

Doc closed his eyes, turned from the fire, and nodded in pain. As did Rob Dundas. Which meant it had to be Gaelic. A curse. Something dramatic. And almost without consciously remembering, Nina pulled out the one Gaelic curse that *she* had learned, and spat it out as phonetically as she could remember.

"*Ma-here! Syall a kinn gonna!*"

More of the distant crashing and heat from the fire made her turn her face, so she didn't see at once. Then she did.

All the rest of her group had turned to look at her. Even Richard. He'd raised his head and now stared with his face twisted but making no sound.

"Sorry," Nina said and swallowed. "It's the only Gaelic I...sort of...got. Read. My first day here, I think."

"Was this it?" Richard finally croaked, and he said the phrase closer to how she remembered Angie and Dougan reading it to her, like a single flowing word.

"Yes. 'My father lies here. Look closely on it.' Something like that?"

"And you read this where?"

"On your father's tombstone."

"Which Tommy paid for," Doc said slowly, looking up at the smoke and sparks streaming into the sky. "Which he chose the inscription for."

"What?" said Rob Dundas through his snuffles. "What's it all about then?"

But Nina and Richard ignored him, staring hard at each other. Then they looked past the still-streaming line of advancing Mackie's Cove residents, past the town of Mackie's Cove itself even. They looked all the way to the bluff on the south edge of town and the abandoned church there, and the scarcely visited cemetery where Tom Mackenzie, joker that he was, had left a pointer to his stolen loot after all.

Richard closed his eyes. "I'll be damned," he said.

41

COME ON, EVERYONE, Richard urged the others. *Dig!*

But even with him leading in a kind of frenzied desperation, it took Richard, Nina, Clive, Billy Cuddy, Jovie McAlister, and Crumpet Davies nearly forty-five minutes to dig up Strachan Mackenzie's coffin. The bastard had been buried deep.

What were you doing, Tommy? Why here? Why fucking here?

At least when they finally hit the wooden lid of the casket, it was surprisingly easy to clear a trench around the lid. Davies and Cuddy, who'd been the ones in the hole at the time, climbed out and let Richard and Nina jump down to pry the lid open. Not locked. No gaskets forming an airtight seal. And the old bastard, dressed in what was probably his one Sunday suit, was barely decayed. He just looked moldy all over. Smelled like rotten meat.

And his eyeballs were pretty much gone. No more drunken stares. No more anything.

"Richard?" Nina said. "We just going to stand here staring or search it? Him."

He turned his head to look at her. It felt like his he was high up out of the hole somewhere, staring down at the scene. "It. And if nothing's here?"

"Then we'll think of something else."

"Like...?"

"I don't know, damn it! *You're* supposed to be the strong one. Pull yourself together."

Her anger and the tear he saw spring out the corner of one eye so surprised him that he grounded back in his body, sudden and hard. "You start at the feet," he said roughly. "I'll work from the head down."

She nodded, but whispered to herself, "Oh, God."

Crouching over the body, he forced himself to breathe through the overwhelming waves of putrescence, and began feeling around it and under it. Nina copied him, on the other side. The storm clouds hadn't let loose, thankfully, so at least the process was dry. Richard just had the feeling that at any moment some part of the old man was going to split open and a stream of squirming maggots would spill out.

Minutes later, they'd searched the whole way down both sides of the body and Richard had actually squelched the corpse up to reach fully under it, creating a squelching noise and another wave of smells that as bad as anything he remembered from the battlefield.

Nothing.

Richard was almost ready to conclude they were chasing nothing at all, when Nina slumped back against the dirt walls of their pit, wiped her forehead with the back of her wrist, and said, "'Look closely *on* it.' Not around it. Not under it."

Richard stared at her, then shrugged and began going through his dead father's pockets.

He found it down the front of his father's pants.

A clear Ziploc bag, extra large, around what looked like a smaller brown velvet bag. A sheaf of typewritten pages were packed in around the inner bag, along with some kind of map.

After he and Nina did one more thorough search of the casket and the corpse, they pulled the casket lid back on and climbed out with

"We open the bag for you all to see," Richard told his digging crew, "*after* the dirt's all back in and we've washed our hands."

So they shoveled back the dirt. And when it was done and the dirt tamped down, they all walked over to Billy's house, because it was closest. They shut the doors and locked them. They pulled all the curtains. They took turns at the kitchen and bathroom sinks. Then they sat around the Cuddy's cleared-off kitchen table, opened the outer, plastic bag, and unwrapped the cloth ties from the inner velvet and revealed...

~~~~

Rubies.

Deep, blood red. All uncut.

A few are the size of Nina's thumbnail. One is the size of her fist, enclosed in its own separate plastic bag with an inscription "Do not touch! Refer to note." There are also dozens of rubies the size of a pea and smaller.

And when Richard unfolds the accompanying note, signed by Tommy, he reads out loud that these are true rubies. They are a thousand times more valuable than spinels or sapphires. More valuable than any gems but diamonds.

Valuable enough to change a nation.

Because these rubies are from Afghanistan, where rubies were once the pride of the nation before the veins ran out and war and opium production took over. But if significant new veins of rubies were to be located in this mountainous country, Tom writes, the entire Afghan economy could shift. No longer would opium and heroin production the only irresistible resource. No longer would the Taliban and Russians run the country by running its drug routes. No longer would all the Coalition efforts be spent hunting drug lords versus delivering aid.

In fact, developed properly, and linked to other mineral resources which have been too difficult to justify mining on their own, the ruby mines of Afghanistan could generate enough immediate revenue to rebuild the ancient irrigation canals that had once made Afghanistan the breadbasket of the Middle East. They could be the first step in turning the entire region towards peace.

"Note," writes Tom, "that the uncut rubies in this bag I've stolen from Senator Gordon Farthering and his partners in crime—"

~~~~

"No!"

Nina's hand on Richard's arm clutched so tightly her nails drew blood, but he didn't push her away. He remembered her going to Farthering at the party, speaking to him like he was a surrogate father. Like Doc had been to Richard. Or Castinages.

Even the surrogates let us down, didn't they.

Maybe it hurt even more because we *chose* them.

~~~~

"—the uncut rubies in this bag I've stolen from Senator Gordon Farthering and his partners in crime could possibly fetch a million dollars on the open market. Maybe more.

"However, the true wealth of this packet lies not in the rubies so much as the enclosed map.

"The rubies are the proof that there's something there. The map details where the mines are.

"The full reasons why Senator Farthering and his partners do not want this map and the evidence of its veracity shared are not as obvious as one might think. But I unfortunately cannot go into them in detail here, as they are part of a much broader investigation into Senator Fathering's dealings and could be misinterpreted if taken only in part.

"Accept that this package is physical evidence of crimes detailed elsewhere. The largest ruby in this package is marked, I believe, with the fingerprints of the Senator himself. It will be critical in building a strong case against him.

"For the rest, I've compiled the findings from my investigations into a more easily accessible set of files, redundantly stored in a number of locations and able to be unlocked only with keys held by myself, my wife, and my daughter, the only individuals on this planet right now whom I both trust and have close to hand.

"If you've found this package, I'm hoping you're one of the others I trust but couldn't leave a key with. If not, well then I guess, in the words I've often heard my brother use, we're fucked.

"God bless. Do the right thing."

~~~~

Senator Farthering? Pops?

No. Damn it. No. Please no.

Lost in the horror of what they'd just read, Nina barely reacted when Billy said uncomfortably, "I guess Tommy go'd a bit strange when your da died."

"An' what was he doing messing with Afghani-bloody-stan?" said Clive.

"What they call it when you don't trust no one?" said Crumpet. "Padenoid, right? That what he was?"

Jovie said nothing but kept staring at the rubies like he was wondering how many he might casually steal away and how he could sell them.

"Put them away, Richard," Nina said quietly.

Richard glanced around at the others, nodded and complied, carefully pouring them back into their velvet bag, putting the fingerprinted monster ruby in with them, tying the bag up. Then he turned to Nina with his eyes glittering.

"You know what this means," he said.

"What?"

"We've got the bargaining chip we need. To get Janine back. To get our lives back."

Nina felt so much weight on her chest that she could hardly speak. "Not if they know about this note. About hidden files? About Janine having the key?"

Richard looked at her steadily, finally seeing her upset but obviously not understanding. "They don't know. They would have killed her outright if they knew."

"No. Like you said, they think we've got these. And duh, we do."

Richard stared at her, then turned to the others in the room. "I'm taking Nina for a little walk. And it may be obvious, but I'd advise that nobody here say anything about what we've found. Not, at least, until we've decided what we're going to do with these things."

He hesitated a moment, then handed the bag of rubies to Clive for safekeeping.

When he'd gotten Nina outside, he turned to her. "Okay. What is it?"

Nina grabbed his sooty shirt. "Jesus, Richard. Didn't you *read* it? Tommy's wrong! He's fingered Senator Gordon Farthering? Gordon...Pops is my godfather! I know him. I *know* him. He couldn't do this. He couldn't kill my sister! That's too much!"

Richard looked left and right and Nina just held on tighter.

"You know Tommy was mistaken," she insisted. "Or lying?"

Richard brought his face back to hers. "Tommy didn't lie. Not about things like this. I can't expect you to understand, but something about what we lived through as kids made it hard to back away from making hard choices, doing the right thing."

"I know that!" She hit him on his chest and it was like hitting warm concrete. Living concrete. With a beating heart. That loved and cried and hurt and... Damn it, he was human. Just so damn hard to live up to.

She buried her face into his chest and smelled the charcoal, the fire, the dank earth he'd pushed through to get to the truth and Janine. He would have gone down that mine shaft after Major Castinages, too. "N-nothing stops you, does it," she said, hanging on tight. "Nothing would make you turn away?"

"From getting Janine?"

She thumped him again. "Of course not from getting Janine. But after that...after we get her...is it going to be justice at all costs?"

He still hadn't raised his arms to hold her. "What are you suggesting we do?"

"I don't know! Just...I don't want everyone to die. Not me, not you, not Pops."

Richard turned his face away again. "I don't know if Tommy had the right read on what the rubies and map could do over there, in Afghanistan. But it he did, and if your godfather is in the way..."

"If and if and if. We're talking countries and millions of people Tommy's guessing about."

"And the man who probably ordered Tommy and your sister killed."

Nina shut up, but then couldn't help herself. "Probably. Not certainly."

His hands still hadn't come up to hold her and Nina wondered if they ever would again.

"Let's go back inside," Richard said. "For now we've got to convince the others to let us take the rubies. Then we have to figure out what to tell the police so they won't keep us here."

42

THERE WERE NO BODIES OR TRACES THEREOF found in the devastation above ground, and Richard doubted they'd get far enough into the mine shafts for months to find what was left of Castinages.

About his and Nina's kidnaped niece, Richard stuck close to the truth—that he'd seen one of the men who took her drive off with her in a big blue sedan. He expected the Tauredaux family, which was fairly wealthy, to receive a ransom demand from the man shortly, and Richard and Nina had to be back down in Washington, DC to help them deal with it.

They gave Nina's mother's house as a contact number. He figured he might as well give Farthering et al. a heads-up that he was coming down to see them.

But even with this announcement, they kept the journey off the radar, carrying out their original plan to boat south on the *Mary-Hester*. It hauled ass compared to the lobster scow they'd had on the way up.

This was good, since when they reached the Maine coast, Richard kept motoring them further and further south, seeking a cheap used car to drive to DC in. It had to be out of their dwindling pile of cash. He was not about to part with Clive's boat, despite the old man's gifting it to him.

It also gave Nina a few extra days to accept what her godfather had done and decide that maybe he deserved getting shot after all.

They ended up moored not far from Atlantic City and driving a 1986 blue Buick LeSabre on the short hop through New Jersey and Maryland before heading south down the I-95.

Nina, who'd visited the Farthering residence many times as a child, but less so as a teen, audibly marveled over how much smaller her godfather's "giant white castle" was than she remembered, and how much more beautiful.

Fall leaves had started to blanket either side of the long drive past the pillared gates. Their crisp scent filled the air and crunched under the tires as Richard and Nina drove in. The autumn gardens of royal-purple bushes, Virginia sweetspire, spider-shaped flowers with hazel blooms, and long swaths of silver-blue switch grass, spoke of a full-time gardener and a gentility that only came with generations of money.

It made Nina wonder out loud why her mother hadn't married Gordon all those years ago. Unless she'd smelled the rot at his core even back then. Snuggle close to power, but not too close.

Richard chugged the Buick LeSabre to a stop near the front steps of the Farthering mansion, tugged down the unfamiliar lapels of his new sports jacket and climbed out. Nina grabbed her small black purse and followed. Half a beat later, the mansion's doors were flung open and Gordon Farthering himself came hurrying down to greet them.

They'd called ahead. Told him they had the rubies. Would he please have Janine there waiting for them?

43

The Farthering estate
Fairfax County
Virginia

A ND HERE THEY ALL WERE, Nina saw. Gentility in the midst of hell.
As soon as a Russian-looking thug had finished patting down
Richard and her, relieving Richard of the pistol he'd put in a rear-waistband
holster, but missing the tiny gun hidden in the false bottom of Nina's purse,
Pops ushered them in through the south double doors of his west sitting room.
He led them to a set of four high-backed armchairs on either side of a Louis
XV side table in slender curves and intricate rococo carvings. Framing them,
the room's twelve-foot-high picture window and the bright gardens outside.

Pops clapped his hands and a servant appeared through a modest, single
door on the east side of the room opposite the windows. He carried a silver
tea service to the high side table between the armchairs and set it down.
Exited.

As Pops began pouring the tea, he called out and a set of other guests
entered through one of the double doors in the north end of the room, the
senator introducing them as they did—Leonard Junk with the NSA; one
Gregor Lechenko, formerly of the Soviet KGB, now a private businessman
operating a multinational business doing some business in both the Middle
East and America; and one Byron Jones, a gemologist with Eguaine-Asia, an
expert on eastern hemisphere rubies. Lechenko took the northernmost chair.
Jones took the one beside him. Junk remained standing.

"Now, Princess..." Pops began but Nina cut him off.

"*Don't* call me that. Never again. Do it one more time and we're walking."

"Without little Janine? Come, come, Neens. I know you better than that, whether you want me to or not."

And he went back to pouring his tea, serving it around as if he were some kind of English butler. Or Jesus, maybe. The greatest shall serve. Wasn't that something he did? Was that how Pops—no, *Farthering*, the bastard—saw himself? The awful thing was just how much Nina had always adored his genteel attitude of noblesse oblige. Had longed to emulate it.

"Where's Elaine?" she said.

Farthering smiled. "My wife? She and our son are off riding horses today. Did I mention that we finally discovered he was our little intel leak? 'Deep Throat' I believe he called himself? Treacherous little scamp."

Richard glanced quickly at Junk and touched Nina's hand, holding her back, but she shook him off.

"Speaking of treachery, Senator Farthering," she said, dripping the Senator with as much disgust as she could muster, "where *is* the six year old girl whose parents you killed before you terrorized and kidnaped her?"

Farthering smiled broadly at her. "Ah, Nina. Always given to dramatics even when you were my little Bhudda g—"

"Shut up!" Nina snapped. "No more of that either. Where is she?"

Again Richard's hand. Why? Was Lechenko over there frowning at her? Was Junk going to suddenly be more than a porridge-faced mind-messer? She hadn't once reached into her purse to check on the pistol there. She was standing here in her pretty floral dress, in her treacherous godfather's sitting room, and she hadn't once kicked, scratched, or spat on him.

"All right," Fathering said slowly. "If you have absolutely no sense of historic moment, Nina." He clapped his hands towards the north door again and called, "Denise?"

The double doors at that end of the room opened and Denise d'Alvay stood there in her obnoxious little pixie-bob, today wearing black high heels and almost Goth makeup. With one hand she held up the hand of a very silent, very pale Janine. With the other she held a gun that was in size somewhere between Nina's hidden pea-shooter and the honking big revolver Richard had first trained her on. D'Alvay had the gun pressed up against Janine's head.

Nina tamped down the urge to cry out to Janine. Instead she allowed herself a puzzled look and said sweetly, "I thought this bitch was aide to Congresswoman Reis."

"Appearances and realities, my dear," said Farthering. "This is Washington."

"You really going to blow her brains out if we're difficult?" said Richard beside her, the first time he'd opened his mouth since they'd come in.

"Why not?" called Lechenko from where he sat, holding a cup of tea. "Whether you cooperate or not, you won't get out of here with the rubies."

"Assuming we have them."

"If you don't, I think we might just kill you now," drawled Lechenko and looked to Farthering.

Nina's godfather shrugged and sighed. "Necessities and time being what they are…"

Richard pulled open the right side of his sports coat and pulled out the plastic baggy they'd found in Strachan Mackenzie's coffin.

Byron Jones, who'd been sitting stiffly like a schoolboy awaiting his lessons, jumped up and stepped forward with his hands out.

"Not quite so fast," Richard said.

"Give us Janine," Nina said.

In answer, Farthering waved at d'Alvay and the bitch stepped back into the far room, pulling Janine behind her. Leonard Junk walked from where he'd been a virtual statue and shut the doors.

"Now," said Farthering, holding out an imperious hand. "Come on. You'll get Janine after we've certified you've brought us back the actual stones and map."

"Like hell you will," said Richard. "Because you know it's just the knowledge of the rubies' existence that's the dangerous thing, don't you. You get the rubies and map and then you kill us, right?"

What was he doing? Looking for a reason to kill them all now? Because even without his gun, Richard could no doubt still find a way. Some way. Somehow. But it wasn't what they'd agreed to! They were just supposed to get Janine, drop the rubies, and split. Richard had *promised.*

"Richard," she hissed.

"It's all right, Nina," Farthering said, clearly not understanding how close he was to death. "He doesn't trust us. You don't trust us. Nor should you. But I'm telling you simply, Mr. Mackenzie, that once we've got the stones and map, we're happy. It doesn't matter who else knows. Gregor here takes control of the trade with the help of his Taliban friends. I get Gregor's money in return and, more importantly, his political support. And you and Nina and Janine walk out of here as if none of this ever happened." His smile turned hard. "Now give me the package."

~~~~

It was all Richard could do to not just step forward and deliver a killing blow to Farthering's larynx. Nina's godfather was so full of shit his eyeballs were swimming in it.

Let them walk out of here? In a shitty pig's eye.

Despite what he'd agreed to with Nina, he'd always figured their chances of rescuing Janine and all three of them getting out alive were minimal. But then the chances of he and Janine surviving Tommy's house had been minimal. Surviving the attack at Mackie's Cove had been virtually nonexistent. For all the mission planning he'd learned in Afghanistan, sometimes you just accepted your limited options and hoped that the randomness of life threw new possibilities your way.

Like now.

Something had caught his attention a minute ago. On the bottom exterior of the picture window, he'd seen something he hadn't seen since before he joined JTF2. It was an exterior bug, probably just strong enough to pick up conversations close to the window, probably low frequency enough that the operator had to be somewhere close by.

Which meant what? The FBI listening in? He hadn't dared contact them himself since he had no way of knowing who was clean and who was in Farthering's employ. But maybe they'd caught onto Farthering without him. Or maybe some other branch of the Justice Department had picked up on Tommy's work?

Most critical—was the bug active now? Was someone out there listening?

"You're telling me, Senator," Richard said a little louder, "that this is all about the money and power. You're handing Afghanistan over to the Russian mob, and our soldiers over there can just keep on doing what they're doing."

"*Plus ça change,*" Farthering said. Shorthand for the French, *The more things change, the more they stay the same.* But the Acadian French near his home never said that, did they. Maybe they'd learned better that life could come up suddenly and hit you in the chops. Things *did* change, like they had for Richard recently. The trick was being the one in control of the change.

"Now, for the last time, Mr. Mackenzie, let us have the stones please."

"And for the last time, Senator," Richard said with the same tired tone as he stepped forward with disconcerting speed, whipped out a hand to grab Fathering, and yanked the senator to him in a spinning move that put the man between himself and the others, Richard's forearm locked across Farthering's throat, "give us Janine first."

~~~~

You could hear a pin drop right now, Nina thought.

Everyone in the room had frozen solid. Except Richard. He looked relaxed. Focused. So Nina took her cues from him and nodded at her godfather.

"We'll still give you the stones. We don't want them. But we want Janine *first*. That's simple enough."

Richard inclined his head, agreeing. They'd talked about this much, at least. They had to have Janine before they gave up the stones. It was probably their only chance of getting out of this alive. And if Farthering was telling the truth about not caring, then he should really just—

The door the tea service had come in by, the one directly behind Nina, suddenly slammed open. Nina barely had time to half-turn and register Denise d'Alvay running in before the woman had one hand around Nina's shoulders, holding her close, while d'Alvay's other hand pressed her black pistol into Nina's temple.

She spoke past Nina's face at Richard. "Want to see if you can choke him faster than I can pull a trigger? Let him go!"

"Uh-unh," Richard said.

"Then I'll just shoot her, I guess."

Almost without breathing, though, Nina had slid her left hand into her purse, under the edge of the false bottom, and come out with the little handgun Richard had bought her. She pressed it now into d'Alvay's stomach and cocked the trigger.

"It's a North American Arms Pug," Nina said, cooler than she felt. "Only shoots .22's, but those should be enough at this range."

Junk reached into this pocket and Richard tightened his grip on Fathering, growling, "I'll kill him now."

Junk removed his hand from his pocket and held both hands up to show they were empty, but d'Alvay hadn't so much as twitched when Nina had shoved her gun into the aide's belly.

Farthering's face, meanwhile, was turning slowly pink from the strain or Richard's hold. Nina saw him cast a pleading look at Lechenko. Finding nothing but boredom there, however, Nina's one-time godfather attempted a nervous grin.

"Nina?" Farthering quavered. "What are you doing? This man has obviously had a very bad effect on you. You know better than this. Don't humor him."

"I'm not laughing," Nina said, her mouth dry.

"But *I* am," d'Alvay said, inches from Nina's right cheek. She ground the barrel of her gun harder into Nina's temple. Nina pushed the smaller barrel of the pug hard d'Alvay's gut.

Farthering *hss-t* both to them, then said, "Nina. I know you. I've watched you grow up. It's your pattern to chase difficult men, to win them, to tire of them and find a way to have them dump you. That's what you did with Tom. It's what you did with that lawyer out in San Francisco, all your coworkers. But this is the first time you've actually hooked up with a truly dangerous man who doesn't understand the meaning of intelligent compromise. Think about what it is he is doing here."

Nina wavered. It was too close to her own thoughts about Richard's inflexibility and too hard to think clearly with d'Alvay's gun shoved against her temple. But...Pops's comments about her, were they true, too? Had she really tried to win Richard, strongest of the strong, just to prove she *could*? Just like her mother.

No. Nina hadn't married one man while loving another. Nina had loved, lost, and now loved again. Honestly. Despite what Pops thought.

And she wasn't here just for Richard, anyway. She was here for Janine.

But still she wavered, mouth dry. Because any second Lechenko was going to pull his own gun, or d'Alvay was going to shoot her in the head and try for Richard, and wouldn't that be a stupid way for everything to end?

"Give me assurances, Pops."

"Nina, look. The first thing you have to understand is that your sister was never supposed to die. Tom was never supposed to die. It's just...the man we worked with who stole the rubies in the first place..."

"Major Castinages," Richard supplied.

"Thank you," Nina's godfather said coldly. "The man was a psychotic. He was dying. He actually believed the U.S. was winning its war against the drug trade in Afghanistan and that the ruby trade was just going to make it harder. More money, inevitably, for the Taliban. But we convinced him we could divert that flow northward, out of Taliban hands..."

"To your good, Russian, neighbors," Lechenko said and laughed. "Because we also control much of the voting here in this country, when we choose to, yes?"

Farthering shot him a withering look before turning his attention back to Nina. "We appealed to Major Castinages's warped patriotism and it got us some hyper-violent results. It was tragic, Neens. But with violent men, things sometimes get out of control."

He held out his hands to her, long and graceful. Hands that had picked her up so many times when she was a child. "It's done, Nina. I know you hate me for it, but I still love you as a daughter and I always will. Just...get your own violent man here to let me go, I'll have Denise lower her gun, and we can wrap this whole thing up in twenty or thirty minutes."

"Richard...?"

And suddenly Junk was pulling a pistol out of his own shoulder holster. "Kill the woman, , Denise," he growled. "And then—"

~~~~

For Richard, time slowed.

Junk raised his pistol towards Richard...and a neat round hole appeared in Junk's forehead, blood spattering out the back. Junk's body crumpled.

It was so clean, and Richard was watching Nina spin and duck in d'Alvay's arms as Richard shoved Farthering aside to lunge towards them, that it took a second for him to confirm the crack of glass that preceded it. Then Richard had tackled d'Alvay hard, and tumbled with her back towards the tea service door, knocking her gun away from both or them. As he rolled up, he saw Junk's killer running across the garden lawn.

Impossible.

The raging square bull of the man who simply *would—not—die.*

Coming straight at them.

~~~~

Get them. Get them. Get get get them get...
Legs pump.
Security coming from post right.
Fuck 'em. Shoot 'em.
Don't slow.
Don't.
Window coming up. Tuck the head and...

~~~~

The window exploded with as big a boom as the mine cart bomb Nina thought had killed this freak a thousand miles from here.

But here was Major Misha Castinages, never say die.

He landed in the shower of glass that knocked over the Louis XV table, two of the chairs, and all the people who'd been on or around them.

Then Castinages sprang to his feet like a ripped-up zombie on crystal meth, assault rifle in his hands, teeth bared, mouth foaming. Jones, the gem appraiser started to scramble up from the knocked-over table and Castinages shot him.

Farthering cowered behind one of the upright chairs, Lechenko behind another, finally pulling his own gun.

D'Alvay yelled "Fuck!" and scrambled after her gun, so Nina aimed her little Pug two-handed, the way Richard had taught her, and shot her in the knee. D'Alvay screeched in pain and dropped to the floor in a fetal position.

And Castinages was suddenly on Gregor Lechenko, dragging him out from behind the chair with a roar and throwing him away from the window in the direction of Nina and Richard. Then he lunged after him and, before the Russian could get his feet under him, Castinages punched his gun stock into the man's nose. Nina heard the bones crunch and the Russian dropped like a bag of rocks near Nina's feet with a blank look in his eyes. As Richard dove for the Lechenko's gun, Nina raised her tiny pistol to aim at Castinages.

"Stop!" she shouted Nina.

Castinages laughed hoarsely, then ran back to grab Farthering before Richard could stop him. He jerked the older man to his knees and Castinages wrapped his cut-bloody arm around Farthering's neck much as Richard had done. Then the commando's face, so scraped, cut, and burned as to be almost unrecognizable, started a strange dance. It ducked back and forth behind Farthering's head. Like a gorilla using a chimp for cover.

"This wasn't the deal!" Castinages croaked, his voice shot. He pointed his assault rifle at Nina, at Richard, then at Farthering's temple. "We were going to win the war on drugs over there! You hear me, Mackenzie? None of that shit Farthering said!" He tapped his ear.

"You were listening in. The microphone on the window was you."

"We were going to end the fucking war!"

"I hear you," Richard said.

Farthering's face had gone white as a sheet, both hands raised before him in unconscious surrender. Castinages coughed, spasmed into a hard series of wracking coughs, then ducked his head back immediately behind Farthering again.

Nina finally realized that Richard was holding back, not taking any of the many shots he could have. Because he had Lechenko's gun raised, casually aimed in the Major's direction. And Nina had seen him in action more than once now. Knew his cold, absolute focus when it came to matters of life and death.

He *was* dangerous, like Pops had said. Dangerous to the insane and evil in the world.

Why was he holding back now?

"I fought my whole fucking life," Castinages rasped, his big back heaving up and down. "Got into the Army, the Green Berets. I did what they wanted. Killed. Blew things up. Fucking generals."

"Ends and means, Sir."

Castinages's thick head bobbed. Coughed into Farthering's neck. "Ends and means. Just wanted to win this fucking stupid war."

And maybe it got to Nina too. Maybe it explained why neither she nor Richard saw Denise d'Alvay, still supine and sweating, red faced, finally retrieve her dropped pistol. Not until she had half-raised herself up and pointed the gun at the massive wreck of a man holding her boss by his neck.

"I never loved you," d'Alvay said, and shot Castinages as dead as Junk.

~~~~

Richard spun and shot d'Alvay in the chest, knocking her down. Nina ran and took her gun away from her. The aide was still breathing.

~~~~

Heartsick, Richard walked to the fallen Castinages, who'd dragged the senator down with him and tugged Major Misha Castinages's huge, bloody hands off Farthering's neck.

Farthering drew in a shuddering breath and grabbed Richard's hand. "You don't want to kill me, Lieutenant," he said.

"You don't think so?" Richard growled.

"No. Because you've never killed a person who wasn't trying to kill you or someone you loved, have you? You're too noble for that. It's why you'd never last in politics. You have no flexibility."

Richard shut out the sound of Farthering's voice as he grunted the Major back a few feet and laid the big man flat across the rug. When the Major was down, Richard knelt beside him for a moment and took heavy breaths. He searched for something in the dead man's face.

When he couldn't find it, the heartsickness that had grabbed him when Castinages fell threatened to overwhelm him completely.

Until he looked up and met Nina's eyes again.

~~~~

Lechenko's gun, a SIG P220.

Nina's little NAA Pug.

Denise d'Alvay's chunky black Glock 23.

Junk's two-tone Smith & Wesson 9mm.

Misha Castinages's M16, and the sniper rifle he'd left out in the bushes somewhere.

Plus the Glock the Russian thug (whom Nina had expected to come running in by now but hadn't) had taken off Richard when they'd first arrived.

"I'm glad you taught me how to shoot one," Nina said as Richard scooped up all the guns present but hers, naming them for her as he did, and sticking three pistols into his pockets and waistbank. He held the M16 like an extension of his right hand. "But I hate guns."

"You can't hate guns," Richard said. "That's un-American."

"I love you," she said.

"That's just sick," moaned d'Alvay. She lay on her back near the east wall where she'd fallen. One of the ground's security guards had come in through the shattered window with an advanced medical kit and shot her full of morphine. He also seemed to have the training to do first aid on what was actually a shoulder wound. Nothing vital hit.

Nina almost wished she'd shot her when she'd had the chance, but now figured her still being alive might make their final negotiation with Farthering easier. Make it possible that Nina, Richard, and Janine could still walk out of her alive.

"We need to get Janine and leave," she whispered to Richard when he came close.

Richard nodded and turned to Farthering. "Where is she?"

The senator called, "Bring her in, Grace!" and the double doors at the north end of the room opened. Nina's mother, pale-faced and shaking, walked in with Janine holding her hand.

Nina almost collapsed.

"I'm so sorry, dear," her mother said. "None of you were ever supposed to get hurt. Things got a bit out of control."

"You think?" said Nina. "When? Before or after you dropped Dad for this loser?"

"Gordon is a great man, my dear. And sometimes great men—"

Nina had pulled her little pistol from her purse again and aimed it at her mother. "Just hand over my niece."

Grace Tauredaux paled and released Janine, who ran straight to Nina and hugged her legs quickly. Then to Richard's legs, where she hugged and held on.

Richard turned to Farthering with the M16 raised up. "So do I kill you now, or do you let us take her and walk out?"

The man Nina had once revered as being the model for a fatherly God, ran a hand delicately around his long neck. He held out a hand. "The rubies and map?"

"Lechenko's dead," Richard said.

"There will be others to fill his place," Farthering said. "The package. If you want to get off this estate alive."

Richard nodded, drew out the plastic bag, and handed it over.

"Good," said Farthering. "On this understanding..."

"What?" Nina said, adding silently, *You evil, murdering bastard.* She shoved the pistol back into her purse before she was tempted to use it. She hated guns. Hated the false power they made you feel.

Farthering saw what she'd done and smiled. "You stay away for a while. Let me negotiate my little deals. Let my partners set up their controls over things. In return, in a month or two, you get your lives back. And everything goes back to being just the way it was. More or less."

"Minus a brother and sister," Richard said.

"Sadly, yes." Farthering paused. "Or, as you say, you can kill me now and prove to Nina that you're everything she fears—a cold and emotionally scarred warrior, as ideologically obsessed, in your own way as Major Castinages. Do you really think she'll stick with someone like that for long?"

Nina opened her mouth to tell Richard no. She loved him be*cause* of his principles, not despite them. But with Janine tugging hard on Richard's pant legs, the future that had to be protected, healed, and grown at all costs, Nina knew the decision was already made.

Hanging his head like he admitted the race was finally over, Richard said, "It's not like there's a hell of a lot we could do at this point anyway, is there?"

Then he lifted Janine into his left arm, and motioned for Nina to follow him out through the smashed sitting room window.

They picked up Castinages's sniper rifle on their run to the car.

44

One degree of separation

ON AUGUST 10TH, the high commands of the various American and Coalition forces still in Afghanistan received a letter informing them of the packages being simultaneously delivered to the Asian Development Bank in Kabul, an Amnesty International office in Kandahar, the Islam Development Bank in Herat, and the UN Assistance Mission in Jalalabad. Each package was a tightly-wrapped cardboard envelope routed out of a small town in Maine. Inside was a single small ruby with a note, a list of the other local recipients, and a photocopy of a map.

A similar cardboard envelope without the list or map made it to Doc Klein's house. But instead of containing one ruby, the envelope held several which, along with the other four rubies and photocopies of the map, had been taken from Tommy's package before Richard had handed it over to Farthering.

The note in the Mackie's Cove package indicated the rubies were to be shared with the town. It also both sought and offered total forgiveness. A chance to make a new start.

45
Collard
South Carolina

THREE WEEKS LATER, while the *Mary-Hester* bobbed gently at a local wharf off the coast of South Carolina, a scruffy-looking Richard Mackenzie introduced himself as Bobby Smith and slid up on the old-fashioned diner stool. His little mute girl jumped up onto the seat beside him. He ordered burgers for himself and his daughter and one to go for their mother who was staying back at the boat on account of feeling a bit poorly.

While they waited, "Bobby Smith" watched the television on the shelf over the ice cream fixings. This being September and a time for mid-term elections in Collard, it was election coverage all day, every day.

"...say that Gordon Farthering, former Republican frontrunner for the Presidential nomination in 2012, cannot go far enough in his criticism of the nation's military deficit."

The news reporter vanished and a clip of Gordon Farthering appeared, his leonine head of white hair virtually glowing in the light of the flashbulbs. "We *cannot* play the game of pacifying Muslim extremists any longer!" he said. "You think they're going to use the newfound wealth they're discovering in their hills to foster *peace?* No! This is not something..."

But whatever rant Farthering was on now got lost as Bobby Smith saw his little daughter's eyebrows shoot up and her fingers point to the screen.

The camera had cut to the crowd at the rally—dancing and screaming right-wingers, half of them waving stuffed eagles at the cameras, or their video-phones displaying their streaming-web pictures of the eagles being filmed.

"What?" Bobby Smith said and grinned at his little girl. "You think Snuffles is jealous? You think he wants to get on camera too?"

The girl's mouth opened and closed excitedly, her lips moving like they were trying to remember exactly how. Then she said, as clear as the announcer cutting into the television footage: "Snuffles knows dot com."

~~~~

Just off the coast
South Carolina

Speaking.

That's what Janine kept doing off and on as Richard piloted them slowly down the sun-glittered, populous part of the coast. Richard kept them close to shore. They were sure to find a good wireless internet connection soon.

Nina, who hadn't yet developed Richard's love of the sea and insisted they dock in a safe port every night, was nonetheless bubbling more than she had in weeks. She sat barefoot and cross-legged on the hold cover now, their new laptop open on her lap. Janine sat beside her, one hand on Nina's still-flat belly.

"Baby boy?" Janine said.

Richard heard it and turned in time to see Nina blush and whisper, "Maybe."

He looked back to his piloting with a smile that he knew went deep. Happy. With him and Nina drawing Janine out just a bit at a time. Didn't want to scare her silent again. Didn't want—

He felt a tug on his sleeve and looked down to Janine's serious face.

"Come," she said.

Quickly dropping anchor, he hurried out of the wheelhouse to find Nina grinning and their laptop happily connected to the great electronic ether. For as long as the battery held out, they were golden.

"Anything?" Richard asked.

"Not under snufflesnose. Snuffles.nose gets me a plastic surgery site. Snuffles_nose gets me a redirect. Trying it with a 'k', for knowledge versus proboscis."

"I know what that word means, you know."

"Only because you've read like a zillion more books than anyone else," Nina shot back. "How about snuffles_knows..."

There was an ominous pause, a blank screen, and then a single question popped up:

How old is Snuffles?

Richard looked at Nina, she looked back. They both turned to Janine and read her the question.

Janine smiled and chewed on her lower lip. "Five zillion years old," she said. Obviously a private joke she and her daddy had shared.

Nina typed it in while Richard jotted it down on a pad of paper. A second question came up Snuffles's favorite food (green grapes), about his favorite color (purple), favorite cereal (Multigrain Cheerios), favorite hockey team (Montreal Canadiens), favorite uncle (Richard, thank God, even if he *was* the only one.), and what Janine was going to name Snuffles's kids if Snuffles ever had any (Zoolander if it was a boy, and Nina if it was a girl).

After the last answer the screen went blank for so long that Richard worried they'd lost their connection, but then a "loading" sign appeared, and suddenly Tommy's face appeared, waving at the screen, with Marie-Ange poking her head in behind and waving, saying, "Hi, JJ! Hi, honey! Hi, darling!"

Richard couldn't speak and she saw Nina had gone still, but Janine just crossed her legs and waved at the screen. "Hi, Mommy. Hi, Daddy."

Then, while the video kept playing, chunks of text began appearing beneath, starting with:

To whoever reads this—
Okay, you got here. It probably means I'm dead and the bad guys have taken over. But just in case there's still time, I have to tell you about Senator Farthering's 2012 campaign irregularities and how he single-handedly tried to screw a foreign people out of their heritage just so he could have a better shot at the White House.

Included are a bunch of data links and decryption codes you'll need to access various proofs I've squirreled away online—N.S.A. telephone recordings, scanned letters, strings of e-mails, photographs, video clips, numbers for bank accounts that fund this Senator's "black ops."...

When the last one was done, Richard looked up to find Janine lying down with Snuffles and Nina, staring at him with an inscrutable smile.

"Knowing Tommy," he said, "it'll be enough to take him down. Maybe give us back our lives. But there's always risk. You game to try?"

She smiled. "If it will get me off this boat, hell yes."

"Me too," Janine called out suddenly. "Get the bad guys!"

"That's our girl," Nina and Richard said at once, laughed, and Richard loped up to the wheelhouse to raise anchor.

Terri Darling lives with her family in the Pacific Northwest, where she writes sensual, suspenseful, and sweet romance. You can find more about her and her work at www.terridarling.com.

And in the meantime, check out the following exceprt from her novel *Second Chances*.

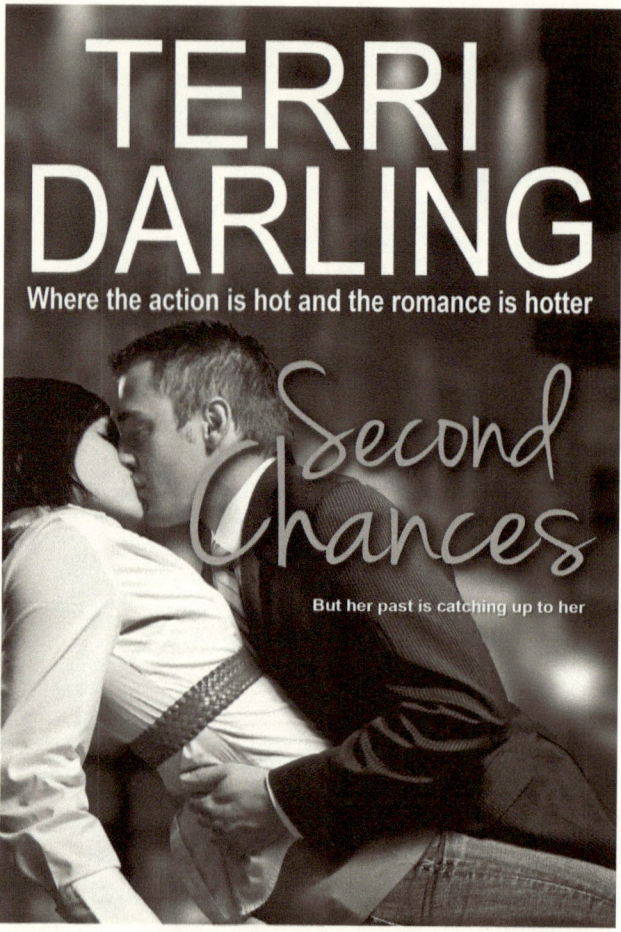

A former teen prostitute.

An uptight corporate lawyer trying to do everything right.

They had a brief fling once upon a time back in high school. Now they're meeting again in the middle of a biker-gang turf war in Vancouver's seedy east side.

And this time *no* one is backing down.

SECOND CHANCES

Terri Darling

Copyright © 2011, 2013 by Terri Darling

1

Almost five p.m. She was going to lose her job if she was late many more times. And still she was here. Back in the stench of urine in the stairwells, the itchy paranoia of the guys you passed on the second floor.

It was too much like...coming home.

"Third floor. C'mon." Micky waved her long, ruby red fingernails at her to hurry up.

Sharon winced and nodded. But as she hurried up the worn wooden stairs, she couldn't help feeling that the guys on second? They'd recognized her. They'd seen past the clean gray university sweats and zip-up fleece, seen past the clean skin and hair, and recognized one of their own.

"I'm *not*," she muttered.

But you're here.

She shook her head. "Shut up."

Reaching the third floor, she saw Micky clack down the hall in her high-heeled boots and in through a door at the end. Sharon followed. The four unmade beds inside, the wasted girl in one, the thick smell of unwashed clothes and unfinished food containers strewn around on the floor – they all triggered in Sharon a sudden, intense need to smoke. Worst cravings she'd had since she'd quit a year ago.

She jammed her hands into her fleece pockets and focused on the bed with the girl.

"Hey," Sharon said.

"Who're you?" the girl whined back. She was probably trying to sound tough, though she couldn't have been more than sixteen. The sunken eyes and pinched face made it hard to tell. She looked sick. Otherwise, she'd have been down on the street tonight.

"Shut up," said Micky, unknowingly mimicking Sharon's earlier command to herself. Micky scooped up a half-empty pizza box with disgust.

"Jamie'll kick your–"

"I said shut *up*! You talk and I'll cut you while you sleep."

The girl huddled back in her blankets and shivered. Sharon pursed her lips and nodded, remembering how you had to enforce discipline on the street.

Micky obviously saw it on her face because she turned with a kind of smug tolerance to acknowledge her. "Rose," Micky said, gesturing at the wasted girl in the bed. Something in the gesture said the older hooker probably considered herself Rose's surrogate mother. She'd just never show it, because that wasn't how you survived on the street.

God, Sharon *really* needed a cigarette.

A noise out in the hall signaled the arrival of Angel, the other prostitute Sharon had befriended over the last two months. She stumbled in through the door and grabbed the jamb, panting and looking around with her eyes wide. Unlike the hard little Micky, Angel was a good head taller than Sharon but fine boned and a natural dirty blond, like a swaying willow tree. Beautiful. Delicate. Clear signs she hadn't lived on the street long.

"Wow!" Angel gasped at last. "You showed up!"

Sharon half-smiled and nodded. "Yeah."

"Oh, but hey!" She straightened up. "Jamie! Someone said they saw him coming back from Commercial Drive. We got, like, two minutes!"

"Figures," said Micky. She crossed her arms over her chest and turned towards Sharon. "So? We're all here. What d'you got to say?"

"Nice place," Sharon said. "I'm sure you'd hate to leave it."

"Yeah, right."

Sharon's gaze flicked around the room and settled on the bed that, at first glance, looked like the others. Same sort of filthy mattress and box spring on a metal h-frame. Rumpled sheets and no mattress cover. But this one was more bowed in the middle – the abuse of regular male weight, plus.

"Jamie's bed," she said, pointing.

Micky and Angel looked at one another.

"We gotta *go*," Angel moaned suddenly. Probably not just from fear of Jamie, but from drug withdrawal too. Worse even than quitting smoking. Angel would be anxious not to miss her jailer/punisher/pimp/supplier. Just as Sharon was anxious *not* to meet him. Besides which, Sharon was going to be late for work if she didn't get going soon.

"In a minute!" Micky snapped. But her hard eyes actually betrayed a glimmer of hope as they looked at Sharon. They looked at Sharon's cropped, dyed-black hair, semi-goth. Tried to fit it with the clean clothes, the lack of makeup, the careful speech.

"You really did this?" Micky said.

"Nearly four years of it."

"Not here."

"No."

"Where?"

Sharon shook her head. She'd use her past this much, to get them to listen to her, but there was no way she was going to risk that past ever finding her again. "I was lucky enough to have someone help me get out."

"And we're payback," Micky said.

"You could say that."

The hard woman nodded.

Sharon pushed it. "You said something was changing on the street. New girls. New pimps. You've been thinking about my offer?"

"Shit," Angel burst out. She was dancing into the room now like she had to pee. "Come *on*."

Micky ignored her. "This 'safe house' you been working on," she said to Sharon. "It's the hotel over the bar where you work, right?"

"Yes." Sharon forced her hands out of her pockets. Body language - nothing to hide.

"Why would we go there? What would we get?"

"It's a first step. A place to chill. You talk to people. You work out a plan. We get you on methadone...."

"Methadone!" Angel shrieked. Her long body shook, feet unable to stop their little dance. "I don't want metha-shit! They tie you down and pump you up!"

"You tell her," said an accented male voice from the door.

"Jamie!" Rose yelped from her bed.

The other three women whirled towards the door and Sharon felt her careful confidence shot through with ice. Whatever she'd told herself about who she was now, however much she'd made a new life, the situation and cues presented right here and now took over her like she was nothing but a puppet. She wanted to run so badly she thought she'd vomit.

It was all she could do to hold her ground. But she did, breaking out in a cold sweat over her forehead.

The girls' pimp lounged against the doorjamb – skinny, male, late twenties, dark-skinned with a black burn mark on his upper lip, Arab looking. He had none of the height Sharon's pimp had carried. None of Daryl's shoulder breadth, the rusty red moustache and crazy-ass glint in his eyes.

But this pimp was still just like him. In the threat. The attitude.

"Jamie" was tugged a little white baggy from inside his jean jacket pocket and called softly to Angel. "Hey, baby. A little nanoo to cook."

He tossed it and she scrambled for it. Then he turned to Micky. "How about you? You are ready for some wings?"

"Don't," Sharon whispered. Not sure if it was to Micky, to Jamie, or to herself.

Micky swallowed and hesitated and Jamie's lips snarled up. He came towards Sharon with an odd sideways gait, snapped out a hand, and grabbed Sharon's upper arm. "Why are you here? You want a taste? Or you are just trying to fuck up my income?"

"No...," Sharon said.

It was all she could manage. Like the ice in her veins had wrapped around her vocal cords when he'd grabbed her. Like she was seventeen again and knowing that the way to avoid getting beaten was to simply stay as still as possible.

"We came up to check on Rose," Micky said from somewhere. "Sharon here's a nurse."

"Yeah?" said Jamie, the acrid smell of him washing over her, his bony hand still clenching her upper arm.

The hint of hesitation in his voice, Micky speaking her name, broke up just enough of the ice that Sharon managed to focus and clear her throat. "Rose...has pneumonia. It's serious and contagious. You could all get it. She needs antibiotics. I could take her. I–"

"No." Jamie threw her arm away from him and sidled over to where Rose huddled. "Micky will take her." He ripped the covers off the shivering girl. "Get up!"

Micky stepped close to Sharon and whispered, "Get out of here."

Sharon, trembling head to foot as the broken ice still flowed through her, nodded. She couldn't do this after all. She wasn't strong enough.

Then she glanced at Angel, who crouched in the corner, with a small jug of water, a hypodermic needle she'd found somewhere, and the baggy Jamie had thrown her. At Micky, whose hard eyes were scared silly underneath.

And she quickly reached to the zipper of her fanny pack, unzipped it, and slid out the little slip of paper she'd prepared. Her cell phone number.

"Take it," she whispered, and shoved it at Micky.

"Go," Micky whispered back.

"Call me. Or just come see me where I work."

Jamie suddenly gave an eerie, high-pitched roar and kicked at the bed Rose lay in, Micky stuffed the number into the top of her Spandex pants.

Sharon wavered, feet wanting to run. Needing to. "You remember where–"

"The Red Owl Bar," Micky whispered. "Yeah. Fuck. Go."

Sharon ran.

***

Cross & Shiptite? Delivered. Done.

Griffin Walsh flipped the final file closed on his glass-topped desk. Then he loosened his tie, planted one Vigotti-shod foot on the lip of the desk, and pushed himself back on his chair with a bit of a spin, riding it like a cowboy until the wheels reached the edge of his carpet protector and bumped to a halt.

Griffin thumped down his feet, stood up and walked to the narrow, but very tall, window.

The whole of north downtown Vancouver spread out before him, from the Wall Building to the line of glass condos lining Coal Harbour, with Stanley Park beyond. It was hard not to feel a bit godlike up on the twenty-third floor. Hard not to feel, given the bonuses he'd be receiving this year, that he was already into the good life barely three years out of UBC Law.

Which was the danger, of course. Exactly the sort of things he'd begun warning some of his greener clients about, something passed on to him from his own parents: *Never let the people you're playing with seduce you away from your goals.*

The question was which people were trying to seduce Griffin here?

He tugged on his right ear. Was it his current bosses at Greene McNamara, with their fabulous performance bonuses and the incredible support staff and reputation that let him punch way above his expected class? Or was it – tug the left ear – Mr. Majo – hard "j" – Cruz, longtime friend and law school buddy who was dangling the classic temptation of starting up their own firm where *they* would be the managing partners and answer only to their clients and the law?

Greene McNamara – money, clout, solid career path.

Majo & Walsh – freedom and control. Though maybe no money, no career, business failure in two years.

Hmm, as his first year Commercial Law prof was wont to say, usually using one hand to hold his chin and tap his nose rather than tugging on his ears.

Hmm.

Without a knock, the door to Griffin's office opened and Griffin swung around to see the craggy form of Burt Lester swagger in. Lester, fourth partner on the letterhead. He rarely came down to the juniors' floor. In fact the grapevine said the appearances of this former football star were getting rarer and rarer in the office, even up on twenty-four where the other partners worked.

Not that anyone was surprised. The aging quarterback's main skill seemed to be looking great in an expensive suit.

"You broke their defense," Lester said, as if it was obvious what he was referring to. Which of course it was. The Cross-Shiptite merger. The same deal that had slipped through Lester's own fingers eight years earlier.

"Yes, sir," Griffin said and waited.

Lester stared at him, nodding his large head until Griffin decided to put him out of his misery.

"There was a sudden opening of the Chinese wheat barriers," Griffin said.

"Ah."

Since it was clear Lester still didn't understand, Griffin explained how Chinese shipping giant CSCL had found itself short and needed a fast deal but wouldn't go multiple because of government pressures. Which had led them to Cross, which had already been looking at Shiptite again.

"Since you'd already laid the groundwork for their merger the first time around," Griffin offered, "I mostly acted as facilitator."

Lester, who'd been leaning forward intently as Griffin had talked, now huffed, as if about to take credit, then laughed with a snort and straightened.

"From anyone else, you know, I'd call that a major suck up."

"It's not, sir. It's just the truth."

"I know! That's what's so incredible. I couldn't believe it when I read your reports, but now, seeing you again, hearing you talk, damned if you're not just like they say."

"How's that, sir?"

"Goddamned humble. Goddamned honest. And goddamned self-confident. Supposedly smart too. That's why they all come to you, you know. They chose you because they know you play it absolutely straight with them."

"Thank you, sir. I like to think I provide good legal advice too."

"Oh, sure, sure." Lester shook his head and shoved his hands into his Hugo Boss trouser pockets like he was fishing for a football in there somewhere. "But this obsessive honesty thing... I've read the reports."

A hard tightness slipped around Griffin's shoulders. "Sir?"

"You really did use some of the templates I'd worked out for the deal. A little bit from there, a little bit from other deals."

"I...did say it wasn't that complicated."

Lester turned on him and his craggy shoulders hunched forward. It made him look like he was calling Griffin into a huddle. "You could have called in more help, stretched it out, covered more contingencies, billed for research time. My God, man. You just closed a merger between two of the biggest marine players out here and you billed them the same as some of the other juniors bill mom-and-pop stores to set up a franchise!"

The old man was shaking all over as he finished, like he expected Griffin to shout, "Yes, *sir!*" and run for position.

Griffin didn't. But the tension in his shoulders had spread right down his arms and chest now. And his office felt very narrow. "You want me to artificially inflate the cost of our services?"

"It's called *commercial* law, Mr. Walsh. The top lawyers cost top dollar. So if you want to be a top lawyer in our ranks..." He hovered over the thought, letting the hint of a sooner-than-expected partnership sink home. "You want to be a top lawyer, you have to learn not just to think like one, but to bill like one.

"Is that clear?"

Griffin's neck was too stiff to nod even if he'd wanted to. Keeping his voice neutral, he said, "Yes, sir. Very."

"Good," said Lester and hovered a moment longer, as if expecting Griffin to deke around him. "Good."

When Griffin didn't move from his stance behind his desk, Lester finally nodded his big head, swiveled about like a quarterback about to jog back down the field after a touchdown, and walked out the door.

For almost a full minute, Griffin stared after him. Then he walked to his desk, clicked up a number on his computer screen, and dialed the phone.

The other end picked up after two rings.

"Cruz here."

"Majo," Griffin said. "It's me. We gotta talk. Where?" A pause. "The Red Owl? Give me the address...Fine. Half and hour."

2

The Red Owl Bar & Hotel had been built in 1903 and looked like it hadn't been washed since then. Four stories tall, it shared a wall for the first three floors on its east side with a meat shop that did decent business, but had heavy bars fixed over its windows.

On the Red Owl's west side, all four floors shared a wall with a poured-concrete garment factory that had been shut down for years, half the windows smashed, the bottom boarded up. Squatters and drug dealers usually accessed the factory's interior via an upended bedframe in the alleyway that let them reach the second floor windows.

The Red Owl itself, for all its dirt, was in decent repair. Above the tatty awning that advertised the first floor bar, its stucco facade rose up, patched and re-patched. A number of the windows looked newer. Most of the original simple cornice still ran across the top undamaged, and the tops of the three flat faux-pillars that bounded the two columns of windows – six windows, six rooms – still butted up under them.

It looked, all told, like a grumpy old man who'd squatted down a long time ago and refused to budge since.

This despite the deterioration of Vancouver's downtown east side into a skid row, the establishment of a major cop shop two blocks away, and the evolution of the nearby "pigeon park" into a place where mothers were afraid to walk their children for fear of stepping on a discarded heroin needle or crack pipe.

The Red Owl continued.

***

Sharon got to the Red Owl's back alley door still running.

Her heart pounded so hard inside her that her chest hurt and her lungs forced her into a racking cough. It was as if all of her had been thrown into the past – her mind, her lungs. She hadn't been that scared since Julia Morrow had helped her get out of Kelowna. Hadn't coughed this hard since the first days going cold turkey on smokes.

Even her face, burning and running with sweat in the thick air, seemed clenched into the kind of mask she hadn't worn since Kelowna. She shook her head hard and blew out over and over again through her lips. She was *not* that girl any more. Hadn't been for almost five years, damn it.

She rubbed and slapped her cheeks then looked, embarrassed, up and down the alley. Two guys lolled at the rear of the garment factory just south of her, but they were too interested in their little tube with a Brillo pad – a homemade crack pipe – to see her. They probably wouldn't even be able to stand up soon.

Sharon coughed and spat on the pavement. Wiped her nose. At least...at least she'd never done that, thank God.

Desperately pulling herself back together, she grabbed the rough metal handle of the Red Owl door, squealed it open, and slipped inside. The greasy bustle of the kitchen cramped around her. Pushing past the six metal barrels of house draft and boxes of bottled beer, mostly Coors, she headed for the staff room.

Her friend Lisa caught her at the discharge rollers of the dishwasher, swinging the tray she was carrying around and up like a stop sign.

"Gotta *use* them tenny runners, hon! We was all beginning to wonder if you were coming in at all tonight."

"I'm not that late. It's only–"

"Fourth time this month. Henry's pissed."

"Shit."

Lisa tossed back her big, back-combed, blonde hair with a dramatic sigh and used her free hand to tug down her low-cut, tight tee-shirt. "Pete and Digger brought in prob'ly twenty-five Hard Riders for dinner. I barely got an ass left, all those boys pinched it so much."

Sharon smiled despite herself. If there was one thing Lisa Doigis, ex-pat Texan, never had to worry about losing, it was her substantial tits and ass. They were "her meal tickets" as she said. And they did indeed seem to have supported her since she'd fled her home state with her five-year-old son, Danny. Exactly what she'd run from she'd never volunteered and Sharon would never ask. Any more than Lisa would ask her where *she* had come from.

"I better run," Sharon said.

"Damn right." But Lisa grabbed her arm as she started to move. "Gotta talk to you sometime, okay? Just you'n me. Sunday?"

"Sure. Everything okay?"

Lisa couldn't answer because the latest young Chinese girl Henry had hired (going through them like firewood – he obviously didn't pay them enough) came jabbering back at them in Chinese, shooing them away from the girl's dishwashing station and towards the front. There Elrad, the cook, greeted Sharon and slid a basket of chicken wings along the counter towards Lisa.

"Clucks up!"

Lisa leapt over, caught them onto her tray, and rolled her eyes at Sharon. "Pete's, of course. Most of the others skedaddled but Pete and Digger just keep on–"

The door to the main room banged open and Henry's bulk stood there, white sleeves rolled up on impressive forearms, thick-lipped face bulging red. "Doigis! Finish your–" He saw Sharon. "Well fucking nice of you to show up."

"I–"

"Thirty seconds, on the floor, you want to keep your job!" He slammed back out to the bar proper.

"Mr. Wonderful," Lisa said, backing out after him. "But you better hurry, hon."

Sharon took a deep breath. Great. She wanted to press Henry about leasing rooms upstairs for which she didn't have financing yet, and he was ready to fire her. She was batting a million tonight.

She chewed her lip and went to the staff corner to strip off her fleece, track pants, and purse. Thing was, she thought as she got them off and balled them into her box, Angel and Micky, and now Rose, couldn't wait long. Even if things *weren't* sliding on their block, street life was always touch-and-go. Sharon had to get things moving. Maybe she could talk to Henry tonight after all. After she'd put in a good night of sucking up to customers, making the Red Owl's usual clientele feel happy and horny.

Things she was unfortunately good at.

She straightened her own white, stretchy top, adjusted her skimpy black shorts, switched her runners for the black shoes she kept at the pub, and did a quick spike gel on her hair.

Then she grabbed a serving tray and headed out.

***

The dive reeked of sex, Griffin thought.

Why was that? And why had Majo chosen this particular place to meet?

Griffin let the grimy door of the Red Owl Bar & Hotel bang closed behind him with a jingle of the bells attached to it, and tried to figure it out. The room had eight old wooden tables, five of them occupied. Dark wooden walls. Door to the hotel stairs on the right wall. Dim light. Wood-shuttered windows. Seventies Elton John, "Goodbye Yellow Brick Road" playing somewhere.

Above it all wafted a greasy food smell cut with cigarette smoke, even though smoking wasn't allowed in Vancouver pubs.

The drinkers on the right side of the room looked like bikers with elaborate jean jackets, a stylized HR crest on the back. The left side of the room had just a few wasted-looking men at the tables and two female customers at the straight slab bar that looked like it had a Formica top and thick plastic front.

The sour-looking bartender behind the bar was eyed Griffin like he was some kind of foul roadkill.

Majo was nowhere to be seen.

And the sex?

Griffin grimaced. Obviously all in his mind. Even the two waitresses by the right end of the bar near the kitchen door had their backs turned to him as they whispered to one another. Both had truly fine rear ends displayed in shorts that might as well have been thongs, they rode up so high. But one was a big-haired blonde, and the other a spiky, black-haired model. Neither his type.

Nor did Griffin have *time* for sex. Especially not now. Majo may have initiated this meeting and chosen the place, but it was Griffin with the plan, Griffin who'd become unshakably gripped with a sense of destiny after Burt Lester's visit this afternoon.

It was a time for great beginnings. Here and now.

Just as soon as Majo showed up.

The waitresses still hadn't seen him, so Griffin made his own way to an empty table in the far left corner. The first item of business after putting this deal together would be finding a better place for social meetings.

He just got his trench coat and suit jacket off, tie loosened, when Majo

Cruz came strutting into the pub. He spotted Griffin, waved, winked at the two women watching his entrance from their barstools, and sauntered over. "*Ola!* " he said.

Griffin rolled his eyes but still stuck out his hand to his darker-skinned law school buddy, whose conservative Mexican parents were probably rolling in their graves at the way he let everyone give his name a hard J. *Ma – joe.*

"Whaddya think?" Maj said as he gripped.

"About...?"

"The place! This pub! My all-time favorite downtown hangout!"

"Which caters currently to six bikers, three grizzled men who look like they work at the meat shop down the block, four underage Asian kids who followed you in, and two hookers at the bar trying for the Wednesday night after work crowd. Oh, and the thug-like bartender and two waitresses who are *still* ignoring us. Very nice."

"Isn't it."

"You troll for clients here?"

Maj slapped a hand over his heart. "I'm hurt. I'm mortally and morally wounded by that remark." He grinned and slipped off his own trench and sports coat. His tie had a dancing Hawaiian girl on it. "Actually," he said and sat, "I did pick up a client here. Bar fight. Clear case of self-defense. I slipped him my card while he was sprawled over by the bar, waiting for the cops. He was very grateful when I got him off quietly. He was a married stockbroker. The *cabrón* who attacked him was the boyfriend of the babe he'd brought here."

"Delightful." Griffin snorted.

"But mainly this place is close to the cop shop, so I come here to hang out and meet the other side."

"Business lunches."

"Exactly. And the prettiest barmaids in Vancouver." Majo swiveled around and tried to catch the eye of one of the two waitresses. "Yo! Customers here!"

Griffin sat back to watch his friend with amusement. Majo had always been the brashest of their law school group. Never the smartest, or most responsible, and rarely politically correct, you still had to admire him. He had guts, charm, and street smarts. No one had been surprised when he articled in a top criminal law firm and got hired back.

Most critical for Griffin, though, was that Majo's heart was in the right place. He cared about his clients. His ethics were solid. That had been the final kicker to–

"Hey, Sharon!" Maj stood up and cupped his hands around his mouth. "Come on! My friend's dying to meet you!"

Griffin frowned. The spiky-haired waitress had turned, seen them, then turned back like she wanted to hide. Something about the name... "I don't think–"

Majo cut him off with a grin. "Trust me on this one."

***

For the second time that night, Sharon felt like a young girl again, her heart pounding. It couldn't be him. Not here. Not like this. It had to be Majo's fault. She'd kill him for this. God, she wished she had a cigarette.

Henry leaned over the side of the bar to poke her and she almost shrieked.

"What?" Henry said. "Majo's calling for you."

"What is it, hon?" Lisa said.

Sharon turned even more towards the wall, trying to hide her face. "I can't."

"S'only Majo," Lisa said.

"It's not him."

"The other guy? What? Looks like a hunk to me. Ears stick out a little."

"I know him!" Sharon said.

"Yeah?" Lisa lifted one eyebrow. "Tell me on Sunday."

It was apparently all the interest she could muster. Her shift was done. She'd been just telling Sharon how Danny's after-school daycare was getting antsy about the times she showed up late. And, despite the usual Texas attitude, she was bagged. No help from that quarter.

Sharon was almost tempted to run into the back to grab one the young Chinese girls from the kitchen, but they all kept their heads down around men and spoke little English. No help from there either.

"Dekker." The big bartender's voice had an edge now, and some or the closer bar patrons were watching. You did not want to get this big man riled. "You with us? Or you like unemployment?"

"I'm going," Sharon said.

She straightened her bra under her the tight stretch of her top, tucked her tray under arm, and rubbed what felt like some sort of crap stuck to the corner of her mouth. Probably the fries she'd quickly scarfed in the kitchen for dinner in between

Pete's food orders. Between that and her sweat from her run here earlier, she knew she looked like hell.

Of course, it wouldn't matter. Griffin Walsh – If it was really him. *Of course it's him.* – wouldn't even remember her. It had been what? Nine years? Ten? And she doubted she'd even had a real impact on him in high school. Despite her best efforts.

Sharon Dekker wasn't the sort of girl the Griffin Walshes of the world remembered.

She took a big breath, then strode out across the floor, circled the biker's table where Pete and Digger whistled at her, ignored the cackles of Brittany and Phyllis at the bar, and the crude stares of the kids near the back whom she was surprised Henry even let in the door. They looked underaged.

Then she was there, right beside Majo's elbow. She gave him and his buddy a quick, fixed smile. "Hi, guys."

And she'd been right. Griffin didn't remember her.

God, but she sure remembered him. Still square-jawed and serious, but firmed up now, with an adult set to his shoulders and a sky blue shirt that looked like Egyptian cotton or something. And when he looked up at her with those dark blue, serious eyes, it still made her knees weak and whole body respond. Like she was back in high school in Vernon, not virginal but innocent, and he was agreeing to be her debate partner in social studies. Twelfth grade. Her final desperate play for brainy, unattainable Griffin Walsh. Virtually raping him behind the bleachers in the gymnasium. Ignoring her dying mother's advice that a girl who gives it up too easily loses everything.

She'd sure proved that right, hadn't she.

Now his vague smile nailed it home. He didn't even give her the usual male once-over of her body. She was nothing to him. Less than nothing.

"Sharon Dekker," said Majo. "Like you to meet a buddy of mine from UBC Law. Griffin W–"

"Walsh," Sharon completed. "Yes. I know."

She forced herself to lean onto one hip in exaggerated expectation and said nothing. She did drop her arms so he could fully look at her. She knew the tight top Henry encouraged her and Lisa to wear did good things for her figure. She wasn't huge up top, but was slim-waisted, and the low scoop and push-up bra gave her the cleavage of a pin-up girl.

Or a slut?

Her blood rushed from her toes up to her face. Her ears burned and she fumbled her hair back over them. But she still didn't back off. Majo, she noted, was goggling back and forth between Griffin and her. Somehow there were always spectators to her worst humiliations.

"I...um...," Griffin mumbled.

Majo plunged his face into his hands. "*Está fregado*," he moaned.

Sharon swallowed and made it even worse. "Vernon High. Ms. Robertson's social studies class. You and I worked together for a debate–'Whether Canada's military should assist in non-combat third world countries.'"

"Ri-i-i-ight," Griffin stalled, obviously wracking his brains. "Sharon Nells. No...Neal? Sharon Neal."

"You are pathetic, man," Majo said, raising his face. "I told you–"

"Griffin's right," Sharon said and Majo shut up.

"You dropped out before the end of the school year," Griffin said. "You didn't graduate."

"That's right," she said. A whole lost world behind that.

Yet for a moment even *that* was irrelevant. Beyond all reason, her mind and body were back in little girl mode around this man, back in high school when the world still had promise.

"You don't remember anything else?"

He met her eyes. Something there. She saw some...

He shook his head and everything crashed around her again - the rejection, the behind-the-hand whispers about her from his high school friends, her father finding out, and the whole snowballing, out-of-control mess that her life had become. It hadn't been Griffin's fault any more than it had been her own. But he didn't even re*member*?

Face burning now from anger as much as embarrassment, Sharon flipped her bar tray up in front of her and took a deep breath to steady herself. "So what'll you gentlemen have?"

Griffin started but Majo recovered immediately. "Beer. Whatever's on tap. Nice tall glass. Foaming head. Better music. You."

He grinned so pleadingly that Sharon gave him a laugh, glad to be looking anywhere other than at Griffin. "Coming up," she said, and hurried at a near run back to the bar.

But as she went, her insides steamed.

To keep reading, look for the novel at your favorite retailer in e-book or trade paperback editions.

www.ingramcontent.com/pod-product-compliance
Lightning Source LLC
Chambersburg PA
CBHW030924050726
47498CB00003BA/886